ACT
OF
GOD

Other John Cuddy novels by Jeremiah Healy

Blunt Darts
The Staked Goat
So Like Sleep
Swan Dive
Yesterday's News
Right to Die
Shallow Graves
Foursome

Published by POCKET BOOKS

JEREMIAH HEALY

ACT OF GOD

POCKET BOOKS
New York   London   Toronto   Sydney   Tokyo   Singapore

This book is a work of fiction. Names, characters, places, and incidents either are products of the author's imagination or are used fictitiously. Any resemblance to actual events or locales or persons, living or dead, is entirely coincidental.

 POCKET BOOKS, a division of Simon & Schuster Inc.
1230 Avenue of the Americas, New York, NY 10020

Healy, J. F. (Jeremiah F.), 1948–
    Act of God / Jeremiah Healy.
        p.   cm.
    ISBN: 0-671-79558-9
    1. Cuddy, John Francis (Fictitious character)—Fiction.
    2. Private investigators—Massachusetts—Boston—Fiction.   3. Boston
(Mass.)—Fiction.   I. Title.
PS3558.E2347A65   1994
813'.54—dc20   93-47451
                                                                                        CIP

First Pocket Books hardcover printing June 1994

10 9 8 7 6 5 4 3 2 1

POCKET and colophon are registered trademarks of
Simon & Schuster Inc.

Printed in the U.S.A.

For Robert J. Randisi,
who's done more to help each of us
than we have ourselves

ACT
OF
GOD

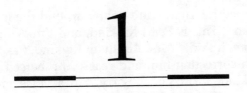

1

USUALLY THEY CALL FIRST. CLIENTS, I MEAN. SEVENTY, MAYBE eighty percent of a private investigator's work comes in through law firms, and attorneys rarely do anything without an appointment. On top of that, almost always you're the one who has to visit their offices.

That Tuesday afternoon, though, the knock came before the telephone rang. I looked up from my desk, which had on it what I'd been able to gather about a teenaged runaway from Vermont. The pebbled-glass part of my door was still shaking against the wooden frame, the stenciled JOHN FRANCIS CUDDY, CONFIDENTIAL INVESTIGATIONS dancing a little. That was odd, too, because most folks will rap on the wood, not the glass.

When I said come in, they did.

A woman and a man, she entering as he held the door open for her. The man nearly had to nudge the woman across the threshold so he could come in, too, and close the door behind him. People are uncomfortable bringing their troubles to a stranger, but from the awkwardly polite way

1

the two of them moved around each other, I got the impression they weren't used to being together, either.

The man said, "Mr. Cuddy?"

I stood up. "Yes?"

He cupped his right hand gently around the left elbow of the woman. "This is Pearl Rivkind, and I'm William Proft."

The woman said, "Mrs. Abraham Rivkind," as though she were both correcting him and reassuring herself.

To Rivkind, Proft said, "Sorry," in a voice more formal than sincere. Then he looked to me. "I wonder if we could have a few minutes of your time?"

It's a good idea to be wary of off-the-street business, but a bad idea to turn it away automatically.

I closed the file on the runaway and eased back down. "Please, take a seat."

My office has two client chairs that face my desk and two windows that overlook the Park Street subway station at the northeast corner of the Boston Common. Rivkind and Proft sat so that each was in line with one of the windows behind me.

Pearl Rivkind was barely five feet tall, even with high heels. Into her mid-fifties, she wore heavy makeup that did little to hide her age and nothing to hide a lantern jaw that would make Jay Leno wince. Her hair was tinted a few shades redder than brown and chopped stylishly short. The silk dress was stylish, too, and went with the warm, late June weather outside, but the clinging silk only accentuated a body that would have seemed dumpy in a bulky bathrobe. It was her eyes that caught you up close, though. Big and brown and deep, the whites were bloodshot and bulged with the irritation of someone who'd lately spent a lot of time crying.

William Proft was tall and lanky, taking a while to lower himself into the other chair. Thirtyish, his hair was sandy but balding front to back over a long face, hollow cheeks, and prominent lips that curled a little, a perpetual grin that you could grow tired of very quickly. He wore a seersucker jacket over a buttoned-down shirt and solid black tie. The jacket rode up on him as he finally got settled, as though he didn't usually wear one or didn't get to sit in it much. Up close, Proft's eyes caught you, too, but more like the guy at the next table in a restaurant who's constantly staring at the food on your plate to be sure he's ordered the best item on the menu.

I said, "How did you find me?"

Rivkind said, "My lawyer, he called around, got a a recommendation on you."

"Is there some reason he didn't contact me himself?"

"Yeah," she said, leaning forward in her chair. "He doesn't think it's such a hot idea, my coming to see a private investigator. Neither does my son or anybody else, for that matter."

I was beginning to like Rivkind. She'd corrected Proft on the introductions, and she wasn't afraid to be direct with me.

Proft said, "Perhaps if I summarized our situation, you could get a sense of what's involved here."

I was beginning not to like Proft much, but I said, "Go ahead."

He crossed his right leg over the left, showing Hush Puppy shoes I hadn't noticed before. "Two weeks ago—that Thursday, actually, so almost three weeks now—Mrs. Rivkind's husband was brutally murdered during an attempted robbery at his furniture store. This past Saturday—three days ago—my sister, Darbra, who worked as a secretary at the store, came back from vacation and seems to have disappeared."

At his mention of the husband, I looked to Rivkind and nodded in sympathy. Her jaw came out a little more, but she nodded back.

To Proft, I said, "You have reason to think the two are related?"

3

"Frankly, no. But Mrs. Rivkind came to my pharmacy yesterday to have a prescription filled—"

"Sedative. My doctor, he said, 'Pearl, no matter what, you've got to sleep.' "

Proft took the interruption in stride. "She and I began talking about the, well, odd coincidence at best, and we thought it might make sense to consult someone like you."

"There a reason you didn't call first?"

They exchanged glances. Rivkind came back to me. "It seemed kind of hard to talk about over the phone." Her eyes drifted toward the window. "Kind of hard to talk about, period."

She said the last in a neutral way, like she'd had a lot of practice with the phrase over the last few weeks.

I said, "What exactly is it that you'd like me to do?"

Proft said, "Well, since Darbra's disappearance may be tied in with Mr. Rivkind's death, we thought you could investigate them together."

Rivkind said, "Kind of a package deal, right?"

I turned my chair to look out the window that shows the top of the State House over some shorter trees on the Common. The capitol dome was dedicated two hundred years ago, Paul Revere sheathing it in copper when the original wooden shingles fell off. Just after the Civil War, some gold leaf was applied. They regilded the thing every twenty years or so until 1942, when it was painted gray to protect us from German bombers or U-boats, nobody seems to be sure which. Now the most recent gold leaf from the late sixties is peeling so badly it should be replaced, but the new fiscally responsible governor who succeeded the old fiscally responsible governor doesn't think the quarter of a million needed would go over too well with state employees who haven't seen a pay raise in five years.

Proft said, "Mr. Cuddy?"

4

I shook my head and turned back to them. "Representing joint clients isn't a great idea."

"How come?" said Rivkind.

"First, it's tough to give equal time to each side of the problem."

She said, "You can't kind of . . . use your own judgment on that?"

"Yes, but then there's the problem of conflicts."

Proft said, "What conflicts?"

"If the death and the disappearance have nothing to do with each other, then I'm wasting somebody's money looking into the other side of this. If the death and the disappearance are related, then it's possible, even likely, that I might find out something that helps one of you but hurts the other."

In the neutral voice, Rivkind said, "I don't think I can hurt worse than this. I hope not, anyway."

I didn't say anything.

Proft arched his shoulders forward in the chair. "Couldn't you work on our problems together until a conflict—what do they do, 'arise'?"

He said the last with the lips curling a little more than they had been.

Before I could answer him, Rivkind wrung her hands together, the four rings on her fingers clicking against one another. "I don't like saying this to a man I never met before, but I . . . I don't know if I can go through this with another investigator."

I looked at her. The makeup was cracking over the muscles in her jaw and cheeks as she tensed them to keep from crying. The woman was doing what she thought was right, despite other people bumping her the other way.

I said, "How's this. Let me interview each of you separately. Then I'll maybe have a better take on whether it makes sense for me to go forward for both of you."

William Proft got up a good deal faster than he'd sat

down. "Why don't you begin with Mrs. Rivkind, then? She's had her problem longer, and I can slip out for some coffee." At the door, he said, "Can I get either of you anything?"

I told him no, while the widow just waved a hand and bit on her lower lip.

2

AS SOON AS THE DOOR CLOSED BEHIND PROFT, PEARL RIVKIND fumbled in her handbag for a tissue. She used it to dab at her eyes, once to the right one, once to the left, then again to the right before swiping it twice under her nose. Gripping the tissue in her left hand, she said, "I'm sorry."

"Don't be. There's nothing you have to apologize for."

She tried to nod. "What do you need to know from me?"

I brought a notepad to the center of my desk. "I can get the details from the police, but it would help if you could tell me a little more about what happened."

A better nod, resolute. "My Abe, he's part—he was partners in Value Furniture. It's a store down in the Leather District."

A small, commercial neighborhood lying between Chinatown and South Station. "Go ahead."

"It's a beautiful building, built a hundred years ago, back when they knew how to make them. He was working late on that Thursday—they stay open till eight, Thursdays—and somebody tried to rob him. They hit him ... they hit him

7

over the head with the poker from the fireplace in his office. The bookkeeper found him, lying on the floor, all his blood ..."

I didn't want to push her. "What do the police say?"

A shrug and more work with the tissue. "They don't, except what I told you already. They figure somebody came in the store, hid somewhere till closing, then went to the office after the money."

"If the store was closed, how did the person get out?"

Another shrug. "Through the emergency door at the back. Beverly and the security guy heard the alarm go off."

"Beverly?"

"Beverly Swindell." Rivkind pronounced it "Swin-*dell.*" A bleak smile. "First time I saw her name written down, I said to Abe, I said, 'Abe, you're hiring a bookkeeper with a name like 'swindle'?' He got a big kick out of that. Abe always loved my little jokes."

"Do you know the name of the security guard?"

Rivkind shook her head. "He was new. An Irish guy, big like you, only not here very long."

"Here?"

"In this country. He came over from Ireland, I don't know, like less than a year ago?"

"Have the police made much progress?"

"I don't know from murder, Mr. Cuddy. They tell me they're looking into things, what do I know to ask them? Nobody saw anything, and whoever it was just ran away."

I waited a minute. "What exactly is it you want me to do?"

A judicious nod this time. "After Abe ... died, I went through his bills. The charge stuff, you know? Joel offered to do it for me, but I thought I should ... get a handle on his debts, whatever."

"Joel's your son?"

"My ...? Oh, no. Joel's ... Joel was Abe's partner. Joel Bernstein. They worked in the furniture business for other

8

people, then got together twenty years ago and bought out the owner of Value. Anyway, I'm going through Abe's papers, and there are ..." Rivkind made another couple of passes with the tissue. "There're these receipts and things for restaurants and bars, only like too many of them."

"What do you mean?"

"Well, Abe was a great boss, he took the people for drinks, dinner at this local place, Grgo's, you know it?"

The name came out "Gur-go's." "I don't think so."

"Well, you'd have to look good for it, he don't advertise much. I've only been there a couple, three times because we live in Sharon, it's easier to head up to Dedham, but all the people from the District eat at Grgo's. The thing is, though, there were too many receipts in Abe's papers from there and some bars and other restaurants I don't remember him ever mentioning to me."

I wasn't nuts about the direction this was taking. "Mrs. Rivkind—"

"I don't mean to interrupt, but would it be okay ... Is it still professional and all if you call me 'Pearl'?"

I looked at her, the big eyes brimming a little.

She said, "The last two weeks, I've been having everybody call me 'Mrs. Rivkind this' and 'Mrs. Rivkind that,' and it'd just be kind of nice to hear my first name from a man."

I leaned back. There was no come-on in what she said, just a sincere request. "Sure. And I'm John."

The tears stood down. "Thank you, John. Now, you were going to say what?"

"I was going to ask you what you thought the extra receipts meant?"

"I don't know what to think. If Abe didn't get ... dead, I never would have seen them, and he'd know that. He took care of all the bills, always did. But—it's not that we ... that I don't have the money to take care of them. It's just ... I don't understand them."

9

"Pearl, are you sure you want to?"

The jaw jutted. "You think he was having an affair on me."

"I'm just saying, are you sure you want to know?"

"John, my Abe and me were together thirty-one years. You get to know a man pretty well, thirty-one years of watching him get up and go to sleep and head for the bathroom. You ever married?"

I thought of Beth and said, "Once."

"How long?"

"Not long enough."

Rivkind looked at me. "Oh, John. She died, too?"

"A time ago. It . . . passes, mostly."

The woman became almost animated, maybe distracted from her own grief by being concerned for someone else's. "Oh my God, I'm sorry. I didn't mean to . . ." Then Rivkind seemed to remember why she was in my office. "Anyway, I knew my Abe pretty well. The last couple of months, it was like . . ." Rivkind turned her head, as though she were concerned about the State House dome, too. "This is very embarrassing to have to say."

"You don't have to tell me anything you don't want to."

Rivkind came back to me. "Abe and me, we always had a good marriage. I mean in . . . in the bedroom. The last couple of months, though, it was like he didn't have his usual . . . pep, you know what I mean?"

"I think so."

"I asked him, was he worried about work, he said no. I asked him, was it me, he said no. I already went through . . . the change, five years ago, so I didn't think it could be that. I even bought some magazines said they had articles about men when they're older—don't get me wrong, Abe wasn't old, he was only fifty-seven—but these articles, they talked about 'testosterone,' so I thought that might be it. I even asked him once. . . ." Rivkind looked down toward her hands, maybe at the band and diamond on her left ring

10

ACT OF GOD

finger. "I said to him, I said, 'Abe, you being unfaithful to me?,' and he said 'No,' and so I figured that was that."

"Pearl—"

"You see, my Abe, he never lied to me. Never, not once. He survived the camps, John, the Nazi camps. Buchenwald. To live you had to lie, every day, every way. He never, ever lied to me once during our marriage, John. He never lied to anybody. Ask his partner, Joel, ask our son, Larry. Everybody called him 'Honest Abe.' The store didn't already have a good name when they bought it, they would have changed it to 'Honest Abe's.' Believe me."

"Then I don't see what you want me to do."

Rivkind deflated a little. "I don't know, can you find out who killed him. It's so . . . random. Joel, he said to me, 'An act of God, Pearl. An act of God, who can explain these things?' But maybe you can, and if you can, I want to know. I want to know who killed my Abe."

"Pearl, the police are a lot better at that sort of thing than a private investigator. They have the resources."

"Resources?"

"Squads of detectives, laboratories, access to other criminals who might give the killer up to cut a better deal for themselves. I'd have to get awfully lucky."

"Okay then. Like I said, I don't know from murder, except what I see on TV. This kind of thing, it never . . . touched me before. So you don't find out who killed my husband, I'd understand. But it seems to me there's one thing you can find out. You can find out did my Abe lie to me. You can find out, was he having an affair on me."

"Pearl—"

"Look, I know what you told us before, about your conflict thing. And I know if I was sitting where you are, I'd be worrying, 'Is this Darbra that one client wants me to find also the woman that my other client wants to know had an affair with her Abe?' Well, I don't care who the other woman is. I mean that now, and I'll mean it all the way

11

through. I just want to know did my Abe lie to me, and I got to tell you, John, I don't think I can go through this with somebody else if you won't help me."

Pearl Rivkind crumpled what was left of the first tissue and dipped into her bag for another. With all the practice she'd probably had recently, she still didn't do it very well, and somehow that kind of persuaded me.

I said, "How was your coffee?"

The corner of his lips curled a little more. "Excellent. I found the most charming hole-in-the-wall place with a hazelnut blend that was out of this world. I really would have been happy to bring you some."

"Thanks anyway."

"Mrs. Rivkind said she'd be back in fifteen minutes. The poor woman, you can just see how badly she's taking all this."

I watched William Proft. He spoke without emotion in his voice, as though he were reporting accurately rather than caring at all about her. It reminded me of how we used to talk in class during my one year of law school.

"Mr. Proft, can you tell me what you know about your sister's disappearance?"

"Certainly. I got a call on Monday—yesterday—from the furniture store. I guess they had a line on their application form about 'next of kin,' and when Darbra didn't show up for work after her vacation, the other owner called me."

"Would that have been Joel Bernstein?"

"Yes."

"What did he say?"

"Oh, not much. Just that Darbra was due back from vacation that morning but hadn't shown up for work, and did I know where she was."

"Did you?"

"No. In fact, I called a woman who lives in Darbra's apartment building and sort of looks after things if she's gone for a while. This woman—she's actually a girlfriend of Darbra's. You'll want her name, I suppose?"

"Please."

"Traci Wickmire. That's T-R-A-C with an 'I,' last name W-I-C-K-M-I-R-E."

"And what did Wickmire tell you?"

"Just that Darbra returned from vacation sometime Saturday, but never got in touch with her."

"Address?"

He gave it to me, a building near Boston College.

"Have you been to the police?"

"Called them, actually. Started with headquarters, then got shunted around. The official message was that I'd have to wait awhile before I could file a missing-persons report. The unofficial message was that the matter would not be given a particularly high priority."

His choice of words was precise, the way you might expect a lawyer to talk. I know pharmacists have to be precise, too, but Proft's demeanor suggested he'd rehearsed this, not for fear of being too nervous to present it accurately, but rather because he wanted to be sure I had all he thought I needed.

"And so you decided to come to me."

"Well, Mrs. Rivkind and I decided together, as we said."

"Whose idea was it?"

Proft looked at me and blinked, as though he were trying to figure whether I would have asked Pearl Rivkind the same question. "Well, I suppose it was my idea that we go to a private investigator, and her idea, through her husband's lawyer, that we come to you."

Cute. "Tell me, Mr. Proft, did you ever study law?"

The lip finally uncurled. "Briefly. I found it too . . . uncertain for my taste, except for tax, which I found uninspired. There is a certainty in my current profession that is rather satisfying. Measuring the proper dosage for a prescription and knowing that you're right."

13

"Quantity over quality."

The lip recurled. "If you like."

A hard man to bait. "How long have you known Mrs. Rivkind?"

"Oh, a few years. Her old pharmacy closed, and mine in Sharon got most of the business from it."

"You own the pharmacy?"

"No. I work there."

"How well did you know Abraham Rivkind?"

"I didn't. Never met the man. Mrs. Rivkind did all their business at my . . . the pharmacy."

"Mr. Proft, now that we're alone, I'll ask you again. Do you have any reason to believe your sister's disappearance is related to Abe Rivkind's death?"

"Let's say I have no real evidence, Mr. Cuddy. Traci did mention that Darbra was upset about his death and therefore really looking forward to her vacation."

Traci mentioned. "You didn't talk to your sister directly about Rivkind's being killed?"

"No."

"Are you and your sister close, Mr. Proft?"

"Evidently not, by your definition. But I am her brother, and I am concerned about her."

Nice deflection. "Aside from Traci Wickmire, do you know any of the people in your sister's life?"

"Not really." A glint came into his eyes. "Darbra does fool around a bit, even in these plague-ridden times."

"Might Wickmire be able to help me there?"

"Probably. And, of course, the people at the furniture store."

Proft seemed to anticipate the question I didn't want to ask him. "One thing, Mr. Cuddy. I didn't know Mr. Rivkind, but I do know my sister. It would not be impossible for her to have some . . . beyond-business relationship with an older man. If so, so be it. If you wish to tell Mrs. Rivkind what

14

you find out, that's fine with me. I just want to know what may have happened to my sister."

Very thorough, relieving me of any conflict I might be feeling. "Maybe you should have stuck with the law, Mr. Proft."

"Perhaps. I would have been good at it, if not particularly happy doing it."

"Any other relatives your sister might have contacted?"

"Contacted? No."

"Any other relatives, period?"

"Our father . . . well, 'ran out' would be a polite expression for it. Our mother is dead. We do have an aunt who runs a curio shop up in Salem."

"Her name and address?"

"Darlene Nugent. I believe she lives above the shop, and that's called 'Sixties,' on Bowdoin Street."

He believes. "I take it you're not too close to your aunt, either."

The lips curled some more. "Closer than Darbra."

"You have a recent photograph of your sister?"

"Unfortunately, no."

"Any thoughts on where I can get one?"

"All roads lead to Traci Wickmire, Mr. Cuddy. She has a key to my sister's apartment, and I'm sure you'll find something useful there. If you decide to help Mrs. Rivkind and me, I'll be happy to give you whatever authorization you need to do what you have to do and take what you have to take from Darbra's place."

"Your sister has an unusual first name."

"I noticed that you've avoided using it."

It troubled me somehow that he was right.

Proft got the glint back in his eye. "Something almost . . . sinister about it, isn't there?"

I said, "Was she named after your aunt?"

"Partly. Darbra's twenty-eight—four years younger than I am. I was named after our father, but my mother's second pregnancy—with Darbra—was what caused him to 'fly the

15

coop,' as I think they used to say. Accordingly, Darbra got her name partly from my aunt—my mother's younger sister—and partly from my mother, who was named 'Barbra,' like Streisand. Could have been worse, don't you think?"

"I'm sorry?"

The lips curled so much they nearly bowed. "Well, how would you like going through life as 'Barblene'?"

I asked William Proft to wait outside until Pearl Rivkind came back. I turned in my chair, slid out my secretarial pulltray and put my feet up on it. As always, there were a lot of people milling around the subway station. I raised my window a couple of inches.

Two sketch artists, maybe Cambodian, were sitting in sand chairs next to their easels out of the sun, hucking the people who walked past. "Hey, lovely lady, we do your portrait? Seven minutes, no waiting."

An elderly black man, in broken boots with no laces, leaned against the wall of the station, talking loudly to nobody in particular. "No, I never *did* live there, man. Not in the *new* New York. Nossir, I lived in the *old* New York, the days gone by when New York was mostly white and all polite. My brothers and sisters of color, man, they ruint that city, ruint it for everybody."

In front of the black man, a carrot-haired boy in his late teens was ballroom dancing with a life-sized female doll wearing a white gown. Her high-heeled slippers were strapped to the tops of his Nikes as he whirled her around their cement dance floor, smiling proudly at the passersby as he gracefully avoided them.

I went back to the notes on my desk. I don't do divorce cases for the same reasons that Pearl Rivkind's request troubled me, but I only had to think of Beth lying in her hillside overlooking the harbor in South Boston to know I'd already made up my mind in Rivkind's favor. I could turn down William Proft, wanted to on personality grounds, but having

16

a missing-person case as a cover would make it a lot easier to deal with the Homicide Unit regarding Abraham Rivkind's death, and having Proft's authorization would allow me to get into both problems faster and smoother.

The knock on the pebbled-glass itself had to come from Proft, and when I said "Come in" this time, he had to hobble himself to allow Pearl Rivkind to enter first. Without my saying anything, they took the same chairs they'd chosen the first time.

Rivkind already had a tissue in her hand. "Well, what do you think? Can you help us?"

Proft didn't speak, maybe sensing that Pearl made the better ambassador.

"Let me spell out some ground rules first, then you can decide."

Rivkind said, "Go ahead."

"First, I'll need my money up front. I don't care how you arrange that between yourselves, but I won't be allocating my time so much to the Rivkind side and so much to the Proft side. Second, I'll consider a call or report by me to either of you to be a report to both."

Rivkind looked at Proft. "That's okay with me." He nodded back.

"Third, I'll keep going until I think it's hopeless or until I see a conflict staring me in the face. If a conflict comes up, I have permission from both of you to stay with one side of the case and tell the other good-bye."

That seemed to give Rivkind a little trouble, but Proft nodded quickly, and she followed suit.

"Fourth, coming at this from two sides will make it impossible to keep my investigation confidential. Given that, I'll want you to lay groundwork for me with the people at the furniture store and Darbra's apartment house."

Proft's lips curled contentedly as he and I both realized I'd finally used his sister's name, but Rivkind just said, "Whatever you need."

17

"Fifth, and I think last, since this is an open homicide, I have to start with the police."

Rivkind said, "I hope so."

"But, since Ms. Proft's disappearance is the fresher trail, I'm probably going to visit her apartment before hitting the store."

Rivkind's eyes told me she had more trouble with that, but she said only, "Whatever you think."

I looked at both of them. "So, we're agreed?"

Final, vigorous nods. As I asked them for the addresses and phone numbers they wanted me to use, I found I wasn't nodding myself.

3

I HAD A DATE WITH NANCY MEAGHER FOR THAT NIGHT. SHE'D been a little vague about what we were doing, just saying I should leave my Honda Prelude at the condo I rented in Back Bay. After my new clients left, I closed out the file on the runaway from Vermont, locked up the office, and went down to Tremont Street. It was barely five o'clock, but the relentless waves of summer commuters heading for the subway already had swamped the sketch artists, the New Yorker, and even Fred Astaire.

I walked up Tremont on the east side of the street, the sun still hot over my left shoulder. I passed Dunfey's Parker House and King's Chapel and probably the best tobacconist still surviving in these politically correct times.

Across from the curving red brick building called Center Plaza, I looked up to see vapor rising from the Steaming Kettle. The coffeeshop under the kettle emblem had been a favorite of Boston trial lawyers weary of battle in the Suffolk County courts, but the shop closed several years ago after the owner died. Somebody still pumps steam through the spout of the kettle itself, a massive copper replica of a teapot, supported over a doorway by steel braces and guy wires. My father used to buy coffee there when Government Center was still known as Scollay Square and an honest cup cost two cents. I wondered where all the lawyers went now that the Kettle and Purcell's in City Hall Square and Slagle's on Milk Street had all gone the way of the dodo.

Nancy worked in a unit of the Suffolk County District Attorney's Office in the New Courthouse building. I cleared the Sheriff's Department metal detector inside the revolving door downstairs and took the elevator to the sixth floor.

She was already at the front desk, a half-moon of oak with a computer, a telephone, and two plainclothes security guys who didn't take their eyes off me until Nancy nodded.

I said, "All this and punctual, too."

"I don't want to miss the preview."

"We're going to the movies?"

A shake of the head. "Nineteen questions left."

When Nancy shook her head, her black hair swayed just a little but never strayed across her face. Which is fortunate, because if it did, you wouldn't get to see the wide-spaced blue eyes or the batwings of freckles under them or the easy way her lips have of showing you what good teeth can add to a great smile.

"So where are you taking me?" I said.

She clucked her tongue. "Objection, ultimate issue. You wasted that one."

I walked up close and took her hand in mine. It fit just right, the nails on her fingers cut only as short as they had to be for working the keyboard on her computer comfortably. "Sounds like somebody had a difficult day in front of some judicial officer."

"A lot harder for the defense, actually."

"Want to tell me about it?"

Nancy checked her watch. "As we walk."

Through the office door and down the elevator and out into the passably fresh air, she summarized the armed robbery case she'd been trying. The jury had come back against the defendant the prior afternoon, and given the guy's record, the judge had ordered a sentencing hearing that morning.

"So what did the defense lawyer have to say?"

"Not much. He was pretty much reduced to arguing that his thirty-one-year-old client had been an altar boy from ages seven to nine."

"You're kidding?"

"God's truth."

No pun intended. "I guess being an altar boy doesn't carry quite the résumé value it once did."

Nancy took my arm, letting my bicep rub against something that felt awfully good under her summer-weight blazer and blouse. "How would you know?"

"How? I was an altar boy, Nance."

She stopped dead, dropping my arm. "No."

"God's truth."

"No pun intended."

"You know, I'd been thinking that but had the restraint to—"

She took my arm again. "You really were an altar boy?"

"I was."

"In South Boston?"

"I was a little young to ride circuit through the outlying parishes."

"John, I don't believe it."

"Why not?"

"Well, you are kind of an eagle scout, but altar ... I just can't imagine it."

"I can prove it."

"How? Your age, all the priests you served with must be dead by now."

"Canonized, most of them. But the way you can really

21

tell if a kid was an altar boy is if he has some embarrassing stories to tell about it."

"And you have some."

"Many."

"I want to hear one."

"Why don't we bail out your car first."

Nancy gave the attendant her ticket, and he let us find the Honda ourselves. Instead of my old-style Prelude, she had a hatchback Civic that was comfortable, quick, and still got as many miles to the gallon as a go-cart.

Once we were in traffic, Nancy started weaving, the little car like a roller derby star. We stuck to the city streets rather than the jammed Central Artery, always mending southward.

I said, "We're going to the beach."

"You're down to seventeen questions."

"That last one wasn't in the form of a question."

"Doesn't matter." She swerved around a beer truck. "Let's hear the altar boy story."

"One of the many."

"Any one of the many will do."

"All right. It was a Saturday morning Mass, the nine o'clock with Father Dolan. Nobody wanted to do that shift, because Dolan was a real stickler for ceremonial detail and the timing wrecked your day off from school, but I was low man on the totem pole, so I drew it. Well, you were supposed to wear dark slacks under your cassock, but I'd forgotten and worn some beige Levi's that didn't quite do justice to whatever feast day it was. I knew Dolan would crucify me, but fortunately I remembered that one of the other kids about my size left a spare pair of pants hidden in a corner of the sacristy, just behind the armoire with the priests' robes in it. So I stripped down to my briefs and was crawling back there to get the spare when a nun walked into the room and screamed. On my hands and knees, I turned my head to see her and said, 'It's okay, Sister Regina, I'm just waiting for Father Dolan.'"

22

Nancy didn't laugh. "Is that a good example of altar boy humor?"

"It was the best I could do at the time."

We passed the street where Value Furniture would be. I craned my neck but couldn't see it.

Nancy said, "What are you looking at?"

"Looking for. I got a case in today that might involve the killing of the store owner down here a couple of weeks ago."

"The busted robbery."

"That's the one."

"We aren't on it yet."

"I don't think the cops have anybody yet."

Nancy nodded, and I could see the wheels turning toward changing the subject. One of the limitations our professions impose on our relationship is that I can't talk about any cases that she, or even her office, might end up litigating. It's a good limitation to observe, especially for her.

Nancy said, "No more curiosity about where we're heading?"

"South is south."

The smile of a cat that hadn't eaten the canary but had just figured out how to work the latch on the cage door. "This will be an education for you beyond geography."

It was held in a union hall about six miles below Boston, and you could see the whole layout from the entrance. The main part of the room had folding chairs in long rows with a center aisle. Around the perimeter of the hall in the back were some folding tables with paper cloths and paper plates, tuna sandwiches for a dollar and cans of Pepsi or Sprite going for the same. They charged us four bucks each to get in the door, Nancy paying since the evening was her treat. We were given two cards with three-digit numbers on them. I promptly folded mine in half and secured it in a pocket of my suit jacket. Nancy also got a listing of all the items for the night by lot number.

23

I said, "An auction?"

"Can't fool you."

"What are you going to do, put me on the block?"

"Only if you tell another altar boy story."

"Seriously, Nance, what do you need from an auction?"

"John, have you ever looked at the furniture in my apartment?"

Nancy rented the third floor of a three-family house from the Boston Police family that owned the building.

"Frequently."

"Have you ever noticed the chest of drawers in my bedroom?"

I just smiled at her.

She said, "You were going to say, 'Nance, I've never been in your drawers,' weren't you?"

"Not after the Father Dolan story."

"Good. Maybe you are educable after all."

"So we're here to look at bedroom furniture."

"Among other things. Come on, this is the preview time."

"Oh boy, oh boy."

We walked slowly past tables against the other walls of the room with junk on them that reminded me a lot of the tables with the tuna sandwiches. There was red glass and blue glass and broken glass. There were old milk bottles emblazoned with the names of dairies long out of business and old comic books with the cover art of superheroes long out of favor. Ladies' hats with veils and feathers in the colors and workmanship of the twenties and thirties rested next to helmets of the armies from both world wars. The furniture ranged from vinyl kitchen chairs to lacquered Chinese cabinets.

Nancy had her eye on a pair of maple bureaus, but she shook her head and made a note in her program. Then she spotted a gigantic one in mahogany with brass handles. It stood on curved, carved legs and probably had about twenty pounds on her Honda. Nancy opened all the drawers and

examined the joints and tapped on the bottoms. She tried
to rock the thing at the top. Didn't budge.

There were three other dressers. Nancy opened the drawers and examined and tapped, but without the same spirit
she'd shown for the mahogany. I had the feeling she was
sold, and I prayed God for other bidders to have deeper
pockets.

As we made our way back to the folding chairs, I said,
"Don't you think you ought to measure the thing?"

"The mahogany one?"

"Yes."

"No, that'd be too obvious. Besides, I thought I'd put it
on the long wall in my bedroom."

"Nance, I meant toward it fitting in the back of the car."

"Not to worry. I have a good sense for that sort of thing.
You see anything you like?"

"Just the sandwiches."

A stony stare as she sat down. "Can you spring for a
couple? I want to save my pennies toward the bidding."

"Pepsi or Sprite?"

"I always prefer an un-cola with poultry or fish."

I went to the rear tables and decided I should show a
little more enthusiasm for our venture. Back at the chairs
with the sandwiches and drinks, I said, "Got you two
napkins."

"Thanks."

As I sat down and she took a bite of her tuna, I said,
"You know, this was the first meal we ever shared."

Nancy looked up from the program in her lap. "You remember that?"

"Your office, when you were arraigning Joey D'Amico,
and I was there for the insurance company on the arson."

Her eyes got soft. "I can still see you that day, even exactly what you wore."

I thought about closing my eyes for effect, but decided
that I liked the effect in front of me better. "You had your

hair longer then, pulled back into a bun. Gray suit, just two pieces, jacket and skirt."

Nancy smiled the great smile. "You know what I thought about you that day?"

"I know you made a pass at me."

"But you said you weren't ready yet."

"I wasn't."

"I know. That's what—"

"Good evening, ladies and gentlemen, and welcome to tonight's showing. My name is Hank Jeffers, and I'll be acting as auctioneer."

Jeffers was a round little guy standing on a box behind a podium so that you could see his head, shoulders, and the saddle and sleeves of a loud sports jacket. "There will be no reserve on any lot number unless it is so indicated in your program. Please be sure to read the other rules listed in the program before you bid by raising in your right hand the card with your number on it."

There didn't seem to be a sequence to the things brought out. It took me ten minutes of reading the program to realize that items in a given category, say bone china, were sprinkled throughout. I guessed that was to encourage each component of the crowd to arrive early and stay late, the more to see specific treasures to spark their impulse.

Nancy observed remarkable discipline, bidding only on a crystal wine decanter from Austria and dropping out when Jeffers got a thirty-dollar wave from an older woman a few rows in front of us. The decanter eventually went to the older woman for forty-five.

I tugged on Nancy's sleeve and whispered, "Probably not dishwasher-safe, anyway."

"I don't have a dishwasher."

"There's one coming up in Lot Two-twenty-seven."

She smiled in spite of herself, and I took the hand that wasn't holding her bidder card and rested it against my thigh.

After another fifteen minutes, I noticed that some things

went for practically nothing and seemed to be great bargains. On other lots, though, there were some people in the room who jumped into the bidding for a while, usually to start it or in the middle, then routinely dropped. I asked Nancy about them.

"Maybe dealers, who know how much they can get retail and don't want to tie up more than X percent of that to buy it here. Maybe also just friends of the auctioneer, shilling."

"Is that legal?"

"I don't know. I'm not here professionally."

Just then the mahogany bureau came up, and at least three other people around us leaned forward. Nancy let go of my hand so both of hers would be free.

Jeffers asked for and received a starting bid of fifty from the older woman who'd gotten Nancy's decanter. I saw a determined look come into both of the wide-spaced blue eyes, which I thought was a bad sign. Then a middle-aged Hispanic man put in a bid of sixty, which the auctioneer recognized just before Nancy raised her card for seventy. They played leapfrog up to one-fifty, by which time two of the dealers (or shills) had jumped in and out, leaving the field to Nancy and the decanter woman.

They slugged it out for another hundred, the older woman turning around awkwardly in her chair to see who the stubborn competition was. I caught her attention and gave my best "what're you going to do?" shrug, hoping that might persuade the woman to drop out before she broke the bank. She gave me back the same look Nancy had, which I thought was a very bad sign.

All told, the bad signs topped out at three hundred even, Nancy winning. Kind of.

I said, "Nice job."

"It's worth twice that, maybe more."

"I believe you."

*　　*　　*

27

Driving north, she said, "I told you it would fit."

Another couple had to help us get the bureau off the ground in the parking lot, but it did slide into the back with about half an inch to spare on each side. Nancy stuffed the margins with a blanket I didn't remember her keeping back there and tied the hatchback down with a couple of bungee cords I knew I'd never seen before.

I'd already told her I thought it weighed as many pounds as it had cost her dollars to buy the thing. "How come the desire for new furniture now?"

She glanced away from the road just long enough to gauge something. "All the stuff I have is from when my mom was alive. I'll still hold on to most of it, but there's a time to pull away from the old, and I decided that this was it."

"As long as the pulling away doesn't include me."

Her right hand left the stick shift and squeezed my left forearm. "Not likely."

"So, I told you about my embarrassing youth, how about you telling me something."

"I wasn't allowed to be an altar boy."

"Something else then."

Another glance, followed by a worried look that seemed only half feigned. "I don't have any embarrassing stories."

"Everyone has some, Nance. Don't worry, I won't tell anybody."

"You'll laugh."

"I promise I won't."

A deep breath, and the determined look came back. "When I was in high school, I . . ."

No need to push her.

A third glance. "I played the clarinet in the marching band."

I didn't laugh. I also didn't say, "What, somebody else already have dibs on the accordion?" but I was thinking it. "Were you any good?"

28

An edge in her voice. "Not very."

"Did you enjoy it?"

"Not much."

"Because you weren't good at it?"

"No, because . . ." Nancy seemed to realize how sharply she'd spoken and toned down. "No, because I really wanted to play the saxophone, but the music director thought the sax was a 'boy's instrument,' so I couldn't."

I thought back over the evening so far. "That also why you didn't find the altar boy story funny?"

"Because I wasn't eligible to be one?"

"Yes."

"Probably." Another glance, but this one full of warmth and heart. "God, could it be that I've fallen for a man who actually gets it without having to be beaten over the head with it?"

"Probably. Otherwise, you wouldn't have fallen for me, right?"

"I retract the last implied compliment."

We arrived in front of her house a few minutes later. There were empty spaces up the street, but given the weight of the bureau it seemed more sensible to double-park, which she did. Nancy went inside while I played with the bungee cords and the blanket. She came back with a long face.

"What's the matter, Nance?"

"Drew Lynch is on the four-to-twelve."

"Meaning he's not here to help us with this."

"He just swung on today. I should have called him, but I knew he'd been working days all week, and—"

I put up a hand. "Not to worry, we can handle it."

"John, it is awfully—"

"Hey, Nance, it doesn't weigh more than both of us put together, and besides, why do I do Nautilus if I can't manage some stevedoring once in a while."

"I don't think this is exactly stevedoring."

"Whatever. We'll work with you on the upside and me

29

JEREMIAH HEALY

on the down. There's a carpet runner on the stairs, so we just have to slide it, and we can rest a little on each step and a lot on the landings. Okay?"

"Maybe we should just wait for Drew to get home."

"And do what in the meantime, stand guard out here over a Civic with a dresser sticking out of its trunk?"

A smile toyed with the corner of her lips. "Hatchback."

I smiled back. "Hatchback."

"If you really think we can."

"I do, but why don't you take my jacket inside and change into shorts yourself so we can maneuver this thing more comfortably."

"Good idea."

She gave me a hug, took another look at the bureau, and trotted to the front door, returning changed with a pair of gloves for each of us.

"This pair should fit you. Drew uses them in the garden."

We slid the dresser out of the car carefully, no scratches I felt or heard. Carrying it on relatively level ground wasn't too hard, but I didn't look forward to heaving it heavenward a step at a time.

We set the thing down so Nancy could prop open the front door, and again inside so she could close it. As she was doing the door, I surveyed the staircase. A lot steeper than I remembered from simply climbing it.

Rocking the bureau, I moved it enough so that Nancy could get on its upstairs side. We lowered the back of the dresser onto the carpet runner. It took a lot of pushing from my downstairs end to move the thing up just one step.

"John, this isn't going to work."

"Sure it is. We just have a problem with the friction coefficient of your carpet runner."

She gave me the sort of withering look lawyers reserve for scientific information.

I said, "Tell you what. Go out and move the car to a legal space, then bring back the blanket."

30

Nancy climbed over the bureau and left, returning two minutes later, blanket in hand.

"Okay, now what I want you to do is put the blanket on the next step, and we'll use it as kind of a flat roller under the thing."

We tried that. A little easier to move it up the second step.

"Nance?"

"What?"

"Let's try it with the blanket again, but this time with the bureau on its side."

"That won't scratch it?"

"With the blanket, I don't think so."

We got the dresser on its side and made better, but still slow, progress as I had to recover the blanket every two steps and toss it back up to Nancy, the strain on my shoulder, back, and legs pretty impressive. We finally covered the rest of the steps to the first landing. Halfway home.

"John?"

"Yes?"

"My arms and legs are pretty tired."

"Blame it on your desk job."

We rested for five minutes, then started in again. It was harder after the rest, but we'd gotten only two steps from the top, from Nancy's landing, when I heard her foot skid and her voice yell my name and her bottom hit the deck. The full weight of the bureau slammed into me, my left shoulder feeling as though someone had drawn a razor blade across guitar strings, my left knee buckling as I managed to stop the slide after only one step lost.

"John, are you all right?"

"My shoulder and knee aren't great. You?"

"I think I'm just going to have a bruise on my rear end. What should we do?"

"Try to get this the rest of the way up."

"Can you?"

"I think going up will be easier than sliding back down."

She heard something in my voice that made her say, "John, thank you for this."

Using my right shoulder this time, I managed to drive the dresser back up the remaining steps like it was a blocking sled on an inclined football field. At the top, we got it upright, and Nancy maneuvered around the thing to give me another hug.

"That was above and beyond the call of duty, sir."

"I'll remember that."

When Nancy opened the apartment door, her gray-tiger cat scuttled out. Renfield was getting used to his rear legs not working quite right from an operation he'd needed on them, so he could move crablike pretty well. The sight of the bureau at first intimidated him, making him hide under the kitchen table. Then, once we had it against the wall in the bedroom, he couldn't get enough of it, sniffing and rubbing against the carved legs.

I said, "A good thing you had his front claws removed."

"Yes, but you know how they have to do that."

"No."

"They actually chop off the first knuckle of his toes."

"Hope they won't have to do that with me."

"Why?" she said, slipping out of her shorts.

"Because of the grievous injuries I suffered on your staircase."

"Yeah, right."

"I mean it, Nance. This may have to go to court."

"Forget it. The legal fees would eat you alive."

"I could represent myself."

A laugh.

I said, "Does that mean that if I represented myself I'd have a fool for a client?"

Nancy undid the buttons on her blouse. "John, anybody who represented you would have a fool for a client."

"Care to kiss a fool?"

"And then some." She opened the blouse and reached

32

both arms up and around my neck. When she applied a little pressure on my left side, the shoulder twinged and the knee started to buckle again.

Breaking the kiss, Nancy said, "What's the matter?"

"My shoulder and my knee can't seem to take much weight."

She canted her head. "Does that mean no hanky-panky for the assistant D. A. tonight?"

"That may depend."

"On what?"

"On how much you remember about playing the clarinet."

Nancy canted her head the other way. "John Francis Cuddy, I do believe that is the raciest thing you've ever said to me."

"The circumstances demand it."

"So long as you never do."

"Never."

She smiled the great smile. "I think . . . a concerto, then."

4

"How's the shoulder?"

I opened my eyes. Nancy was standing over me, holding Renfield against her blouse, the skirt to a blue suit, panty-hose, and dress shoes already on below it.

"What time . . . ?"

"Going on eight."

"You should have gotten me up, Nance."

"I wanted to be able to use the bathroom first. Besides, after the 'grievous injuries' last night, I thought your body could use the healing power of sleep." She narrowed her eyes. "Seriously, John, how do you feel?"

I rolled my left arm a little on the bed. "Okay, I think."

"And the knee?"

I flexed it. "No pain."

Nancy exhaled. "I'm so glad."

"Of course, I may have a relapse."

The canted head. "Calling for an encore on the clarinet?"

"It's rapidly becoming my favorite instrument."

"We'll see how frisky you are tonight."

"Tonight?"

She looked at me, a little strangely. "I thought I'd take you out to dinner, to thank you for all your help. Of course, if you have other plans . . ."

"I don't. It's just—"

"Fine, then," she said, but a little subdued, then checking her watch with a very upbeat "I've got to go. Occupy Renfield till I'm out of here, then help yourself to the fridge."

Easing the cat onto the bed, Nancy kissed me good-bye, but only on the forehead.

Renfield's eyes followed her out of the room. As soon as the apartment door closed, he nuzzled my hand, then began licking it, his tongue like sandpaper.

"Hey, Renfield, leave a little skin on that, okay?"

He squinted up at me, purred, and doubled the tempo of his licking.

When his hindquarters got hurt, Nancy took him to the vet's for the curative operation, but she had to be out of town when it was time to pick him up. When I did, he'd been in bad shape: shaved from the belly downward, groggy from the anesthetic, and hurting from his rearranged legs. I'd stayed up with him that night, and he'd "imprinted" on me, the vet called it. Now it was like he embraced me every time he saw me. I'd never been nuts about cats, but there was something about his attitude that . . . Jesus, what was wrong with me?

I rubbed Renfield on the head, then snapped my fingers a couple of times at the edge of the bed, the signal he'd learned for getting down. I threw back the sheets, hopped out of bed, and hit the floor. Literally.

My left knee had collapsed under me as soon as I put weight on it.

Renfield scuttled about six feet away from the noise of the impact, then came back cautiously to investigate, making a little moaning sound in his throat. I stayed on the floor, gingerly stretching out the joint. No pain still as I flexed it, and there had been only a brief, searing jolt when the knee buckled. Renfield nuzzled my left leg. I pushed him away, but he kept coming back. I got up using my right leg, very carefully shifting my weight onto the left one. No pain, no apparent weakness, and I found that I could walk fine so long as I kept my weight exactly over my feet.

Reassuring Renfield that everything was okay, I went out to the kitchen and had some toast and juice. I showered and found a clean shirt I'd left at Nancy's. Getting dressed in the bedroom, I made another unwelcome discovery. Putting my right arm into the sleeve of my suit jacket and grabbing the right lapel with my left hand to pull the jacket on, nothing happened.

There was no strength in my left shoulder. I couldn't draw my left hand across my chest against even the minimal resistance of the jacket sleeve on my right arm. There was just a clicking noise and the same twinge inside the shoulder I'd felt the night before with the bureau.

I looked at Nancy's newest piece of furniture. Walking over to it, I kept my weight centered. Then I kicked it in the part of its legs I took to be its shins.

What's the matter, John?

I raised myself awkwardly from where I'd laid the tulips crossways to her headstone. "Had a little problem hauling furniture, Beth."

You're getting kind of old for Pepsi Generation moving parties, aren't you?

"The ones in front of a rented van where beautiful people are smiling and the dog catches a Frisbee in its teeth?"

That's what I had in mind. A pause. *But that's not the whole story, is it?*

"No." I told her about Pearl Rivkind and William Proft.

Sounds like you think you did the right thing and made a mistake, all at once.

"Maybe not the only mistake, either."

The furniture moving again?

36

"Only partly, Beth. It's more Nancy and me."

Another pause. *How do you mean?*

"There've been some . . . I don't know. It's just that sometimes everything's just right and other times I'm not sure we're on the same wavelength."

What does she say?

"About what?"

About your . . . wavelengths.

"We haven't talked about it."

Sure you have, John. You just don't realize it.

I looked away from the grave toward the edge of the harbor below us. A Styrofoam board was crashing against the rocks, so weathered and battered it was hard to picture what it had been before going into the water.

John?

"Still here."

But trying not to be?

I looked back, not toward the headstone, but below that, to where she was. "What do you mean?"

You have a way, you always did, of closing off things you don't want to hear.

I shook my head. "Beth, I wouldn't have gotten this far, not as an MP or a claims—"

I don't mean professionally, John. I mean personally. You close off and miss things.

"Like what?"

Like whatever you and Nancy should be resolving.

"Which is?"

That's something you'll have to see for yourself. With her.

I watched the hunk of Styrofoam bounce off a few more rocks and started to empathize with it.

"John, how you doing?"

I looked at Elie, holding a clipboard behind the counter at the Nautilus club I'd joined a while before. He was the manager, his black hair, olive skin, and blue eyes the kind of mix he'd told me was typical of his Lebanese background.

"Not so good, El."

His face darkened. "When I didn't see you for a while, I figured it had to do with that gang . . . thing."

I'd been involved in a bad situation, a shoot-out with some members of a street gang into drug-pushing. "This is different, El. There's something wrong with both my shoulder and my knee."

"What happened?"

I told him.

"Gee, John, I don't think you'd better work out till you get things looked at."

"You know any good doctors?"

"Mostly just people at the Sports Medicine clinics. There are a couple of them, but you don't really have a sports injury, you know?"

"I know, but I'll need to be able to run and work out after whatever some doctor does to me, so I may as well start there."

He tore a sheet of paper off his clipboard. "Let me give you the one I'd go to."

I went back to the condo I was renting from another doctor doing a two-year residency in Chicago. Changing suits, I called the number Elie gave me, reaching a receptionist who sounded frazzled. She said they had a cancellation for later that same Wednesday and did I want it. I said I did. Then I walked downstairs, carefully, and got the Prelude out from the parking space behind the building.

"Yeah?"

I opened the door that had LIEUTENANT ROBERT MURPHY on it. He was sitting behind his desk, the penholder in front of him sporting a miniature American flag. Murphy wore a crisp white shirt with short sleeves, his black skin

38

contrasting with it and the gold-toned watch and wedding band. His paisley tie was snugged tight against the collar button, the pen in his hand hovering over a report he seemed to be revising.

"Cuddy. Forgive me for not getting up."

"That's okay, Lieutenant. Mind if I sit down?"

"Go ahead. Actually, it's kind of kismet, you know?"

I closed the door. "Fate?"

"Yeah. I was just doing the biyearly here."

"The homicide report?"

"Right. It's—what's wrong with your leg?"

"I had a little accident."

"The gang thing?"

"No. Nothing from them or anybody else about that."

"Good." He leaned back in the chair, lacing his fingers behind his neck. "Just as soon not have you any more in the statistics than you already are."

"How are things looking?"

"Not so bad, actually. A lot of cities, they had a banner year last time 'round, but we've been dropping since we hit the record with one-fifty in 'ninety."

"Nice to know it's safer out there."

"It isn't."

"I don't follow you."

"It isn't any safer. Used to be, the perps used sawed-off shotguns, then went to .380 automatics. Now the nine mil's the weapon of choice, account of the firepower. Fifteen, even eighteen rounds some of them, and you can pick one up for a hundred on the street. Shit, Uzi'll go for only twice that, and I was talking to a fed from ATF said they found a guy in Hyde Park with six MP-5's in his car trunk."

"That's the German thing?"

"Heckler & Koch. Light as a pistol, accurate as a rifle, and it'll fire thirty slugs in two seconds flat."

Christ. "How come the homicide statistics aren't going up, then?"

"We're getting better at handling the victims. More cops on the scene faster, more EMT's getting the wounded to hospitals, better trauma units once they get there. Hell, Cuddy, Boston's geographically small and our medical care's the best there is."

Glad to hear it. "I don't want to keep you from the paperwork too long."

"Meaning you want something."

"Just a little cooperation and understanding."

"Let's hear about the understanding part first."

"I've been hired on a missing-person case that might be tied to an open homicide."

"Which one?"

"Abraham Rivkind, the furniture guy got killed about three weeks ago."

"Cross drew that one."

"I thought she was on your squad?"

"So did I. Then the commissioner, he noticed he had exactly two so-called minorities in Homicide, so he decided it'd look better if the one black male and the one white female weren't both crowding the same three-person team. We reassigned folks, and with her already being a sergeant and all, Cross got to be head of her own squad."

Cross had a first name, "Bonnie," but I'd never heard him call her other than by the last. "She around?"

Murphy's eyes went to slits. "I'm guessing that brings us to the cooperation part."

"Lieutenant, I don't know if the killing and the missing person are related, but I figure the best way for me not to step on your toes is to find out what you've got and stay away from what you're watching."

"Cuddy, how come it always sounds so nice coming from you in the beginning and blows up by the time you work your way round to the end?"

"Kismet?"

A grunt. "Best you talk to Cross, then. Be her toes you'd

be stepping on, and I don't much like your chances for a life long and happy, you do."

"What?"

"Nice to see you, too, Sergeant."

"Cuddy, what?"

I sat in the chair beside her desk. On the desk were stacks of manila case folders and a box of assorted Dunkin' Donuts Munchkins. Behind the desk, Cross sat in a black, padded swivel chair with her elbows on the blotter. The elbows were even with her shoulders, which didn't need any padding to fill out the camel's hair blazer or the buttoned-down brown blouse underneath it. Her hair matched the blouse but was pulled behind her neck in a careless ponytail. She wore small pearl studs as earrings, no other jewelry except for a Timex on her left wrist, the face of the watch peeking at me as she reached for a powdered cinnamon and popped it into her mouth.

Around the Munchkin, she said, "For the third time, what?"

"I just talked with the lieutenant. He said you'd drawn the Rivkind killing."

"He ought to know."

"I've got a missing-person thing that might be related to it. I was wondering if we could talk some."

Cross stopped chewing and looked at me, then swallowed and brushed off her hands. Moving a file, she delved into a short stack of folders and came out with one that she opened in front of her. "Related as in a relative?"

"No. A secretary at the furniture store named Darbra Proft. Her brother's hired me to find her."

"*The* secretary."

"Don't get you."

"Proft, she's the one and only secretary they had, and she left work the day of the killing at like five-thirty. She was with a friend of hers at the movies when the boss got it."

I took out a pad. "Friend's name?"

"I've got Wickmire, Traci. Want the spelling and address?"

All roads do lead to Ms. Wickmire. "Thanks, already got them from the brother."

Cross closed the file and looked at me. "Guess that does it for you, then."

I returned the look. "How about some details on the crime."

"How about them?"

"Meaning, I've got just the secretary with an alibi, how come I'm still sitting here."

"Cuddy, you're still sitting there account of I haven't thrown you out. The question is, how come you're still interested in the homicide when it doesn't look like the missing person has anything but coincidence going for her with it?"

"The widow's also asked me in."

"The widow. Mrs. Rivkind?"

"Yes."

Cross dropped the eyes and the voice. "You know, I really feel sorry for her."

"How come?"

She passed a hand over the file like a magician disappointed with a trick. "Woman's lived her whole life for a man without knowing what the hell was going on in his."

"What was going on?"

Cross raised her eyes again. "Number one, the store was going to hell in a hand basket."

"Recession?"

"And the big suburban discount houses. Talk to the partner on that, Joel Bernstein."

"Number two?"

"Two, I've got enough smoke to make me think there was a little fire between the decedent and your Darbra there."

Shit. "Which is why you checked about the alibi."

"That and the phone call."

"What phone call?"

"The night he was killed, within probably ten minutes of him being attacked, there was a call placed from his office phone to her apartment."

"Who made the call?"

Cross smiled, some powdered sugar lodged at the corners of her mouth like dried foam. "That's a good question, isn't it? Abraham Rivkind or somebody else or whoever killed him. New England Tel records show the call was completed, but—"

"But how could it be, if Proft was out to the movies with Wickmire?"

A better smile before it disappeared around a honey-dipped Munchkin. "You're almost getting good at this, Cuddy."

"Practice."

"Yeah, you and me both. Anyway, Proft told us she had her tape machine on that night, and when she got home the message light was lit." Cross jumped her tone two octaves, " 'But like it was five minutes of just like dead space, you know?' "

"A direct quote?"

Cross answered in her own voice. "Afraid so."

"You believe her?"

"No. But it seemed kind of stupid for Proft to have an accomplice call her at home from the victim's number, so I didn't follow up much."

"Aside from the telephone call, any other connections with Rivkind?"

"She worked there, they were all smiles, and they were seen together a lot at this local restaurant."

"Grgo's?"

"That's the place."

"Who else was in the furniture store that night?"

"Salespeople were gone. Only ones left were the decedent, the partner, the bookkeeper, named Swindell, Beverly, and the security guard, named Quill, Finian."

I wrote down the guard's name. "What are their stories?"

"Pretty consistent. Decedent was killed in the office he shared with Bernstein on the fourth floor of the building. The windows are fireproofed, so they give light but no access or egress. Bernstein says he was in the crapper, also on the fourth floor. Heard the security alarm for the back door on the first floor go off, and finished up as fast as he could to run down there. Swindell says she was in her office on the fourth floor, down the hall from the partners' office. When she heard the alarm, she ran to find them."

"Why?"

"She'd been counting the cash from the day's take, and got panicked when she heard the alarm, so she went for Rivkind or Bernstein. She was pretty shaky by the time we got there."

"What about the guard, Quill?"

"He says he was on the first floor, near the front doors, where he's supposed to be, case some customer got so turned around they didn't realize the store was closing."

"So he could let them out."

"Without anybody else getting in."

"What was his reaction?"

"He says he was there at the front entrance when he heard the alarm. He ran to the rear of the building and went through the door, hoping to catch the guy going down the alley."

I tried to picture it. "How did Quill know it was a guy?"

"He didn't. He figured it's just somebody pulling a prank. They'd had a few lately, so he wanted to catch the guy or kid or whoever was doing it."

"Quill actually see anybody?"

"He says no. He went all the way down the alley, but the guy must have gone up and over the fence and God knows where after that, maybe for some *dim sum* at the Dynasty around the corner."

"And Bernstein joined Quill?"

"No. Bernstein says he started to go downstairs, then heard Swindell screaming."

"And so . . ."

"And so Bernstein goes down the fourth floor hall to her while Quill comes up the backstairs."

"Quill heard her, too?"

"Yeah."

"From the first floor?"

"The sound carries down the staircase. It's their fire stairs, they don't have an escape because of the windows not opening."

"So Swindell was screaming . . ."

"Because she's the one found the body, and she's screaming till she gets to the fire stairs, then opens that door and screams some more."

"And Quill and Bernstein join her."

"And basically destroy the fucking crime scene in the partners' office, though truth to tell, if they hadn't, we would have."

"How do you mean?"

"Oh, you know how it is, Cuddy. Alarm goes off, here comes the fire department. Then 911 gets a call, you got uniforms and EMTs and even media swarming all over the place before one of us gets there. Then it's like trying to orchestrate a fucking circus, all the people traipsing in and out. This one, though, it was more stupidicide."

"The killing itself, you mean."

"Yeah. Granted the perp must've panicked when he saw Rivkind still in the office, but he could've just run. He used the poker from the fireplace, not some weapon he brought in."

"The poker was the murder weapon."

"No question. From the location and angle of the wound, M.E.'s pretty sure Rivkind was at his desk, back to the door, when the killer comes in and picks up the poker. Rivkind's turning and standing as he gets it across the left temple, goes down onto the floor."

45

"Just the one blow."

"One was enough. Fractured his skull like an eggshell."

"How did Mrs. Rivkind take it?"

Cross started to say something, then didn't. "You know what the hardest part of this job is, Cuddy?"

I thought back to my time as an MP in Saigon. "Notifying the families."

"No, but I can understand why a civilian—" She shook her head. "Sorry. Forgot you were overseas. I can see what you mean. No, for us, the notification isn't the hardest part, because it's over quick. The people are so much in shock, they don't get emotional right away, and we're usually out of there before the real impact hits them. No, the tough part is dealing with the survivors, over the months and even years after the killing."

I nodded. "You don't think you're going to close this one, do you?"

"FBI says something like thirty percent of all homicides nationwide never get solved. Of the ones we do close, most of them are made on eyewitnesses, which we don't have here. Hell, there isn't so much as a physical description of the perp, and he didn't take anything away, not even the poker, which doesn't have but smudges on it, no readable latents or even partials. First twenty-four, forty-eight hours, you've got a good chance something new'll turn up. But now we're at what, three weeks tomorrow? Things get awful stale, that kind of time goes by and fresh bodies come in, barking at you for attention."

Cross shook her head. "No, that's the hardest part, Cuddy. Getting the calls from the family when you know the case isn't going anywhere, them asking us if we've checked things we already told them we checked, us telling them again. Some of the guys, they duck those calls, but I can't. Nobody wants to talk to the survivors, but I've got to, you know?"

Knowing her I knew. "Anything else you can give me?"

Cross thought about it, taking another Munchkin to help her. "We ran checks on everybody. Swindell had a continued-without-a-finding on a receiving-stolen-property back fifteen years ago, not even a traffic ticket since. Nobody else showed anything, but I thought this Quill breathed a little easier when he realized we weren't from INS."

"You think maybe he has an immigration problem?"

"Cuddy, you didn't know it, let me tell you. Half the brogues in this city have some kind of immigration problem, either in illegally or in legally and overstaying. Quill, though, I just had that feeling about him."

"I appreciate it, Cross."

"So how about your Darbra, what's the line on her?"

"I don't know much. She went off on vacation, she came back, then disappeared."

"And her brother hires you to go fetch."

"At least go find. Any other tie-ins to Ms. Proft from your end?"

"No, but she's a flashy one."

"I haven't seen a picture."

"Kind of blank face, a 'so-what-did-I-do' look on it. But big green eyes and legs to her chin and the kind of walk you can't be taught."

Cross said it like she'd once tried to learn it.

I stood up. "I find out something you should know, I'll be in touch."

She reached for another cholesterol ball. "Have one."

"Thanks, but my body's a temple."

Cross regarded the Munchkin like it was something precious. "My body used to be a temple. Now it's a ruins."

I left her chewing.

"What kind of day am I having, John? Let me tell you what kind. I'm having a Sol Wachtler day in a Woody Allen week, that's what kind of day I'm having."

"Sorry to hear it, Mo."

47

"Huh, tell me about it." Mo Katzen interrupted himself to set down his newspaper, whisk some tobacco ash from a dead stogie off the front of his vest, and lunge for a war memorial lighter on his desk. The lighter was the only functional thing on the desk, awash in the quasi-paperwork of baseball programs, playbills, sandwich wrappers, and God knows what else from fifty years of reporting, the last ten or so at the Boston *Herald*. "I tell you, John. I'm tired, dog tired."

Mo had been saying that since I'd met him, wearing the same outfit of the pants and vest to a three-piece suit without ever being seen in the jacket. His feet were up on a corner of his desk, the rickety manual typewriter still on the secretarial pull-tray, the old warhorse resisting computerization like it was the glue factory.

"Mo—"

"I mean, it's not just the hearing aid, which I still got to wear, God knows why. Actually, I know why. It's because I couldn't hear you talking to me, I didn't have the little bugger in. And it's not just old age, though I'm a lot sharper than most of these little shits snickering behind their hands because they can work the computers and they think I can't. I'll tell you why I'm so tired, you want to know."

"I want to know, Mo."

"I'm so tired, John, because I find myself bereft of ideas. That's a nice turn of phrase, don't you think? I first heard it from an old editor I had, Bissington, Jonas Bissington, as WASP as they come, but willing to give a Jewish kid a chance if the kid was willing to work and able to write a decent lead. Bissington, he sat me down one day, and he said to me, he said, 'Mr. Katzen'—he was a real formal guy, John, all the younger men Mr. this, all the women, younger or older, Miss this or Mrs. that. Anyway, Bissington, he says, 'Mr. Katzen, someday this will happen to you. Someday you will be in need of a column, a story, a bylined article, whatever'—he didn't say 'whatever,' John, that's just me, giving you the sense of it—and he looked at me and he said, 'Mr. Katzen, I stand before you, bereft of ideas. Provide me one.' Not 'provide me with one.' Oh no, Bissington was a stickler. But he was dry, John, pumped dry of ideas, and I was so taken back—taken 'aback,' Bissington would say—that I couldn't think of one. Not one idea, and me an energetic young man at the start of a promising career. So Bissington said to me, he said, 'Mr. Katzen, then I shall have to stoop, *stoop*, to reading the . . .'—and Bissington paused, John, and he made a face you wouldn't want to see over a meal. Then he finished by saying, '. . . the *class*-i-fieds.' I tell you, all things considered, it was not a pretty scene."

"I can imagine. Why—"

"Imagine? Imagi-*nation*, that's the problem, John. To get a new idea, you have to have imagination, an imagination, some imagination. Well, I got to tell you, I'm all out. Not that there haven't been plenty of newsworthy events. Last Wednesday, we had those three honor students killed in the drunk driving thing on Route 2. That night the North Shore woman supposedly lost overboard from a sailboat turns up tied and weighted down next to some lobsterman's traps. And then Friday, that airliner heading from here to D.C. hits the flock of geese down there, crashes, and kills half the people on board. Picture that, John, a flock of birds. I got a friend on the state police I can call on the students thing, another friend in the Coast Guard on the woman, and a contact over at Logan in the agency investigates air crashes. Great stories all, John, but they've been covered, every last one. And now I'm like Bissington. One toe in the grave, and pumped dry of ideas. So I'm stooping, *stooping* to reading the . . . *class*-i-fieds."

Katzen passed his hand over the pages he'd been holding when I came in, so much like Cross's gesture with the case file that I felt for him. "I don't get it, Mo."

"Don't get what?"

"How do the classifieds help you?"

"How? How? You just got to read them. Look."

Or listen, as Mo picked up the paper and traced with his now-dead-again cigar down a column. "Here, here's one. 'For sale or trade, four polar-bear rugs. Skins dingy, but all teeth, claws, and'—I love this, John—'eyes in good shape.' Now, you see what I mean?"

"There's a story in that ad."

"There's got to be a story. Who the hell has four polar-bear skins? How'd they get them? Where've they been? What are the chances of other ones being out there? It's like that, all through the ads. Oh, you're going to have ninety, ninety-five percent duds, but then that one comes up for you, and boom, you've got your idea."

"And you're no longer bereft."

Mo aimed his cigar at me. "Somehow, that doesn't sound too good coming from a man your age, John."

"Sorry, Mo. Listen, I was wondering—"

"I mean, a man your age shouldn't be bereft of anything except the foolishness of youth. That's a quote, too—from somebody else, not Bissington—though it wouldn't surprise me much, he was to have said it back when I knew him."

"He probably did. Mo—"

"You knew Bissington?"

"No, I—"

"Of course you didn't, you were born way too late. You shouldn't do that, John."

"Do what, Mo?"

"Try to confuse a tired old man like me. It makes us go off on tangents."

"Sorry, Mo."

"That's okay. Now, what brings you here?"

"I'm working on a missing-person/murder case."

"I don't get you. The missing person is dead, they're not missing anymore, right?"

"No, Mo—"

"Unless, of course, somebody stole the body after the person dies, but then it'd be a 'missing-body' case, right?"

"Right, Mo. I—"

"You ever have one of those?"

"One of . . . ?"

"A missing-body case."

"Not yet."

"The day will come, John. The day will come."

As all days do. "I was just wondering if you could get me into your paper's morgue for some stories on a killing that happened a few weeks ago, a killing that might be related to the missing-person case I've got now."

"Sure thing. Why didn't you say so in the first place?"

"My oversight, Mo."

He got me the issues for the days after Abraham Rivkind's death. The stories didn't tell me anything I hadn't already learned, and the obit with Pearl Rivkind mentioned prominently just reminded me of why I agreed to take the case to start with.

5

When I called my answering service, there was a message from William Proft. He'd reached Traci Wickmire, and she'd told him that I could come see her anytime that afternoon. I took the Mass Pike a few miles west to avoid the downtown traffic, then wound up Western Avenue and Harvard Street to Commonwealth Avenue.

Commonwealth stretches for a lot of miles and is featured prominently in the Boston marathon. The avenue starts at the Public Garden in Back Bay, where it's lined with stately townhouses and mansions that were once single-family, a few remaining so even today. Within a mile, though, Commonwealth winds through Boston University and Kenmore Square, just a bad hop from the Red Sox home at Fenway Park. After that, it's fast-food and electronics stores and mostly closed car dealers before doglegging left and climbing the long, slow hill toward Boston College, where Father Drinan once headed the law school and Doug Flutie once guided the football team, though not many alums would put the two men in that order.

About a mile from BC, the numbers approached the address Proft had given me for his sister's apartment house. It turned out to be a three-story stucco with a Bauhaus look to the beams in the walls. I found a parking space about a block away and walked back to it.

The entryway was recessed under a peaked miniroof. There were ten buzzers and mailboxes, none marked superintendent. I found WICKMIRE, T. under the button marked 31 and PROFT, D. under 21. Enough of the last names had full male first names after them that I wasn't sure the women were fooling anybody by using only their first initials.

I pressed 31 and heard an internal ringing. Then the glass doorway buzzed at me. I pushed through just before the buzzing stopped, entering a hallway with white and black diamond tiles and no rug except for a remnant that served as makeshift welcome mat. The bulb in the fixture overhead was maybe twenty-five watts, and it took a minute for my eyes to adjust to the central staircase in front of me. It had a steel bannister and posts painted black and a carpet runner that could have started almost any color but now was dirt-brown.

From an upper floor came a woman's voice that trilled like a dolphin's. "I'm on three."

I walked past a black door with a couple of locks showing through it and a single brass "1" at eye-level, a red blotch in the outline of what might have been another "1" next to it. After a full morning of using my knee, the joint seemed okay going upstairs, wobbling only on the way down them, but I still took it easy. At the first landing were three doors marked in brass 21, 22, and 23. Climbing to the second landing I could see only a 32 and a 33, because the door to 31 was swung in.

I knocked on the jamb of the open door.

From somewhere inside, the trilling voice said, "That's why I left it o-pen," a lift to the last syllable.

The apartment had a short corridor beyond the door, which I closed behind me.

The voice said, "Just throw that bolt, o-kay?"

There was a deadbolt, and I turned it.

"Find me if you can," again with the last syllable rising.

I found myself not looking forward to spending time with a Flipper impersonator.

At the end of the short corridor, the apartment branched right and left. To the right was another short, darker corridor with two doors, both closed, that I assumed led to bedroom and bath. To the left was brighter, a gift of sunshine from the front of the building having southern exposure.

Walking left, I entered a living room/dining area. A small gateleg table and one straight-backed chair stood outside a kitchen barely big enough for the appliances in it. The scent of potpourri wafted from the stovetop, the gas on underneath it even though the outside temperature was pushing seventy-five. The living area had framed, artsy photos of women in aerobic tights on the walls and sectional furniture upholstered in what looked like the hide from Tonto's pinto pony. The furniture was arranged in no apparent pattern, with a corner piece facing me, two side pieces together against a wall, and a second corner piece literally facing the corner, a plush dunce chair.

In the center of the room, on another side piece, a petite woman sat Indian-style, her ankles under the opposite thighs and a small computer on what there was of her lap. She had kinky hair that ran to strawberry blond, barely shoulder length but tousled like she'd just gotten out of bed. Her clothing consisted of blue jeans with tears through the knees and a green flannel shirt so many sizes too big that she had to roll the sleeves twice for them to end at her wrists. The woman inclined her head downward, consulting a spiral notebook that lay folded over next to the little computer.

"Ms. Wickmire?"

She looked up, big eyes and a broad nose over a coy smile on thin lips. "Found me."

"I had a lot of hints."

The smile lost some of its coyness, then regained it. "You're the detective, right?"

"Private investigator."

"What's the difference?"

"Detectives are on police forces. I don't have any official status."

"Is that like a *Miranda* warning?"

"Is what?"

"Your telling me you don't have any . . . 'official status.' "

"No. As long as I didn't show any hoked-up ID or misrepresent myself, I could let you go on with whatever false impression you drew yourself."

"Wild Bill told me your name was Cuddy."

"John Cuddy."

"Does that mean that I get to call you by your first name?"

More coyness, but without any body language to go with it, as though she were trying to act out a *Magnum, PI* or *Rockford Files* but had been given only her dialogue, not any stage directions. "Ms. Wickmire, you can call me anything you like."

"Why do I get the feeling you're *not* flirting with me?"

"Maybe because neither of us is."

Wickmire lost the smile entirely, then hit a few keys on the computer and a switch on its side. "Since it looks like you'll be here awhile, I'll conserve the battery."

I took her comment as an invitation to sit, which I did in the corner piece in front of me. "That a laptop?"

She shook her head. "Next generation. A 'notebook,' though I'm told there're now 'subnotebooks' for the executive who's really on the go."

The lifting voice again, the sarcasm more evident face-to-face. I said, "And you're an executive not on the go?"

Wickmire closed the cover of the computer and set it and the spiral notebook aside, bringing her feet out from under her. The feet were bare, the nails painted a salmon pink approximating the shade of her hair. "Wild Bill didn't tell you much about me, did he?"

I took out a pad just a little smaller than hers. "You can speak freely."

She seemed to catch herself starting to smile, then didn't. "I'm a free-lance writer, Mr. Cuddy. Right now I'm working on an article for *Boston Magazine* about the local charities. We're going to separate the needy from the greedy."

"Catchy."

Wickmire seemed to measure something. "You aren't exactly trying to butter me up, are you?"

"No."

"Why?"

"When I came in here, you played at being playful without seeming to mean it. Then you seemed to settle down somewhere around witty, so I'm just going along till I figure out what's going on."

"I don't think you'd be a fun interview."

"I don't know how much your audience would be interested in reading."

"Somehow I doubt that. But, like you said, let's 'figure out what's going on.' Darbra's what's going on for you, right?"

"I've been hired to find her, and most of the people I've talked with seem to point me toward you."

"Ask your questions."

"How did you and Ms. Proft come to know each other?"

"Boy, we're starting way back, huh?"

"It's usually the best place."

"Okay. How. We met in college. Drama class. I was taking it because I wasn't sure what I wanted to do with myself: actress, playwright, muckraking journalist. Darbra was a little more focused, and, of course, she went further with it."

"How do you mean?"

56

"Oh, she used to do summer stock on the Cape or up in New Hampshire, Vermont. You know, *The Fantasticks* and that kind of schmaltzy stuff, where you fiddle around with the costumes and makeup while you're also the star for the week."

"How long did the acting last?"

"Not long. Darbra's big on looks, but short on talent. I saw her once. She kind of . . . overplayed things, in order to stand out, you know?"

Pretty frank for a good friend talking to a stranger like me. "You stayed in touch after school, then?"

"More or less. We both settled in the area. She bounced around, workwise. Mostly Mac-jobs."

"I'm sorry?"

"Mac-jobs, like the fast food. Office temp, morning shift in a health club, the kind of short-term stuff that's all your generation will let our generation have the chance to do."

I'd forgotten. "How long have you lived here?"

"About a year? Yeah, about. We were both looking at the same time, and these like identical one-bedrooms came up in this building. I guess I saw the ad first, in the paper, and Darb was having lunch with me, and we came over together to see them. We liked both places, so we tossed a coin, and I won."

"You won?"

"The higher-floor unit. Less noise from the street."

"You both were looking at one-bedrooms?"

Wickmire suddenly grew cautious. "That's right."

"Why?"

"What do you mean, why?"

"Well, a free-lance writer and a free-lance everything, I'd have thought two college friends might try to room together, save some money."

A shrug that didn't quite come off. "Prices were right, the recession and all. Besides, our allergies don't match."

"I don't get you."

57

"Darb has a cat. I'm allergic to their dander."

"What's her allergy?"

The coy smile. "I'll let you guess when we see her place."

Moving right along. "Ms. Proft talk with you much about work?"

Another shrug, this one real. "What's to tell? Boring, boring, *bor*-ing, except for one special somebody."

"Who?"

"She won't tell me. Darb's like that. I came in on her once, on the phone, talking baby sweet talk to somebody. She was rolling her eyes, and I tried to make her laugh, but she held on till she hung up, then she and I roared till I thought we'd pee our—uh-oh, did I shock you?"

"Not yet."

"Gives me something to shoot for."

Again the rising voice. "Ms. Wickmire—"

"I decided I'd rather you call me 'Traci.' "

"Traci."

"I mean, if I can call you anything I want, you should be able to call me anything you want, right?"

The rising voice was the only coloring on the flirting lines, because she didn't deliver them with anything else. "Traci—"

"And I'll call you 'John.' "

"Traci, she never told you who at work it might have been?"

"No, I just asked her, 'Who the fuck was that, your sugar daddy?' Oh-uh, I just used 'fuck.' Now I have shocked you."

"My generation doesn't shock that easily, all the practice we've gotten holding yours back."

Wickmire rubbed the knuckles of her toes. "I think you're a lot more clever than you show at first, John."

"What did Ms. Proft—"

"As long as we're so flexible with names, can we call her 'Darbra'?"

"Fine."

"I mean, it's a super name, and there's at least a chance she's dead, so why not speak nice about her?"

The air felt a little cold. "You think she's dead?"

"I don't know. But she is missing, and you started me way back in college with her, so I have to think you believe it's a ... 'distinct possibility.' Why do you think I've been telling you all this so straight?"

"Traci, what exactly did Darbra say when you asked her who the man on the other end of the phone was?"

"I don't know, something like, 'Yeah, kind of.' "

"Kind of what?"

"Kind of her sugar daddy, I guess."

"Do you remember when this was?"

"A month, six weeks ago. It was no big thing with Darb, John."

I took some notes. "What was no big thing?"

"Talking to a man on the phone. She had her share."

No lift to that sentence. "She saw a lot of men?"

"Saw them, touched them, fucked them. There, if that doesn't shock you, I don't know what will."

"How many?"

"We could check her bedpost for notches."

"How many recently that you know of?"

"How many. Well, sugar daddy, whoever he is. The married guy, and—"

"What married guy?"

"This guy, lived out in the suburbs somewhere. They were a thing almost since we moved in here. I used to see him when he'd come in to Darb's for a little ... what did you call it when you were young, 'trysting'?"

Not even formally. "Can you describe him?"

"Yeah, but wouldn't his name be a little more help to you?"

I looked at her. "It would."

"Okay. His name's Roger Houle. It sounds like 'jewel,' but it's spelled like French."

59

"H-O-U-L-E?"

"I think so."

"Address?"

"I don't know, but you can find out easy enough."

"How?"

Wickmire looked at me as though I should be sitting in the sectional piece facing the corner. "They used to phone each other all the time to set up 'logistics,' Darb said he called it. All you have to do is check with Ma Bell, right?"

Not quite as easy as that. "Okay—"

" 'Course, he's not going to be much help to you, John."

"He's not?"

"Uh-unh. Darb broke up with him, oh, a month ago, maybe?"

I thought about it. "Before or after the 'sugar daddy' call?

She took a moment. "After. I remember thinking, 'Well, it's a good thing she still has her sugar daddy.' "

"Did you say that to Darbra?"

"No." Wickmire seemed indignant. "That would have been pretty insensitive of me, don't you think?"

"Whose idea was it to break up?"

"I don't know, but probably Darb's."

"Why?"

"Men who are stupid enough to get involved with her don't usually walk away from her. She said it was a real screamer, though."

"What was?"

"The breakup. In a restaurant yet, can you picture it?"

"Which restaurant?"

"Some place over by her job. Funny name . . ."

"Grgo's?"

"That's it. Yeah."

I didn't really want to ask the next question. "This special somebody from the furniture store, the 'sugar daddy,' could he have been the man who was killed there?"

Wickmire wiggled her toes. "I wondered about that, even

kind of hinted around it, you know, but Darb won't say. I can tell you this. She was really upset about it."

"About the killing, you mean?"

"Yes."

"You were with her that night?"

"The night the man was killed, you mean?"

"Yes."

"Yeah, we went out to the movies."

"What time?"

"About seven, got back at nine-thirty, ten, and I'm just about through my apartment door when she calls to tell me the cops were on her answering machine about it."

"The cops were."

"Right."

"No other messages?"

"She didn't mention any."

"But she was upset."

"Yeah, but you have to know Darb."

"What do you mean?"

"Well, she was more like 'Aw fuck, what do I do now?' not 'Ohmigod, my poor boss just got killed.' "

"Okay. So we've got the sugar daddy and Roger Houle. Any other recent men?"

"Just her new boytoy."

Boytoy. "Who's that?"

"Rush Teagle."

For some reason the name sounded familiar. "You know how I can find him?"

"You're probably sitting about thirty feet above him."

One of the names by the mailboxes. "He lives here."

"Basement apartment. That way he can practice without driving the rest of us nuts."

"Practice what?"

"Guitar. He's got this band. I think he'd like to call it 'Rush,' but that was already taken, you know?"

"How long has Darbra known Teagle?"

"I'm not sure. He's been sniffing around her awhile, but I don't think they were making it until a few weeks ago."

"After the breakup with Houle?"

Wickmire gave the impression she was concentrating hard on my question. "About the same time, I think."

"By 'boytoy,' I take it you mean—"

"Sex toy. Human dildo." There was a trace of bitterness before the coyness kicked back in. "Oh, that got you a little, didn't it? Darb once said to me, 'Trace, if Rush had a CB in that convertible, his handle'd be Wagon Tongue.' Let me tell you, John, she has quite an appetite that way. Just another reason why it's more fun to be with her than to live with her."

As if Wickmire needed another reason beyond the dander allergy. "Tell me, Traci, if Teagle was seeing Darbra and lived in the building, why didn't she ask him to feed her cat?"

"Why?"

"Yeah, you having the allergy to it and all."

"Outside of bed, Rush isn't what you'd call the most reliable guy in the world."

I glanced through my notes. "Any other men?"

"Not that I know of, John, but that doesn't necessarily mean there weren't any."

"When did Darbra leave on vacation?"

"Let's see . . . Week ago this past Saturday."

"You're sure?"

"Well, that's when she said I was supposed to start feeding Tigger."

"Her cat."

"What else would you name 'Tigger'?"

"Did you see her that day?"

"No, but she called me the night before, to make sure I was going to be able to do it."

"Feed him, you mean?"

"Right."

"So she called you before she left a week ago Saturday."
A nod.
"How about when she got back?"
The coy smile. "Not a word."
"When did you expect her back?"
"She was supposed to be gone a week, so Saturday or Sunday, I wasn't sure."
"When did she get back?"
"Saturday, four days ago."
"How do you know that?"
"When I fed Tigger Friday night, her clothes and stuff weren't on the bed. When I came in Saturday night, they were."
"You feed him Saturday morning?"
"Yeah."
"Did you check the bedroom?"
"In the morning, you mean?"
"Yes."
"No, I didn't."
"But you did at night."
"Right."
"Why?"
"It's a small apartment, John, but you're responsible for it, you like to make sure everything's okay. Like nobody broke in through the win-dow?"
The sarcastic lift. "You know where Darbra stayed on her vacation?"
"No, but I think there's a way we can find out."
"How?"
"There might be something in her mail about it."
"Her mail?"
"Yeah. I picked it up all week and put it on her table."
"Which table?"
"The one outside her kitchen, like mine there, only she doesn't have a gateleg. Hers is a—"

"You collected Darbra's mail all week and left it on that table?"

"That's what I said, John."

"Was the mail still there Saturday morning?"

"Huh?"

"Was her mail still—"

"Oh. Oh, I get it. To see if she got back Friday. Hey, that's pretty good, you know?"

"Was the mail still there?"

Wickmire closed her eyes, really squeezed them shut. "I don't remember." She opened her eyes. "Sorry."

"That's all right."

"But I know where the mail is now."

"Where?"

"On the bed, with her clothes and stuff."

I folded my pad. "Maybe we'd better take a look."

"That's what you came here for, right?"

The sarcastic lift as she left her sectional piece and moved toward the kitchen.

6

———————

"HEY, YOU ALL RIGHT BACK THERE, JOHN?"

"Yes, fine." My knee had buckled as I took the first step down the stairs behind Wickmire.

"Good. Last thing I need right now is medical bills."

At the second-floor landing, we stopped in front of the door marked 21. Wickmire made a production of putting the key in the two locks and turning it with gusto each time. Pushing the door a crack, she kept her foot, now wearing sneaker and sock, in the opening.

"Keep back, Tigger. Stay inside, now."

Looking down, I could see an orange tabby's head and forepaw struggling against Wickmire's foot before giving up and disappearing.

"Tigger always tries to get out, and it's a pain to catch him on the stairs."

Wickmire let me go inside first, the cat starting down the short corridor, then returning to blink curiously at me. Closing the door behind us, Wickmire said, "Believe me, seeing

65

a strange man come into this apartment is not the trauma for Tigger that it might be."

I walked down the oriental runner that covered most of the short corridor. At the end of it, the floor plan of Darbra Proft's apartment seemed identical to Wickmire's. I turned left first, into the living/dining area.

There was another oriental rug, a big one with a marble coffee table in the center of it and a hunter's-print couch and love seat grouped around it. The drapes over the windows picked up a minor color of the rug and the print. On the walls were etchings, artist's proofs. The small table outside the kitchen was antique cherry with one ladderback chair, a mate to the chair next to a Governor Windsor desk in the corner, the drop leaf closed. A television, in a big wooden cabinet like you don't see anymore, but no stereo or . . .

"Darbra doesn't have a VCR?"

"Uh-unh. Can't work it."

"Just the clock, or the whole thing?"

"Whole thing. She's hopeless with remote control stuff, and she's barely computer literate. I don't know how she gets along at work."

I tried to take in the living area as a whole. Lamps, end tables, miniature shelving with lots of figurines, like Hummels, jade elephants, and bronze tigers. Even the knick-knacks looked pricey.

"Nice furnishings."

Wickmire looked around casually. "Darb got some big bucks when her mom died. My guess is this is all that's left from it."

I indicated the cherry table. "That where you piled the mail?"

"Yeah, but there wasn't so much that you'd exactly call it a pile."

The sarcastic lift. I walked from the living area past the table into the kitchen. Hard not to notice the table as I did.

"Tigger, beat it, willya?"

I looked back at Wickmire, who was trying to shoo the cat away with her sneaker.

She said, "They can always tell when you can't stand them, you know?"

There was a strong smell of used cat litter in the air. "If it's tough on your allergy, I can do this part without you."

"No. I mean, I'm okay as long as I don't try to cuddle with him. Besides, you're in here because I let you in, and so I'm feeling kind of responsible."

"Where's the cat food?"

"You serious?"

"Yes."

Wickmire went past me into the kitchen. Bending down, she opened a cupboard next to the sink and came out with a box of dry cereal and two cans as examples. "Cat food."

I thought about Nancy's Renfield. "Dry food in the morning, canned at night?"

"Right."

"Are there as many cans as you saw Friday night?"

"Of course not. I've fed Tigger ever since Monday."

"Monday?"

"When Wild Bill called me about Darbra not showing up at work."

"What I meant was, are there any cans missing other than the ones you used?"

Wickmire stared at me for a moment, then looked down at the cans in her hand and back into the cupboard. "I don't know. There's six, seven, eight—eight left now. I couldn't tell you if there used to be nine or ten, if that's what you're getting at."

"What I'm getting at is whether Darbra might have fed him since she got back."

"Oh. Oh, I see what you mean. No. I mean, I can't help you on that."

I walked around the living room. Something was both-

67

ering me. After not being occupied for a week, a room should be a little musty, and this one was, but there was something else.

"Traci, any of the windows open when you came in on Saturday?"

"No, not morning or night."

Odd, you're away on vacation, come back to a musty apartment, then don't air it out. But the room was different beyond that. Aside from the cat litter, it had no real smell, as sterile as a no-smoking room in a hotel.

I moved back through the place to the corridor that I assumed led to bedroom and bath. I tried the door on the right first. A small bathroom with a tub/shower unit, hopper, and sink installed with a sense for space that would have done a submarine designer proud. The only available floor was occupied by the litter box, pretty full.

I said, "Any spare kitty litter around?"

"Beats me. Why, you want to change it?"

No, but I'd have thought a person returning home from vacation and using this bathroom might have.

Above the little box were blue and white tiles, blue and white towels. I felt the towels and a face cloth hanging from a wire shelf on the shower head. Bone dry. Same for the soap. I took a deep breath through the nose. Same sterile sense. I picked up the soap. No scent at all.

Behind me, Wickmire said, "You're getting warm," with the teasing lift at the end.

I turned and looked at her, then put the soap back into its dish and crossed the hall to the other door. It led to a bedroom with a mahogany four-poster high enough to need a little two-tiered step stool next to it. The posts had carved pineapples at the top. The bed was covered with a quilted comforter, the sheets underneath soft and supple. At the center of the bed an old hard-sided suitcase was opened, envelopes scattered next to it.

I looked around the room. The bureaus, a highboy and a

lowboy, were also mahogany and reminded me enough of Nancy's new one that I felt it in my shoulder and knee. Wickmire used the stepstool to get up onto and sit at the edge of the bed.

I walked to the lowboy. A four-by-six photo in a stand-up frame showed a man in his early twenties and a woman in her early thirties. The man had dishwater-blond hair worn long and parted in the center, a lecherous grin on his rugged, tanned face, and a chain of what looked like human teeth around his neck. He was dressed in a black T-shirt and black jeans, the butt of an elaborate guitar resting on his crotch. The woman had auburn hair, worn just past her shoulders. Leering at the lens, she was dressed only in a bikini bottom and midriff halter top without a bra, her body draped around his left arm and shoulder, her own left hand seeming to stroke the barrel of the guitar.

In a tired voice, Wickmire said, "The one and only."

"Darbra and Rush Teagle?"

"In one of their family-entertainment moments."

"How long ago was this taken?"

"She bought the bikini for the vacation, so just before she left."

Only a few weeks ago, then. "He looks pretty young."

"He is pretty young. Twenty-two, maybe."

I focused on the woman in the shot. "Darbra looks older than twenty-eight."

"It's not the years, it's the mileage. And by the way, that's not exactly the first photo in that frame."

I turned to her. "Who else was there?"

"Old Rog, for one."

"That's Roger Houle?"

"Right. Posed with Darbra, of course."

"I don't have a recent picture of her. Can I take this one?"

"I guess so."

I slid the backing from the frame. It did come off rather easily. I put the photo in my jacket pocket and looked back at the top of the bureau. China ashtray that held coins and subway tokens, hair brush, hand mirror; woven Easter-egg basket with a pair of sunglasses, bracelets, earrings, a Swatch watch.

The taller bureau had on it just another photo in a stand-up frame. This one was eight-by-ten, though, and showed two women in the bathing suits and hairstyles of the early sixties. One was a little more stolid than the other, but there was a striking resemblance of one to the other and both to Darbra.

"Who are these people?"

Wickmire said, "Darbra's mom and aunt."

"Do you know which is the aunt?"

"The heavier one."

"Darlene Nugent?"

"I think that's her last name."

Which confirmed what William Proft had told me. No photo of him, though. And as I took a breath, the rest of it hit me, too.

I looked back at the lowboy. "No perfume."

"Bing-o."

I looked at Wickmire. "That's Darbra's allergy?"

"To all kinds. She nearly sued this department store, one of their cosmetics whores tried to spray some on her in an aisle once."

I moved to the suitcase on the bed. It had been jammed with clothes, because they rose up from both sides of the clamshell. Shorts, tops, blouses, swimsuits, underwear, all mixed together and wrinkled.

"Did Darbra usually pack like this?"

"Like what?"

"All jumbled."

Wickmire looked at the opened suitcase and shrugged. "I don't know. She wasn't the world's neatest person, and after all, she was coming back, you know?"

"Coming back?"

70

"From vacation. I mean, it's not like she was packing to go *on* vacation."

Made some sense. I crossed back to the lowboy and opened the top drawer. Underwear, jumbled. Next drawer, shirts and blouses neatly folded. Next drawer, cotton sweaters and one wool, neatly folded. The highboy had paperwork crammed into its top drawer, bundled in rubber bands. I pulled out a couple of bundles. Bank statements and rental receipts, but even the most recent was well over a year ago.

The next drawer had shorts and T-shirts, all jumbled. More clothes in the next three, alternatingly folded or jumbled, with the key seeming to be the more casual, the less neat.

I opened her closet door. Dresses and blazers and skirts neat, laundry in a heap at the bottom over a few dozen pairs of shoes, also helter-skelter, and three handbags.

I said, "Do you know how Darbra keeps her keys and money?"

"How she keeps them?"

"Yes. Key chain, wallet, what?"

"She's got a key chain, and a wallet, sure."

"You seen them around since she got back?"

Wickmire's eyes roamed the room. "No."

I came back to the bed. "You said you didn't know where she was on vacation. You think the mail would help?"

She ticked a couple of envelopes with a fingernail. "That's where I'd start."

The mail wasn't very much. Junk mail from contests telling her she may already have won, a couple of credit card solicitations. No charitable ones, though, and only one real bill.

Her tab from New England Telephone.

I opened that. The local calls wouldn't appear, and I'd need a court order or police intervention to get them from the company. There were a few message units early in the

71

billing period to an exchange in Meade, a suburb southwest of Boston where I'd had a case a few years ago. No charges for anything out-of-state.

I said, "Does Roger Houle live in Meade?"

"Yeah, now that you mention it. That on there?"

She looked at the bill. "I guess that's him."

Wickmire kept looking at the bill even though she'd answered my question.

I said, "Something wrong?"

"No, it's just . . . Well, I thought she might have charged the call she made to me, but I don't think the statement goes that far."

"What call?"

"Last week. Darbra called me from wherever she was, and I kind of thought she might have charged it to her home phone, you know the way you can?"

"You spoke to her while she was away?"

"That's what I said."

"What did she say?"

"Just the usual. How's Tigger, what's the weather like up there, you know?"

"When was this, Traci?"

"Well, let's see. I went out for drinks last . . . Tuesday? No, Wednesday. So it was Tuesday, like she was checking up on me."

"Checking up?"

"Making sure I was taking care of Tigger."

"She ask you any other questions?"

"No. She didn't even come right out and ask about me feeding the cat. Darbra's kind of like that."

"Like what?"

"Always being indirect. She likes to come at you from the side, or behind, if it suits her."

"She didn't say where she was?"

"No, just the town."

"What?"

"I said, just the town."

"I thought you told me before that you didn't know where she was staying on vacation?"

"Yeah, but I meant I didn't know *exactly* where. She went to this beach town in New Jersey, but I don't know the motel or whatever."

I tried to keep the impatience out of my voice. "Which town, Traci?"

"Sunrise. Or Sunrise Beach, if there's a difference."

"A difference?"

"Like with Miami and Miami Beach. She used both names."

"Both."

"Both Sunrise and Sunrise Beach."

I glanced again at the current phone bill. "You figure all her old bills are in the top of the highboy?"

"I think those are just the way-back ones. The more recent things she keeps in the desk in the living room."

Before leaving the bedroom, I went through the open suitcase. Nothing but the clothes and a toilet kit and a little sand that had sifted down into the corners of the case.

Wickmire followed me back along the corridor to the living area. At the Governor Winthrop, I lowered the drop leaf and positioned the chair for sitting. The cubby-holes held rubber bands, pencils, a Flair pen and two Bic ballpoints, a small calculator, stamps, and blank envelopes.

I raised the drop leaf. The first drawer had bundles of bills, these more current. I went through her charge card statements for the past year. Lots of clothes purchases, not much else, and no entertainment items. Either she paid cash or got treated. Same for her bank statements, but no indications of checks being deposited beyond her salary, which was only five-ten and change take-home twice monthly. It seemed she spent her money on rent and clothes and that's it.

"Traci?"

"Yeah—Tigger, will you quit it? What?"

"Darbra have a car?"

"No. Can't drive either."

"Can't or doesn't?"

"Well, I guess I'm not sure she *can't*, but I've never seen her."

"Then how did Darbra get to New Jersey?"

When Wickmire didn't answer, I turned around in the chair.

She said, "I don't know."

I went back to the bills, this time the bundle for the telephone. Over the months, more calls to Meade, including some, in fact the majority, to a different number in the same town.

"Does Darbra know anybody else in Meade?"

"Besides Old Rog?"

"Yes."

"I don't know. But he was in business out there, real estate, I think, so maybe she was calling him both places. She's so dar-ing."

There were no calls to any New Jersey number going back to the earliest statement in the current bundle. There was one from the middle of March to a Salem exchange, where William Proft said his aunt Darlene had her store. The other calls would take a while to sort out, probably by my calling them, if it came to that.

"Traci, I'm going to take these phone bills and the one from the bedroom as well."

"Help your-self."

Finishing with the other drawers, I sat at the desk a minute. There was something bothering my pants cuff.

I looked down to see the cat, looking back at me with a curious expression on his face. "I don't know either."

Wickmire said, "What?"

"Skip it. You think I can find Teagle in his apartment?"

She glanced out the window. "He doesn't have a practice studio, and it's a little early for the club scene, you know?"

74

"He's a full-time musician?"

"No. He's a part-time musician and a full-time nothing else."

"Unemployed?"

"More like unemployable. But wait till you meet him, form your own impres-sion?"

I wasn't sorry to be saying good-bye to Trac-i.

7

AROUND THE CORNER FROM UNIT 11 WITH JUST THE SINGLE BRASS "1" was a narrow staircase going down steeply. My knee started to give again on the fourth step, and I felt another twinge in my left shoulder as I reflexively grabbed the bannister to steady myself.

In the basement, there was only one door that wasn't marked BOILER-ROOM or STORAGE, and it didn't have any brass number or letter. The noise coming from behind it was reassuring, though.

Electric guitar, doing chords in no particular order that I recognized.

I knocked on the door. With no break in the guitar-playing, a smoky male voice said, "Go away."

I knocked harder. The voice said, "It's the middle of the fucking afternoon. I can play now unless there's a fire."

"Fire" came out sounding like "far." I knocked harder still, and the playing stopped.

The voice said, "I told you to fuck off!"

With the flat of my hand, I started banging on the door

like Krushchev with his shoe at the U.N. No more playing, but a bolt got thrown on the other side, and the door flew open.

The young guy from the photo on Darbra's bureau stood in front of me. Six-two plus, we were eye-to-eye. He was naked to the waist, his torso and arms tanned and husky but not muscular, torn shorts with gawky but tanned legs underneath, as though upper and lower bodies had come from different people and been sewn together, then baked to an even brown.

Into my face, he yelled, "I told—who the fuck are you?"

I gave him a flash of my ID holder. "My name's Cuddy. Darbra Proft's brother reported her missing, and I'm here to talk with you about it."

Teagle tried to follow the ID as I refolded its holder. There's no badge in it, state law says there can't be, but I already had his attention.

The eyes were wary as he looked back at me. "I don't need no hassling from the cops."

"Best way not to get hassled is to cooperate, Teagle."

"I don't got time. I'm like working here."

"Here" sounded like "her."

"I heard your work. We can talk now, or I can pull you off a gig somewhere when it suits me. Your choice."

Teagle mulled that. The expression in the photo was a pose, as most photo expressions are. In real life, he had a hard time maintaining anything but an air of confused stupidity. I thought about Cross calling Abraham Rivkind's murder "stupidicide," and I wondered.

"Awright, awright. I'm getting a little tired anyhow."

"Tired" came out "tarred." As he led me into the apartment, I said, "Where are you from originally, Teagle?"

"What difference does it make?"

"That doesn't sound like cooperation to me."

"Fuck. I'm from Baltimore, awright?"

Ball-a-more. The inside of his apartment was low-ceilinged

77

and sooty, probably from the wood stove in the corner. The stove didn't look very professionally mounted on the bricks underneath it, the fireplace tools lying on the bricks instead of in their upright stand behind the stove itself. The room was a modified studio, with a king-sized bed, covers unmade, in another corner and a couple of dinette chairs grouped around some music stands near the center. There was a stack of stereo equipment next to a nineteen-inch TV with a VCR, viewable only from the bed. Spoiled smells came from a galley kitchenette, dirty pots on the range. A bathroom, with towels hung over the shower rod and wadded on the floor, was visible through a half-open door in another wall. There were no windows, and the only light fell from a faint overhead fixture and a candle burning on a heap of dark, bagged shapes.

Teagle sat in one of the dinette chairs, carefully easing into a soft-shelled black case the guitar from the photo on Darbra Proft's bureau. "So, like what do you want?"

I took another chair and straddled it, my forearms resting on its back. "What led you to come up here?"

"What, you mean like to Boston?"

"That's what I mean."

"I was on tour, man."

"Tour."

"Yeah. Me and some of my buddies from the old group were opening for this mega-band. Maybe you heard of it." He named the band; I hadn't. "Anyways, we went all around the northeast, playing tight and getting raves, man, raves. But their drummer, he like OD'ed one night doing a college gig up here, and the manager stiffed *us* on the bread, like it was our fault their drummer couldn't balance his shit. My buddies kind of freaked, but I'd saved my money and stayed on up here when they went back to Maryland."

Murl-lind. "They leave you their equipment?"

"Huh?"

78

I inclined my head toward the heap of bagged shapes. "The instruments?"

"Oh, not. Those are for my new group, man. Bass, drum kit, and keyboard. I'm lead."

"Lead guitar."

"And vocals."

I looked at the heap again. "Seems like a lot of cases for just instruments."

"It's not just the instruments, man. We got to bring our own amps and effects rack and all when we play a club. House just provides monitors and mikes."

"Monitors?"

"Like the speakers, you know?"

"You play a lot around here, Teagle?"

He got cagey. "We do awright. What's this got to do with Darbra?"

"Never know till I ask. And you answer."

Teagle worked his jaw. "I did answer, man. You asked me if we play a lot, and I said we do awright."

"How'd you spend this past weekend?"

"Spend it? I went out Friday night."

"Where?"

"No place in particular. We could of had a gig Friday night, but we turned it down."

"Why?"

"Aw, it was at this queer place."

"A gay bar, you mean?"

"Yeah, only they try to pass it off like it ain't. It's mostly married guys from the 'burbs come into it, buying the hustlers drinks like they were big brothers to them, counseling them instead of feeling them up. It's disgusting, you ask me. That's why we call it the 'Fag Dad Café.' Got the nickname from that weird movie like a couple of years ago about the diner in the desert."

"*Baghdad Café?*"

"Yeah."

"They also made a television series from it."

"You say so. I don't watch TV."

I looked over at the nineteen-incher. "What's that?"

"Oh, I just like use it for tapes, maybe check out what the hot groups are doing for videos."

Teagle smirked at me for no apparent reason.

I said, "And Saturday?"

"Huh?"

"What'd you do this past Saturday."

"Oh, we had a gig at this place in Kenmore."

"Kenmore Square?"

"Right. We were boss, man."

"You see Darbra when she got back from her trip?"

Teagle stopped. If my jumping around threw him, he wasn't making much effort to cover it. "No. Like I said, I was out."

"So you don't know if she did get back?"

"Huh?"

"She left a week ago Saturday, and supposedly came back this past Saturday. You didn't see her, you don't know if she's back or not."

Teagle worked his jaw again. "Sure I do, man."

"She called you?"

A pause. "No. No, she like left me a note."

"A note."

"Yeah. Under my door here."

"What'd it say?"

Another pause. "Not much. Just like, 'I'm back, call me. Darb,' you know?"

"Can I see it?"

"See what, man?"

"The note."

"Oh, man, I didn't like keep it. What for?"

"You threw it away?"

"Yeah, sure."

"Would it still be in your trash?"

80

"My trash?"

"Yes." I looked to the messy kitchen. "Doesn't seem like you've taken out the garbage for a while."

Teagle was clearly trying to think his way through something. "I, like, I didn't throw it away here."

"You didn't."

"No, man. I took it with me upstairs, and knocked on her door, then pitched it outside when she didn't answer."

"Pitched it where?"

"In the street, man. You gonna get me for littering?"

He tried, but like one of Traci Wickmire's lines, the light tone just didn't quite come off.

"When did Darbra leave you the message?"

"I don't know, man. She didn't like time-stamp it or anything."

"When did you notice it?"

Again he seemed to be thinking something through. "After I got up."

"Which day?"

"Saturday, man. I was a little hung from Friday."

"Hung over."

"Right, right. So I didn't get up till like maybe two in the afternoon, and there it was."

"Could it have been there when you came in the night before?"

Teagle smiled, like he'd been smarter than he thought. "Yeah, yeah. Coulda been. I was kinda lit coming home."

"Friday."

"Friday."

"After your clubbing."

"Right."

"Did Darbra tell you she was going away on vacation?"

"Yeah, she told me."

"She say where?"

"Where she was going?"

"Yes."

Cagey again. "Just Jersey somewheres."

"But you don't know where."

"Uh-unh."

"You hear from her while she was gone?"

"Never did."

"You think about going with her?"

Teagle weighed something. "Not. Darbra and me, we're both sun freaks, you know, but you don't like bring sand to the beach, and you don't like take a date on vacation."

"You and she were seeing each other back here, then?"

"On and off."

"For how long?"

"I don't know."

"Estimate."

"That's what's tough, man. I think she like had her eye on me from Jump Street, but didn't make her move till maybe a month ago?"

Her move. "You see each other a lot?"

"Man, we don't exactly go out for a malted, you know? It's more like a physical thing."

"How did you spend the week?"

"Huh?"

"How did you spend the week she was gone?"

An elaborate shrug. "Just hung out."

"Where?"

"Beach, clubs, practiced like always."

"With the other guys in the band?"

"Uh, no, actually. They couldn't . . . we couldn't all get it together for a session this week."

"You played a club on Saturday without practicing together all week?"

"Yeah, man. We had plenty of time for a good sound check, and like I said before, we're tight."

"And you were boss."

Teagle didn't like the way I said it. "Right."

"You make enough money from the music not to need a day job?"

"I don't need much, and I write some songs."

"Songs to sell, you mean?"

"Yeah. You gotta do that, otherwise the band you're in breaks up, you don't have any product except a couple of audition tapes, you doing the leads on them."

"So you sell your songs to other groups?"

"Yeah. I'm not into the political shit, man. Like, I don't know nobody, I don't owe nobody, and I don't blow nobody. I just write the music people want to hear, the basic pure. Rock and roll."

"How much do you get from a song you sell?"

"That's not really the point."

"It is if you have to pay the rent."

"Like I said, I don't need much, and I saved from the tour, remember?"

"When did the tour end?"

"I don't know."

"You don't know when you started living around here?"

"Awright, awright. It was like . . . March, maybe?"

"Three months ago."

"Man, when you're young, you don't worry so much about time."

"Darbra ever mention any other men to you?"

"Not."

"You think you're the only one seeing her?"

"Man, what she does is her business, what I do is mine, awright?"

"No jealousy?"

A smirk again. "I'm too young to worry about time, and too young to worry about love, man. That'll like work itself out, you know?"

"You have a key to Darbra's apartment?"

"No. Why should I?"

"You've been seeing her."

83

"When she gets the urge, she calls me. When I get the urge, I call her. It works out, it works out."

"You like her cat?"

"Her—Tigger?"

"Yes."

"Not especially."

"Why not?"

"Darb lets him sleep in her bed. Not the kind of pussy hairs I like in my mouth come morning, you know?"

A really special guy, Rush. "She ask you to feed him while she was away?"

Teagle paused again. "No, I think Traci was taking care of that."

"Seems kind of odd, Darbra leaving you a note she was back but not telling Traci."

Rush Teagle stared at me. "Darbra, she like don't always do the considerate thing, you know?"

8

A VOLUNTEER AT THE INFORMATION DESK INSIDE THE PNEUMATIC doors suggested I'd find the Orthopedic Associates by following the yellow line past the gift shop to the elevator, the elevator to the third floor, and the yellow line again to a clearly worded sign. I did as I was told and found myself standing at a counter behind a Hispanic woman leaning forward on crutches and a black man leaning sideways on a cane. When my turn came, I told the woman in the print dress staffing the counter the name of the doctor Elie had recommended. The woman found my name near the end of what upside down looked like a long list and handed me a clipboard with an even longer printed form to fill out. After she told me to take a seat and I would be called, I asked her when that might be, and she gave what I took to be an honest shrug.

Thanking her, I risked losing whatever priority I had and took the clipboard and the elevator back down to the gift shop. Their choices of magazines were slim and their paperbacks slimmer, but I found a Lawrence Block novel Nancy hadn't bought for her own library and went back upstairs. As I hit the waiting area, a woman in a nurse's white pantsuit with a stethoscope around her neck was calling my name.

"Right here."

The woman gave me a measured look. "Where were you?"

I gestured vaguely with the clipboard. "Bathroom."

She didn't take it well. "This way, please."

I was led around a corner to a little alcove with a plastic formed chair like those in the waiting room, a water cooler, a scales, and some kind of vertical post that rolled on wheels. The nurse pointed at the scales.

I said, "With shoes or without?"

"Doesn't matter."

I got on the scales and she niggled the counterweight. "One-ninety-eight. Hold still for your height."

She slid the horizontal piece down until it slanted at some angle off my head. "Seventy-six inches."

"Between six-two and six-three, actually."

She didn't respond. "Sit down for your blood pressure, please."

I asked her if she wanted me to roll up my sleeve.

"Doesn't matter."

She wheeled the vertical post over, wrapped the black leather bandage around my sleeve at the bicep, and starting pumping. Then she placed the stethoscope pad on my arm and released the pressure slowly. "One-twenty over eighty."

"Is that good?"

"It isn't bad. Please return to the waiting area and have a seat until the doctor can see you."

"Do you know how long that'll be?"

She said, "No."

"Doesn't matter."

"What?"

"Never mind."

* * *

"Were you waiting long, Mr. Cuddy?"

"About seven chapters."

"Sorry?"

I held up the book.

"Oh, I see."

We were in a windowless, characterless examining room with one of those padded tables, a desk, and two chairs. The doctor sat at the desk, me next to it. Reading through the form I'd completed on the clipboard, she paused with the eraser of a pencil on certain lines. About five-foot-three and Asian-American, a Chinese surname appearing before the "M.D." on the tag above the breast of her labcoat. Attractive with short black hair in a shingled haircut, she also was a good decade younger than her patient.

"Mr. Cuddy, you say here you served in Vietnam?"

"Yes."

"Any wounds?"

"A couple, but I doubt they're involved with my knee or shoulder now."

"Just the same, could you describe them?"

"Mortar shell took a little chunk out of one thigh, knife—"

"Which thigh?"

"Right."

"And it's your left knee that's bothering you now?"

"Correct."

"You started to say knife?"

"Slash wound, across the ribs."

She nodded. "Any others?"

"Not from the war."

"Tell me."

I did. She had to turn the form over to use the other side.

"How about other injuries, sports or accidents first."

We went through those, a lot shorter list.

"Mr. Cuddy, I'm most concerned about the bullet wound to your left shoulder."

"It healed fine."

"Well, we're going to have to take the shirt and pants off sometime. Let me step outside while you strip down to your briefs and put on this johnny coat, open side to the back. Feel free to leave your socks on if you like. Some people find the floor a little cold."

I did as she said, at first leaving my socks on, then realizing I looked like a bad imitation of Jack Lemmon in an early sixties comedy. The doctor knocked before she came back into the examining room.

"Let's start with the knee."

As I repeated how I'd hurt it on Nancy's stairs, the doctor manipulated my leg until the joint had bent at all the usual angles and a few that made me squirm. She couldn't have weighed more than ninety pounds, but she knew how to use leverage to achieve the effect she wanted.

A frown. "Patella feel like it's floating a little?"

"If that's the kneecap, yes."

"And the buckling occurs mainly going downstairs?"

"Going down, period. Even just getting out of bed."

"But not on level surfaces or upgrades?"

"Not so far."

"Good. Let's try the shoulder now."

She started on it. "I see the scar." A look at my back. "Went clean through?"

"Yes."

"Loss of function?"

"Not after a few months."

"Any physical therapy?"

"Nothing professional. Just exercise, Nautilus equipment for a while now."

"You were very lucky on that, Mr. Cuddy. Most people don't realize how complicated, and easily destroyed, the workings of the shoulder are. Now, let's see about the current problem."

She began manipulating, this time massaging as much as

moving the joint, then doing the equivalent of isometric exercises with it. More frowning.

I said, "What do you think?"

"I'll know better after X-rays. Can you stay for them today?"

"Yes."

"We'll send you down now, then. Take this out to our counter here, and Natalie will tell you the rest. Just be sure the technician in Radiology knows I'm waiting for the plates."

"I take it I get dressed first."

A small smile. "We generally insist on it."

Hector said, "First, we do the knee."

He had me stretch out, face up, on a table. Unlike the one in the examining room, this one was rigid instead of padded and had what looked like a glass window in it. He slid something under the table, then laid a heavy, thick apron over me from ribs to mid-thigh. "Protect the future generations, you know it?"

"Thanks."

"Hey, we got to think of these things."

He then adjusted an almond-colored cone on a flexible arm over my knee. The cone was about the diameter of a volleyball, and the arm was attached to a track system on the ceiling. The tracks allowed the arm and cone to move in roughly the same patterns as a rook in chess.

"Okay, man. We gonna shoot maybe five pictures of your knee, so just relax and breathe in and out when I tell you from behind the wall there. I'm gonna come out in between, bend your knee this way and that some. You gonna hear a buzz sound, like when you step in the dentist's office."

"Great."

Hector went through the sequence, then moved the cone out of the way and had me step down off the table. "Now we gonna do the shoulder, man. Just stand up in front of

89

this screen here. Little to the left. Good. Now we put the lead skirt on, velcro like . . . so. Good. First one's gonna be head-on, then we play around a little."

After shifting this way and that through five or six of the short bursts from the cone, Hector pronounced me finished with him.

"The doctor said I should tell you she's waiting for your . . . plates, is it?"

"Yeah, plates." He looked down at the paperback. "You enjoying the book?"

"Yes."

Hector seemed glad for me.

"How many chapters now?"

"Fifteen."

"We shouldn't be too much longer today."

"Better to get it done."

The doctor nodded at me without conviction, then went back to studying the X-rays against a lighted screen in the examining room. "Well, I've got good news and inconclusive news."

"Let's start with the good."

"You want it in Latin or English?"

"English would be nice."

"Plain and simple, your kneecap's just lifting a little from the kind of sponge it rests on in there. We tend not to see this so much from a sudden trauma like you had with the bureau on the stairs, more typically it's from people who are marathoners."

"We didn't talk about this, but I ran the marathon a few months ago."

"You did?"

Her inflection said she was less upset that I hadn't mentioned it and more surprised that I'd actually done it.

The doctor added a note to my form. "Well, that's more

consistent, but anyway not much to worry about. I'm going to write you a prescription for an anti-inflammatory."

"I'm not much for pills, Doctor."

"These will just reduce the aggravation in the joint. They have a very slight tendency to make you nauseous, so be sure to take one with meals."

"And that's it?"

"No. No, I'm also going to give you a prescription for a neoprene sleeve."

"A what?"

"A neoprene sleeve. It's a kind of leg brace, made from the same stuff as a scuba wet suit. You've probably seen basketball players with them all the time. Football and baseball players wear them, too, but they don't show as much under the uniforms."

"Why do I need a prescription?"

"You don't, but a prescription will make it easier for the medical supply house to fit you. Also, this way the brace will be mostly covered under your health plan."

"Thanks."

"That buckling sensation will go away by itself, but just be sure to wear the brace whenever you jog or do anything athletic on the knee. In fact, a lot of men wear them all the time, since they don't show much under pants, like I said."

She must have seen something in my face. "Mr. Cuddy, believe me, it's no big deal. You'll get used to it and not even notice it's there."

I nodded. "How about the shoulder?"

"That's the inconclusive part. The pills should help you with that as well. The X-rays don't show any major damage, but then they often don't. You might have nothing more than a pull, but your description of the guitar-string sensation makes me believe it might be more serious."

"Like what?"

"I'd hate to speculate without an MRI."

"What's that?"

"Magnetic Resonance Imaging. Kind of an expanded X-ray. What's the matter?"

"Nothing."

"Mr. Cuddy, if you have any questions, I'd be happy to try to answer them?"

"I guess I have only one."

"What's that?"

"How soon can I have one of these MRI things?"

From the look she gave me, I could tell neither of us thought that was my only question.

"What's the occasion?"

Nancy said, "Does there have to be an occasion?"

I took in the restaurant. Il Capriccio is in a suburb named Waltham, just off Main Street. From the outside, you see just a flat storefront with white, vertical blinds. Inside, though, there's a foyer with twelve-paned windows looking into a cozy dining room done in rust, gold, and pastel green. Wall sconces throw muted light onto the sprigs of fresh wildflowers on the tables, giving the place an exotic, romantic feel. I'd been there only once before. Expensive, but great gourmet Italian food.

I said, "I'm glad it's your treat."

A tall, attractive woman in a white blouse and flowing black skirt greeted us warmly in the foyer, introducing herself as "Jeanne" and showing us to a table for four that fit nicely into a corner with a commanding view of the dining room. Nancy sat so she could see the room, I sat so I could see her.

"John, what's the matter?"

"Nothing."

She reached her left hand across the table, resting the palm lightly on the back of my right one. "I want to enjoy taking you out for dinner as thanks for wrestling with the bureau, and I won't enjoy it if you sulk."

"I'm not . . . sulking."

"Then what are you doing?

Nancy said it quietly, not at all nagging, but it still irritated me. "I just . . . It's been kind of a long day, okay?"

She kept the same, quiet tone. "Can you tell me about it?"

I thought of Traci Wickmire and Rush Teagle. "Not without maybe compromising you on an open case."

"Okay. Consider that buried. Now, what else is bothering you?"

I was saved by Jeanne, bringing three types of bread in an oblong wicker basket and olive oil in a tall, black bottle. Nancy asked for the wine list, and Jeanne lifted it out from under my menu, saying she'd be back in a minute.

Nancy opened the leather holder. "White or red?"

"Red."

She didn't try to restart the conversation until Jeanne came back, took her order for a bottle of Gattinara 'seventy-four, and went to get it. "John, please don't spoil my treat, huh?"

I bit back what I was about to say, took a deep breath, and let it out. "I saw a doctor today."

Nancy seemed surprised. "Why?"

"About what happened last night with the bureau."

"I thought you were okay this morning?"

"Well, I'm not."

Nancy waited a moment before asking, "And?"

"And what?"

"What did the doctor tell you?"

"She said I'd have to wear a brace on the knee for . . . probably forever."

Another moment. "What kind of brace?"

"Basically a rubber legging. It's got a hole for the kneecap and this felt horseshoe inside it to support the joint."

"You already have it?"

"Picked it up this afternoon after I left the hospital."

"How does it feel?"

"It felt restricting."

"Meaning you're not wearing the brace now."

"Right."

"And is that what the doctor suggested?"

"I don't care."

Jeanne returned with our wine. Nancy went through the motions of approving the label and sniffing the cork. Jeanne swirled a little in both our glasses before draining what she'd swirled into a third glass. After we tasted the wine, Jeanne poured for us, reciting specials like spinach and herb dumplings in broth, porcini gnocchi, and roast pork with braised fennel.

When we were alone again, Nancy raised her glass and said, "To your once and future knee."

"Not funny, Nance."

"It wasn't meant to be. It was meant to be a recognition."

"Of what?"

"Of your mortality, John."

"Terrific."

"No, face it. You're being pissy with me, and you're never like that. At least, you haven't been with me."

"I'm not being pissy."

"And if you are, it isn't because of your knee."

"Right."

"Great reasoning path, but I'm not what you'd call convinced."

"Why not?"

"Oh, John. I've seen you after you've been beaten up, chased by cars, even shot."

"Twice."

A creeping smile. "Twice. Once with me, if you'll remember."

"I'll never forget, or forgive myself for—"

"Not why I brought it up. What I mean is, I've seen you when you've had every reason to be down or depressed, after you've *killed* people, for God's sake, and you've never been petulant before."

"I thought I was being pissy."

94

The smile crept further. "Take your pick. You're such a good man, but such a little boy, too."

"And the little boy's afraid of something."

"Yes. Afraid that his time as an athlete or whatever is drawing to a close."

"That's not it, Nance."

"That's part of it."

"Maybe. But it's more . . ."

"More what, John?"

"More that—I don't know, if I'd stayed with law school, it wouldn't matter whether my knee's a little shaky or my arm won't work right. It—"

"Your arm?" She looked at me. "What do you mean, your arm won't work?"

"Nance, I could barely pull my jacket on this morning."

"From last night, too?"

"That's right. It's something with the shoulder, but the doctor doesn't know what's wrong, and she won't without some more high-tech X-rays."

Nancy paused. "So what's the worst case?"

"Worst case?"

"Yeah. The worst case, you need surgery, and you do end up suing me."

"Nancy, I'm not going to sue you."

"I'd rather that then see you be so pissy."

"I like petulant better."

The hand that wasn't holding the wine glass reached across the table again. "John, look at this objectively, okay? You're a little like a professional ballplayer. To a certain extent, you make your living with your body, and for the first time, after all it's been through, parts of it are starting to fail. Not in a big way—"

"Ask me after the next time I have to block a punch."

"Or scramble up a ladder or break down a door. John, at some point, all that has to stop. But chances are that point's

95

a ways off, because this doctor can probably tell what's wrong with you and fix it."

"She certainly spent enough time manipulating me today."

"Manipulating you."

My turn to pause. "Well, more a diagnostic massage, I guess."

"She attractive?"

"Stunning."

Nancy's hand left mine. "Did you tell her you're already spoken for?"

"Kind of."

"What does that mean?"

"I told her my heart belongs to another—"

"Good."

"—but that the other organs are up for grabs."

"Maybe she can do a radical circumcision." Nancy opened the menu. "I think I'll order for you."

"What am I having?"

"The fillet of jerk strikes just the right note."

"Does it come on a bed of sour grapes and crow?"

Nancy lowered the menu enough to let me see the smile creep all the way across her face. "I'll speak to the chef."

9

THE NEXT DAY WAS THE THIRTIETH OF JUNE, ONE OF THOSE CLEAR, bright mornings that make you believe that enduring another New England winter was worth it after all. While Nancy used my bathroom, I slid on the knee brace and then my pants over it. I tried bending and flexing the leg, but the brace was as restricting as the day before, allowing me to walk only on the verge of limping. I'd tried one of the anti-inflammatory pills with our dinner at Il Capriccio, and I had to admit both the knee and the shoulder felt a little better for it.

Nancy and I walked together from my place down Beacon to Charles, then up the slope of the hill to the State House. We kissed good-bye there, Nancy continuing on Beacon toward the courthouse complex, me watching her until the other pedestrians wrecked my line of sight. Then I went past the monument to the 54th Massachusetts, the Civil War regiment memorialized in the movie *Glory*. The monument is a bronzed frieze, the scene depicting the white commander on horseback, the black soldiers marching with rifles at shoulder-arms around him. The commander doesn't look much like Matthew Broderick, but two of the soldiers are dead ringers for Morgan Freeman and Denzel Washington.

I bought a muffin and hot chocolate from probably the same place William Proft had gone for his coffee when he and Pearl Rivkind had come to see me. I popped another pill on the way to my office on Tremont Street.

Upstairs, I opened the two windows to prolong the fresh-air feeling from walking into work. After checking with my answering service and skimming the prior day's mail, I took out Darbra Proft's telephone bill and dialed the more frequently called number in Meade. I got a real estate brokerage and asked for Roger Houle.

The woman at the other end said, "I'm sorry, but Roger won't be in the office for a few more days. Can I take a message?"

"No, thanks. I'm afraid it's a personal matter."

She hesitated. "Are you calling about . . . are you a friend of the family?"

"Not exactly."

"Then perhaps if you called back at the beginning of next week."

"Sure. Thanks."

After she hung up, I tried the less frequently used number. If another woman answered, I was prepared to apologize for a wrong number, but there was no answer and no tape machine.

I thought about it. A few more days, a friend of the family. Then I took out the MetroWest telephone directory and matched the number that didn't answer with a residential address in Meade.

The Houle house was imposing, the kind of suburban manse that was built on four acres in the nineteen-teens, with complementary houses on their respective four acres around it. Mostly red brick, the white Doric columns supported both a main entrance and the roof to a broad porch. The driveway was wide enough for two cars to dance in, curving along the house and disappearing about where a detached garage might be. It looked as though the trim around the bricks had been recently repainted and the mortar between the bricks recently repointed. The only cause for neighborhood concern would be the lawn, which hadn't been mowed in a week.

I left the Prelude at the curb and went up the flagstoned path to the front door. The knee brace had broken in some on the walk into work and the drive out to Meade, the neoprene not nearly as stiff at the back as it had been. However, I felt a little queasy, probably from the pill, and decided not to take another for a while.

Next to the front door and above a bell button was the name HOULE. When I pushed the button, there was a deep, bong-bong chiming somewhere in the house, but nobody came to the door, and I didn't hear anything else.

As I started toward the driveway to check the garage in back, a female voice said, "May I help you?"

A chunky blond woman was standing in the driveway for the house next door. She wore a pair of corduroy pants, cotton blouse, and wool sweater, all earth colors and a little too warm for the mild morning. As I got closer to her, she seemed to be about sixty, with a kind, creased face, the hair that brassy color a natural blonde gets as she ages.

"I'm looking for Roger Houle, Ms. . . . ?"

"Mrs. Mrs. Thorson, that is. And you are?"

Thorson had an almost courtly manner. I took out my identification holder. "John Cuddy. I'm a private investigator."

She studied the printing, the creases around her mouth growing deeper. "Oh, my. Now what?"

"Now what?"

Thorson handed back the holder. "I hope that after all Roger's been through, this isn't more heartache."

"Excuse me, ma'am, but I don't know what you mean."

99

She reached into the cuff of her sweater for a handker-
chief, to tend to eyes that suddenly had filled with tears.
"His wife died last week."

"I'm sorry."

Thorson didn't return the hankie to her cuff. "Caroline
was such a dear. We'd been neighbors for just ages, and I
was so happy when she and Roger met and got married,
she just . . . beamed is the right word, Mr. . . . ?"

"Cuddy."

"Cuddy. Yes, of course. I'm so sorry, it's just that she was
very nearly my best friend, even though she was ten years
younger than I. As you get older, the years between you
don't seem to matter as much, somehow. She was really like
a younger sister to me rather than a neighbor—both of us
were natural blondes, you see, so people mistook us for
sisters sometimes—and I just wasn't prepared . . . but, of
course, nobody could be."

"Her death was sudden, then?"

"People have tried to tell us that, and I do hope it's true,
but it still must have been horrible."

"What was horrible?"

"Why, the—oh, there's no way for you to know that, is
there? Caroline was on that plane that crashed near
Washington."

Mo's airline story. "You're right. I didn't know."

Thorson didn't need much prompting. "It's just such a
tragedy. She was on her way to . . . It was the twentieth anni-
versary of her brother's death, you see."

"Her brother?"

"Yes. He was killed in Vietnam, and Caroline decided she
should go down to see the memorial. I believe it's called
'the Wall'?"

"It is."

"You've seen it, then?"

"Not yet."

Something about the way I said that made Thorson pause.

Then she shook her head. "A tragedy upon a tragedy. Caroline had been planning this trip for months, to coincide exactly with her brother's death. I wasn't sure it was such a good idea, and Roger decided to build her the potting shed she'd been wanting, so that she'd have a lift when she got back."

"He didn't go with her, then."

"Oh, no. No, this was something Caroline felt she had to do herself. *For* herself, to . . . exorcise the demons, I guess. The ones still there after all these years."

"How's Mr. Houle taking it?"

"Her death? Oh, very hard. Very, very hard. They were so much in love, you see."

Thinking about his supposed affair with Darbra Proft, I said only, "I haven't met him."

Thorson looked off. "Roger was at our house. We were having a barbecue. Nothing elaborate, just a few of the neighbors. This has been a very . . . stable neighborhood, Mr. Cuddy. Most of us have been here four generations, five in my case. But that afternoon, we were all in the back, on our patio. My husband was taking drink orders before we started the coals, and I was videotaping everybody—for Christmas, my husband bought me one of those wonderful zoom kind that you can play in your own VCR? I've been having such fun with it ever since."

"Mrs. Thorson?"

"My husband was at the barbecue, and I was videotaping, and Roger had his cellular phone with him, because he and Caroline always called the other when one was traveling, and he didn't want to miss the drinks after he'd worked so hard all afternoon. Well, he was sitting there, we were all talking and joking and listening to WCDJ—that marvelous jazz station?—and suddenly the news announcer broke in with a bulletin about a plane crash, and we realized it was Caroline's flight, and Roger, he . . . his face just . . . crumbled."

101

Thorson went back to her hankie. I gave her a minute, then said, "I'm really sorry to intrude at a time like this, but it's important that I speak to Mr. Houle. Do you know where he is?"

She finished with the hankie. "The last time I saw her, I'll never forget it. Roger had come over to borrow a tool, and we were at my front door there. The taxi was pulling away to take Caroline to the airport, and behind the window she gave me her wave, a very gay wave—in the traditional sense of that word, Mr. Cuddy. That's the kind of person she was, on her way to revisit a tragedy, and she could think only of letting me know she was all right."

I gave the woman another minute, then said, "Mrs. Thorson?"

Something behind her eyes seemed to register that she'd been out of the conversation. "I'm sorry, yes?"

"Excuse me for pressing on this, but I really need to see Mr. Houle about another matter. Can you tell me where he is now?"

"Where he is?"

"Yes."

"The same place he's been since he got back from Washington. We've picked up his newspaper from the sidewalk and his mail from the box. My husband and I even talked about cutting the lawn, but that would seem somehow . . . macabre, with Roger sitting there."

"Sitting where, Mrs. Thorson?"

"In the back." She gestured with her hand. "Staring at Caroline's garden."

Stopping at the corner of his house, I watched him for a while. From the rear, Roger Houle was a teddy bear of a man, even slumped in a redwood lounge chair. Almost bald, brown hair in a fringe around the ears and back, matted and sticking up above the neck of his T-shirt and on the thick forearms. The arm of the chair was wide enough to

102

hold a drink, but there was no glass or bottle on it or in either hand.

He seemed to be staring at the garden in front of him, a kaleidoscope of blooming flowers and plants with vases and pots in front of the rock-studded border. To his right was a half-finished shed, the vertical posts sunk into concrete footings, the lean-to roof framed but not yet planked, only a couple of boards nailed at the bottom as the beginning of its walls. Outside the shed were big, empty plastic bags that might have held peat moss; long-handled shovels; half-hoes; and small trowels. The variety of sizes suggested that Caroline Houle had been a meticulous gardener.

As I moved closer, I could see that one of the vases by the rocks was less a flower pot and more an urn, its cover sitting on top of it. "Mr. Houle?"

No reaction.

I moved closer still, now only about ten feet away, and spoke a little louder. "Mr. Houle?"

The head moved, but if I hadn't spoken I wouldn't have taken it as a response.

"Mr. Houle, I'm sorry to disturb you, but I need to talk about something with you."

This time he turned to face me, a growth of stubble on his cheeks and throat like a prospector three days out of town. The eyes didn't have any spark to them, and the lips parted only enough to say, "What do you want?"

Sometimes the best way to explain things to someone in shock is simple, declarative sentences. "My name's John Cuddy, and I'm a private investigator from Boston."

"Boston."

"Yes. I've been hired to find someone by her brother, and I'm hoping you can help."

"Help."

I wasn't sure he was really following me or just repeating the last thing he'd heard each time. "Would it be all right if I sat down?"

103

There was a second lounge chair closer to the shed. He waved at it, and I pulled it over so that I faced him from a three-quarters angle instead of head-on. "Mr. Houle, your neighbor told me about your wife. I'm really sorry."

He looked at me, the empty eyes. "You can't begin to know."

"Actually I can. I lost my wife, young, to cancer."

Something moved behind his eyes, as with Mrs. Thorson out on her driveway. "Cancer. So, it took a while?"

An odd question, but I wanted to bring him out if I could. "Yes. Months."

"Well, it didn't take months for me. Took a second. Or minutes, I guess, they're not real clear about that." He looked at me, through me. "You know how they do it?"

"Do what, Mr. Houle?"

"Handle the identification of the body."

"No, I don't."

"They tell you how sorry they are, and then they fly you down there. They say they'd be happy to arrange for any kind of transportation you want, but how the hell else are you supposed to . . . So they fly you down, free, of course, and then somebody from a government agency meets you and tells you how sorry he is, too. Then they take you into a room. Not *the* room, not the . . . morgue place. No, this is a room with just another guy from the government and a video monitor and a table and some chairs in case you keel. . . . And they stand on either side of you, and they tell you it won't take long and are you ready. And when you say you are, you know you're not, really, but what can you say, it has to be done. And then they kind of hold on to your arms, just a little, like they're ready to catch you. And the camera comes on, or the screen, I guess. And there are some guys in green smocks and masks, like an operating room, only they're around this white slab with a green sheet over it. Then they pull back the sheet and you see . . . You see her face, and one side of it's gone like a burnt-out tube from an old TV, just collapsed and black, and the other side looks just like her, just like she's sleeping next to you on the other pillow. And they say, 'Can you—,' Only you don't let them finish the sentence, you just say, 'It's her,' and they say, 'Thank you,' like you're saving them a lot of time and trouble. And then the one government guy leads you out, and there's somebody else waiting there, outside the door. Somebody else who had someone on the plane, waiting to go in and watch the show."

Houle closed his eyes.

I watched him tell it, and I felt him tell it. There was no faking this, no act. I'd lost the person I thought I'd spend the rest of my life with, and you can't fake that or act through it.

A grasshopper or cricket started chirling in the garden, and Houle opened his eyes. "Sorry. I guess I kind of zoned out on you there."

"Forget it. When did you get back from Washington?"

"When? Sunday . . . Sunday sometime, I think. They flew me back after . . . after I arranged things down there. Why?"

"Do you know that Darbra Proft is missing?"

"Missing?"

"She went away on vacation, maybe to New Jersey, but it looks like right after she came back, she disappeared."

Houle held my eyes for a while, as though he were trying to follow me again, then shook his head and looked back at the garden. "I haven't. . . . The last time I saw Darbra was when we broke up."

"I know this is difficult for you, Mr. Houle."

"Difficult. Actually, talking about Darbra is easier than thinking . . . about all this."

I took it that I could continue. "How did you meet?"

"What, Darbra and me?"

"Yes."

"It was maybe a year ago. She was in the market for a condo. Her mother'd died a while back, and she—Darbra—

got some insurance from it. Had to split it with her brother, which irked her some."

"Irked her?"

"Yeah. She and Wee Willie didn't exactly get along."

"Wee Willie."

"Her nickname for the guy."

"Any idea why they didn't get along?"

"No. She told me she really hated him, though."

I filed that. "You sold her a place?"

"No. No, when she found out how expensive things still were, she decided to rent. But we'd spent half a day or so together, and we ... Well, it sounds so stupid, so fucking stupid now, but she came on to me, and I ... responded. She was ... Darbra's beautiful, but she's also ... beguiling?"

"You began seeing her?"

"Seeing her. Yeah, I guess you could call it that. I'd take her out for dinner here and there, up to Rockport, down to Plymouth, far enough to be ... safe. But mostly we'd just ... I'd go to her apartment, and we'd ... make love."

Houle brought his hand to his face, rubbing.

I said, "You saw her regularly, then?"

"Regularly. Yeah, once a week, once every two, if I was traveling or Caroline and I had ... things to do, you know, conflicts in scheduling."

"Your wife worked, too?"

"Caroline? No, she had a ... bad leg. Polio. Just a limp, but she never worked. Told me I didn't have to, for that matter, all the money she got from her father. She never had to split anything with *her* brother, either. Poor guy, got killed in Vietnam a long time ago, before her father died. That's where she was going when ..."

I'd gotten that from Mrs. Thorson, and I didn't want Houle drifting too much on me. "When's the last time you saw Darbra?"

"The last time? When we broke up—what, three, four weeks ago?"

106

"How did that happen?"

A lost look. "You tell me. I still don't understand it. She'd been acting distant for a while, kind of . . . distracted, maybe. We were expecting to go out that night, but she said she had to work late, could we have dinner at this restaurant by where she worked. I said sure, it was . . . safe, you know?"

"As a place for you to see her?"

"Right, right. It was down in the Leather District, and I didn't know anybody from the store."

"So you met her for dinner where?"

"This place called Grgo's. Funny name, but I'll never forget it."

"What happened?"

"I don't know, like I said. We're having dinner, and Darbra's acting real . . . distant. Kind of . . . I don't know, play-acting? Then she picks a fight with me."

"About what?"

"About nothing. That's what I mean. She said I made so many demands on her time, when we were seeing each other just the same as we always did, the weekly sort of thing. Then she gets mad, and it still seems kind of like she's onstage. I mean Darbra was seething, and she throws a glass of wine in my face, and looked like she was thinking of overturning the table, except the owner, this guy 'Grgo,' he comes over and kind of breaks it up, and she storms out of there."

"And what did you do?"

Houle exhaled. "I went to the men's room, tried to clean the wine off my shirt, couldn't. Then I came home."

"And that was your last contact with Darbra?"

"Yeah— No, wait a minute. Not the last contact, no."

"What do you mean?"

"I called her, at work once after that."

"Why?"

"I didn't understand what happened, I wanted to see if I could patch things up or at least leave them on a better basis than the restaurant thing."

"What did Darbra say?"

"Not much. Just that I'd already embarrassed her enough with her job, like I was the one who threw the wine."

"With her job?"

"Yeah, turns out somebody from work was there that night."

"In the restaurant?"

"Right."

"Do you know who?"

"No. I mean, I didn't know anybody from the store by sight, and she sure didn't introduce anybody to me over dinner."

"Do you remember her exact words?"

"I don't get you."

"When Darbra told you about somebody from work seeing the fight."

"Oh. Let's see. . . . Just, 'And this woman from work had to be there, too.' "

"That's all?"

"I think so."

"Any indication of which woman it was?"

Houle shook his head. "No, but I wasn't paying a lot of attention to that part of the conversation, and she hung up on me right after she said it."

"And you didn't have any further contact?"

"No." Houle let his gaze move to the covered urn. "No. In fact, after that, I took the scene in the restaurant as kind of an omen."

"Omen?"

"Yeah. I mean, the whole time I was seeing Darbra, Caroline never found out. I paid all the bills, so she never even knew about the telephone calls, you know? I figured that maybe the fight was an omen, that it was time to break up with Darbra anyway before she broke up my marriage. But then . . ."

"Mr. Houle—"

"You know, they won't even let me spread the ashes here."

I stopped.

He looked from the urn back to me. "When I ... after they finished with ... Caroline, I ... they cremated her at this place down in Washington, and I carried her back with me. But they told me it's against the law to scatter her ashes on a garden in a 'residential area.' "

Houle's hand rubbed at his eyes again. "She lost her brother to a war, and her life to a plane crash, and she can't even become part of the one thing ... this garden here."

I said, "Mr. Houle?"

Without looking up, he said, "Yeah?"

"Did you know about any of the other men in Darbra's life?"

The head snapped toward me. "The what?"

"The other men Darbra was seeing?"

"What are you talking about?"

He seemed genuinely confused. I said, "I'm told she has a boyfriend, a musician named Rush Teagle."

"No."

Houle's response seemed more like "No, she doesn't have a boyfriend," rather than "No, I don't know him."

I tried to be softer about Abraham Rivkind. "Did Darbra talk with you at all about the other people at her job?"

"No."

"Not even about her boss?"

"I think she has a couple of bosses, the two men who own the store."

"Yes, but she didn't talk to you about the one who'd been killed?"

Houle nearly came out of his lounge. "Killed? What're you saying?"

"One of her bosses, Abraham Rivkind, was killed."

"What ... ? How?"

"He was working in his office, and the police think a

robber hit him over the head with a poker from his fireplace."

"Jesus Christ. When . . . when did all this happen?"

I told him.

"That would have been . . . That would have been when I was in Denver. For my company. After the fight in the restaurant, I thought it'd be a good . . ."

Now it made sense. "I'm sorry. You never would have talked with Darbra after the killing."

Houle rubbed his face. "Jesus, maybe the fight was an omen."

I had only one other question to ask him. "Can you think of any place Darbra might go, might take off for without letting anybody know?"

"No." He seemed to be struggling with something. "No, I can't . . . think right now."

I rose. "Mr. Houle, I'm really sorry to have to put you through this."

He started to get up. "No, no really. It was almost . . . good for me, actually. Got my mind on something else."

We shook hands. "Take care."

Houle sank back down. "You know, it's true what they say, though."

"What's that?"

"When God decides to shit on you, it's like he took an Ex-Lax."

I left Roger Houle in his chair, staring past the urn at his wife's garden.

10

I STOPPED AT A PAY PHONE IN A STRIP MALL JUST BEFORE ROUTE 128 and tried to reach William Proft, partly to report in but mostly to ask about how Darbra and him not being "particularly close" had matured into her "hating" him. When I got the drugstore, though, the pharmacist on duty said Proft wasn't scheduled to work that day. As I hung up to try his home number, two acne-faced teenagers wearing different T-shirts but identical hiking shorts and Oakland A's baseball caps sauntered up to the phone. I finished dialing and got just a very reserved outgoing tape message with William Proft's voice on it. I left my name and number, but also said I might not be reachable.

While I dialed Pearl Rivkind's number, the bigger of the two teens hiked his baseball cap and said, "Hey, man. You gonna be all fucking day or what?"

I smiled sweetly. "Might be. I've been trying the new José Canseco hotline in Texas, and I've just now managed to be put on hold."

The bigger kid looked enough like he wanted to take the

111

phone away from me that the smaller kid tugged on his shirtsleeve till his friend tore away from the staring contest and walked with him toward the other end of the mall. In my ear, a male voice said, "Hello?"

"Hello. Can I speak with Pearl Rivkind, please."

"Who is this?"

The voice reminded me of the bigger kid's attitude, but I remembered my client mentioning a son, and I tried to put myself in his frame of mind three weeks after his father had been murdered. "This is John Cuddy. I'm working on a project for her."

"What kind of project?"

His tone didn't change for the better. Then, from offstage, Pearl Rivkind's voice said, "Larry? Larry, who is it?"

The kid's voice said to me, "Look, I don't want you bothering us, you hear me?"

"Larry? Who?"

Pearl's voice sounded closer.

I said, "Can I please—"

"I'm gonna hang up now."

Pearl said, "You don't hang up on somebody's calling me. What'd they teach you at that college? Hello?"

"Pearl, it's John Cuddy."

"Oh, yes."

"How are you?"

"Oh, so-so, just so-so."

From offstage, "Mom, what're you—"

Away from the receiver, Pearl said, "Larry, that's enough already. I'm on the phone here."

To me, she said, "Sorry."

"That's okay."

A little color came into her voice. "You find out something?"

"I'm afraid not."

The color waned. "Guess it's kind of early."

"Kind of. I was hoping to stop by the furniture store

112

today, and I just wanted to make sure that you'd paved the way."

"You bet. Everybody knows you're coming, and most everybody's there all the time, so don't worry about before lunch or after or whatever."

"It'll certainly be after."

"That's okay." She became a little more subdued. "You need me there?"

"Probably not."

A breath. "Good. It's real hard for me to just stroll around the store like I was shopping it, and it's just impossible for me to try to . . . spend time in Abe and Joel's office there."

"I understand."

"Anybody gives you trouble—they shouldn't, but they do, you call me here, okay?"

"Okay."

"Oh, and John?"

"Yes."

"Thanks."

"You're paying me well for what I'm doing."

"No. I mean, yes, I know that. I meant more . . . thanks for thinking to call. I appreciate it."

"You're welcome, Pearl."

I hung up the phone, knowing I'd been at least half right in taking the case. Then I took out Darbra Proft's phone bill and tried the number listed in Salem.

A gravelly woman's voice said, "Sixties."

"Who is this?"

"Who's this?"

"I just wanted to know your hours of operation."

"We don't do any 'operating,' but we're open ten to six weekdays, ten to five Saturdays, closed Sundays. That about do it for you?"

Real warmth. "Thanks, Ms. Nugent."

"Hey, how did you—"

113

I hung up on her and went toward the Prelude to head north on Route 128.

Darlene Nugent's store was off Route 114 on Bowdoin Street, just short of the bridge that takes you into downtown Salem, the county seat of Essex. I was in the superior court there once, testifying on a case for Empire Insurance. The courtrooms were straight out of Dickens, and the lawyers' library had a fireplace tall enough for me to walk into without having to stoop. I couldn't say the same for "Sixties."

It had a lot of windows, as though a miniature Woolworth's had originally been on the site, but I had to duck to get under the door lintel, and the cowbell on the frame made for a less than grand entrance. To my right stood album covers of the Beatles, the Rolling Stones, the Zombies, and groups that trailed off from there. A laminated page from *Billboard* magazine showed Creedence Clearwater Revival, Blind Faith, and Iron Butterfly having records in the top-ten LP category. Across the room hung posters from *Planet of the Apes, 2001: A Space Odyssey*, and *Barbarella*, the last showing Jane Fonda in a French-maid pose wearing less clothing and holding a ray gun that looked like the prototype for a portable hair dryer. There were racks with bellbottoms and tie-dyes and leather vests and bowler hats, clogs and sandals and Carnaby Street two-tones on shoe shelves under them.

"Help you?"

I turned to see where the gravelly female voice came from. She was about my age, standing in front of a display with various forms of kitsch on it. Black hair parted in the center and combed long and straight like Michelle Phillips used to wear hers, a peasant dress from the Mama Cass collection brushing the ground at her feet. It was hard to tell with the dress, but the woman seemed to be below medium height and above medium weight, with a virtually boneless face and a flower in her hair over the left ear. You wouldn't have placed her even as the heavier woman from the photograph in Darbra Proft's bedroom.

"Darlene Nugent?"

She stood a little straighter, nearly upsetting a lava lamp by her elbow. "You're the one on the phone."

"That's right."

"I got a can of Mace under here."

"Oh, my."

The voice to my right belonged to an elderly woman with hennaed hair and a conservative suit, holding a hand to her mouth.

To the elderly woman, I said, "Nothing to worry about, ma'am."

Reassured, the woman faced Nugent. "I came in here to purchase something for my grandson, because he lived in San Francisco during the summer of 1968. However, I must confess that I cannot bring myself to do so."

Nugent said, "How come?"

"There are pornographic photos back there for a play entitled *Oh, Calcutta,* I believe it is, and others with a naked white man kissing an oriental woman in all sorts of . . . poses."

"And you're offended, right?"

"That's right."

Nugent nodded her head. "So fuck off, blue-hair."

Stunned, the elderly woman teetered a bit in her sensible shoes, then stalked out of the store, the cowbell jangling wildly as she slammed the door behind her.

I said, "Great customer relations."

Nugent came back to me. "Who are you and what do you want?"

"My name's John Cuddy. I'm a private investigator from Boston."

She glanced at my ID, but seemed to be forming a thought before she did. "*Mannix,* huh?"

"Not like on TV, Ms. Nugent. This is real."

A sweep of the hand that took in her inventory. "This is real, too, pal. It just isn't reality. See the difference?"

"This is history, but real. Only today is reality."

"That's right." She seemed to relax a little. "You ever have somebody do your chart?"

"My chart?"

"Your astrological chart. You know, signs and moons and which houses things are in."

"Not recently."

"Too bad. I got this woman, she's Armenian, but a real wiz with the zodiac. All the biggies used them. Marilyn, Janis . . ."

"Nancy."

"Nancy?"

"Reagan."

A hand to the hip, like a pregnant woman trying to relieve some pressure. "You're one of those, huh?"

"One of those what?"

"One of those guys, demonstrated against the war in 'sixty-nine, then voted for Death Valley Days in 'eighty."

"Wrong on both counts."

"Both? You weren't against the war?"

"I wasn't against it until I was in it, and by then it was a little late for leafletting at shopping centers."

For some reason that seemed to soften her. "Okay. What can I do for you?"

"I've been hired by your nephew to find your niece."

"My . . . ? Will-yum?"

Everybody seemed to have a different derogation of my client's name. "That's right."

"So where's Darbra off to?"

"That's what I'm trying to find out. She went to New Jersey for a vacation, came back, and disappeared."

"And you figure *I* know something about it?"

"You're a close relative."

"I'm her aunt—Jesus, that still sounds odd to hear me

say, you know? That I'm aunt to somebody in her twenties. Anyway, I'm Darbra's 'aunt,' but that doesn't make us close."

"She called you a few months ago."

Nugent moved away from the lava lamp, swinging her hips slowly, like a teen walking through a meadow with her first beau. "You've done some homework, huh?"

"A little."

"So you're wondering, why did she burn a toll call on me, we aren't that close."

"Yeah, I wondered."

"Well, I'll tell you, I wondered, too. I mean, it was my birthday and all—the Ides of March, like that Shakespeare thing?—but as soon as I heard her 'baby-girl' voice on the other end of the phone, I was trying to spot her angle."

"She had to have an angle to call an aunt on her birthday?"

"Aunt and godmother. Barbra—that was my older sister? She made me promise at the christening that I'd always look after her little 'baby.' Thank God she never made me promise the same thing about Will-yum."

"I take it you're not nuts about him, either."

"Hah. Will-yum's like a . . . nonentity, you know? My guess is he'll go out like a Viking."

"Like a Viking."

"Yeah. He'll die with his sword in his hand."

"Ms. Nugent—"

"Whacking off, get it?"

"I get it. Ms. Nugent—"

"I mean, Will-yum, he's the kind of guy couldn't have gotten laid during the Summer of Love."

"Can we go back to the phone call?"

"The phone call?"

"From Darbra."

"Oh, right. What do you want to know?"

"Why else would she have called you?"

"That's what I was wondering. I was upstairs in bed, had a cold, a cold on my birthday yet, and the phone rings—there's an extension up there for down here, easier that way—and it's my loving niece, saying how are you and how's business, and I said sucky and suckier."

Which must have warmed things right up. "And then?"

"Then she asked me, have I heard from Will-yum, and I said, 'Yeah, he sent me a card and some flowers, that soft touch, why?' And she said, 'Oh, no reason. I just haven't heard from him in a while.' Then she finally got to it."

"Got to what?"

"The real reason she called me, the angle."

"Which was?"

"The insurance policies."

"The policies?"

"Yeah. Didn't your client Will-yum tell you about them?"

"Not that I recall."

A smile. I realized Nugent hadn't shown her teeth to me, because the two canines would have been tough to miss. They stuck down a little farther than the others, giving her a Bride-of-Dracula look. "When Barbra's husband ran off—good riddance, he was a fucking bum, dropped more acid than a whole block of Haight-Ashbury—she kind of obsessed about financial security, you know? Took out these policies on herself and each of the kids, Darbra and Will-yum both. She—Barbra, my sister—made me promise to always keep up the policies, so that the kids wouldn't have it as rough as she did."

"But her husband didn't die, he just took off, right?"

"Yeah, but same difference, he isn't there to provide for his family."

Not really. "So there were policies out on all three?"

"Right."

"For how much?"

"I don't know what the premiums were back then, but they

118

must have been peanuts, because Barbra kept all three up till she died, and I've been paying on the other two ever since."

I worked through that. "What are the face amounts?"

"You mean, what the policies would pay?"

"Yes."

"The same for everybody, a hundred thousand."

"Payable?"

"Half to each."

"So when your sister died . . ."

"Darbra got half, and Will-yum got half."

"And now?"

"And now Will-yum dies and Darbra's up a hundred, and vice versa."

"You don't participate?"

"Hey, I pay the premiums, pal, which isn't so easy, this place not exactly being Tiffany's, you know? Matter of fact, I may have to expand the stock."

"Expand?"

"Into the seventies. God, it makes me gag. Imagine having to put up posters of the Bee Gees and Travolta and carry fucking leisure suits?"

"But you don't get anything if either your niece or nephew dies."

"No, like I said. I promised Barbra, and a promise is a promise, but I think it's kind of . . . I don't know, ghoulish to bet against the generation behind you, despite all this stuff I try to peddle from when we were young."

I didn't quite follow her, but I didn't want to get involved in another talk about inventory. "Ms. Nugent—"

"How about 'Darlene,' okay? I feel ancient enough already with this conversation."

"Darlene, I'm sorry to have to open old wounds, but how did your sister die?"

"How?" Nugent began to play with the ends of her hair, which were down around her waist. "The how's easy. She went off the roof of her apartment house."

"Where?"

"Down in Quincy. That was the Nugent sisters for you, both of us ended up living in historic towns, Barbra down by the Adamses', me by the witches."

"Suicide?"

"Not how the cops saw it. She was up there to sit in the sunshine, bathing suit and all. Two kids into their twenties, and Barbra still had a figure for it. Not like..." Nugent let go of the hair. "Anyway, she was up there on a weekday, by herself, and they figure she went to get up from her chair and pitched over the edge. Ten stories to the ground."

Nugent's voice had become elevatorlike, no emotion at all in it. I said, "Before, you started to say 'the how's easy.' "

"What?"

"You said the how's easy."

"Oh, right. The how is she fell like a hundred feet. The why is like a hundred thousand."

"The policy."

"Yeah. Or I guess fifty thousand, huh, since they never liked each other enough to get together and plan something."

"You think Darbra or William killed your sister?"

"Right. For the money."

"But the police didn't."

"No. There was one, he kind of swung with me on it. But the cops couldn't do anything about it, and the insurance company had to pay, too, because there was no—what do you call it, 'physical evidence'?"

"And no eyewitnesses."

"Except the one who did it. Either could have given Barbra that push. Imagine that, killing the woman who brought you into this fucking world?"

"Do you remember the names of anybody from the insurance company?"

"Are you kidding?"

"How about the police officer?"

"You mean the one who was with me on it?"

"Yes."

"Christ, no. That was what, five years ago? Let me tell you, five minutes after you leave, I won't even remember yours."

"How about the name of the insurance company?"

"Same."

"You don't remember that, either."

"No. No, it's the same company as now, as the policies on Darbra and Will-yum."

Nugent reeled off one of the big national outfits, which would make things both easier and harder. I said, "The police officer was from Quincy, though?"

"That's where it happened."

"I mean, he wasn't from the State Police."

"Oh. Let me . . . No, no he was from the Quincy cops, account of I remember that's what it said on his car."

Time to change the subject. "Can you think of any reason your niece would disappear?"

"Not unless it had to do with a man. Darbra's a slut, you could even see it in her as a kid. We'd go shopping or ride the train—she loved the trains, even just the subways like the Red Line from Quincy into Boston? And you'd watch her, and she'd be watching the men. Any size or shape, age or color. She'd just watch, really like . . . concentrating. At first I figured it was because she never knew her own father, you know? She didn't have one around the house—and my sister was real good about that, though my guess is she'd had her fill of men with her husband and how he turned out—but Darbra now, she wasn't just watching them, she was . . . studying them, maybe? Trying to figure out what they were like, maybe *what* they liked. And she found out they liked her, and she became a real slut. Sorry, but there's just no other word for it."

"Darlene—"

"Hey, you know the difference between a slut and a bitch?"

"No. I—"

"A slut is somebody who sleeps with everybody in town. A bitch is somebody who sleeps with everybody in town except you."

I waited for her to finish laughing. "You know any of the men in Darbra's life?"

"Not by name. Not at all, in fact. I just know there must be some, nonstop and probably overlapping. The kids nowadays, they have an expression for people like Darbra. They say, 'A-tisket, a-tasket, the condom or the casket.' Thank God we didn't have to worry about that kind of stuff in our day, huh?"

"Right. You know anything about your nephew's life?"

The two vampire teeth gleamed at me. "And whether there are any men in it?"

"Whatever."

"No. No, if anything, I like Darbra better, for all her faults, than Will-yum. At least with her there's some . . . action, some living. Will-yum, he's like one of the Body Snatchers, you know?"

"The movies?"

"Yeah. One was in the fifties, and the remake was the seventies, so I don't have anything on them here. But he goes around the way the people did after they went through the pods, kind of . . . dead inside. Robots who did what they did, imitating life."

I looked at her.

She said, "That's why I was surprised to hear you say Will-yum hired you. He's always been pretty tight with a buck. A buck, hell, Will-yum wouldn't pay ten cents to see Christ ride a bike."

I kept looking at her.

Nugent said, "What's the matter?"

"I was thinking, if either your niece or nephew did kill your sister, you must have thought about which one it was."

The vampire smile again. "I've thought about that a lot,

you know? One of them a murderer, and here I'm paying for insurance policies on each of them because the one that *got* murdered made me promise to. But I finally gave up and decided I'd just wait."

"Wait for what?"

"Wait for one of them to collect on the other. Then I figured I'd know for sure."

As I opened the door to leave, the cowbell reminded me of another movie. *Monty Python and the Holy Grail*, the scene where Eric Idle walks along behind the plague cart, ringing a bell and calling, "Bring out your dead."

Only this time it didn't strike me funny.

11

CRAWLING SOUTH IN THE TRAFFIC ON ROUTE 1 BACK TOWARD BOS-
ton, I pieced together what I'd learned so far. Five years
ago, Barbra Proft dies in a fall that her sister, Darlene, believes was murder. William and Darbra split a hundred
thousand dollars of insurance proceeds. A year ago, Darbra
moves to the Commonwealth Avenue building with Traci
Wickmire and starts an affair with Roger Houle. Then three
and a half months ago, in mid-March, Darbra calls her aunt
to check if the remaining policies on her and her brother are
still in force. A month or six weeks ago, Wickmire overhears
Darbra's half of the "sugar daddy" telephone conversation.
Some time later, Darbra breaks up with Houle in a melodra-
matic scene at Grgo's restaurant and about the same time
starts an affair with Rush Teagle. A week or so after that,
Abraham Rivkind is killed at the furniture store. Another
week later, Darbra leaves for vacation in New Jersey, mode
of transportation unknown, calling Wickmire in the middle
of the week from Sunrise or Sunrise Beach. Then Darbra
supposedly returns on Saturday, Teagle saying she left him

a conveniently lost note, nobody else hearing boo from her. Darbra's suitcase and accumulated mail are on her bed, but none of the other things you'd expect a returning vacationer to do seem to have gotten done.

There might be a pattern in there somewhere, but I couldn't see it.

After leaving the Central Artery at South Station, I found a parking space in the Leather District. Until the 1830s, the area was known as South Cove, and with good reason, since it was under water and provided wharf space for merchant goods. Then the cove, like Back Bay, was filled in to create more livable land. After a fire in the 1870s, the area was rebuilt as the center of the shoe industry, which gave the district its name. Now most of the shoe manufacturers and their warehouses are gone, replaced by artists' lofts, galleries, and restaurants.

I treated myself to a heavy lunch at the Loading Zone, a converted warehouse on Kneeland Street with hustling waitrons, great barbecue, and a wide selection of ales on tap. Then I walked over to Value Furniture.

From the curb, the store also looked like it was converted from a warehouse, but what a warehouse. Four stories tall, the windows were bays on the first three floors and Palladians on the top, with ornate, flagged spikes like medieval lances guarding the roof. The facade was marble, curlicues and other detail work around the sills and corners. The entrance was two massive brass doors, and I tugged open the one on the right.

I was barely across the threshold when a pert young woman with a smile like a toothpaste commercial and a hairstyle like the national boundaries of Iraq met me. "Good afternoon, sir, and welcome to Value Furniture. My name is Karen. Can I help you in any way?"

"I'm here to see Mr. Bernstein."

"Fine. Mr. Bernstein is on the fourth floor." The smile never wavered. "If you'll just follow me, I'll show you to his office. We can take the elevator, or"—she gestured with her hand to a central staircase, the kind you'd expect Vivien Leigh to descend in a flowing gown—"we can see some of the store."

"The stairs, I think."

"Please watch your step, then."

Karen's smile had wavered, and I got the impression most office visitors opted for the elevator over three flights of Tara. Actually, though, as we climbed from the first-floor living room sets toward the second-floor dining rooms, the grand staircase trimmed down significantly, becoming pretty utilitarian as we left the dining rooms behind and moved into the bedroom suites on the third floor. At the fourth floor was a set of padded-leather café doors with brass tacks to the left and more furniture to the right.

"This way, please."

She led me through the swinging doors and into a tiled corridor with a men's room, a ladies' room, and a water fountain the size of a wastebasket mounted on the wall between them. At the end of the corridor was a less inviting steel door with a small porthole window at eye level. This door didn't seem to require any key as Karen pushed it open into a broad hallway, this one carpeted. What looked like offices lined both sides, another steel fire door, this one with a panic bar, at the far end. We walked to an open doorway, my guide frowning as she looked into it.

"I'm sorry, but I don't see Mr. Bernstein."

From the hall, the office was impressive, afternoon sun streaming in through the Palladian. The sunshine bathed a huge partners' desk, where I guessed Rivkind and Bernstein had worked like Siamese twins. Old, bustle-back chairs for each partner that you just knew would crackle when you sat on them and creak when you swiveled in them, captain's chairs for visitors. Currier and Ives prints graced the walls around a marble fireplace with a screen and tool holder. Dangling from the holder were a brush and tongs but no poker, and the lush red carpet was bleached in an oval spot near one of the chairs.

"Can I help you?"

A precise, female voice from down the hall. I turned to see a light-skinned black woman standing outside one of the other doorways. Fortyish, she would have been about five-six without the two-inch heels, in a yellow blouse and maroon skirt. Her hair was between brown and blond, brushed stylishly into a wave that rode toward the back of her head.

Karen said, "Mrs. Swindell, this gentlemen's here to see Mr. Bernstein, but—"

"Mr. Bernstein had to go out. Is it something I can help you with?"

I said, "My name's John Cuddy, Mrs. Swindell. Maybe Mrs. Rivkind talked with you about me?"

Swindell's head bobbed once. "Karen, I think you can go back downstairs now."

"Sure. I mean, yes. Thanks. A pleasure to meet you, Mr. Cuddy."

"Same. Thanks for the tour."

"You're welcome."

As Karen walked away, Swindell came toward me. "Beverly Swindell, Mr. Cuddy."

Up close, Swindell's eyes matched the color of her hair, something in them making me push her age a few years higher. The nose was proud, the nostrils prominent, giving her face a little more character than beauty. Her handshake was firm, but reserved.

"Sorry to have to be here about this."

She bobbed her head again. "We all are. Joel won't be back for a while. Can I . . . I don't know what, get you started?"

"Maybe in your office?"

"Of course. Please."

Her room had the same Palladian window effect, but you

127

stepped from the late nineteenth century harshly into the twenty-first. A computer system sprawled over two similar hutches of beige plastic. In front of each hutch was one of those ergonomic chairs that looks like a Catholic kneeler with an attitude. There were a couple of calculators awash in a sea of green and gray printouts with single metal rings through one of the three holes punched in their sides. Dozens of loose-leaf notebooks stood upright on shelves in some kind of color-coded order that escaped me. The small amount of empty wall space was barren, no prints, no photos, nothing personalizing the place.

"Have a seat, please."

I looked at her, but she was pointing at the corner of the room to the left of the door. There were three conventional chairs around a circular conference table. I took one of them, Swindell another.

"How can I help you, Mr. Cuddy?"

"Did you talk to Mrs. Rivkind directly?"

"I did. Pearl said you were looking into what happened here for her and into Darbra's disappearance for her brother—Darbra's, I mean."

"That's right."

"What happened that night, it's not easy for me. But if it'll help, I'll do what I can."

"Let's save that for a minute and start with Darbra. How long has she worked here?"

"About three months, but I could get the exact date from the payroll records."

"Could you?"

Swindell went over to one of the computers, clacked awhile, then said, "March twenty-eighth, a Monday."

Two weeks after Darbra Proft's telephone call to her aunt, checking on the life insurance policies.

Swindell came back to the table.

I said, "How did she get the job?"

"I think Darbra's brother knew Pearl from town—the

town the Rivkinds lived in, Sharon. Her brother mentioned that Darbra was looking for a job, and Pearl said to speak to her husband, maybe there was an opening at the store."

"Was there?"

Swindell closed in a bit. "Was there what?"

"An opening."

She seemed to choose her words carefully. "We had to use secretaries from time to time, usually got them from temp agencies. I guess Joel and Abe decided it would be a good idea to have somebody full-time."

The way Swindell said it, I had the feeling she didn't think it was such a good idea. "How have things worked out?"

"With Darbra, you mean?"

"Yes."

"I don't have that much to do with her. Most of my time is on the computers, and they produce about all the paperwork I deal with. I started here fifteen years ago, nobody thought about computers for anything but space shots down at Cape Canaveral, you know? Now I don't see how we could live without them."

I had a different feeling, like I was being steered away from something. "With what you've had to do with Darbra, how does she strike you?"

Swindell didn't say anything.

I took a breath. "Look, Mrs. Rivkind told me you all would do your best to help me here. There's not much I can do for either of my clients without everybody telling me what they can."

A bob. "Darbra is . . . manipulating. Or manipulative, I guess."

"How do you mean?"

"She's bright, but not in a . . . productive way? She gets into a situation you've handed her, and she tries to do you one better, but not necessarily in a way that does her job better."

"Can you give me an example?"

"Couple of times, I've asked her to kind of sort things, put invoices or whatever into reverse chronological order, make it easier to see where we stand on shipments."

"And?"

"And she does almost what I tell her."

"Almost."

"Yeah, but she'll put this twist in it, like sort the things into two piles instead of one."

"Which didn't help you."

"And which maybe didn't hurt me, either. I mean, hurt what it was I was going to do with the things. It's just that she has to . . . manipulate the job somehow, like she's trying to do your idea one better."

Swindell seemed to be opening up a little, speaking in a more relaxed tone. I took a chance. "I understand there was a fight in a restaurant around here?"

"A fight?"

"An argument between Darbra and a man?"

"Oh, that."

"You saw it, then?"

"Yes, it was pretty embarrassing."

"How so?"

"Well, I was sitting in Grgo's, a table in a corner like this one is, away from the center of the room. All of us eat there a lot—it was Abe's favorite place—but I'd never seen this man before, and it was, well, kind of like Darbra was . . . showing him off?"

"Showing him off?"

"Yes. She introduced him to Grgo—the owner? Then she made a real production about getting seated, not right at the center, but toward the center and across the room from me."

"You said that people from the store ate there a lot. Was anybody else there that night?"

"From the store?"

"Right."

130

"No, not that I saw. No, definitely."

"Do you think Darbra saw you?"

"Yes. But she made a real effort not to look over at me, like she was an actress and I was the audience."

I thought back to the phrase Roger Houle had used. Play-acting. "Go on."

"Well, I was already halfway through my meal, so I thought I'd just finish and leave. Before I could, though, Darbra raised her voice."

"Raised it."

"Yes, like she was angry about something. I looked over there—you can't help yourself, somebody acts up in a restaurant—and I saw her throw some wine at this man and stand up and throw down her napkin and kind of stomp out of there."

"Stomp."

"Yes, but like she was putting it on, acting rather than just acting up, like I told you before."

"And the man?"

"He seemed kind of shocked, fumbling around for a couple of seconds. Then Grgo was right there, kind of toweling him off with another napkin. Then the man left, too."

"Could you hear anything that was said?"

"No. Just like her voice, not the words to it."

"Did you see her at work the next day?"

"Yes."

"How did she seem?"

"She, I don't know, kind of pouted, like I'd put some insult on her."

"She didn't mention the fight?"

"No, and I didn't bring it up."

Understandable. "Mrs. Swindell, I need to ask you about what happened here the night Mr. Rivkind was killed."

She lifted her chin an inch higher. "Ask."

"I've read the police reports, but you're the first person

131

I'm seeing who was here that night. Can you tell me what you remember?"

"I remember too much, but I'll tell you what I can. It was a Thursday—we're open till eight, Thursdays, kind of a tradition but hard to justify on the business we do once the commuters head home. Anyway, I was here in my office, working on the dailies."

"The dailies?"

"The tabulations, department by department, of what we had in. Abe insisted on that, always wanted to know how we'd done before he headed home."

"So you were working here."

"Yes. With my door closed."

"Why?"

"Abe and Joel always liked to talk at the end of the day, and they always kept their door open. I don't close mine, I can't concentrate."

"Okay. Then what?"

"I was sitting here, working, and I guess they were down in their office."

"You guess?"

"Well, that's where they'd be."

"All right."

"I was just finishing with the dailies when I heard the back door alarm go off."

"The alarm for the back door of the building."

"Yes. It's got one of those school-door things on it, sets off an alarm when you hit it."

"What did you do?"

"I tried to phone Abe and Joel."

"Why?"

"Well, I guess it could have been a fire, but we'd been having problems with kids coming into the store and hiding out. One of them had a knife once, and that's why Joel said we needed a security guard, especially for Thursdays."

"That would be Finian Quill?"

132

"Yes, Finian. Anyway, Abe said, if I ever hear the alarm, I should just sit tight and lock my door."

"Did you?"

"No. Like I said, I wasn't sure, was it a fire or was it kids? When Abe and Joel didn't answer, I thought it might be bad, so I ran out into the hall here, and the noise from the alarm was real loud, we've got those siren things on every floor, and I went down to Abe and Joel's office."

"Even though they hadn't answered the phone?"

"Yes. They should have—answered, I mean, and I wanted to see if anything was wrong."

"And?"

"And I didn't see anything, at first." Swindell bit her lip. "Then I stepped into the room, and saw Abe. He was on the floor by their desk, and he had this big . . . gash upside his head . . . and . . . I don't know, I guess I started screaming. I remember I ran down the hall, busted open the door there—"

"Wait a minute. Which end of the hall?"

"The end by the back stairs. I busted open that door with the school handle and yelled for Finian."

"For the guard."

"Yes."

"Why?"

"I thought he might be down there by then, checking on things."

"By 'down there,' you mean the first-floor back door?"

"Yes."

"Did he answer you?"

"If he did, I couldn't hear him over the sirens. My dear God, it was deafening, once you stuck your head out there, worse than even in the hall."

"Then what?"

"I started to turn around, and Joel was there, shaking me by the shoulders, asking me what was wrong."

"He didn't know about Mr. Rivkind."

"No. Not then, because when I yelled at him—you had to yell, to make yourself heard—he put up his hands, like 'What, what?' and so I ran back to their office and . . . and showed him."

"What was Mr. Bernstein's reaction?"

Swindell looked at me hard. "His reaction? He was—" She stopped. "Actually, I was so shocked myself, I guess I'd use that word for him, too. He covered his face with his hands, then grabbed the poker."

"The poker."

"The one from their fireplace. It was on the ground by Abe . . . by Abe's body. And Joel just grabbed it and threw it to the side."

"Where did he grab it?"

"What?"

"The poker. Where did Mr. Bernstein grab it?"

"I don't know. I may have . . . no, no I didn't—I couldn't see, because he—Joel—got down on his knees between me and Abe . . . Abe's . . ." Swindell waved her hand, warding off the memory.

I waited, then said, "Where was Finian Quill all this time?"

"I didn't know. I mean, we've all talked about it since, so I know Finian was in the alley in back, looking for whoever it was, and Joel was in the men's, but that's just because we talked about it. I didn't see any of it."

"Mr. Rivkind, he was dead when you found him?"

"I don't know. Joel said we should move him, try to . . . resuscitate him? But . . . I helped him move the body a little, got some blood on . . . on me, and I wasn't too good after that."

I waited longer before saying, "Mrs. Swindell, how do you think the killer got out?"

She shook her head. "At first, when the police were talking to us, I figured whoever it was must have gone out the front way."

ACT OF GOD

"The front way?"

"The swinging doors we have back out to the store."

"Past the rest rooms."

"Yes, and then when the main entrance on the first floor was locked and he couldn't get out, he went back through the store to the back door and set off the alarm. But that was because I didn't hear anything before the alarm went off."

"You did have your door closed, though."

"That's right. That's what I mean. With the door closed and all, I guess the man could have gone by my office, then down the back stairs and out."

"Setting off the alarm."

"Right, but the alarm goes off up here, too."

"You already told me that."

"No. No, I mean—what's the best way to say this? We hear the alarm all over the store, that's the idea of it, to warn everybody. But it gets set off by opening any one of the doors to the stairs."

I tried to picture it. "Any one of the doors to the back stairs sets off the alarm?"

"I'm pretty sure."

I made a mental note to ask Bernstein and Quill about that, but there were still a few questions I had for her, ones I'd saved till the end because I didn't think she'd like them. "Mrs. Swindell, have there been any problems with the business here?"

She stiffened. "Problems?"

"Money problems, debt problems, you tell me."

"I don't think I will, Mr. Cuddy. I'm the bookkeeper, and I don't think it's my place to comment on that."

She'd gone back to the reserved, precise tone of her profession. "Different question, then. There's no easy way to phrase this. Do you think there was anything beyond business between Darbra Proft and Abe Rivkind?"

Stiff became rigid. "Let me tell you something, Mr. Cuddy. When I was young, and my husband got sent to

135

prison, the judge was going to send me along with him. He might have had grounds, too, some kind of accomplice charge. Well, I'd been taking some courses at one of the business schools over in Back Bay, improve myself, but I needed a job. The probation officer back then, he knew Abe from the temple they belonged to, and he asked Abe if he'd stand up for me, give me a job." Her anger seemed to burnish itself. "Abe met with me, talked with me, and hired me. Nowadays, all you hear about is the friction, the hate. Farrakhan and the JDL. Even back then, though, it still meant having a black woman in a Jewish business, but Abe gave me a chance, and that means something to me, Mr. Cuddy. So you have that kind of questions, you can ask them to somebody else."

A male voice boomed off the walls of the corridor. "Beverly? Beverly, you all right down there?"

Swindell took the edge out of her voice. "I'm fine, Joel, but there's somebody here I think you ought to meet."

Footsteps barely sounded on the carpet outside, even with the office door open. I said, "One last thing. What's your husband's name?"

She spoke softly, contempt lacing the words. "Swindell, Samuel E. He did a short ten at Walpole, and I haven't seen or heard from him since he got out. What's more, I hope I never will."

12

THE MAN FILLING THE DOORWAY TO BEVERLY SWINDELL'S OFFICE literally had to turn himself sideways to walk through it. About five-eight, he was obese, his stomach swinging in front of him like the bass drummer for a marching band. In his mid-fifties, the hair was still black and lay in clotted curls on his head. The eyes were sweeping the room, as though he expected to hear a joke about his weight and wanted to spot the joker. He wore pants with suspenders, and a shirt that strained at the waistline but billowed on the arms.

He addressed Swindell. "What's happening?"

She said, "Joel, this is John Cuddy, the investigator Pearl hired. Mr. Cuddy, Joel Bernstein."

I stood to shake with him and nearly flinched at the strength of his grip. I had the feeling he was putting more behind it than just a businesslike firmness.

Bernstein said, "You know, I don't approve of this, right?"

"Mrs. Rivkind told me that was the general opinion."

"Well, Abe was my partner but her husband. She wants

137

to spend their money on you, it's hers to spend. You and Beverly finished here?"

"For now."

"Come down to my office then, get this over with."

I thanked Swindell and followed Bernstein into the corridor. "Who has the offices across the hall?"

Over his shoulder he said, "What?"

"The offices on the other side of this hall. Who's in them?"

"Nobody."

"Can I see them?"

Bernstein let out a deep sigh, then fished around in a side pocket, coming out with a chain that held at least twenty different keys. He walked back to the door opposite Swindell's office, having no trouble choosing, the first time, a key that opened the cylinder lock on it. He swung the door open for me.

I looked into an office that wasn't just unoccupied but abandoned. Two old desk chairs, each missing a wheel, a couple of plastic chair runners with broken-off corners and deep cracks in the plastic, a framed landscape somebody had sliced through with a knife, three old IBM standard typewriters. The dust on the linoleum floor looked undisturbed, the view out the windows that of the red brick building next door.

I said, "Hasn't been used in a while."

"Try decades."

"How about the other one?"

Bernstein locked that door and moved on up the hall to the one across from his and Rivkind's office. Same key, so far as I could tell.

"A master?"

He said, "What?"

"The key. A master for all the doors on the floor?"

"Oh. Yeah. Easier that way."

He didn't elaborate, but did swing this door open for me, too. More modernly appointed, no obvious junk, carpet on

138

the floor so no dust layer to disturb. "Who used to have this?"

"Our day manager."

"Where'd he go?"

"To Heaven, I hope. More directly, St. Michael's in Roslindale."

"The cemetery."

"Right."

"How long ago?"

"Two years. Heart attack, went out like a match."

I looked at him. Bernstein said, "I know what you're thinking."

"That it's odd you haven't replaced him?"

"No. This economy, it was a break he went so quick, we didn't have to lay him off and could give his bonus to the widow. No, what you're thinking is, 'Sight unseen, I'd have bet Bernstein'd have the big one before this other guy,' am I right?"

"No."

He made a derisive face. "You're telling me, you saw me walk into Beverly's office, you weren't thinking about some kind of fat joke?"

The bass drum image came back. "I thought about it. Not exactly a joke, but I thought about it."

Bernstein said, "All my life, I've been like this. I weigh three-ten now, have for twenty years, and before that it was two-seventy, two-eighty, around there. I go for a plane, they try to make me buy two tickets. I go shopping in the food market, people watch what I put in my cart. I was in school, the other kids made oink noises when I tried to eat in the cafeteria. You live a certain way long enough, there's nobody can fool you about what they're thinking."

"I'm thinking, who else has a key to this office."

"This one? Abe had one, a master like mine. The big Irish has one. . . ."

"That's Quill?"

139

"Right, right. Security. Beverly's got hers."

"Also a master?"

"Yeah. It just makes it easier, like I said. Who else? Probably Pearl and Larry, though when they ever used theirs I couldn't tell you."

"Darbra Proft?"

"No. She was just a secretary, not here long enough for that."

"To be trusted with a master, you mean?"

"With any key, except to her own door."

I pointed to the closed door next to the partners' office. "That one?"

"Yeah."

"I noticed you said 'was.' "

"What?"

"When you mentioned Darbra, you said she *was* just a secretary."

"Right."

"Why past tense?"

Bernstein looked at me hard. "Because she doesn't show up for work, doesn't even do us the courtesy of calling in, and this after she got a week's vacation only three months into the job, she doesn't have a job in my mind anymore."

"Can I see her office?"

"All right."

He used the same key to open the final door on the corridor, the one closest to the swinging doors back to the store. A cubbyhole more than an office, with just a desk and computer terminal and the collection of paperclip holder and stapler and in-boxes you'd expect.

"Mind if I have a look?"

"What, at her desk?"

"The drawers."

"The hell could her drawers have to do with Abe?"

"I don't know, but I'm guessing Mrs. Rivkind also told you I'm looking for Darbra at her brother's request."

"She told me. And I told her it sounded like the rest of it, cockamamie."

"Can I look?"

"Look. Look all you want. Long's I'm standing here, see what you find."

Hard to argue with that. The center drawer had a ruler, staple remover, and assorted blank papers and forms. More papers and forms, these with envelopes, in the left-hand top. Second drawer had tissues; a bottle of aspirin; cough drops; plastic spoons, forks, and knives; two different brands of granola bars; and the menus from three take-out places. The third drawer had a collapsible umbrella and a pair of Lady Reebok aerobic shoes with short white cotton socks.

"Any treasures?"

"No."

"Then come into my office, we can get this over with."

Bernstein locked Proft's door. "It's genetic, you know."

"Genetic?"

"The obesity. I'm not fat, I'm obese, account of three-ten's way more than a hundred-twenty-five percent of my ideal body weight. But it's not like I got some control over it. Just metabolism, you've got it in the family, you're born with it. You can diet, you can exercise, doesn't matter. Whatever you lose, you pay for it in the side effects. It's like Biafra, or that Somalia now. Most people spend all their time thinking about food, obsessing over how good it'd be to have this or that. Me, I was cold."

We moved into the partners' office. "Cold?"

"Yeah, like shivering. Teeth chattering even, middle of summer, didn't matter. I tried the diets and I tried the exercise and thank God I finally got this doctor, straightened me out. He told me they did this study on obesity, something like ninety percent of the people in it said they'd rather be blind than fat. Blind. You know why?"

"No."

"Because when you're blind, people want to help you out.

141

Nobody thinks to help a fat person because they figure it's your own fault. But it's not."

"Genetics."

"Like I said. So now I'm just content being me, with some pills here and there for high blood pressure, whatever."

Bernstein glanced at the bustle-back chair with the bleached spot near it, then shook his head as he lowered himself into the other, mirror-image chair. The seat crackled, the springs creaked. "You know, he was the only one."

"I'm sorry?"

"Abe. Take a seat."

I pulled over a captain's chair. "Mr. Rivkind was the only one?"

"To never make fun of me. He never once looked at me like he didn't want to be like that, fat. Obese. You know why?"

"No."

"He was in one of the camps as a kid. Buchenwald."

Bernstein pronounced the "w" as a "v." I just nodded.

"Abe, he was like a little kid, and he starved, like all the rest. Things were awful then, unimaginable. I mean, my dieting? Nothing. These starving Africans? Horrible, but at least nobody's putting them in ovens. Nothing compared to the camps, to hear Abe tell it. That's why he hired Beverly, you know."

"She said a probation officer put in a word for her."

"Yeah, that's how come Abe got asked. He handled hiring, running the store. Me, I'm more the merchant, the guy who makes the buying decisions on the stock. But Abe hired her because he never forgot the Liberators."

"The airplanes?"

"No, no. The black troops, our boys, end of World War II. This battalion of tankers, the 761st, I think was its number, but they called themselves the Black Panthers. Maybe that's where the political guys, the revolutionaries, got the name, I don't know. They—the soldiers, I mean—they came up to

142

Buchenwald, and I guess the guards—the Nazis—tried to make a fight of it, and the tankers just took them out, crashed through the gate. Abe, he showed me a picture of that gate, somebody took for him later and sent him. There was what looked like an office over it, then a clock with a picket fence and a flag flying over that. I guess the soldiers crashed through the gate, then saw the bodies piled up inside it. The prisoners the Nazis shot beforehand. Piled up like so much firewood, Abe said. 'Flexible firewood, Joel,' was how he phrased it. Well, now, Abe, he'd never seen a black person in his life except in the cinema—funny, Abe never called it 'the movies,' always the cinema, though you wouldn't really hear his accent, you didn't listen close on some words. But there came our boys through the gates, liberating the camp. And they see all these prisoners, heads shaved, ribs sticking through the tattered clothes or no clothes, hands clasped to God, giving thanks for deliverance. The soldiers were crying, these big black American kids, crying their eyes out. 'Angels,' Abe called them. 'Weeping angels.' "

Bernstein suddenly, violently, made a blubbering sound, but no tears. "Anyway, when his friend from the temple said he had this woman, needed a job, Abe just had to take one look at her, and he knew—hell, I knew—she had the job. The Black Panthers, they liberated Abe. Abe, he had to give the black woman a chance. And, turned out, she was terrific."

"How about Darbra?"

Bernstein made the derisive face again. "Not a waste, but not so far from it. Could do the simple things fine, but give her something a little complicated, needed any kind of judgment, and it was a miracle, you got back what you wanted. Beverly felt the same way, maybe she told you."

"Why keep Darbra on, then?"

"Abe's side of the business, like I said. He did the hiring

and the firing. He also said, 'She'll get better, Joel. She'll get better.' Only she never did, and now this."

"This?"

"Not showing up and not even calling."

"What's she like as a person?"

"What, Darbra?"

"Yes."

"There was something a little ... off about her."

Past tense again. "How do you mean?"

"Like ... like milk can get, you know? Not exactly spoiled, just you open the carton and stick your nose in and you wouldn't drink it, you could buy some more."

I had the same questions for Bernstein that I did for Swindell, but I also thought to save them for the end. "Can you take me over what happened the night Mr. Rivkind was killed?"

"I already told the police all this."

"Sometimes it helps to hear it again fresh."

"I don't know how fresh it's going to be—what, three weeks later already?"

"I'd still appreciate your trying."

Another deep sigh. "Okay. We're open late Thursdays. We'd had some problems, kids hiding in the store, then doing some vandal shit and banging out the back door, two A.M. the cops or the fire department calling me out of bed with the news about our alarm going off. So Abe hires the big Irish—I'm sorry, no offense, it's just that's what Abe and I called the guy."

"That's okay. Go on."

"Anyway, Abe and I are up here, trying to talk our way out of the recession, and Finian's down below, walking through the place, looking for stowaways—I guess the store's not going anywhere, they're just 'hideaways,' huh?— and Beverly's doing the dailies so we can see where we stand. I get up to go to the head—these pills I take, they

ACT OF GOD

don't make me constipated, just kind of . . . irregular, you
know?"
"Which bathroom?"
"Which? The men's room, of course."
"I mean, the one in the corridor past the fire door?"
"The only one we got. What's the matter with that?"
"Just seems kind of odd, the management using the same
facilities as the customers."
"Abe's idea."
"Abe's?"
"Yeah. We bought this store together, going on twenty
years ago. It doesn't matter, but you'll see what I mean.
When you looked up at the outside, the facade, you notice
anything?"
"Just that it's a nice building."
"Nice? Huh, this is a Despradelle."
"A des . . . ?"
"Despradelle. French architect, came over near the turn
of the century. This whole area, the Leather District, I mean,
it burned in 1872, and the warehouse they rebuilt on this
site, it burned, too. So around 1900 or so somebody got
Despradelle to design this building to replace it. The top of
the facade's got that spike effect, 'finials,' Abe said they
called them, with the flags. Now do you get it?"
I thought I did. "The way you described the gate."
"That's right. That's absolutely on the button. This building, it looks like Buchenwald's front gate, only now Abe
could be in the office looking down. We bought this store
because we were in the furniture business, but I got to tell
you, we bought this place because of the building more
than the business. That's what I meant about Abe being
like that."
"Resolute."
"What?"
"Decisive, determined."
"Right. Resolute, yeah. That was Abe. He had to have this

145

building, he had to offer Beverly the job, and he had to take Darbra on, too."

"Because he'd made up his mind."

"And believe me, it was easier to go along with him than to try to change it."

"Why Darbra?"

"Why?"

"Yes. I understand about the building and hiring Mrs. Swindell, but why Darbra Proft?"

"I think it was Pearl. She was doing a favor for somebody."

"Darbra's brother?"

"I think that was it."

"You never found out for sure?"

"Like I said, with Abe, it was just easier to go along. He wasn't a big guy—he always figured the time in the camp, the starvation, it stunted his growth—but he made up that mind of his, you couldn't change it with dynamite."

That sudden blubbering sound came again from Bernstein, but again without any other sign.

"So," he said, "what else you need to know?"

"We were talking about the night—"

"Oh, right. Right. Sorry, where was I?"

"In the men's room."

"Right, and I was telling you—look, that was another of Abe's ideas."

"What was?"

"Us sharing the men's room with the customers. Or Beverly and the female salespeople with the women. The idea was, you'd overhear things that might help you with the business."

"Like what?"

"Like, 'I really like a print on a sofa better than plain, don't you?' Or, 'Man, blue leather is just so *in,* I gotta have it.' Like that."

"So, you're in the men's room that night."

146

"Right."

"For how long?"

"How long? I don't know. Was it ten minutes? Could have been. Fifteen? Maybe. These pills, they make it . . . unpredictable, you know?"

"Did you hear anything?"

"Not till the alarms went off."

"Alarms?"

"Yeah, the—well, I guess there's just the one alarm, but we got sirens everywhere, and it just about deafened me in there with all that tile."

"What did you do?"

"Started cursing. We'd had this trouble before, like I said."

"Then what?"

"Well I—I finished up as quick as I could, then went out to the head of the stairs and yelled for Finian."

"The head of which stairs?"

"The store stairs."

"Through the swinging doors."

"Right. But I don't know if he could hear me. I sure as hell couldn't hear him. So I walked back through the doors into the corridor here."

"The office corridor."

"Right. And I see Beverly down at the other end, and I yell to her, but she doesn't hear me."

"What's she doing?"

"She's got the door open—the door to the back stairs, now—and she's yelling for Finian, too."

"You could hear her?"

"Yeah— No, no, as a matter of fact, I couldn't. Couldn't hear what she was saying, I mean, just her voice over the alarm. I guess she must have told me later what she was saying. Anyway, I see her at the door, and when she doesn't turn around after I yell at her, I go down to see what's what."

"You didn't see your partner."

"No. I was watching her. I glanced in the office here probably, but I don't really remember doing it now."

"You glanced in here but didn't see anything?"

"Like I said, I maybe didn't even glance in. That alarm, it makes everything kind of fuzzy, you know?"

"Go ahead."

"So I get to Beverly, and it's like she's seen a ghost or something. She's yelling and crying, but I can't make sense of it, except for the one word."

"Which word?"

" 'Abe.' "

This time I was ready for the blubbering sound, but Bernstein didn't make it. "Then what happened?"

"Beverly turned around and started running back up the hall, so I followed her to our office here. She stopped at the door, and I—I don't know exactly what I did. All I know is that I saw the poker thing we never should have had in the first place because the goddamned fireplace doesn't draw—Despradelle, he was great on the facades there, but not so hot on the heating system. And Beverly and I moved Abe around and we tried to ... but he was gone. You could see it."

The blubbering sound, more than once, then a steady chorus of it, but still no tears.

When Bernstein finished, I said, "Then what?"

"Beverly called the police, and Finian got here—the office here, I mean, and he said he went out the back door after he heard the alarm but didn't see anybody."

"Does the alarm sound when any of these doors is opened?"

"You mean the doors to the back stairs?"

"Yes."

"Yeah. Some kind of fire regulation, account of we don't have fire escapes. Every door to the stairs has to be wired into the alarm."

"So you wouldn't know which door the guy went through?"

"I don't know if they can tell that. The cops went through all the floors when they got here. At least, that's what I was told afterward."

"Other than a panicked robber, you think of anybody who'd want to hurt your partner?"

"Abe? Hurt him? You never knew the man. Listen to people who did, me almost thirty years. He grew up in the camp, in Buchenwald. He grew up knowing violence, knowing what provoked it. Knowing the kind of person who got off on it. He also knew how to avoid it. He was the kind never to give offense. Never a harsh word. And he never lied, either. Never, not once in all the years I knew him. Abe . . . Abe . . ."

The blubbering again. It hurt you to hear it.

This time I said, "About the business."

A shrug. "I'm gonna carry it on, long as the economy'll let me. It's what I've got. No family, just this."

"What kind of shape is it in?"

A darkening. "You need that for what you're doing for Pearl?"

"It might help to know."

"What's to know? We're floundering. A lot of the big furniture places, they've already closed their Boston stores, like Paine's there on Arlington Street? Never thought I'd see that. Others can't make it in the suburbs even, they closed down altogether. Beauty of this place, it's ours. The building, I mean. We own it, still free and clear, so I can last as long as I can cover the rest of the overhead, like payroll, utilities, and all."

"And if you had to close?"

"At least it wouldn't be bankruptcy court, like a lot of others. We'd hand out the pink slips, lock the doors, and sell the building for what it'd bring."

"Did you and Mr. Rivkind ever talk about that?"

149

JEREMIAH HEALY

"Abe? Are you kidding or what? This place *was* Abe Rivkind. He'd never even consider . . ." Bernstein paused. "Wait
a minute. What are you saying?"

"I'm not saying anything."

"No, but you're implying something, aren't you? You're
implying that Abe would have kept the store running, even
if it meant a lot of debt and bankruptcy if it did have to
close. Well, let me tell you something, Mr. Investigator. Abe
wanted to do that, he was the boss, as far as I was concerned. I would have let him have his way, because of how
he went through the camp and because of how he treated
me. You've been thinking, how come Joel's not crying over
his partner of twenty years, am I right?"

"Yes."

My not trying to dodge that question seemed to throw
Bernstein off a little. "You're a direct son of a bitch, I'll give
you that. Well, I'm not crying for Abe because I don't cry,
Mr. Cuddy. I learned not to cry when the other kids in
school threw food at me and tripped me and just-for-the-
hell-of-it beat the shit out of me. And I didn't cry for Abe,
I don't see me ever crying again over anything. But that
doesn't mean I didn't love him, and it doesn't mean I had
reason to kill him. Now get out of here."

"Mr. Bern—"

"Get out! You want to go through the store, do what you
gotta do for Pearl, fine. But you get the hell out of my
office right now or I'll put you through one of Despradelle's
windows there."

I stood up. Either I'd really struck a nerve with him, or he
was very good at sensing a question about any relationship
between his partner and Darbra before I could ask it.

150

13

I LEFT THE OFFICE COMPLEX THROUGH THE FIRE DOOR TO THE REST room corridor. A man came from the swinging doors and bent over to take a drink at the water fountain. His footsteps weren't much more than clicks as he'd come toward me, and I went into the men's room as he walked back toward the swinging doors. From inside, I couldn't hear him at all, and I wasn't even in a stall, like Joel Bernstein had been, where the walls would be another barrier to sounds.

I left the rest room and moved back into the store. I dawdled a little on the fourth floor, fending off two eager salespeople, then risked my knee to climb down to the third and did the same. I confirmed what I'd thought on the way up with Karen: plenty of places for somebody to hide until after Value Furniture closed for the night.

I was moving gingerly down the staircase, the knee seeming pretty stable inside the brace but me not wanting to press my luck. On the last flight to the first floor I saw Karen at the main entrance, pointing up toward me as she spoke to a kid in his early twenties with clean-cut good looks over a golf shirt and blue jeans. He came up the steps two at a time, bouncing on the balls of his feet like a dancer and smiling at me. I smiled back, and the kid hit me in the stomach with his right fist.

As I doubled over, Karen screamed and ran out of my sight to the left. The kid swung his knee up toward my face, and I parried it with my right palm, pushing forward so that he went backward down the stairs. He stumbled at first, regaining his balance as I straightened back up, my left knee not even wobbling. He charged and decided to try another punch, this one a swooping left cross. I blocked it with my right forearm and slipped my hand up and under his arm at the triceps, pinning his wrist and hand at my underarm and lifting up just enough to let him know I could dislocate his elbow if things didn't calm down.

"Hey, hey that hurts!"

The voice was familiar. I said, "It's supposed to."

"Let go. Let go of me!"

"Not just yet. Who are you?"

"Fuck you."

I lifted a little more.

"Ow. Ow! I'm Larry Rivkind, all right?"

The son from the telephone. "Why did you attack me?"

"Let me go."

"Same question."

Exasperation, then resignation. "My mother shouldn't have hired you, and I don't want you going around, trying to throw mud at my father."

"I'm not. I—"

"You are, if you're here asking questions. He never had any affair. He told her he didn't, and my father never lied."

"So people keep telling me."

"Now let me go."

"If I do, you going to behave?"

"Yeah. Yeah, come on."

I let him go as I backed away on the step. He rubbed his

152

arm a little, then said, "I'm telling you, butt out of this. Butt out now."

I expected that Karen had gone for help, and she returned with a husky guy about thirty in a powder blue, short-sleeved shirt and dark blue pants. There were no patches or badges on the shirt, but the forearms were corded with muscle, and the nose looked like the next break might take it into double figures. His hair was red and cut in an old-fashioned butch. The brows were so fair as to be almost invisible, the eyes under them more playful than wary.

He said, "What's this, now?"

"Nothing," said Rivkind, moving down the stairs but not rubbing his arm anymore with company having arrived. Taking the last few steps two at a time, he went out the door.

I said to the guard, "Why didn't you stop him?"

"They don't try leaving with a lamp under their arm, they're welcome to go." The brogue was thick, the voice syrupy with that harsh edge that makes you pay attention to it. "Besides, he's family of the owners. And who might you be?"

"John Cuddy."

"Ah, the one we had the call about."

"Probably."

"Finian Quill. I suppose you'll be wanting to hear my side of it, won't you?"

"I would."

Quill looked over to where he'd come from. "There's a place in back might suit us."

"Kerry. And your family, now?"

I said, "Cork, both sides."

Finian Quill nodded. He was sitting on a recliner chair in an employees' lounge furnished comfortably with pieces that looked too expensive for the purpose until you noticed a tear here or a ding there. His hands were folded casually over his belt, his head resting back at the half-mast position in the chair.

153

I shifted my rump on a leather love seat. "How long have you been in the states?"

"Oh, you lose track of that sort of thing pretty fast, you do. This beautiful country, it intoxicates, makes you forget most everything that came before her."

Despite the nose, the smile looked to have all its teeth.

"Mind if I see your registration card?"

"What, my green card?"

"Right."

His teeth flashed at me again. "I'm thinking neither of us has a badge here."

I was thinking how a man like "Honest" Abe might react to finding out he'd broken the law in hiring his new guard. "How illegal are you, Quill?"

"How might 'Finian' and 'John' strike you for conversational purposes?"

"Fine. How illegal?"

"Well now, I'm not sure there's levels of that where the Irish are concerned, John, but I've heard tell of streets in Dorchester where a man could buy himself a lovely package of Social Security card, voter registration, and the like for about a hundred dollars."

"Which makes you look like a citizen."

"So long as the one doing the looking isn't too demanding. Now, with what I'm told is my strongish accent, I'm not so sure I could pull that off."

"So you have a green card."

"Not quite kelly green, but it will do."

"Let me guess. You came over on a tourist visa good for what, three months?"

"More like six."

"And you decided to overstay your welcome."

"As I said, an intoxicating country."

"So long as somebody else is buying the drinks."

A flash of more anger than teeth. "Easy words to your lips, born to the advantages here because of the sacrifice of your forebearers. Let me tip you to a few things, eh? First, I'd been wanting to come over for ten years now, but your grand immigration policy, it said I needed an immediate family member already here. That may help the Mexicans and the Chinese, but not so much the Irish, the last wave of us being forty years and more ago. Second, when the policy seemed to loosen some a few years back, I queued up like a good lad and waited my turn, but wouldn't you know it, by the time my turn came, there were no more of the right kind of visa. Can you imagine that, John? Some forty million—*million*—of your countrymen trace themselves back to the Auld Sod, but now there's not enough room at the inn? So I'm looking hard at my own thirtieth birthday and wondering how many years I've left on this planet, and I decided it was time. I got myself a green card, never you mind just how, now, and that means I can have a job doesn't require me to work for less than the minimum wage under the table."

"What happened to the nose?"

"Ah, the old honker? A bit of rugby, a few differences of opinion over a pint here and there. A small price to pay for enjoying oneself, don't you think?"

"How did you come to be working here?"

The face went sly. "You're a man who changes gears a lot, eh?"

"Depends on the terrain."

"That it does, but this question's a bit easier than the first few you've asked me. I saw an advert in the newspaper."

"And responded."

A nod. "Came in to see Mr. Rivkind. He liked what he saw."

"And what was that?"

"Come on, man. You look at me, you see a lad can handle himself as a bouncer but mostly just act as a scarecrow. That's what the owners had in mind."

"When did you start here?"

"Two months ago tomorrow."

A month after Darbra Proft. "Any trouble?"

"None to speak of. Couple of scamps, figuring to cause some mischief is all, and they came to see the error of their ways soon enough."

"So Mr. Rivkind's death was the first big problem."

"Far as I would know."

"Can you tell me what happened that night?"

"I can. Would you rather I walked you through it, though?"

"Yes."

Quill got up and led me back into the first floor of the store. "I'd already locked up the front and turned off the elevator when the alarm sounded."

"Hold on a second. What's your routine?"

"You mean for closing up, now?"

"Yes."

"Pretty simple, actually. I wait until eight-fifteen, eight-twenty, when the last of the customers appears to be gone. We're supposed to close at eight, but this economy, it doesn't do to rush the good people out."

"Go on."

"By eight-forty-five, even all the sales clerks have gone, and I turn off the elevator and lock the front entrance."

"The only way in and out?"

"No. We've also the loading area out back, for delivering the pieces to the store. But that's closed and locked by five."

"Okay. Go on."

"Well now, I've turned off the elevator, and I'm starting my rounds here—"

"You work from the ground floor up?"

"What's that?"

"Your rounds. You work from the ground floor up?"

"Ah, that's right."

"Why?"

"Mr. Rivkind's idea, it was. He liked me checking every-

156

thing and ending up there on the fourth floor with him and
Mr. Bernstein so I could walk them to their cars and Mrs.
Swindell to the subway."

"Did you come down the stairs then?"

"You mean on a regular night?"

"Yes."

"No. I'd turn back on the elevator, and we'd all ride
down together."

"Why was that?"

"Well now, Mr. Bernstein, he's not as partial to stairs as
some might be."

"Okay. You're on this floor that night, doing your rounds.
Where are you when the alarm goes off."

"Colonial."

"Sorry?"

"I'm in the colonial section. Over this way."

Quill took me to a display of living room sets that had
lots of rural prints and burled wood.

I said, "Then what?"

"Well, I hear the alarm and I figure it's kids, as what
happened before. So I run over to the back door."

"Show me."

Quill started running. With the knee, I walked fast behind him.

I caught up outside another set of padded café doors with
an illuminated FIRE EXIT ONLY—ALARM WILL SOUND
above them.

He said, "I've often thought the sign's a challenge to them,
but I'm told it's another of your fine country's laws."

Quill pushed through the café doors, showing a steel door
with a panic bar like the one on the fourth floor. To the
right was a staircase leading upward.

"These the stairs that go to the fourth floor?"

"And each one in between, if that matters to you."

"All right. What did you do when you got here?"

157

"What did I do? I went through the door and into the alley, to see if I could catch the lads."

"You thought there was more than one?"

"That's what Mr. Rivkind told me when he hired me. He said, 'These kids, now, Finian, they hide in the store and then bust out, like it's a game with them.' "

"But you didn't actually see or hear anything before the alarm itself went off."

"No. If I had, I would have come running sooner, wouldn't I?"

"Can you show me the alley?"

"I can."

Quill took out some keys, nearly as many as on Bernstein's chain, and stuck one of them into a silver and red metal box near the top of the door. "Deactivates the alarm, now."

"If you didn't do that, how quickly would the alarm sound?"

"Matter of seconds."

He removed the key from the box and used his hip to press the panic bar. The door opened onto a broad alley with a wooden stockade fence bordering it. To my right were two garage doors about six feet off the ground, the lip of the building sticking out just below the bottom of the doors.

"Loading bays," said Quill.

I looked around the alley area. Potholes that held oil-slicked rainwater, some food wrappers and smashed bottles at the margins by the fence.

"No way for anybody to come through the bay doors?"

"Padlocked, inside and out."

"Nor the front entrance."

"Not once I've turned the key in her."

"So this is the only other way out."

"It is."

"Show me what you did that night."

"Well now, I came through the door—"

"Without bothering to deactivate the alarm."

"No need to. She was already sounding because somebody had gone out the door."

I looked at him. "Then what?"

"Then I ran down the alley."

"Leaving the door open?"

"What was that?"

"Leaving this door open behind you?"

"Ah, no. I let her close because I had a key in my collection here to get back in."

"Which way did you run?"

"To the right."

"Why?"

"Why to the right, do you mean?"

"Yes."

"That's where the driveway is for the trucks."

"The delivery trucks."

"That's right. I figured the lads might take the low road out rather than try to hop the fence."

"Did you hear them?"

"Well, I don't figure now it was just young vandals, John."

"I mean that night, did you hear anybody running in front of you?"

"Couldn't very well with the alarm, could I? She wails like a banshee."

"Even once the back door closed?"

Quill gave me a funny look. "My ear were still ringing from the noise."

"When you got to the driveway, what did you do?"

"I went out to the street, to see if I could spot the lads running away, but I couldn't, now."

"And then?"

"I came back around here."

"To the back door."

"That's right."

"Running?"

"Me running, do you mean?"

"Yes."

"Well now, no. No, I don't suppose I was. Not till I got close to the door, that is."

"What happened there?"

"I could hear Mrs. Swindell screaming."

"You could hear her?"

"Yes, like through the door, even all the way down here. I understand she was up at the door on the fourth floor, screaming her heart out over finding Mr. Rivkind."

"What did you do then?"

"I went up the back stairs here, quick as I could."

"Can we do that?"

"We can." Quill unlocked the door with a key, ushered me inside, then closed it behind him, using another key on the red and silver box again. The stairs in front of us were concrete, gray with black rubber treading, the paint on the walls yellow. Emergency lighting boxes, like camping lanterns, lined the top of each landing.

As we climbed the stairs, I said, "You didn't stop on the second or third floors?"

Quill turned to give me the funny look again. "And why would I do that?"

"You knew the screaming must be coming from the fourth?"

"Of course I did. That's the only place anybody would be."

We reached the fourth-floor landing. "What happened when you got to here?"

"I opened the door."

"With your key?"

"That's right. These doors, they're all designed that way, to lock when they're closed so that nobody on the stairs in a fire would get out before they reached the bottom and safety."

I watched Quill. "Go on."

"Well now, I couldn't hear anything over the alarm."

"Which was still sounding?"

160

"Nobody had turned her off, man. I would have down below when I came back in, but I could hear Mrs. Swindell screaming, and I didn't want to take the time."

"Was she screaming the whole time you were coming up the stairs?"

Quill stopped. "No, no, in fact I didn't hear the lady at all once I was back inside downstairs, which made me hurry all the more."

"Why?"

"Why? I thought there might be more troubles on the fourth floor, and I was right."

"So you're up here on the fourth floor—"

"And I open this door, and I hear somebody yelling— well, I know now it was Mr. Bernstein and Mrs. Swindell. In the owners' office, they were, and when I got down there, they were trying to move Mr. Rivkind— Ah, a horrible scene it was, John. Horrible."

"What did you do?"

"Well, I went in to help them, but Mr. Bernstein, he was on his hands and knees, blood on his hands, too, and so I stepped in and moved the poker so he wouldn't kneel on it."

"You picked up the poker?"

"Yes. I was almost going to kick it, then picked it up before I saw the . . . the gore on the working end of it. Then I'm afraid I dropped it pretty fast."

"Did Mrs. Swindell see that?"

Quill stopped again. "I couldn't swear to it either way. I think she was on the telephone by then, calling for the police. Didn't have to, of course."

"Why not?"

"That alarm, I expect it would have brought the cops, too. We surely got more than our share of firemen out of it."

I pictured the scene. A madhouse, as Bonnie Cross had described it.

Quill fingered his key ring. "You want to see the fourth floor, too?"

161

"Already have. Wait a minute."

"What is it?"

"How could we go through this door without setting off the alarm?"

"How? By using my key, John." He waggled the thing in front of my eyes.

"This key opens the door from the stairwell side without the alarm sounding?"

"And from the store side as well."

I didn't reply.

"John?"

"Who else has one of them?"

"One of the keys, do you mean?"

"Yes."

"Let me see. Mr. Bernstein for certain. Mr. Rivkind had his, too. I suppose that's all. Anything else, now?"

"No, I don't think so."

As Quill turned to go back down the stairs, I said, "I'll have to take these a little slowly."

"A bit gimp in the knee, are you?"

"A bit."

"I noticed from the way you held yourself on the stairs with Master Rivkind there."

"Tell me, you know much about him?"

"The son, now?"

"Yes."

"Nothing but what I saw of him at the funeral. Never really came around the store. Of course, I can only say about the last two months."

"What did you think of Abraham Rivkind?"

"The salt of the earth, and gentle as a spring rain. The last man you'd hope would depart this world on the wrong end of violence."

Not exactly the question I'd asked. "How about his relationship with the staff?"

162

"The staff? He was an easy man to work for, if that's what you mean. No airs, very natural."

I had the feeling I'd get less from Quill than I had from Swindell on that count. "How about Darbra Proft?"

"Darbra? Well now, I wouldn't be seeing much of her, would I?"

"You tell me."

"She was a secretary on the fourth floor, John. Not much need for me to be up there, and almost none for her to be wandering the store where I'd be."

The past tense from Quill, too. "Do you think there was anything between Mr. Rivkind and Ms. Proft beyond boss and secretary?"

"It's not good to think about such things, John. Like the priests and the nuns used to tell us."

We reached the first floor and came through the padded doors back into the store. As we moved toward the front entrance, Quill said, "Will that be all, then?"

"Maybe one more thing. Is there a way to tell if the fire doors had been opened?"

"The alarm tells you that."

"I mean, if the alarm was set off by one of the doors, is there a way to tell whether a particular other door was opened?"

Quill stopped. "Well now, that's a good question, isn't it? I don't know. But I don't see that it matters very much."

"Why is that?"

"Well, I opened that downstairs door, didn't I, when I went out after what I took to be vandals. And Mrs. Swindell opened the fourth floor door to call for me, she said, and I surely opened it to go to Mr. Rivkind. So one way or the other, both the doors you care about got themselves sprung by people with a right to be inside the store."

Finian Quill flashed the big smile at me, but I somehow didn't find it very warming.

163

14

ON MY WAY OUT OF VALUE FURNITURE, KAREN GAVE ME SIMPLE
directions to Grgo's. It was only around the corner from the
store, but without her specifics, I would have walked right
on by.

The door to the restaurant was six steps below street level,
the name on the jamb in calligraphy so small it could have
fit on a three-by-five index card. The door was locked, so
I knocked.

It was answered by a wiry little man wearing a white
shirt, black tie, and black pants. Shrugging into a black Eisenhower jacket and opening the door, he said, "No dinner
before five, please."

"I'm here to see the owner."

A brief nod. "Come in, please."

I did, the man locking the door behind me. "You wait,
please, I bring him."

The man hurried through an empty dining room with
tables for two and four, all covered with heavy white cloths.
The tables were positioned for privacy, cutting down on

164

the number of people who could be served, surprising in downtown. On top of each cloth were silver place settings; a delicate, spiraled vase with one bloom in it, all tulips; and a candle with burgundy wax. The walls were painted the color of the candles and held portraits of medieval knights and aristocrats in dull golden frames. The largest frame held a flag, horizontally striped in red, white, and blue with a crest of red and white checkerboard centered in the upper half. There was a sense of being in a foreign land that you've never visited and know little about.

My greeter appeared from what I took to be the kitchen with a portly man in a double-breasted gray suit and silk tie. This one had black and gray hair worn thick and full, with a matching beard that was either just coming in or had been freshly trimmed. The portly man dismissed the other with a pat on the arm and came toward me.

"I can help you?"

Up close, his irises were almost black, with dark smudges under the eyes and on the hooded lids above them. "Are you Grgo?"

"It is my pleasure owning this establishment. And you?"

"John Cuddy." I showed him my identification. "I'm here to ask about a couple of your customers."

"Which of these?"

"Abraham Rivkind and Darbra Proft."

He pursed his lips. "This will need some time, yes?"

"Probably."

"Come."

I followed him to a square table for four in a corner, him pulling back a chair for me, then pushing it in under me and taking the one to my right. Unlike the other tables, this one had no silverware, just the tulip vase and candle and a large brass ashtray like an emperor's crown with a pair of dry-docks for cigars and more for cigarettes.

From a jacket pocket, Grgo took out two cigars. "You will join me?"

"No, thanks."

He didn't ask if I minded his smoking. "This city say I must have my table in 'Smoking Section.' If I not sit here, they charge me and I must pay fine."

My greeter came over and hit his boss's cigar, puffs of bluish smoke drifting upward. When we were alone again, Grgo said, "So, you come from Mrs. Rivkind."

"Yes."

"What you want from me?"

"How about your last name?"

"Easy. Radja."

"Like the basketball player?"

"The one the Celtics love to get play for them, but I don't think so. He make too much money for Italian team. We very distant cousins, I think."

You get a person talking, it's good to keep them talking. "Croatian?"

"Yes, so. From Zagreb, me. You know the country?"

"Never been."

"You should not go now. It is disaster."

"You've been back since the war began?"

A vigorous puff. "Yes, so. When we hear the Serbs attack us, three of my Hrvat friends—'Hrvat' is what one Croat call another—three my friends from here and me go on plane there to fight."

"To fight?"

"Of course to fight. The Chetniks—this is our word for Serb fighters—the Chetniks attack city of Vukovar across the Danube. We fight so long as we can. One my friend from there, we go school together in Zagreb before I come over here, he is on ambush with me, but I don't know this before he look at me, he say, 'Hey, I know you somewheres.' And Mate and me realize we friends from thirty years before. And so we want to talk, about relatives, friends, but we cannot. The Chetniks come with their trucks and hardened cars—no, cars like tanks?"

166

"Armored cars?"

"Yes, so. They come up the road, and we kill them. We kill first the front car with shoulder rocket, big boom, then the last car, boom-boom, then the Chetniks jumping out from all trucks. We kill very many, but my friend Mate, he killed, too. Thirty years, and he killed after we see each other again five minutes."

Radja shook his head and sculpted his cigar ash on the tray. "The Serbs, they are stupid, they celebrate their big holiday, you know what it is?"

"No."

"It is day in year 1389 they lose the big battle to Turks at Kosovo. They lose, they live under Turks five hundred years, and they celebrate. They animals, too, I tell you. Vukovar fall, they come to hospital there, they take three, four hundred people out from hospital. These some Hrvatska—Croatia—soldiers, many civilians, all wounded and no guns no more. The Serbs take them to pig farm, then kill them, bury them in cornfield with bulldozer." He looked up at me, the hooded eyes moist. "Bulldozer for grave. The Serbs for their own, they build grave houses."

"Grave houses?"

"Yes, so. Little houses like big house you live in, only small, over grave. They put in there things for dead person to use, like radio, refridge, these things. Then they go out, have celebration like picnic at house on the Days for the Dead, but their church—the Orthodox—their church don't like it."

"How long were you in Croatia?"

"Two, three months. There was no more bullets for guns, no shoulder rockets, no shells for—what is word, 'artillery'?"

"Yes."

"No more for that, neither. Croatia get more bullets, I go back."

"You think the war will last that long?"

A grunt. "The war, it last centuries now already. The

167

Serbs and the Croats and the Muslims. I kill your brother, you kill my family. You kill my family, I kill your village. The United Nations think it can stop this? How can you stop war when neighbors kill you, when neighbors you have in your house, Serb friends like I got from school, Peda or Borislav, come kill you? I tell you, in Sarajevo, the Chetnik snipers with the telescope rifles on the hills, they shoot at their own house."

"Their own houses?"

"Their apartment house. You see, that way the sniper know which window Serb, which Croat, which Muslim, so he shoot at the right windows. And the hate, the hate it is passed down to the children like the good silver and the jewels. What the Serbs do to Vukovar, the city is gone. Sarajevo, soon. The worst, though, this is the *ciscenje.*"

"What's that?"

"The 'cleansing.' The newspapers, the television, they call it the 'ethnic cleansing.' Rape, burn, bomb. I tell you, the Serbs, they rape girls, Croatia girl, Muslim girl, twelve, thirteen years, don't matter to them. They rape like Ford make cars, the 'assembly line' thing. They rape them in front of parents, then kill them. Dead girls can have no children, so no more Croat, no more Muslim after the cleansing. But the Serbs, they don't care which ethnic, so long as she not Serb. Hungarian, Greek, Italian, don't matter to them."

The Croatian Nazi government slaughtered hundreds of thousands of Serbs during World War II, but it didn't seem like the time to bring it up. "Mr. Radja—"

"Grgo, please. Nobody know Mr. Radja, everybody know Grgo. I tell you what you want, you ask."

"You knew Mr. Rivkind well?"

"He was good customer, good man. I open up this restaurant, there not many in Leather District. Mr. Rivkind, he come here once. I recognize him from street, I wait on him myself, he come back. Then he come back all the time."

"The police think he was killed by a burglar, a robber."

"I think so. That night, I hear the alarm noise, even in here. I go out to see, the fire trucks and the police cars come everywhere."

"Did you see anything else?"

"I don't know what you mean?"

"Did you see anyone else that night, anything strange?"

"No. I am in this room until the alarm noise."

I nodded. "Did Mr. Rivkind bring his wife here very often?"

Radja took the cigar out of his mouth, pursing his lips as he scraped off more ash. "Not so much. She live in Sharon, long drive for her to meet him or them to come on weekend."

"How about people from the store?"

"Yes, so. Everyone from store. You work for Mr. Rivkind, I give you discount."

"Did Mr. Rivkind bring people from the store to eat with him?"

"Yes, I just tell you."

"Darbra Proft?"

The hooded eyes became sad again. "Her I don't want in my restaurant anymore."

"Why not?"

"There is . . . argument. She throw things. Not good for business."

"When was this?"

A shrug and a small puff. "Month? I don't know."

"Can you tell me about it?"

Radja looked away from me, toward the center of the room. "She come in, with man I don't see before. Seem nice, but old for her. She come in, make big thing that she know me, that I know her. They sit. Then I am in kitchen, waiter come for me, he say come quick. I see her stand up, throw wine at the man. She is very loud, very . . ." He flapped his hands wildly around him in a limp-wristed way. "She act like end of world. Then she leave, poor man red from wine

169

and red from shame, too. I try to help him, but he want to leave. Who can blame this? No, I tell you, I don't want to see her again."

"Did she come here often?"

A big puff. Around it, "Like others."

"Like the others from the store?"

"Yes, I tell you already."

"Did she eat here with Mr. Rivkind a lot?"

A bigger puff. "Everybody from store eat here with Mr. Rivkind. This is the way he is. He take people out to lunch and dinner at Grgo's."

"Did it seem that they had more than a business relationship?"

"I don't talk on my customers that way."

"Loyalty?"

"Loyal, yes. When I come here from Zagreb, I don't have the two cents. I work hard, I start this restaurant, I starve if Mr. Rivkind don't find me, come back all the time with his people. I go to his funeral, I cry like the babies. Loyal? I learn in Croatia, when you loyal for communist party, for Soviet 'guests,' for anything big like that, it don't get you nothing. It take advantage of you. When you loyal for country, like my Hrvatska, you feel good, even if it don't help you. But when you loyal for person, for person help you, they remember you. Mr. Rivkind remember me, I loyal for him."

One last try. "Grgo, if nobody will talk to me about Mr. Rivkind, how can I help his wife?"

"I don't know this. I just know I don't talk on these things."

"Did Mr. Rivkind ever talk with you about his business?"

"Yes, so. All the time."

"What did he say?"

"He tell me things are hard. He has to tell me? What is this first thing people stop when they lose job? They stop eating in restaurants close to job. Shame to see other workers

170

still there, shame, too, for those workers still have jobs. You not have job, you still need the hair cut, and things to drink and eat, but not at restaurant like Grgo's."

"Many people from Value Furniture lose their jobs?" Smoke wended out his nostrils in two wispy strands. "Enough."

"Any of them angry at Mr. Rivkind?"

"I don't think so. Nobody can be angry at him. He was good man, good to all."

"Somebody didn't think so."

"Then it is somebody don't know him. At his funeral, I think of all the things I learn Catholic in Croatia, good things to say about dead person. But it is Jewish funeral, so I don't think it is right to say them. In Zagreb, a friend of mine from school, he was Greek, and I go to his father's funeral when he die. I am nine, ten years, but I remember my friend tell me what the people say. When it is time to put coffin into ground, they say, 'The earth that fed you now will eat you.' "

Christ. "Did you say that?"

"No. But I think this." Grgo Radja stubbed out the cigar. "Funny thing to think for man who own restaurant, I tell you."

15

LIKE RADIOLOGY, THE DEPARTMENT I WANTED WAS BELOW THE lobby. One wing of the basement had painters doing touch-up work, the sign MAGNETIC RESONANCE IMAGING/ AMBULATORY PATIENTS temporarily propped against a pillar.

Inside the doorway was a waiting area with a receptionist sitting behind a desk. Putting down the Lawrence Block paperback I'd been carrying since the last visit, I gave my plastic hospital card to her, and she used a machine to stamp it through several self-carboned forms. With a pencil she handed me, I filled out a "yes/no" information sheet that seemed interested mainly in whether I had any shrapnel or other metal parts in my body.

An attendant who introduced herself as Maureen came through a set of doors and led me into a locker room with a wooden bench flanked by classy new lockers and dented old ones. Looking at the new ones, Maureen said, "These are from Italy. Paid a fortune for them, but guess what?"

ACT OF GOD

She had an accent like a friend of mine in the army who'd
grown up near Milwaukee. "What?"
"The company over there shipped the things without keys."
"You're kidding?"
"Uh-unh. That's why we have to use these old ones." She
pointed me toward the dented lockers, which looked like
they'd been salvaged from a high school gym just before
demolition.
Removing the key for Number 16, I said, "Are you from
Wisconsin by any chance?"
"No, upstate New York, outside Buffalo."
"Sorry, it's just—"
"I know. We sound like Wisconsin, and we never lose
our accent no matter where we move to."
I got the feeling she thought I was nervous and was trying
to make me feel better, so I just nodded.
"Okay, Mr. Cuddy, please take off all your clothes except
briefs and socks. Put on one of these outfits back to front
and step through that door when you're done."
"Thanks."
I stripped and put on the johnny coat and, a new one on
me, johnny pants. There were also plastic envelopes that
folded inside out to form something like slippers for your
feet. When I was finished, I picked up my book and key
and went through the door.
Maureen was waiting on the other side. "Let me take
those from you. You won't be able to read, and the key
doesn't work so well inside the chamber."
Chamber.
We went into a large room. There was very little in the
way of furnishings beyond a big metal cylinder like an iron
lung from the fifties and a fancy gurney table in front of it.
"Please sit on the end of the table."
When I did, Maureen used a strip of cloth maybe six feet
long to bind my shoulders back. I suddenly had a vision
from Saigon during the Tet Offensive, suspected Vietcong,

173

on their knees in the street, their arms bound behind them at the elbow, causing them to arch forward, like—

"Am I hurting you?" said Maureen.

"No."

"You just grimaced, and I was afraid—"

"No, thanks. I'm okay."

"Good. Now, please scoot back so you're able to lie flat on the table facing the ceiling. A little more . . . good. Now just lie still, please."

I did. Maureen padded my left elbow and taped a circular ring like a juggler might use on my left shoulder, as though my shoulder were my head and the ring a straw hat. Then a triangular foam support was wedged under my calves and restraints strapped across my waist.

She said, "I'm going to slide you in now."

"Be sure to notice whether it's a boy or a girl."

A nice smile. "Mister Originality."

Maureen moved me headfirst into the iron lung. The first impression was being inside a coffin, and I pushed from my mind Grgo's comment about "the earth that fed you." Then I noticed the semicircular top and the indirect lighting and the metal buttresses. Suddenly, it was like a day when I got back from the service and a friend took me through the Callahan Tunnel in his convertible, my head lolling on the backrest, watching the roof of the tunnel as we went by underneath it. Now I had maybe eight inches of airspace between my face and the walls and roof of the machine. Above me, a white disk and then two red dots flashed, and I was aware of the whirring of a small fan somewhere. Then, over a muted public address system, I heard Maureen's voice in my ear.

"Are you all right in there, Mr. Cuddy?"

"Fine."

"Please stay completely still. The first imaging lasts for just three minutes."

There was the sound of radiator pipes clanging, then an

174

arrhythmic bongo sequence, then a constant chattering, somewhere between a sewing machine and a jackhammer. The chattering seemed to get louder as time went by, but that might just have been me.

"Okay," in my ear, "are you still all right in there?"

"Still fine."

"Good. Relax and let me look at this image."

Relax.

She said, "Okay. Good one. This next will take nine minutes. Please remain completely still."

"Right."

Radiator, bongo, chattering. Same sense of escalation as we went through it.

"Okay, Mr. Cuddy. That was the worst of it. How are you?"

"Still no problems."

"Good. The next one is the last. Just four minutes. Ready?"

"Ready."

After the sequence, Maureen said, "Okay. I'll be right in."

I hadn't realized she'd been out.

Maureen slid my table from the machine and unstrapped me. Returning my book and little key, she led me back to the locker room door and left me. On the bench inside, a small boy sat hunched over in a johnny suit that accentuated how thin he was. His face was too old for his body, a lopsided bandage wrapped around his head. The way Beth was for a while after they told us what was growing inside her skull. The boy didn't look up at me.

I said, "It's not so bad. More like going for a ride through a tunnel."

This time he did look up, with the scorn of a veteran for a rookie. "I know."

I shut up, changed, and left him, hunched over on his bench.

*   *   *

175

"John, good to see you."

"Same here, El."

"Shoulder and knee all cleared up?"

"Guess not, I'm still wearing this thing."

He peered over the counter at my brace. "You supposed to work out already?"

"Not exactly. I just need to blow off a little tension."

Elie frowned. "You been to the doctor?"

"Yes."

"Physical therapy?"

"No."

His face showed he'd heard the edge I tried to keep out of my voice. "Well, just use your own judgment, then."

I took myself down a notch. "Thanks, El. I will."

As I did the hip and back machine in front of a mirrored wall, I noticed Elie talking with one of the other members, a real estate mogul named Norm. He was about my size and weight, but he could ride the stationary bike longer than the winner of the Tour de France. Norm lived in the high rise catercorner to my brownstone on Beacon. He seemed to have a lot of free time during the day, because I'd run into him at the club often enough when most folks would have to be working.

I skipped the leg extension machine because of my knee and moved to one of the two leg curls. Norm got on the sister machine next to it. The effect was that we were lying stomach down about a foot away from each other, like men on adjoining massage tables.

"Elie tells me you screwed up your leg."

I did a curl. Count of two on the uplift, four on the down. "And shoulder."

"Bastards, both. When that happened to me, I had to lay off most of the machines and all the running."

I paused on the up, then let it down slowly. "What did you do instead?"

"Got started on the bike. Boring, but it keeps your tone

and wind close to where they'd be otherwise. StairMaster helps, too."

Two up, four down. "What about the upper body?"

"The therapist my doc recommended showed me how to use this thick elastic band. I felt a little silly, but I could do the exercises on my own, and I came back from it."

Two, four. "From the injury, you mean?"

"Right. Takes a while, but you feel the progress, and that keeps you going."

"Thanks, Norm."

"Don't mention it. You stay active at our age, these things are gonna happen to you. Trick is to come back the right way."

"Tell Elie I got the message."

Norm grinned. "What are you doing for the Fourth?"

"Of July?"

"Right."

"No plans."

"I'm having a party at my place, watch the fireworks and concert. You interested?"

About five hundred thousand people jam themselves onto the riverbank to listen to the Boston Pops play in the Hatch Shell and to see the special effects get launched from an anchored barge. "Can I bring a date?"

"Sure, but nothing else. I'll have booze and buffet. Be fifty, sixty people there. Who knows, maybe one of them needs a private eye."

"Networking."

"The way the world turns."

I did a very light circuit of the remaining machines, then twenty minutes on the bike and ten on the StairMaster. Pulling on my sweatshirt, I stopped at Elie's front counter.

He looked up from a newspaper. "How'd the workout go?"

"About the way you thought it should."

"Hey, John, I'm not trying—"

"You were right, El. Thanks."

177

"No big thing. You coming to Norm's party?"
"First my personal trainer, now my social secretary."
A big smile. "Everybody needs somebody sometime."

"How about a movie?"
"Don't feel like sitting, Nance."
She turned a page in the newspaper. "Video?"
"Don't feel like sitting here, either."
Nancy Meagher looked at me across the coffee table in
her living room. We'd just cleared it of dinner dishes, Ren-
field in a ball on her couch, snoozing off the scraps I'd
fed him.
Nancy said, "If you were a little younger, we could go to
one of the rock clubs."
"Funny."
"No, really. Jesus Lizard is at the Paradise."
"Sounds totally awesome."
"How about Sexploitation at the Rat?"
"What do they do?"
"Says here 'retro-dance.' "
"You know what that means?"
"No."
"Maybe you're too old for the clubs, too."
"Here's another—oh, you'll love this one. Look."
I set down the last of my beer and read the name of the
group. Tequila Mockingbird. "I don't get it."
"Say it out loud."
I did. "I get it."
Nancy's voice changed. "I don't."
I looked at her. "What do you mean?"
"I know your being banged up has been—"
"I'm a little more than banged up, Nance. Parts don't
work the way they're supposed to anymore."
"But you're doing what you can about that, right?"
"I can't do anything about it."

178

"Yes, you can, and you are. You've been to the doctor, you had that magnetic thing."

"Magnetic resonance imaging."

"The doctor will read the image or whatever you call it, and prescribe what you should do."

"What if there's nothing I can do?"

"Oh, great. John, it's not like you to be so . . . defeatist. What's the matter?"

I told her about what Norm said at Nautilus.

"So? That sounds encouraging."

"Encouraging."

"Yes. If those things worked for him, there's a good chance they'll work for you."

"Nance, I'm not a real estate wheel who just wants to stay in good shape. I'm a private investigator who has to be able to do things."

"We're back to that, are we?"

Without names or details, I told her the trouble I'd had with Larry Rivkind on the staircase at Value Furniture.

"John, he sucker-punched you."

"And therefore?"

"And therefore it wasn't your knee or your shoulder or your less-than-immortal masculinity that let that happen. Even if you were fine physically, you never would have blocked that punch."

"Granted. But afterward, I was barely able to handle him without hurting him."

"But you did."

"He was just a college kid, Beth."

Nancy's fine blue eyes filled. "You've never done that before."

"Done what?"

"Called me 'Beth.' "

"Jesus. Did I?"

"Yes."

"Nance—"

"Just don't touch me for a minute, okay?"

"Okay."

She used the edge of her forefinger to swipe at the tears. "That's been the hardest part about being with you, John." I hated to ask, but I didn't see it. "What has?"

"That. You're with me, but you're not with me."

"Nancy, I just plain don't get it."

"Look." She clasped her hands in her lap. "When we first met, I understood about you still being . . . attached to Beth. I thought it was—I was going to say 'admirable,' but I really mean 'desirable.' That faithfulness was a character trait that made me . . . that made me think I wanted to love you. And then your other traits started to grow on me, too. Your sense of duty, of ethics, even your sense of humor. And I realized I did love you, and I do love you, but . . .'"

"But what?"

"I get the feeling sometimes, not often but too often, that I'm some kind of . . . stand-in, that I'm not really the one in your life yet."

"Nancy, there hasn't been anybody else, not even close."

"You don't understand. I'm not saying there's somebody else. Or I guess I am." Another swipe with the finger. "You're still tied to Beth, like you haven't really taken hold of me as the person in your real life."

"Nance, I spend all my 'real' life with you."

"But that's just the point, John. You give me the impression you want to spend time with me, but not your life with me."

"How? How do I do that?"

"The auction."

"The auction?"

"Yes. I wanted to go down there with you, not just to have a 'stevedore,' but to have somebody help me pick out a piece of furniture that we'd kind of buy together, a start on nice things that we'd own together and use together and look at over the years together, watch last together."

I let out a breath. "And all I did was take potshots at it."

"At the auction, at the furniture, at me. It was all just a . . . lark, the boy indulging the girl in what she wanted to do and being a wiseass about even that."

"Nance, I'm sorry. Why didn't you say something?"

"I started to, in the car on the way back. But then you seemed to come around, the way you do, and I thought you'd gotten the idea. Then after you hurt . . . got hurt, I couldn't very well be mad at you for your attitude when the thing I bought was the reason you were hurt."

"Nancy, the reason I hurt myself was because I was too stubborn about thinking I was man enough to move that bureau without more help."

She stared at me. "You're doing it again, John."

"Doing what again?"

"Making it seem like you got it, like you're a sensitive man who can be objective about himself. So now we'll start joking and move off the subject and into the bedroom for some tender, soothing sex."

Nancy was right. It was hard for me to see it, much less admit it, but she was right.

I took her left hand, the one she didn't use on the tears, in mine. "I'm not sure this is going to help, but let me explain something to you. Beth was the only woman I ever knew, and not just biblically. She was half of me, Nance, the half that didn't have to be the ex-MP or the insurance investigator. I could relax with her, confide in her, not worry about myself around her. Then she got taken, slowly, and that half of me went with her. It just wasn't there anymore when I woke up in the morning or went to bed at night. In the time we've been together, I've felt some of that half coming back to me, back into me, but it's not all there yet. I do know that from the moment I first saw you in that courtroom, I felt a 'ping' inside me, something I hadn't felt since I'd lost her. You started me back up, Nance."

"Ping and start up. I feel like an ignition key."

"Now who's joking us off the subject?"

"Sorry."

"So I'm back on track, kid, and it's thanks to you. But I'm not to where I was with Beth, and I'm not sure I ever will be. Or can be."

Her stare got a little hollow. "That's the worst thing I've ever heard you say, John Cuddy."

"It's the truth. If you'd rather I lied to you, I'd rather leave."

"Don't."

"Which?"

"Either." She wet her lips. "I know . . . I don't really know what it was like for you to lose Beth, John. I lost my dad when I was too young to understand it and my mom when I was in law school, but those were parents, people I'd taken as given. I don't know what it's like to lose the one person you've sought out, the one you expect to spend the rest of your life with, but I do know this."

"What?"

"I'd know what that was like if I ever lost you."

She put her face in the crook of my good shoulder and started to cry.

I gave her a while. Then, "Nance?"

A muffled sound.

"When I called you 'Beth' before, there was a reason."

Her head lifted enough so she could speak clearly. "What was it?"

I spoke softly into her ear. "When I was having the MRI thing today, the machine is like being slid into a coffin."

"Oh, John, I'm sorry. I didn't—"

"It's okay. It's okay, it's not even really that. It's more . . . when I was finished, and felt kind of, I don't know, relieved that I was through it, there was this kid in the locker room."

"The locker room?"

"Where they have you get ready for the machine. He couldn't have been more than ten, maybe not even, but his

182

face was so ... weary, and he was wearing one of those head bandages, like a turban."

Nancy pushed back some more, so that she was looking me square in the face, her hands resting on my collarbone. "Go on."

"It was ... it was just so much like what ... the way Beth looked the last couple of months, just before she couldn't get up by herself and move around. And he was so little, Nance, and so down. Depressed, I mean. So I tried to lighten it up for him, and he just looked at me. He'd been through the thing before, I don't know how often, but I'm pretty sure that what they told him didn't get any better. And I thought of Beth, of how ... hopeless it was all the time that we wouldn't talk about how hopeless it was. And I couldn't keep talking to the kid, Nance, I had to get out of there. And I went to Nautilus, and that was some help, but not much."

I suddenly realized how long and hard I'd been looking into Nancy's eyes, losing something in them. And getting something back, too. Getting back a lot more than I'd left there. "God, Nance, I just felt ... scared."

"It's okay to be scared."

"No. I mean, I'm not scared of what'll happen with the knee and shoulder. It's more because ..."

Nancy cocked her head. "Because of what, John?"

"Remember when Renfield was hurt, you got drunk and told me how scared you were about leaving him at the vet's for the operation?"

"Because it hit home how fragile life could be?"

"Right. Well, since Beth died, in a sense I haven't been scared."

"You haven't been?"

"Everything I cared about, the one person I cared about, she'd already been taken from me."

"There was no way for anything to hurt you anymore."

"Right. Well, I just realized something."

"What?"

"I don't feel that way anymore."

Nancy's eyes moved left-right-left on mine. "You feel scared?"

"More that I could be scared again. That I could be scared of losing you, because I'm talking with you the way I talked with her, the way she let me talk with her."

"John, you've always been able to do that with me."

"Not quite, Nance. I've always been allowed to talk with you like that, because you were open to it. I've just never been able to feel that I could, and I covered for it by lumping it under professional conflicts of interest, the public prosecutor and the private investigator. I never really opened up with you, because I didn't want there to be another person I was afraid to lose, another person I could be scared to not have be a part of me."

More tears, but through a smile. "You know what?"

"What?"

"I think I like you better when you can be scared."

"From what I remember of it, it's not such a bad way to be."

She came in for a kiss. "Not a bad way at all."

16

MOST OF FRIDAY MORNING WAS SPENT WORKING ON OTHER CASES in my office. About eleven, I went down to the Prelude and took the Southeast Expressway to Route 128, the beltway around Boston. At Route 24, I turned south for Sharon. Reaching the main drag, I found the pharmacy where William Proft worked. There was a pay phone outside it, and I tried Pearl Rivkind's home number. No one answered, and no tape machine broke in to take a message. I hung up and walked inside the pharmacy.

It was the kind of place every town had before the chains took over. Newspapers and magazines in racks at the front, two elderly men casually reading without buying while a young girl yawned at the cash register. On the right wall was a preserved if nonfunctional soda fountain with a gray marble top and chrome accessories. Aisles of greeting cards, hair and skin products, cold remedies, and so on, but without signs to tell you what was where because you'd shopped there long and often enough to know. The prescription counter was at the back and elevated above its cash register,

William Proft's balding, sandy-haired head nearly brushing the suspended ceiling above him.

I stood at the prescription register for a full minute before he looked up from what he was doing and noticed me.

"Mr. Cuddy."

"Mr. Proft."

He looked down in front of him. "I'll be just a moment."

"Your dime."

Proft came back to me. "Or at least half of it is, but still a good point. This can wait."

He descended what seemed to be four steps, then opened a gate in the elevated counter to reach my level at the register. He wore a buttoned-down blue shirt under a white lab coat with a pocket protector and three different colored pens in it. "What can I do for you?"

I glanced around the store. "Slow morning."

"Yes. I frequently say I'm the only drug pusher I know who isn't swamped by customers."

The perpetual grin curled some more, to show he thought his remark clever even if I didn't think it funny.

"Still," I said, "it might be nice if we could speak somewhere a little more private."

A conspiratorial nod. "I'm about due for a break, and there's just the best coffee shop a few doors down."

"Hazelnut blends?"

"You remembered."

"And the coffee shop will be confidential?"

"Ah, no. At least, not assuredly. It is a nice day, though. Perhaps a bench outside?"

"Fine."

I followed Proft to the front of the pharmacy, where he advised the young girl that he was going on break, her acknowledging the information with another yawn. On the sidewalk, he led me to the coffee shop, even treating me to an iced-tea-to-go before we settled on a municipal bench without too much pigeon guano staining it.

ACT OF GOD

Proft tore a small triangle in his coffee's plastic cover, as
though he were worried about spills on a bumpy ride. "So,
have you made any progress?"

"Some. I found out that you and your sister weren't exactly close."

A tentative sip. "I told you that."

"Other people said she hated you."

"Who?"

"People in a position to know."

"Ah, that sounds like dear Auntie Dar."

"I also found out that you and your sister shared a hefty
policy on your mother."

"That's correct."

"Mind telling me how that came about?"

"Mother felt insecure after our father left. The policy was
her security blanket for us."

"How did she die?"

"From what I was told, Mother was sunbathing on the
roof of her apartment house. She got too close to the edge.
Or just tripped."

"Or was pushed?"

The grin curled a little more. "Or jumped, for that matter.
God knows Mother had a hard enough life to justify it. But
I've always preferred 'fell.' "

"Because the insurance company wouldn't have paid off
on a suicide?"

"And for sentimental reasons as well. She was my natural
parent, after all."

"You say you prefer to think she fell. Is that what you
believe happened?"

"Rather late in the game to make a difference, wouldn't
you think?"

"I don't suppose you remember the name of the police
officers who investigated?"

"After six years?"

187

Darlene Nugent had said five. "It would save me some time."

Another sip, less tentative. "And your time is my money, correct?"

"Half of it, anyway."

The grin curled toward the corners of his eyes. "You know, Mr. Cuddy, I do enjoy speaking with you. Sparring, if you like, even if I am paying handsomely for the privilege. But I must say, I don't see what Mother's death has to do with Darbra's disappearance."

"Turns out you and Darbra have crossover policies on each other."

"I'd have been disappointed if you hadn't found out about those from Auntie Dar."

"You might have told me."

"Why?"

"So I had a better fix on why you wanted your sister found."

"No, Mr. Cuddy. My motivation should be immaterial to your investigation. What matters is that you find my sister, not why I want her found."

"Maybe it's material to the condition you want her found in."

"Dead, you mean?"

"A life policy generally requires it."

Proft set his cup on the bench. With a labored sigh, he stretched his long arms and legs, the left hand dangling off the end of the bench, the right trailing along the top of the back rest. "Our mother made Auntie Dar promise to maintain those policies. Why? I'm sure that consciously it was more security blanket, to provide for the survivor in the event one sibling lost the other. However, I'm equally sure that Mother was aware of the . . . absence of love between Darbra and me, and therefore subconsciously Mother was insuring more than our lives. She was insuring, via Auntie

Dar, that in the event one sibling dropped out of sight, the other would have a reason to look into it."

"Money as the motivation for concern."

"It works, Mr. Cuddy. My retaining you is proof of that."

"I also found out how Darbra got the job at Value Furniture."

"My suggestion to Pearl Rivkind, you mean?"

"Yes."

"So?"

"So that would have been another nice thing for my client to tell me."

"For one of your clients to tell you, certainly. But, if you'll recall, you spoke with Pearl first, and when you didn't ask me about how Darbra came to be at the store, I naturally assumed Mrs. Rivkind had already satisfied your curiosity on that point."

Nicely done. Even with some law school training, though, Proft had to have thought the thing through in advance of us getting to the bench. "Why'd you put in the good word?"

"With Pearl, you mean?"

"Yes."

A casual shrug. "I knew my sister was looking for work, and I thought Mr. Rivkind might have a job for her."

"How'd you know your sister was out of work?"

The grin curled a little more. "Given that dear Darbra and I don't get along that well?"

"Uh-huh."

"Ah, Mr. Cuddy, you seem to be better at your job than I could have hoped. I'm very glad I hired you."

"I'd be very glad if you answered my question."

Another sigh. "Darbra called me a few months ago, rather out of the blue."

"About what?"

"Well, Auntie Dar's birthday was coming up—oh, so it must have been more than a few months ago, mid-March to July One . . . yes, three and a half months ago. In any case,

Darbra thought it would be a good idea for me to call Auntie Dar and find out if everything was still in order about the insurance policies."

"Meaning, was Darlene Nugent still paying the premiums on them."

"Precisely."

"And?"

"And what?"

"Did you call your aunt?"

"No. No, I was grateful to be reminded to send some flowers for the occasion, but I thought that checking up on the policies seemed rather . . . tacky, so I told Darbra I'd leave it to her, if she wished."

"Tacky, but you still asked Mrs. Rivkind about a job for her."

"I thought the discipline of a well-managed store might be good for my sister."

My face must have shown what I thought of that one.

"Oh, all right, then. I was just trying to have some fun."

"Fun."

"With Darbra's ways, I thought she might . . . liven things up a bit at Value."

"Stir up trouble, you mean."

"I really didn't know."

"But if Darbra caused trouble at the store, and you'd recommended her to Pearl Rivkind, you might have lost the Rivkinds' business."

"Lost . . . ? You mean, at the pharmacy?"

"Yes."

"You overestimate my sense of . . . entrepreneurship? I'm just a lowly employee, Mr. Cuddy. The pharmacy losing a customer over a little prank on my part really wouldn't trouble me a great deal."

The explanation made sense, so long as you believed William Proft was that kind of guy. "It was your idea that you and Mrs. Rivkind come to see me together."

"I recall I did tell you that."

"You wanted her in on it because you thought I wouldn't take you on alone."

He returned to his coffee. "Because of my personality. Or perhaps lack of it, as some have commented in the past."

"And if I did take you on alone, you were afraid I'd drop the case once I found out the real reason you wanted Darbra found."

"And you would have, wouldn't you?"

I didn't reply.

Proft's grin turned smug. "So, you see, I was right. Having Mrs. Rivkind as a joint client not only saved me half your fee, it also kept you on my case."

"Half right."

"Half?"

"I'm still on the case, both for your sister and Mrs. Rivkind's husband. But I've mostly eliminated possibilities rather than discovered new ones. I think I'm going to have to take a trip to New Jersey."

"I don't envy you."

"But the trip will be for Darbra, not for Abraham Rivkind."

As Proft caught on, his grin evaporated. "But surely the money we've already given you is sufficient—"

"It's sufficient, all right. But the trip to Jersey is going to be funded by you. Entirely."

"Not fair."

"Call it client discipline."

"I'm being punished?"

"Yes."

Proft simply watched me for a minute, the eyes hungry from whatever he was thinking about. "Very well. It's nothing I couldn't have predicted, and had I hired you entirely on my own, I would have had to pay the full freight any-

191

way." Another sip of coffee. "Besides, what can it cost as a percentage of what I might receive?"

As much as I can milk it for, I thought.

After William Proft went back into the pharmacy, I tried Pearl Rivkind's number again with the same negative result. When I called my answering service, there was no message from her but an "urgent" one from Traci Wickmire. I hung up and dialed the number she'd left.

"Hel-lo?"

The trilling voice. "Ms. Wickmire, John Cuddy."

"I thought I told you to call me 'Traci'?"

"Traci, my answering service said—"

"I know. Was 'urgent' the right word to use?"

"What?"

"Was 'urgent' the right word. I never dealt with a private investigator before, and even though I've used 'urgent' as an adjective in articles, I didn't know if that was the right word to get across what I meant."

The upward lilt on the last word. "What did you mean?"

"Well, I went in to feed Darb's cat this morning, right?"

"Yes?"

"Somebody's trashed her place."

"Trashed it?"

"I checked the thesaurus in my computer, and I think 'ransacked' is the right word, but it sounds kind of funny saying it out loud over the telephone. Maybe you should come see for yourself."

"Half an hour."

"I'll be here."

"Ransacked" was the word.

Tigger watched us from under an overturned art book big enough to form a sort of lean-to, the smell of his litter more pervasive than it had been the last time I was there. The place was a mess, but when you looked, the devastation was only partial. For example, the living room had books pulled down and a lot of things upended, but while the cushions were off the couch, nobody had slashed them open or done the couch itself. All the Hummels and animal figurines were intact on their little knickknack shelves, which told me whatever was being searched for had to be bigger than they were. In the kitchen, somebody had gone through the cabinets, tossing stuff from the shelves onto the floor, but the small, opaquely wrapped frozen goods in the freezer hadn't been torn apart.

In the bedroom, the open suitcase was on the floor, whoever it was having rifled through it and scattered its contents around the carpeting. The mail Wickmire had put on the bed also was scattered, but none of it opened. The covers were off the mattress and the mattress off the box springs. The closet and bureaus had heaps of clothing in front of them, but no slashing there, either.

Wickmire said, "Something, huh?"

I turned to her. She was wearing the same overlarge flannel shirt, but untorn jeans this time. The strawberry hair shook as she took in the mess.

I bent down to check through the mail again. "When did this happen, Traci?"

"Not sure. I came in to feed the cat this morning about eight, and it was like this."

"But it was okay last night?"

When Wickmire didn't answer, I looked up, and she gave me one of her coy smiles. "Wouldn't know."

The lilt on the last syllable again but the first time she'd tried the faked flirting this visit. "Why not?"

"I spent the night at a friend's. I mean, it's one thing for me to be a neighbor and keep looking after Tigger, and it's another for the cat to dominate my social life, don't you think?"

I was hoping for a charge card bill that hadn't been in the last batch of mail I'd seen. No luck. "So this could have happened when?"

"Anytime."

"Since yesterday morning?"

"That's right. I left Tigger enough food for all day Thursday and all night. But I'm telling you, the smell of that litterbox is starting to put me off more than my allergy."

I thought about it. "The litterbox still in the bathroom?"

"Disgusting, if you ask me."

I looked at her.

She said, "I mean, sitting on the toilet doing your business with the cat squatting next to you doing his? Come on."

I moved to the bathroom. Somebody had overturned the litterbox, too, and pawed through it. Or the cat had done the pawing.

Behind me, Wickmire said, "Oh, great, just great. What am I supposed to do now, clean it up?"

"That's a thought."

"Why should I have to?"

"Because it won't get better on its own."

We went back to the front door. I'd looked at it briefly as Wickmire had opened it for me. Now I examined the jamb and lock more carefully. "No sign of a break."

"I know."

I looked at her again.

"I mean, that's what's so creepy, you know? I came down here to open the door, and it's locked just fine the way I left it yesterday morning. But when I walk in, it's like—I don't know, 'ransacked' still sounds funny when you say it, and 'pillaged' is even worse."

"Anything taken, as far as you can tell?"

"I never even thought of that."

"Called the police?"

"I called you."

"And I appreciate your doing that, Traci. But you didn't report this to the police?"

"No. I don't like cops. Besides, I don't even know if I'm . . .

authorized to call. I was supposed to just look after the place until Darb got back, and as far as I know, she *got* back."

"You're here most of the day, right?"

"No. I'm in my apartment on account of my allergy to Tigger, remember?"

There was none of the faked flirting this time from Wickmire. "I mean here in the building."

"Oh. Right, I am."

"Did you leave your apartment at all yesterday?"

"I left about four to meet my friend."

"Before that?"

"Just to get the mail. Oh, and lunch. I was on a roll with the charities article, so I ran out and got a sandwich and came back."

"Did you see anybody around?"

"What do you mean, like—what's the word, 'suspicious'?"

"That'll do."

She thought about it. "Suspicious, yes, but nobody who didn't belong."

"I don't get you."

"Well, I saw Rush down by the mailboxes, and he sure as shit looks suspicious to me, but he lives here, too."

"Was Teagle doing something in particular?"

"In particular?"

"That made you think he looked suspicious."

"Oh, no. No, Rush just looks suspicious on general principles."

"You think he's in now?"

"I doubt it. He said he had a sound check today."

Teagle had mentioned the phrase to me. "Like a dress rehearsal with his band?"

"Yeah. They've got a gig down at a club by Kenmore Square, and their sound has to be right."

"You know which club?"

She gave me the name, then sighed. "Maybe Wild Bill."

"Darbra's brother?"

"Yeah."

"You think he might have done this?"

"What? No, no I mean the litterbox."

I looked at her. "The litterbox."

"Yeah. Maybe if I called him again, he'd come to clean it, look after the cat."

"My advice?"

"Yeah?"

"Don't count on it."

The club where Rush Teagle was appearing lay just off the square. I walked in at street level, the linoleum floor sticky from beer and worse. The bar ran along the right wall, a dozen or so college kids and construction workers sitting in clumps of two or three, having a late lunch and a couple of drafts to wash it down. When I asked the barkeeper for Teagle, she said she'd never heard of him. Then I said he was in a band. The keep nodded and said, "Try downstairs."

The stairway was dark, the basement darker still, so much so that I had trouble making out the pony bar that would be directly below the one on street level. The only lights in the basement were above a man with long, graying hair at a control panel halfway to the stage and against the left wall. On the stage, which was really just a platform maybe two feet off the floor, were Rush Teagle and three other young guys I'd never seen before. One, a skinny kid who might have been Korean, had long hair like Teagle, only braided into dreadlocks. The second was an olive-skinned Hispanic boy with short, styled hair. Number three, the drummer, was burly, pale, and clean-shaven, head as well as face. They made an interesting grouping.

Unfortunately, I couldn't say the same for their music. It was awful, atonal rock, with no apparent rhythm or melody. Teagle shrieked into a mike as he raped his guitar, the other long-hair more strumming his instrument while the short-

haired kid pounded a keyboard and the no-haired kid preferred cymbals over drums.

The man at the control panel adjusted a few levers in
front of him and made some notes, then held up his hand
in a stop sign. Everybody saw it but Teagle, who wailed for
a few more chords before realizing he'd gone solo.

Teagle said, "The fuck's wrong?"

The man dropped his hand. "Nothing's wrong. I got
enough, that's all."

"Enough? We're only halfway through the fucking set."

Teagle didn't endear himself to the guy. "Look, pal. I been
doing this twenty-five years, and I've heard enough to know
when I've heard enough. Besides, you're lucky, there'll be
so many assholes shitfaced in this place by the time you go
on, nobody'll hear you anyway."

"Oh, that's real fucking funny. And real professional,
too."

As Teagle glared at him, the older man closed down his
panel and walked toward me. Conversationally, he said,
"What do you want?"

"I'm with the band."

"Christ, you ever read that book?"

"What book?"

The guy gave me a disgusted look and went upstairs.

Teagle now had his back to me, his friends starting to
break down their equipment. I moved toward the stage.

Seeing me, the drummer said, "Yeah?"

I spoke to Teagle's back. "I need to talk with you."

The lead singer turned around. "Well, what do you know."

The keyboardist said, "Agent?"

Teagle said, "Not. This is the fucker who claimed to be a
cop, rousted me in my apartment."

The Baltimore accent made it "A-parr-mum." The other
guitarist, the Asian kid, tried to sound tough. "Maybe we
ought to mess him up a little for you, Rush."

"Maybe we should, Hack."

197

Hack and Rush. I almost wanted to know the other kids' names. "Bad for business, guys."

The drummer said, "So, we take you outside, asshole. Management doesn't give a shit what happens in the alley."

I looked at the four of them, figuring the drummer as the only real trouble, then thought of my shoulder and knee. "Not just bad for the bar's business, boyo. You guys make a living using your fingers."

The drummer grunted. "Some living."

I said, "Suppose even one finger on one hand got broken, how would that affect your playing?"

Hack, the Asian guitarist, swallowed hard. The Hispanic kid at the keyboard wiggled his fingers until he realized he was doing it and stopped. The drummer just smiled at me as Teagle said, "What the fuck right you got, coming in here and threatening us like this?"

"I thought I was the one being threatened, but why don't we just call it a draw. Then you can sit down and talk with me a while."

"And if I don't fucking feel like it?"

"Then I stake out your place, catch you sometime without the U.N. Peacekeeping Force here to monitor my good intentions."

The drummer said, "I still think we ought to beat the shit out of this asshole."

Teagle seemed to be thinking about something. "No, wait. The dude wants to talk, that's cool." Lovingly, he laid his guitar on its soft black case. "How about over there?"

I met him at the darkened bar, no stools for sitting. As I looked around the room, I couldn't see any place to sit, just stand-up counters at elbow height for setting down drinks.

"So man, what's up now?"

Teagle was silhouetted by the stage spots, so I couldn't see his face clearly, but the voice told me he was grinning. I couldn't quite understand the change in his attitude.

As the other three dealt with their equipment, I said, "Why can't you just leave things there for tonight?"

"Huh?"

"Your instruments and stuff. Why do you have to take everything down?"

"Oh. Coupla other groups are playing tonight. Gotta give them the chance for sound checks, too."

"Battle of the bands?"

"Huh?"

"You guys in a contest?"

"Oh. Not. Tonight's like an audition night."

"But the place already hired you, right?"

"Not exactly. It's more like we auditioned with a tape. That's how you do it now, drop off a tape so the houseman or the owner—"

"Houseman?"

"The asshole was working the console over there. A club'll have three, four groups come in from their tapes, and everybody gets to play a set. There's a Sox game tonight, so they'll start early, get people in the mood. But we're the best, 'cause we're an original band."

"Not a copy."

"Right. The other guys, they're just cover bands. They play like the top-forty songs."

"Instead of their own music."

"Right, right. I don't write it, we don't play it."

Teagle was being awfully cooperative, almost as if he wanted my help in return.

I said, "I have a few more questions for you."

"Like ask away, man."

"You seen Darbra since I talked with you last?"

"Uh-unh."

"Heard from her?"

"Not even a note."

I watched him, my eyes adjusting enough to the light to see his now. They seemed eager.

"Did you see anybody out of the ordinary in the building yesterday?"

199

"The building?"

"Where you live."

"Oh. No, man. Ran into, let's see, Traci, some guy on Social Security looks like the next good breeze'll finish him. . . . That's about it."

"Traci the one who told you I wasn't a cop?"

"She mentioned it, yeah."

"How about last night?"

"Thursday? I was out with my band. How come?"

"Somebody went through Darbra's apartment sometime yesterday or last night."

He seemed genuinely surprised. "How do you know?"

"They tossed the place."

"No shit." Something else moved behind Teagle's eyes. "What'd they get?"

"I don't know if they got anything."

"What do the cops say?"

Teagle was definitely as interested in this as I was, and I didn't get the feeling he was acting. "You know any reason somebody'd toss her apartment?"

"Not me, man."

"Somebody with a key."

A smile. "Same answer. Not me, man. Get it?"

"I get it."

"So, anything else you got to ask me?"

"Not just now. You guys aren't touring in the near future, are you?"

"Touring." A laugh, the kind I remembered coming from me when an older relative at a holiday might make a joke he thought I'd enjoy. "No, I'm gonna be around. For a while, anyways."

Teagle pushed off from the bar and swaggered back to the rest of his band, throwing stale patter at them like a bad Henny Youngman warming up a room.

*   *   *

From a pay phone in the upstairs bar, I called my service again. Nothing from Pearl Rivkind, but there was a message from the doctor at the sports clinic. I tried her and got through after only two layers of insulation.

"Oh, Mr. Cuddy. Thanks for calling. I have the results of your MRI."

"That was fast."

"I asked them to push on it."

"And?"

"And they came through."

"The results, I mean."

"Oh, sorry. Can you come by sometime this afternoon?"

"I'm in the area right now."

"Good. How soon?"

I felt a twinge in my left shoulder, even though I wasn't moving it. "Right away."

Her smile seemed upbeat. "How's the knee brace working out?"

"I've gone slowly with it."

"Like what?"

"Light Nautilus, a little stationary bicycle, and StairMaster."

"Good. After you've worn the sleeve for another few days, you might try a short run, level pavement."

"How short?"

"Oh, no more than half a mile. If there's going to be more of a problem, you ought to know it by then."

"Otherwise?"

"Otherwise, just keep wearing the brace continuously until you don't need it anymore for stairs or other every-day things."

"What about the MRI?"

"I've reviewed all the images, and they hold good news."

I felt a relief that surprised me by its sheer size. "What does good news mean?"

"The X-rays showed no fractures, and now we can rule

out a tear of the rotator cuff or other structural damage. I think it's just a matter of torn muscle tissue, though there may be a wayward tendon or two."

Wayward. Where do they go? "So, what should I do?"

"How has the anti-inflammatory worked?"

"Makes me nauseous."

A little smile. "So you stopped taking it."

"Yes."

"That's all right. It's mainly for pain, anyway, so it's your choice, pain or nausea. What I think you should do is go to a physical therapist."

"What for?"

"What for?"

"Yes. If there's no damage, won't the muscles just . . . what, grow back?"

"Well, they'll grow, all right, and mesh. But you want to minimize the scar tissue and maximize your recovered strength, right?"

"Right."

"Well, then, the therapist can show you exercises that will help that, help you to come back sooner and sounder."

I thought about Norm's advice. "Okay. Can you recommend somebody?"

"I can." She paused. "Just one thing?"

"What?"

"The pills you can skip, but the exercises, you really should do them faithfully."

"Or else?"

"Or else you've wasted my time and your money."

That was close enough to a line I'd used with clients in the past to take her word for it.

17

THE INSURANCE COMPANY THAT CARRIED THE POLICIES ON THE Proft family was headquartered in Omaha, but it had a claims investigation office in Hartford. Rather than drive the eighty miles, I got on the phone and drew a semblance of a human being named Nichols.

After outlining to him my involvement, I said, "When I used to work at Empire, we'd keep files ten years."

A laugh. "You were at Empire?"

"Yeah."

"Get laid off when they folded things up in Boston?"

"No. I left a while before that."

"Huh. You're lucky. You bailed out before there was a lotta guys looking to open their own shops. How do you like it?"

"There's not much security, but the pay's fine when it arrives, and you come to enjoy being your own boss."

"Hey, I'm my own boss now, in charge of the department, anyway, and it's not so hot. What do you get for a daily rate up there?"

203

"Depends on whether it's commercial or personal."

"Give me a range."

I did.

Nichols said, "Be lucky to get anywhere near that down here for either kind of work. Well, let's see now, what can I do for you?"

"Can you access your closed files, give me the name of whoever it was investigated a claim out of Quincy for you?"

"When was the claim?"

"Five or six years ago."

"Did we pay off on it?"

"Yes."

"Before or after litigation?"

"Nobody's said anything about a lawsuit."

"Then you're fuck out of luck, pal."

"How come?"

"Maybe—I don't know—three years ago, company decided to shred everything was closed over three years without litigation."

"You weren't computerized then?"

"On the policies, yeah, but not on the investigations. See, they figured, none of our work's ever admissible in court anyway, so why keep the stuff or pay for it to go on microfiche."

"Accounting must have a record of your paying off on the policy."

"Yeah, they would. But it's not gonna have any details like who investigated. Just a claim number and the policy number and probably a picture of the cancelled check."

"And you couldn't access the claim by the claim number?"

"No," said Nichols. "Not until three years back, when we—when Claims Investigation—went on-line, too."

"Any suggestions on who might have been assigned to this one?"

"Why, because of where it came from, you mean?"

"Right."

"Hell, no. Our adjusters and investigators, they turn over every couple of years. Half of them don't like the work, another quarter really wanna be lawyers and leave us for school. Only mules like me stay on long enough to be Head of Claims Investigation for a region."

Which is what I'd done at Empire. "Well, listen. Thanks anyway."

"Sorry I can't help you out."

"There's maybe something else you could check."

"What's that?"

"I'd like to know the status on a couple of current policies."

"These life policies, too?"

"Yes."

Nichols went a little sly on me. "There wouldn't happen to be any . . . uh, relationship between the claim we paid out on and these current ones, would there?"

"Might be."

"Any chance this relationship could maybe get us a shot at recovering what we paid on the first one?"

"To be honest, I doubt it."

Nichols didn't say anything for a moment. Then, "Give me the names of the insureds."

I did.

"I gotta tap these into my terminal here. Omaha's not bogged down, I can probably have the status in like a minute."

"I appreciate it."

About forty seconds later, Nichols said, "Insured: Proft, Darbra, policy number—you want all this shit?"

"Just whether they're paid up currently."

"Yeah, Proft, Darbra and Proft, William. Both current. Premiums billed quarterly to Nugent, Darlene. Want Nugent's address?"

"Got it already. Beneficiaries?"

"Just crossovers. Darbra if William goes, him if she does."

"Nothing for the aunt?"

"The who?"

"Nothing for Darlene Nugent if either Darbra or William dies?"

"No. But we're just one company here."

"What?"

"We're just one company. Look in the Yellow Pages, there's plenty of other places she could buy insurance on a relative's life."

A good point, but hard to check. "Thanks, Nichols."

"Hey, don't mention it. I ever decide to go out on my own, I'll give you a call."

"Fine."

"And Cuddy?"

"Yes?"

"Looks like maybe the, uh, family relationship gives us an angle, let me know, huh?"

"I'll try."

"That's all any of us can do, right?"

"Hey, what's this, I don't see you for a month, and now you're back inside a week?"

He was wearing the same vest and suit pants. I gave him the benefit of the doubt on the shirt and cigar. "How are you, Mo?"

"How am I? Let me tell you how I am. I'm having a Sol Wacht—wait a minute, I already told you that one, right?"

"Right."

"I tell you, John, it's getting harder and harder to remember these things. The short-term memory, the doctors call it. I'm afraid I'm getting a little senile."

"You, Mo?"

"I know, I know. It's hard to believe. But I'm losing it enough, my wife's afraid I'll have Alzheimer's for six months before she notices the difference."

"Mo—"

206

"You still working on that furniture store thing?"

"Yes."

"You know, I gotta give you credit, John."

"Credit for what, Mo?"

"Your thing there. Your case."

"I don't get you."

He waved the cigar like a conductor tuning up his orchestra. "When you were here last time, I was struggling for a story, remember?"

"I remember, Mo. The classifieds."

"The what?"

"The classifieds. You were going through them to—"

"Oh, yeah. Right, right. The polar-bear skins, they didn't pan out too good."

"And they looked so promising."

"Huh, tell me about it. But the lady just had them in her attic all this time. Never did anything about them, only knew they must have been from the former owner who's dead lo these four and twenty years. No way to trace any of the family. Depressing, isn't it?"

"What is, Mo?"

"Families. What the hell we talking about here? The way families drift apart. Son moves here, daughter moves there, all across the country, even the world, all this Global Village stuff. Not like the old days."

"Right. I won—"

"The old days, the families stayed together. Not 'nuclear,' that's . . . 'Extended,' that's the word for it. The families used to be extended, John. Three, four generations under the same roof, pooling their money, watching out for each other, taking care of each other the way the family was designed to. When I was growing up in Chelsea . . . of course, that brings me back to it."

I was beginning to empathize with Mo's wife. "Back to what?"

207

"To my story. John, you gotta keep the thread straight here."

"Sorry, Mo."

"The story idea you gave me."

"I gave you?"

"Yeah. The Irish and the Jews."

"That—"

"Did you know the mayor of Dublin used to be Jewish? No, wait a second, that's not the right way to phrase it. Did you know a Jew used to be mayor of Dublin?"

"I'd heard something about it."

"Well, he did. And then there's all this ecumenical stuff, the archbishop of this and the rabbi of that, breakfasts and lunches and—why do you suppose it's always some kind of food, John?"

"Beats me, Mo."

"Yeah. I ought to look into that. I had to spend a little time on the old days, unfortunately. Like how Boston was one of the biggest supporters of that Father Coughlin character from the midwest in the thirties or our own Father Feeney, out there on the Common, screaming anti-Semitic stuff at the commuters in the forties. Believe it or not, when I was young, there were lots of neighborhoods you couldn't go, the Irish kids would chase you, stone you even, yelling 'Kike!' and 'Christ-killer!' that kind of thing. Fortunately it didn't happen in Chelsea where I was growing up, but then we were maybe three-quarters Jewish and a lot of nice Italian kids, good families."

"I'm glad—"

" 'Course, you still got problems, like that flare-up a couple of years ago between Alan Dershowitz and Billy Bulger over the judgeship, but maybe that's gonna happen whoever you got on one side versus the other." He pointed at me with the cigar. "You were saying?"

"I'm glad you got a good article from it, Mo."

"Yeah. So, you still working on it?"

"On the case?"

"Of course on the case. John, maybe you should come over to the house. The way you're losing track here, you'd make me look good in front of the wife."

"Actually, I was kind of hoping I could get into your morgue again, Mo."

"How far back?"

"Five, maybe six years."

"Let me goose one of the punks we've got outside, can work the computer. Get you a printout. We need an exact date or a name, though."

"Barbra Proft."

Mo was back in five minutes. "Had to nearly twist the punk's arm to get him to stop what he was doing, 'save' his precious paragraphs, whatever 'save' means to the computer. Here it is."

The sheet was a little waxy, like fax paper. The article itself was from almost six years before, just a couple of paragraphs, summarizing what I'd already been told by Darlene Nugent and William Proft. With one exception.

The name of the investigating officer from the Quincy Police Department.

Sergeant Bonnie Cross said, "Quincy wouldn't give it to you?"

"No. They said they don't give out the addresses or telephone numbers of retired officers, and 'Angelo Folino' isn't listed in the book."

"You tried the South Suburban?"

"And the Boston, even the West Suburban and North Suburban."

She had a fresh box of Munchkins in front of her and reached into it, a cinnamon appearing between thumb and index finger. "He used to be a cop and he's retired, it's probably either the Cape or Florida."

"For directory assistance, you still need a town."

Cross popped the Munchkin. "So, what, you want me to get it for you?"

"It would save some time."

"I thought that's how you guys got paid, running up the meter."

"Not when we don't have to."

She swallowed. "And if I don't help you?"

"Then I'll have to bribe somebody with a computer at the Retirement Board, maybe New England Telephone."

"So I don't just save you time, I save you from committing a crime, too."

"Maybe a felony, all I know."

"I have a feeling you know, Cuddy. I have a feeling you've looked up all these things in the General Laws, with classifications and maximum sentences and the whole nine yards."

"A crime prevented is a crime nobody has to solve."

"I like you, Cuddy. You're a pain in the ass, but you're kind of fun to shoot the shit with. Once in a great while."

"Thanks, Cross."

"Spell the last name for me?"

"F-O-L-I-N-O was the way the paper had it."

"Let me make a call."

She dialed, picking up another Munchkin, a chocolate-honey-dipped, and turning it under the light above her desk. Into the mouth before into the mouthpiece with, "Give me Detectives.... Whoever's up there.... Right.... Holman, was it? Holman, this is Cross, Boston Homicide.... No, I don't think we do. You want to give me a callback? ... Good, I don't have time for that kind of bullshit, either.... Look, you got anybody there goes back seven, eight years? ... Yeah, I figured that.... What I've got is an open case here, might have some connection to one you guys had a while ago.... No, no I don't think it went down as homicide. Accidental or suicide, but I understand the detective was on it's retired now.... Folino, Angelo.... No, really? Thanks, that'd save some time. . . ." She reached for a pencil, scribbled on a pad, then scribbled some more. "Got it. . . . Me or a PI named Cuddy. . . . Yeah, insurance is mixed up in it, too. . . . Thanks, Holman. . . . Right."

Cross hung up, tore the sheet off the pad, and flicked the paper to me. "Read my writing?"

"He's just down in Squantum."

A powdered-sugar took its last journey. "Saved you some gas, too."

18

"ADA MEAGHER."

"That has such a personal ring to it."

"John. What's up?"

"You pressed?"

"A little."

"How about dinner tonight?"

"Tonight? Sure."

"You don't sound sure."

"It's just ... no, dinner's fine. Where?"

"How about Commonwealth Brewery?"

"As long as there's nothing going on at the Garden."

"Nance, it's July. The Celtics and the Bruins have a ways to go before they play again."

"Then great. What time?"

"I'm going to be driving in on the Expressway, so how does seven-thirty sound?"

"Perfect. I've got some computer research to do, anyway."

"You've got a computer case?"

"Oh, no. This is a legal research thing. You tell the com-

puter to search the decided cases in the data bank for two
phrases within a certain number of words of each other."

"Why?"

"So you can get all the cases that, say, talk about both
'cocaine' and the 'plain view exception' to search warrants.
That's not a great example, but do you see the time it can
save?"

"I guess so."

A change in her voice. "John, did you see the doctor
today?"

"And the physical therapist."

"And?"

"I'll tell you all about it over dinner."

"Fine. Oh, and John?"

"Yes?"

"Thanks for calling."

"I wanted to."

"I know."

Expressway south to Quincy Shore Drive. After crossing
the Neponset River, a left onto East Squantum Street. Past
the entrance to Marina Bay, a mammoth beige condo building with a slate roof that overlooks the tidal flats. Then onto
the peninsula of land called Squantum that's the easternmost
part of Norfolk County, cradling Boston's Suffolk County
on the west and south.

On Dorchester Street, I paralleled the bay for eight or ten
blocks before winding up Bellevue Road, passing a grassy
strip called John R. Nelson Park and the Star of the Sea
Church. The homes ranged from converted cottages and dis-
guised trailers to sprawling contemporaries with cupolas
and decks offering vistas of the bay and maybe even Boston
harbor over the roofs of their downslope neighbors. There
were anchors for decoration on the lawns, lobster pots for
cocktail tables on the patios, and ten or twelve different
kinds of weathervanes spinning wildly in the gusty winds.

213

Crisscrossing, I found the street I wanted, the name FO-LINO on a post with a smaller PRIVATE WAY sign above it. The macadam angled down toward the water, and I left the Prelude as much off the narrow driveway as I could.

He was sitting on a webbed lawn chair, his bricked patio commanding a view of the ocean as far as the horizon, a harbor island or two visible to the north. The house was one of the converted cottages, green clapboard with white trim, a wind sock standing straight out from its mooring. He'd probably go medium height and a hundred-fifty pounds, his age in the fifties, the facial features even, the hair mostly gray. Wearing a long-sleeved T-shirt over cutoff shorts and shower thongs, he had hairy calves and a newspaper on his lap, the right hand not visible as he distracted me by waving with his left.

"Help you?"

"Angelo Folino?"

"Sign kind of gives it away."

I stopped a respectable distance from him. "My name's John Cuddy. Bonnie Cross from Boston Homicide and I have a case up there I'm hoping you can help us on."

"I got a call. ID?"

Without moving, I said, "Okay if I reach for it?"

Folino smiled, glancing down at his lap. "Guess I'm giving away lots of things, these days."

"No. The wave was right. It's just that Holman at your place wouldn't tell me anything, and I've known some retired cops here and there."

"You yourself?"

"Just military."

"MP, you mean?"

"Yeah."

He watched me for a minute, saw something else, and nodded, a different look in his eyes. "Pull up a chair."

There were three more like his folded against a wall of the house. I opened one and set it conversationally to his left.

214

Folino lifted the newspaper, then carefully laid the Smith & Wesson Detective's Special that had been under it on the brick next to his right foot.

I said, "Not that it's any of my business, but you expecting somebody in particular?"

A shrug that included face as well as shoulders. "One of the guys on the force got the word through a source that a hard-case I put away's out and maybe thinking about it."

"You get a lot of that?"

"What, the threats? Oh, yeah. You get 'em all the time, working a small city like Quincy. It's not like Boston, where usually there's a little space between the cops and the perps. Down here, you shop at the same stores and drink in the same taverns. One guy I put away for armed robbery, his wife'd pour my coffee every morning, this little five-stool joint near the station."

I swung my head around. "Pretty place you have here."

"Yeah, in the family since my grandpa. Come over on the boat, learned carpentry, built this place when all you needed was hammer and nails and sweat, no permit or certificate or variance. My parents winterized it, and I grew up here. When they died, well, I couldn't think of any place else to live. Hey, can I get you something to drink?"

"No, thanks."

"You sure? I don't keep any hard stuff in the house, but I got some cold wine, iced tea maybe?"

"No, but thanks."

Folino seemed to prepare himself a bit. "So, you're the P.I., right?"

"Right."

"Let me guess. Cross, she doesn't give two shits about whatever you're working on, but she owed you a favor, so she made the call to Holman, right?"

"Close."

"She cared about whatever you've got, she'd be here herself."

215

"She would."

"So, what is it you've got?"

"Not much, but I think it might have to do with Barbra Proft."

"Proft. The one who went off the building six, seven years back."

Folino didn't phrase it like a question. I said, "Almost six, from the papers."

"The papers, I don't remember they did much with the case. Just one day in the *Herald* and the *Globe*, two in the *Patriot Ledger*."

"Did it merit more?"

He moved his tongue around inside his mouth. "What makes you ask?"

"The daughter of the dead woman is missing. The son of the dead woman hired me to find her."

"The daughter was the one with the funny name."

"Darbra."

"Right, Darbra. Christ, she was a cold one."

"How do you mean?"

"Well, we get the call. A neighbor in the building's looking out her window, making breakfast, and she sees this Barbra Proft's body on the ground. Medical Examiner figured she fell some time the day before, but she took her dive into the window well, and nobody noticed her till the next morning."

"Nobody heard a scream or anything?"

"We had two neighbors, both retired, both with windows onto the well. One's deaf as a stone, the other's watching *Hawaii Five-O* and God knows what else and said she didn't notice any 'unusual' screams. Some commentary, huh?"

"So time of death's screwed up."

"Enough so everybody's—I mean your Darbra there, the brother—I don't get his name."

"William."

"William, even the spooky aunt from up in witch country.

216

Everybody's got an alibi or doesn't. It's not like on TV, you know, where everybody can account for their whereabouts and you got to figure who's lying. I mean, who remembers where they were, and how can you pin them down if the M.E. can't give you a decent time of death?"

"You can't."

"Of course you can't. Besides, we didn't have any physical evidence. No bruises, nothing missing, nothing where it shouldn't be."

"You got there before the staties and the lab people?"

"Yeah. Four, five minutes after the neighbor called it in, we're at the scene. The roof—it was ten stories, I think. I haven't been by the building in a couple, three years, but I'm pretty sure it was ten. After about five floors, though, might as well be fifty."

"I know."

"Right. Sorry, I forgot you'd been in."

"Didn't mean to interrupt you."

"Hey, don't worry about it. Truth is, I'm on my own here, so a little interruption's kind of a nice change of pace, you know?"

It was more a statement than an opening, so I didn't take it. "Nothing up on the roof, then?"

"Nothing but what you'd expect. A lounge version of what we're sitting on now, near enough to the edge. Some piping they had exposed there, right around the ankles, if you were walking. All kinds of signs, DON'T GO NEAR THE EDGE or some shit like that. You live there a year, though, you don't even notice the signs anymore, much less read them or do what they say. Even had a drink, the ice melted, decedent's prints all over the glass."

"Nothing in the drink?"

"Gin. Just about straight, you figure she must have had a couple cubes in it, chill the booze for her a little, hot day like it was."

"And Proft was sunbathing?"

"Yeah, at least she was wearing a bikini. Your Darbra told me she still had a good figure, too, but except for the legs, which looked all right, you couldn't tell, her hitting facedown and all. That's what I meant about cold."

"Darbra being a cold one?"

"Yeah. The staties, they like to leave the notification to us. We found out from the decedent's address book the kids' names—they weren't exactly kids, your Darbra being early twenties, though she looked older. The brother William, only late twenties, I think, but he could pass for a lot older, kind of . . . pasty. I saw him, I thought he might have done some time, till you talk to him and realize he'd catch a shank the first day on the yard just for being such a tight-ass."

"You run him anyway?"

"Yeah. Clean. Back then, anyway. When I told him—oh, sorry, I was talking about your Darbra, got sidetracked."

"That's okay."

"It's just that an old case, it comes back to you in chunks like that, you know? It's not like it's a whole story, more like little scenes."

"You saw Darbra face-to-face?"

"Yeah. The address book, people almost always put the relatives under the right letter for the last name, but use only the first names. So I looked right away under "P," and found just "Darbra" and "William" with no last names. I remember this decedent, she had nice handwriting, flowery like an old woman who learned her penmanship real well."

"What was Darbra's reaction?"

"Well, that's what I mean. I caught her at work—some kind of temp job, I think—and I broke the news the way you try to, kind of simple and quick but clear, so they don't have to try and ask you any questions? But she asked me how it happened, and I told her it looked like her mom was sunbathing and tripped, and your Darbra, she says, 'Her body, it always got her into trouble.' Just like that, no tears, no break in the voice. Just the observation there."

I had the feeling Folino had been one hell of a cop. "And it rubbed you the wrong way."

"You could say that. Me, the hairs on my arms always tingled, I got somebody I thought was hinky. For you it's rubbing?"

"More like something off in the stomach."

"Yeah. Yeah, I knew a guy was like that. Narcotics. He said it was like he'd just had an extra dessert, something too sweet rolling around down there. Anyway, this Darbra, she was cold, but even so, I thought it might be better to have the son identify for us, being a man and all. So I left my partner with your Darbra, take down her story, and went out to him—a druggist back then."

"And still."

"They didn't get along, William and her."

"And still again."

Folino stopped. "But the brother hires you to look for her?"

"Insurance."

He looked out to the ocean. "He's got a policy on her."

"The aunt does, actually, William as beneficiary. She kept them up as a promise to her dead sister."

"Yeah, well, I wouldn't want to testify to it, but there was more than a little insurance back then, too."

"The brother told you?"

"Not right away. I come into the drugstore where he is, and I break it to him same way as to her. I remember that, because after your Darbra, I wanted to see what his reaction would be, so I used the exact same words with both of them. And he says, 'How far did she fall?' And I say, 'Ten stories,' and he says, 'Well, then, there won't be much to identify, will there?' "

"Cold runs in the family."

"Except for the aunt. Maybe the dead woman, too, for all I know."

"The aunt was different?"

219

"Yeah. I didn't really need her for anything, but you want to do the right thing, not leave anybody up in the air, so I asked William if it was okay to see—I don't get her name, either."

"Darlene."

"Oh, right, right. That's where the daughter's name came from." A couple of sailboats did a ritual dance on the bay, sails changing color a little as they wheeled in the wind. "Christ, I should have remembered that."

"It was six years ago."

"Yeah, but it was my last—Jeez, I was about to say 'homicide.' A city like Quincy, you don't get so many. I don't want to say you're nostalgic about them or anything, but there's something to it when you don't get a hundred a year like Boston or—what, four hundred down in D.C.?"

"More, I heard."

"Christ, can you imagine that? I mean, D.C. proper, it's not even that big."

"I know."

"Well, back to the aunt. I see her and I tell her the same way. Figure to see if it *really* runs in the family, the cold. Well, she's just the opposite. I mean, she goes near berserk on me, crying and screaming about how the kids must have done it, the kids did her in."

"Like, acting together, you mean?"

"I don't know. I mean, I didn't know what the aunt meant right at that moment, you know? She was just screaming whatever came into her head. Took me half an hour, more just to get her calmed down enough to tell me about the policies."

"The insurance company investigated, too?"

Another whole body shrug. "Aw, they ran a routine check, but what can you do? We got no eyewitnesses, no physical evidence, nothing but motive on account of the policy and opportunity on account of no certain time of death. You take that to the DA, you get laughed at. Even the company's lawyer backed off it, said they'd never survive summary something-or-other."

"Summary judgment, maybe."

"Yeah, that was it. You have to have some kind of evidence for your side—on homicide by the beneficiary or at least suicide by the decedent—and we didn't."

I sat back in my chair, letting the salt air wash over me. "Something tells me you didn't stop there."

Folino worked his hands, then replaced them on the arms of his chair. "It was just too pat, you know? I mean, granted the dead woman lives there for years, you still have kind of a healthy respect for the edge of the building. More so, you have some booze in you."

"Autopsy?"

"Enough of the gin so she shouldn't have been driving, but not so much she'd have been stiff. And no note or particular depression beyond her apparently shitty life and shitty kids. But all I had was the policy and the neighbors, who wouldn't have noticed King Kong going by their windows, and the tingling, you know?"

"My stomach's acting up on this one, too."

"Account of the insurance."

"Right."

He gave it a few seconds. "Let me tell you, I can't prove it, and if somebody can sue me, I'll deny I even said it, but I think my decedent had some help going off that roof."

"You said before the aunt claimed the kids did it."

"Only about twenty times."

"What do you think?"

"You mean, were they in it together?"

"Yes."

Folino turned that around, but only a little. "No. No, I watched them at the service they had for the mother. Wasn't more than a 'So long, have a nice day' service, by the way. No, I'd say neither one cared for the mother or trusted each other. Oil and water, at best."

"Could it have been an act?"

"I don't think so. The aunt, neither."

"Darlene Nugent?"

"I don't think she was acting with the screaming and the carrying on and all. And she didn't seem like she could stand the kids, either. Weren't for the aunt, the service would have been over in maybe half the time. This Nugent, she was crying at the coffin—closed, I guess I don't have to tell you that. But the kids, they were sneaking peeks at their watches, and after a while, not even sneaking them, you know?"

I let it settle for a minute.

Folino said, "Sure I can't get you something to drink?"

"Just one more question, maybe. You said you didn't think the kids were in it together."

"Right. And nobody else had motive, far as I could see."

"So you figure if the dead woman had help, it was one of the kids acting alone."

"Off the record?"

"Off the record."

"That's what I think."

"Which one?"

Folino looked me straight in the eye. "Take your pick."

I nodded and got up. "Thanks."

As he was about to say something, there was the crackle of gunfire from a fairly short distance.

Folino said, "You know what that is?"

"Moon Island?"

"That's right. I forgot you guys from Boston have to qualify out there, you want a permit to carry."

"Every five years."

"Let me tell you something, I sit here sometimes, and they're going all day long. It's kind of late today, but last year, when the Boston force was switching over from revolvers to the Glocks? They were sending the guys in for like three days, familiarization firing with the things. Man, you would've thought it was Kuwait City around here. The funny thing is, though, I . . . I enjoyed it. I never once fired my service revolver on duty. Never once in the thirty years. But the sound of the gunfire, it makes me think about being a young cop and wondering if I ever would. You know what I mean?"

"Not knowing what life's going to bring."

"Right. I lived my whole life in this city, Cuddy. Never been west of Worcester, you can believe it. I grew up here and joined the force and just stayed with the folks. I looked after them when they got sick, never married, myself. You?"

"Once."

"Recently?"

"Not for a while."

He nodded. "I been thinking, last couple of years, I should've tried it, too. At least once. Never really missed not having a wife while I was on the force, always things to do and people to see and all the other guys getting divorced when their wives found out about their fooling around on the side."

I was starting to feel uncomfortable. "It doesn't work for everybody."

"No. But then, you never really know till you try. Me, I never did. Just got a little older and more tired and more set in my ways. For years, I looked forward to my pension, and now I have it. And I sit here and I watch the ocean and I wonder, just a little, where it all went."

I thought about Roger Houle staring at the urn in his wife's garden and me visiting Beth's graveside and finally the retired cop sitting in front of me watching the boats go by. I figured I knew what Folino meant, but he looked up at me anyway.

"Get married again, Cuddy. And don't ever fucking retire, you can help it."

I thanked him for talking with me and made my way up the macadam drive to my car.

*   *   *

Roses.

"Pink ones. Mrs. Feeney said the pinks were the freshest."

So they'll last awhile.

"They'll have to, Beth."

Because it'll be a while before I see you again.

"Yes. It's not so much that I'm going away somewhere."

In a way you are.

I stopped, looked down at her. "What do you mean?"

It's been building for some time, John. You're just the last to see it.

"To see what?"

That it's time for you to move away from me and toward Nancy, move toward her for real.

My jaw tightened without me saying anything.

It's okay, John. It's . . . natural.

"That doesn't mean—"

It's right, too. You've been a good husband to me, in life and afterward, for so long.

"I don't regret a minute of that, Beth."

No, but at some point you would, and it's better to see it coming than go through it once it arrives.

I knelt down, placing the index and middle finger of my right hand where her lips might be. "There aren't words."

There don't have to be.

Commonwealth Brewery is on a cross street between the Government Center parking garage and the Boston Garden. The street floor has high ceilings and copper ducts and crimped-copper tables for eating and a long, crowded bar for drinking. Behind the bar are massive copper kettles, though the real work is done downstairs, where another bar has glass walls onto the micro brewery, allowing you to watch the workers in the funny outfits at each stage of the brewing process.

Nancy was standing at the bar on the street level, her briefcase off the shoulder and onto the floor between her legs. She held a pint of amber ale in her hand, talking with a guy in a suit who stood with his hands on his hips so that you could see his designer suspenders. He looked as though he had as many advanced degrees as dimples in his cheeks.

As I moved toward her, Dimples moved away to rejoin his clones down the bar. Nancy went up on tiptoes to give me a kiss, short but sweet with only a slight pong from the ale.

I said, "Who's my competition?"

"He's just perfect, don't you think? The guy managed to mention he has an MBA from Harvard in the second, fourth, and sixth sentences out of his mouth."

"I didn't think they even bothered to call it 'Harvard' over there. I thought it was just 'the B-school.' "

"Yeah, but he heard my Southie accent and probably figured he had to translate for the townie."

"What drove him off?"

"I told him I was your parole officer and we were meeting here because I was afraid to see you anywhere but a public place."

"You want I should rough him up a little before we're seated?"

"Save it for later, help you work off dinner."

I tapped the hostess, and Nancy carried her ale to a table while I ordered a different one from a traveling waitress. As I took the chair across from Nancy, she looked up at me with a glittery, half-tooth smile that always reminds me of Loni Anderson at the switchboard on *WKRP in Cincinnati*, even though the two women couldn't look less alike.

I said, "What are you thinking?"

"I'm thinking that I like seeing you four nights in a row."

"We don't usually?"

"Not usually. Not your fault, either. One or the other of us will have something going professionally, and it's just not feasible."

"That's going to be true generally, you know."

"I know. I'm not so much complaining about that as enjoying this."

She reached a hand across the copper and worked her nails on me. "So, tell me about the shoulder."

"There's not that much to tell, really. The doctor said the X-rays and MRI showed no structural damage, so she sent me to this physical therapist, who beat me up for a while, then tortured me on half a dozen machines."

"Nautilus stuff?"

"I didn't notice the name on them, but different functions that seemed to have more gauges than weight markers."

"Do you have to go back?"

"To the therapist, you mean?"

"Yes."

"No."

Nancy played with her ale without drinking any. "You're sure?"

"Well, I got the impression the guy would love to see me again, given what they charge. He 'assessed' my shoulder and cut a length of red elastic off a roll. It looks like a Bulgarian prince's cross-sash, but it's called a 'Theraband,' and he showed me a 'regimen' of exercises with it to bring back the strength in the joint."

"And you have to repeat this 'regimen' every day?"

"Or so."

The waitress brought my drink, a wheat beer I'd had there before. If you've never had fresh-brewed, think about the last time you went to the trouble of squeezing juice directly from an orange instead of pouring it from a box or bottle, and you'll have the idea.

I held up my pint, clinking it against Nancy's. "To a new regimen."

"Of exercise?"

"Of everything."

19

ASSUMING YOU'RE NOT IN LOVE WITH BUS TRAVEL, THERE ARE BASI-
cally three ways to get from Boston to the Sunrise area in
New Jersey. First, you can fly to Newark and rent a car
there for the fifty or so additional miles. Problem is, with any
kind of luggage, it's tough to make the subway connections out
to our Logan Airport, which means cabbing it through the
tunnel and having to allow about an hour for traffic and more
time to be sure you'll check in early enough to make your
plane. Given those problems you may as well take Amtrak,
which runs from South Station to Newark and then continues
on to Philly, D.C., and eventually somewhere in Florida. The
problem with the train is that you'll still burn four to five
hours and have to see Hertz or Avis for the rest of the trip,
anyway. Accordingly, with luggage, it's easier just to drive
your own car all the way.

To do that, I got up fairly early on Saturday. After Nancy
left, I did the series of exercises with the Theraband tied to
my doorknob, feeling vaguely silly and weak as a kitten in
the left shoulder. I packed casual clothes and one suit, and

the Theraband and the knee brace, then put on a pair of shorts and a polo shirt for the drive. Down at the space behind the condo, I loaded my suitcase into the trunk of the Prelude and headed off for the Mass Pike.

I took the turnpike west to Sturbridge, the traffic fairly light for the Saturday of July Fourth weekend, then got onto Interstate 84, which cuts diagonally southwest through Connecticut. To avoid construction in Hartford, I took the so-called "alternate route," which also had construction on it and added ten miles to the trip. From there it was clear sailing to Brewster, New York, where I picked up 684 south. After half an hour of trees and reservoirs, I maneuvered through the tricky interchanges and terrible drivers that bring you to the Tappan Zee Bridge over the Hudson and one of the grandest water views in the east. About eight miles further on is the turnoff for the Garden State Parkway, a useful road marred by heavy traffic and countless thirty-five-cent tollbooths. Somebody from Jersey once told me that the roadway paid for itself within its first few years of operation in the sixties, the state skimming pure profit from it ever since.

I pulled into a convenient rest stop for gasoline and had a hamburger that was barely warm and a Coke that was clearly flat. Back on the road, I passed a lot of exits, some for towns I recognized like Elizabeth and Union, others for ones I didn't, like Kenilworth and Winfield Park. At the intersection of the New Jersey Turnpike, I stayed on the Parkway, crossing the Raritan River and winding closer to the coast, though I never actually saw any ocean. The cars were bumper-to-bumper, but still doing sixty miles an hour. Gratefully, I took an exit for Sunrise that turned out to be quite a ways from it. After negotiating a couple of traffic rotaries (called "circles" in Jerseyese) and passing three big restaurants, all with plywood across their windows and FOR SALE signs on their doors, I got onto Route 35, which ran north/south along the water.

A few miles later, Traci Wickmire proved to be right: There was both a Sunrise and a Sunrise Beach, which was not great news from the standpoint of checking motels and hotels. Hitting the one where Darbra Proft had stayed might take a while, so to be sure I had a room for the night, I checked into a chain place at about four P.M. It advertised a baseball card show in one of its function rooms, but there were plenty of vacancies, even so close to the beach on the middle of the three big summer weekends. My room was small and clean, with a double bed, shower rather than tub, and cable TV.

After unpacking, I got back in the Prelude and started down Route 35, showing the photo I had of Darbra Proft draping herself over Rush Teagle and his guitar. Four guesthouses and two motels later, nobody had recognized her, and I was hungry again.

I parked the car in front of a motel that had a restaurant next door. The room clerk had never seen Darbra Proft but allowed as how he'd like to have. I asked him about the food at his neighbor, and he told me I'd do better at a seafood place farther south.

I took his suggestion and was glad I did, at least at first. The lot was nearly full, usually a good sign, and the hostess led me past a blackboard with daily specials in multicolored chalks to a tiny table for two in a corner. The cloth was rough paper, and the centerpeice was a Chinese teacup with half-gnawed crayons in it. The place had fishnets on the walls and fans hanging from the ceiling, but the floor was spectacular, richly grained wood in three-inch and wider planks that someone had lovingly fitted in a pattern of lighter, medium, and darker shades of stain. The people around me were mostly families, typically three generations with what looked like grandma, her daughter and son-in-law, and a raft of screaming kids.

I glanced at the menu, which had plenty of choices and

a fair wine list on the back. When my waitress came over, she asked if I'd like something to drink.

"Yes, but before I do, can you tell me what kind of wood that is?"

She looked down with me at the floor. "Huh?"

"The wood. I was wondering what it was. Cherry, beech?"

"Oh. I dunno. I never really like noticed it before."

I decided not to ask her for a recommendation from the wine list. Which was just as well, since of the twelve listed, they didn't have the first three I asked for.

When she brought me number four, an inexpensive chardonnay, it wasn't very cold. I took it anyway and ordered the bluefish with garlic butter, rice, and a salad. Using the Block paperback to close out some of the din around me, I was actually surprised when my meal arrived. The bluefish was fine, but the salad tasted as though it had been made a week ago and frozen since, and about one in every ten grains of rice wasn't cooked, nearly costing me a filling on the first mouthful.

I passed on dessert and left about half the wine in the bottle. Paying the bill, I asked both my waitress and the hostess if they recognized the woman in my photo. Two shakes of the heads.

I went back out to the Prelude, the cars still whizzing by on Route 35. It was pretty early to head back to my room, so I drove south a little more, paying attention when the road became a divided highway of two lanes south separated from the northbound by a block of tiny cottages.

After another five miles or so, the road dumped me into a town called Seaside Heights. There were a bunch of motels and tenement apartments squeezed next to each other. Lots of men and women stood on sidewalks and stoops, the men holding cans of beer and the women one and sometimes two babies. Each small side street ran east/west, ending in T-intersections at Ocean Terrace, the avenue along the beach with a raucous boardwalk beyond it. The north/south avenues seemed to specialize in taverns and discos.

Years ago, I would have stopped in one of the discos, watching the other customers dance, maybe joining in myself. But that was years ago. Even that trip, I might have gone into a tavern to watch the Yankees or Mets in the company of strangers, but in some towns, you never knew what offense a regular might take to an accent from Boston, and I wasn't in the shape or mood to jam with anyone.

Driving north on the beach road, I found a parking place, feeding all my quarters into a meter. I used the ramp to the boardwalk at Lincoln Avenue, the Beachcomber Bar & Restaurant a landmark for where I'd left the car. Then I went south to the end of the boardwalk, turned around, and walked back, giving my knee a chance to recover from all the driving that day.

There were amusement park rides clumped on two piers jutting into the water, many of the attractions with signs that said, "The following people should not ride this ride," including "Those with back ailments," "Pregnant women," and "Those under influence of narcotics." A yellow-on-black computer board advertised fireworks sponsored by a cola company. Near it, someone had assembled a "Portable Sport Climbing Wall," a series of clay-colored slabs stacked vertically with small concavities and convexities for a guy in baggy trunks to scale, tethered to the top by a safety cable. A number of stalls sold saltwater taffy, frozen custard, and fried dough. Even more stalls had games of chance with betting wheels and ringtoss and water pistols as your path to a mountain bike or, more likely, an off-colored stuffed animal.

The clientele was mostly young, the children squealing in genuine ecstasy, the early teens in baseball caps worn backward using the attractions as an excuse to touch each other here and there, the late teens goofing on the whole scene. Sophistication is a very relative concept.

However, if you paid attention, you saw some other things, too. An African-American couple in their thirties, joking and walking on either side of a son who might have been twelve but smallish, sunglasses over his eyes despite the darkness and one hand in each of his parents', his smile if not his sight alternating between them. A Latino kid, muscular but with a blank expression on his face, rap-dancing alone, not bumping into anybody, a Mets cap on his head, the bill turned up like Huntz Hall used to do on the Dead End Kids, moving to the beat of his own internal music. An elderly couple, Italian from the few words I caught, strolling arm-in-arm instead of hand-in-hand, at about the pace they might have gone down the aisle after a ceremony fifty years before.

Feeling pretty mellow, I sat on a bench with white concrete stanchions and cross planks the same color as the boardwalk. Half the benches looked toward the ocean, but mine faced a bar that seemed to have live music inside and a double line of twenty-two-year-olds outside. They wore mostly shorts and T-shirts, the latter showing their colleges. Rutgers, Drew, Monmouth, Douglass. More than a smattering of New York schools. There was a lot of loud talk and foul words and good-natured jostling. I was about to get up to find a quieter spot when some bad-natured jostling broke out the door and through the line.

A blond guy, hair short on top, locks tumbling down his neck, was pulling a young woman by her brunette hair behind him, another couple about the same age trailing in a hesitating way. The blond guy was the size a major college looks for at tight end, a sleeveless New York Giants blue and red sweatshirt showing arms pumped more for blocking than receiving. The brunette was twisting and yowling a little, saying "Greg . . . please! . . . Jesus . . . you're . . . *hurt*-ing me!"

The blond guy said, "Fine. Little pain's fucking good for you."

I looked around, hoping for a cop but not seeing any.

Given the kid's size, everybody else, including the couple apparently with him, was backing off before forming a circle in that unconscious, herd-mentality way we instinctively seem to have by fourth grade. That's when the blond guy stopped and turned. Letting go of her hair, he clouted the brunette on the side of her face with the back of his other hand.

She cried out, then began just to cry. "Greg . . . I wasn't . . . doing . . . *any*-thing."

"The fuck do you call smiling at that bartender?"

There was a little blood dribbling down from the nostril on the side he'd hit her. By the time he'd recocked his hand, I'd joined him and the brunette in the center of the circle.

He looked at me. Small, meanish eyes. "The fuck do you want?"

"I want you to knock it off."

A smile. Crooked, gapped teeth. "Her head or yours, douchebag?"

The girl edged toward the other couple. In ascending order, her boyfriend had me by about two inches, twenty years, and forty pounds.

I said, "Around the time you were learning how to throw up, the Army spent a lot of tax dollars training me to hurt people. Touch her again, and we'll see if Uncle Sam got his money's worth."

Greg seemed to process that. "So what? That make you some kind of hero?"

I liked that he didn't step toward me as he said it. "Doesn't take a hero to handle you, Greg."

He didn't like my using his first name, but he'd lost the momentum, and as a football player, he could sense it. "Get the fuck out of my face, man."

"I'm not in it. We're just standing here talking, everybody watching."

Greg surveyed the sea of faces, didn't seem to find what he wanted in it. Then he noticed that the other couple and his girlfriend weren't there anymore.

"The fuck? Hey, Joey? Annette?"

"Long gone, Greg."

He looked at me.

I said, "Crowd like this, the cops'll be here soon, maybe Joey and Annette bringing them."

He tried to process that, too.

"Wouldn't sit so well with the coach, your hitting a woman, all these witnesses and a formal complaint to boot."

The kid looked around now, more wary.

"I were you, Greg, I'd head north. At the gallop."

He took a last look at me, then started to run, north along the boardwalk, the circle parting for him before he had to shove anybody out of the way.

When I turned around to move toward my car, the black male in the couple with the kid in sunglasses was standing by himself, the woman and the child off to the side.

He said, "Where you from?"

"Boston."

A nod. "Didn't sound like from around here. Which department?"

"None."

He raised an eyebrow? "Never?"

"Just the service."

Another nod, extending his hand. "Nate Imes. Newark."

"John Cuddy." I shook with him. "Wouldn't have been such a smart thing, you diving in with family here."

A grin. "No, but if the Boz there started driving your head through the planks, I sort of figured I'd have to, jurisdiction or no jurisdiction."

"Thanks."

Imes said, "You're a little long in the tooth for us, but you ever think about relocating, give me a call."

"No offense, but not from what I've seen so far."

A sad nod this time. "I can believe that."

* * *

Sunday morning I showered and channel-surfed on the cable while my hair dried. One station was showing *Infectious Disease*, two gray-haired doctors enthusiastically discussing methods of transmittal. Next was something called *Lip Service*, contestants trying to recognize the lips of a "famous" singer belting out a song, after which the contestants got to lip-synch one, being graded on "accuracy," "body mechanics," and "overall entertainment value" by a panel of judges including Linda Blair and Tiny Tim. Next was some kind of law prep program, a female talking-head lecturing in a shrill, nasal voice about essay and multiple-choice questions.

My hair still wet, I had breakfast in my motel's coffee shop and thought about checking out, then decided to burn another night's worth of William Proft's money to give me a base of operations for that day. On my way out of the coffee shop, I saw a bunch of kids in Little League uniforms half-running down the hall toward the function room with the show in it. I checked my watch, then followed them.

It was three bucks to get in the door, but things were just opening up, so I figured to kill some time before starting out with Darbra's photo again. There were tables set up around the perimeter of the room and another group in a square at the center of it, like a wagon train drawn up to defend against Indians. The vendors or collectors already were standing behind their tables, Styrofoam cups of coffee or tea or something a little stronger in their hands but away from their wares. Most of the cards were from the seventies and eighties, encased in plastic or under glass cases like rare gems, which from the prices some of them might have been. The ones that caught my eye, though, were from my time as a kid. Hitters like Mays, Mantle, Musial. Famous pitchers like Koufax and Drysdale, crafty ones like Early Wynn and Bobby Shantz. One man in a Brooklyn Dodgers jersey had a great display of the old Boston Braves, before they moved to Milwaukee in 1953, Warren Spahn and Sibby Sisti and Del

Crandall. A woman in a Hawaiian shirt had a ton of Red Sox, including Ted Williams, Jackie Jensen, and Carl Yastrzemski, some of them autographed in blue ballpoint.

"Can I show you anything?" she said.

"No, thanks. Just remembering."

"Lots of folks do that."

She said it in a way that made it hard to tell if she was putting me down for not buying.

At the far end of the room, several strapping young men were signing autographs. There were eight-by-ten staged poses pinned to the wall above each table, I guess to tell the fans which line to get on for which player once the lines got longer and the players harder to see. Walking by, I heard a black kid introduce himself to the white player behind one table. The kid was about the same age as Nate Imes's boy, but tall and straight and skinny as a beanpole, his jeans riding about three inches above his shoes from the last year's growth spurt.

The player took a baseball card from him. "Seven-fifty."

The kid looked at him. "Say what?"

"It's seven-fifty for the autograph."

The kid fished in his jeans for what looked to be the change from a ten he'd used for the admissions charge. "Ain't got but seven."

The player shook his head, but said, "Okay. Discount, since you're here so early."

Taking the money, the player dashed off his signature. "See, this way the autographed card is worth more to you, because there'll be fewer of them. Most everybody else on the team'd hit you for ten, at least."

"Uh-huh."

Handing the card to the kid, the player said, "So it's really helping you, charging for this."

"Uh-huh."

The player frowned. "You're welcome."

236

"Ain't no need to thank you, dickhead. I bought this, you didn't give me nothing."

Agreeing with the kid, I made my way to the door.

Moving south, I worked a guesthouse, two motels, and three more guesthouses. Zip. Then I turned back north and caught a break at a small motel on the beach.

Taking off her glasses, the woman with the orange hair and pudgy fingers held the photo up to her face, nearly touching her nose with it. "Yeah, I seen her." She handed back the photo.

"Do you remember when?"

A finger scratched the side of her head. "Week ago? No, must have been two. I remember because I was thinking about giving her the room Mr. and Mrs. Pejorek had, but we didn't get that far."

"Why not?"

"This girl, she wanted a VCR in the room. I said to her, 'Honey, you come down the shore to get away from all that, right?' "

"Then what?"

A shrug. "She made this big thing of how she needed a VCR and was there any motel along the beach that had one."

"And?"

"And I told her to try up at Jolly Cholly's."

"Where's that?"

"Few blocks north. Got a sign like a clown's face on it."

I thanked her and left. It was boiling hot in the midday sun, and I'd left the Prelude unlocked with the windows down. As I got to it, a heavyset man in his early thirties was lugging a big Coleman's cooler across the parking lot. He was sweating like a pig, the cords on his neck straining above an already-sunburned back. A woman about the same age was sitting on a blanket she'd spread over the sugarlike sand, using a shoe to anchor one of the corners.

He called out to her. "Stay where you are, Mitzi. I oughta be able to finish this in seven, eight trips."

Over her shoulder, without even looking at the guy. "Don't get on me, Tony."

He reached the blanket. "Get on you? The fuck you think this is, your birthday or something?"

"You get nasty again, I'm taking off."

Tony set down the cooler. "Mitzi, you take off again, I swear I'll drag you by the fucking hair into the fucking water and drown you."

"Fuck you."

Tony turned to go back to wherever he'd come from. "I'm telling you, Mitz', fucking drown you is what I'll do."

I got into my car, wondering if Greg and Tony shared a common gene somewhere deep in the pool.

The wooden sign was faded, and one of the screws holding it up was about to go, but it did sport the face of a crudely drawn circus clown and JOLLY CHOLLY'S underneath. There was a bar next to the motel on one side and a pizzeria on the other. All in all, Jolly Cholly's didn't look like the sort of place you'd choose for getting away from it all.

The motel itself was built on a concrete pier perpendicular to the beach, a row of units at street level and another on the second floor with a white balustrade of rusting metal. I walked up to the door that had a smaller clown's-head sign and the word OFFICE underneath it.

The exaggerated hee-haw of a donkey sounded as I walked through the door. In front of me was a hinged counter with an angled stand holding brochures for restaurants, miniature golf operations for the kiddies, and party boats for fishing. A coffee machine too small for guest use was perking on a table behind the counter. The man who came through the door next to the machine might have been Cholly, but the other half didn't fit.

He was dour and long of face, and his skin was leathery from the sun and age—somewhere in the low sixties, I'd say. His hair was bleached white from gray and black, shag cut in no particular style. His tanned arms were sinewy, strong without being showy, at the ends of the sleeves of a "Seaside Heights" T-shirt with a tear at the shoulder and a food stain between the two words in its legend, as though someone had inserted a sloppy hyphen.

"Help you?"

"My name's John Cuddy."

"Utt."

"I'm sorry?"

"The name's Utt, Frank Utt."

"Oh."

"You figured my name'd be 'Cholly,' right?"

"Crossed my mind."

"Bought the place, it was already called Jolly Cholly's. Seemed a shame to lose the goodwill, given I'd already paid dear for her. Help you with a room?"

His voice had a singsong quality. I said, "You're not from around here."

"From that Boston accent, neither are you. What difference does it make?"

Definitely not the jolly innkeeper. "Not much."

Utt answered me anyway. "From North Dakota, originally. Fargo, along the Red River. Only one in the country flows south to north. Got tired of seeing the thermometer stuck at forty below in the winters, having to plug the car in at night to keep the engine block from freezing."

"You ever heard of Steve Nelson?"

"Linebacker, wasn't he?"

"One of the Patriots' true and few stars."

"Went to North Dakota State, if I remember correctly. Not exactly a football factory, but you got what it takes, you can make it anywheres, I guess."

I said, "What made you come out here?"

" 'Back east,' we'd call it in North Dakota."

"Back here, then."

"Already told you. The weather."

"Yes, but why New Jersey?"

"Heard about the beach. Call it 'going down the shore' here, though. Figured it might make a nice change of pace, kind of a retirement before I retired."

"How's it working out?"

Utt rubbed his chin twice with his thumb and forefinger, but more like the chin was a watermelon pit he was shooting out. "There some reason you're warming me up like this?"

"There is." I showed him my ID. "I'm looking for a woman from Boston."

Utt nodded.

"This is a picture of her."

He glanced down at it, but just barely. "I knew there was something wrong with her."

"She stayed with you?"

"For a week. You took one look at her, you could tell there was trouble, but I figured she might be good advertising."

"Advertising."

"You ever seen her in a bikini?"

"Just this photo."

"Doesn't do her justice. She moved like original sin, twitching her rump this way and that. Near drove her friend crazy to see the other fellows measuring her out."

"Her friend?"

"The long-hair."

I looked down at the photo of Proft and Teagle. "Him?"

"Yeah, him."

I worked on that.

Utt said, "They drove up here in this yellow convertible, said they'd heard I had VCRs in the rooms. Well, I had to do something, didn't I?"

I stared at him. "Something?"

"To draw the folks in. Mister, we've had four bad summers here out of five. Hospital tide, just plain rain, then a couple of winter storms like to wash every grain of sand from the beach."

I thought of the closed restaurants I'd seen coming in from the parkway.

Utt said, "Tourism's down so bad, you have to do something, so I tried VCRs in some of the rooms."

"Just some of them?"

"Well, I figured not everybody'd want one, there are a few who just want to forget about the world. But they usually got the money to help them forget, they head down to Ocean Beach, maybe. Rent a little cottage and not talk to anybody for a week. Your Darbra girl, now she was different."

"How so?"

"She must have introduced herself to everybody on the strip. I had people coming up to me in stores, mentioning she'd been in, telling people how much she liked Jolly Cholly's. I was right, huh?"

"Right?"

"About her being advertising. Even when she wasn't in the bikini, she did me some good here. If only it weren't for the noise."

"The noise?"

"One night they was here. The last night, actually. I remember because I kind of expected her to apologize and all, but she didn't."

"Apologize."

"Yeah. From the noise they made that one night with the movie they were watching. See, they wanted a room with the VCR, but I had only the one on the first floor. I figured, most people who'd want VCRs would rather be on the top floor, no feet thumping above their heads, and that way there wouldn't be so much risk for me from thieves, too, like there might be on the downstairs units. But no, your

Darbra girl and her friend, they wanted a downstairs unit and no two ways about it."

"Why?"

"Be on a level with the beach, I suppose."

I looked around me. "Can I see their room?"

Utt did the pit-shooting routine again with his fingers on the chin. "Don't see why not. Won't even charge you for it."

He reached behind him to what might have been a rack I couldn't see, because he came back with a key on a clear plastic tag. Flipping up the hinged part of the counter, he said, "Come on."

We walked out the door and away from the beach along the concrete sidewalk outside the first-floor units. He stopped at number 123.

I said, "They were willing to take this unit?"

"What's wrong with it?"

"You have second-floor units closer to the water?"

"Available for that week, you mean?"

"Yes."

"I did, even a couple you could see the surf from, you didn't mind craning your neck a little at the window. But like I said, they wanted one on the first floor."

Utt put the key in the lock and turned it, waving me across the threshold. The room had a queen-sized bed centered on one wall. Centered on the other wall was a low bureau with a seventeen-inch Zenith on top of it and a VCR on top of the television. Past them on the same wall was a doorway opened so you could see part of the bathroom. As Utt closed the unit door behind us, I saw a short refrigerator in the corner, a small table with two dinette chairs in the other corner. The air inside the room was cool, but stale.

"Has anybody been in here since Darbra and her friend?"

Utt shook his head. "Just the maid. And me to clean up the sink."

"The sink?"

"I'll show you."

We walked to the bathroom. The facilities were all almond porcelain, but there was a darker discoloration at the bottom of the wash basin.

"Took me most of an hour to get it that good. Damned if I shouldn't check these things before they leave, but you can't always."

"What color was it when you first saw it?"

"The stain?"

"Yes."

"I don't know from colors that well. Kind of yellowish?"

"Any idea what it was?"

"No."

Yellow convertible, yellow paint, maybe? I looked around the bathroom, but it didn't have any character to it, and it had been cleaned since they'd been there.

We came back into the main room. Even with the window closed, the traffic sounds from Route 35 were noticeable and probably annoying, you were trying to fall asleep through them.

I went over to the bureau. "Mind if I go through these?"

"The drawers?"

"Yes."

"Help yourself."

I did. Nothing but contact paper, in little clown shapes. "You said something before about noise?"

"Noise? Oh, right. Their last night here."

"That would be what?"

"Friday."

"Meaning?"

"Meaning nine days ago. I rent the weeks Saturday afternoon to Saturday morning if I can. Out by eleven, do a whirlwind, then in by two with the next one."

"Go ahead."

"Well, it must have been only about ten P.M., and being that it was a Friday and all, I wouldn't have cared too much

243

about the noise. But I had an elderly couple above them, and the old folks come down to me to complain. Fairness to them, I could hear it soon's I opened the office door. So I told the old folks I'd talk to the people in 123."

"To Darbra and her friend."

"Right."

"And did you?"

"Put on a sweater—we get a real chill off the water here, saves like you wouldn't believe on air-conditioning. Back in Fargo, we got our electricity cheap on account of the Garrison Conversion, but around here, you like to save every kilowatt you can."

I didn't want to know what the "Garrison Conversion" was. "So you came down to this room?"

"Right. The noise was so bad, some kind of rock music, I thought the door was going to shake right off the frame. I knock, and I don't get anything, so I start pounding when the douchebag—that's what they call real jerks around here, 'douchebag.' "

"So I've heard."

"I thought of her boyfriend like that. Great name for him, too."

"How do you mean?"

"Well, Darbra, she couldn't have been more sociable. I don't mean coming on to men, either. Just real friendly. The boyfriend, though, he didn't seem ticked off only when she did that. He seemed more ticked off in general, like he wasn't real pleased to be here or like my motel didn't suit his standards."

Having seen Teagle's apartment, I found that hard to understand. "Go on."

"Where was—oh, right. So I'm pounding on the door, and he finally comes to answer it."

"What did he say?"

"Well, I told him we'd had some complaints about the noise, and he said he was real sorry."

"Sarcastic?"

"No. No, just straight, like he really was."

"Not nervous, then?"

"No. Really polite, nice as a six-year-old at Sunday School."

"What did Darbra say?"

"Didn't see her. She was taking a shower."

"How do you know?"

"The douchebag told me, but I could hear the water running, too."

"Over the noise?"

"What noise?"

"From the VCR?"

"Oh, no. No, her boyfriend turned it down before he answered the door."

"Before?"

"Yeah. I tell you, it was kind of weird, like him and me were talking by the door to a church, except for all the beers by the television there."

"So you didn't come in the room."

"Of course not. She was in the shower."

"And you didn't see her then?"

Utt gave me an offended look. "She was a real foxy lady, but I'm no peeper."

"Then what?"

"Then I went back to the office. I got my place behind it."

"No more complaints?"

"No."

"And they checked out the next morning."

"Early."

"Early?"

"Yeah. They could've stayed till eleven, like I said. And since they'd checked in late the Saturday before, just finding me by luck and all, I might've let them stay a couple hours into the afternoon. But it wasn't even nine in the A.M. when Douchebag dropped off the key and bolted out of here."

245

"Bolted?"

"Yeah. They were gone out the parking lot before I ever got to the door. Bastards."

"How do you know?"

"What?"

"How do you know they both left?"

Utt looked at me, then looked at the floor, then back up at me. "Well, I guess I don't. I saw the back of long-hair—I thought of him as that, too, you don't see so many hippie types the way you used to—as he dropped off the keys, but I was on the phone, and by the time I hung up, they—the car, I mean, was going out the back of the lot onto 35 north."

"Could you see if both were in the car?"

Utt looked at me, then the floor some more. "Top was up, so no. And I was disappointed, like I said."

"Disappointed?"

"Yeah, at your Darbra girl. Her not coming by to apologize for the noise or at least say good-bye or something."

I let my eyes go around the room again. "When you came in here after they left, was anything unusual?"

"Unusual?"

"Out of order, messed up?"

"No more than you'd expect. Except for the sink, which I figured was the reason they took off like that, afraid I'd charge them for it."

"But the rest of the place?"

The chin routine. "Bedclothes kind of pulled this way and that, like they'd had a real active night." Utt winked at me, man to man.

"No signs of . . . a struggle?"

He darkened. "Struggle? Hell, no. What are you getting at?"

I looked at him. "I wish I knew how to tell you."

20

I CHECKED OUT OF MY MOTEL AN HOUR LATER, WILLIAM PROFT getting charged for the extra night. The traffic wasn't so bad, Sunday being the middle day of the long weekend, but driving from New Jersey back to Boston I still had more than a few hours to think things through again.

Six years ago, Barbra Proft dies in a fall that her sister Darlene, and a pretty good cop in Angelo Folino, think was caused by either Darbra or William for the insurance. Darbra's share is just about exhausted when she starts an affair a year ago with Roger Houle and moves into the Commonwealth Avenue building with Traci Wickmire. Three and a half months ago, Darbra makes a not-so-subtle call to her aunt to see if Darlene has kept up the premiums on the remaining policies. A couple weeks later, at the end of March, Darbra starts working at Value Furniture thanks to what William thinks of as a prank on his part. Maybe Darbra starts an affair with Abraham Rivkind, too, and maybe she doesn't. A month later, Rivkind and Joel Bernstein decide they need a security guard and hire Finian Quill. A few

247

weeks after that, Wickmire overhears Darbra's "sugar daddy" call. Then, sometime later—and about four weeks ago—Darbra breaks up with Houle at Grgo's, knowing that Beverly Swindell is there to witness it, and starts up with Rush Teagle. Another week goes by, and Abraham Rivkind is killed, with Bernstein, Quill, and Swindell the only people certainly in the store. Nine days after that, two weeks ago, Darbra and Teagle leave Boston for New Jersey. Darbra calls Wickmire midweek from Sunrise Beach to check on the cat. Frank Utt at Jolly Cholly's doesn't see Darbra Friday night, nine days ago, when the noise problem arises nor Saturday morning as Teagle "bolts" after leaving the key. Back in Boston, Darbra's suitcase and mail look like she returned sometime Saturday, but the rest of her apartment doesn't, and Teagle's shaky story about the note from her almost has to be a lie. When Darbra doesn't show up at the store on Monday, Bernstein and Swindell treat her as fired, and brother William uses Pearl Rivkind as camouflage to get me to go looking for his sister in the hope that she's dead and the insurance company will pay off again. Sometime Thursday, two days after I'm working on the case, somebody with a key ransacks Darbra's apartment.

I shook my head. You could line things up that way, or a half dozen others that I tried out on the drive, but none made more sense than another. One thing seemed obvious, though.

Rush Teagle's was the next cage to rattle.

I got off the Mass Pike at Newton and went over Centre Street to Commonwealth. Stopping at a pay phone, I let Nancy know that I was back and that we could go to Norm's party the next night. When I arrived at the apartment house, I found a space on the street. I was pleased to see a yellow convertible across the road and down.

Getting out of the Prelude, I walked over to the convertible, a late-model Ford Mustang with the top up and the look of a nice car poorly maintained. There were some divots and rust spots from minor collisions, but no indication of the vehicle being recently repainted or even retouched. I used my hand to shade the passenger compartment. Amid the litter of fast-food wrappers and soda cans, there was some ragged sheet music; three wires, irregularly coiled, that could have been guitar strings; and a torn road map with something on it that looked an awful lot like the shape of New Jersey.

I crossed back to the apartment house. I didn't want to give Teagle any advance notice, but after five minutes, nobody had come in or gone out through the front security door, so I tried Traci Wickmire's button. Nothing. I pushed it again, longer.

A voice squawked over the intercom, but if I hadn't been expecting hers, I doubt I'd have recognized it. "Who's there?"

"Traci, it's John Cuddy."

"I'm busy. I can't see you right now."

"I want to talk with Rush Teagle, but he's not answering."

"So maybe he isn't home."

"Buzz me in so I can find out."

Nothing. Then, "All right."

Opening the door, I walked through the dark vestibule to the basement stairs. I moved down them slowly, partly for my knee but also staying to the edges in case Teagle was camped at his door, listening for anyone. When I got to his apartment, I waited, listening myself. Nothing. After a minute or so, I knocked. Nothing. I knocked harder. Still nothing.

That's when I got just the faintest whiff of it.

"Jesus." I dropped to my good knee, like a Catholic genuflecting, then all the way down to push-up position. From the little space under the door I confirmed it, nearly gagging as I always did. As everybody always does, no matter what they try to tell you about how they've gotten used to it.

The sweet-and-sour smell of not-so-fresh death, of decomposing flesh.

I got back to my feet and pulled out my shirttail, using it to try the door. Locked.

I stuck the shirttail back in my shorts and climbed to the third floor and Wickmire's apartment. I knocked on the door impatiently.

From the other side came her voice. "Is that you?"

"Open up, Traci. I have to use your phone."

"I can't. I'm—"

"Open up. It's an emergency."

"Look—"

"I think Teagle's dead down in his place. Will you open the door?"

The bolt slid back, and then a chain. She was wearing just a bathrobe, her hair stringy from a shower. "What do you mean, dead?"

I came into the apartment, almost barging past her. Instead of potpourri, there was incense burning somewhere. From the bathroom area came a deep female voice, "All right, Honey-bun, where'd you hide my panties, you little—"

The husky woman who appeared in front of me was just throwing her head back to get the wet hair out of her eyes. She was naked except for the unbuttoned flannel shirt Wickmire had been wearing the first time I'd been there. The shirt seemed to fit her.

The woman said, "Oh great, just great," but made no attempt to cover herself.

"So now you know."

"Traci, it doesn't matter."

"Sure."

Wickmire was sitting on her writing chair, the computer

closed down and on the desk, as though she hadn't been using it for a while. She'd changed into the torn jeans and a blouse. Her friend, first name "Myra," was in the bedroom, maybe getting dressed.

I said, "The police will be here pretty quickly. You know anybody else who'd have a key to Teagle's apartment?"

A shrug. "We don't have a super. The management company, maybe, but by the time they get here, won't the cops have broken down his door?"

"Probably."

"Are you going to tell them?"

"Tell them?"

"The cops. About . . . Myra and me."

"I'm going to have to tell them that you and Teagle knew each other. Or know each other, if he isn't who's dead down there. Then the police will want to know a lot about you, including your whereabouts for the last day or two and who, if anybody, was with you."

"It's not like I'm ashamed or anything."

I thought back to her faked flirting with me the first time I'd seen her and the relative absence of it the second time, as though she'd forgotten to maintain the pose when we went through Proft's ransacked apartment.

Wickmire said, "It's just I like my . . . privacy."

"I'm going to have to tell them what I saw and heard here today, Traci. They'll draw their own conclusions, but my advice, if you want it, is that you tell them the truth right off, because they have a way of finding out later that's usually not as pleasant."

She was about to say something else when her buzzer rang in three strident bursts.

The patrol officers got there first, a single car followed by a sergeant/supervisor and a shotgun guard minus the shotgun. While the first cop and the guard secured the scene, meaning stood outside Teagle's apartment, the sergeant burned up Wickmire's phone wire with calls to every uniformed branch in creation. I suggested they just kick down the door, but the sergeant insisted on waiting for a fourteen-pound sledge from the Narcotics Unit, by which time Bonnie Cross and one of her two partners had arrived. The partner examined Teagle's door, asking about outside windows, then reared back and kicked it in anyway. After that, the uniformed sergeant said he was going outside to assist in crowd control around all the official vehicles.

You couldn't blame him. As the door gave way it whipped inward, then hit its hinges and swung back, fanning a wicked volume of tainted air into our faces. Cross was ready with a hankie doused in air freshener, the rest of us making do with our hands. The younger of the two original uniforms said he had to leave, too.

Cross said, "Cuddy, you stay outside the apartment."

"Fine with me."

She went in, stepping very carefully around the overturned everything on the floor. Pots and pans from the kitchenette, videos and their cassette boxes, but as with Proft's place, smaller items were untouched. The instrument cases had been unzipped and emptied, however, the guitar off its stand near the wood stove and Rush Teagle's body.

Cross said, "It's cool enough in here, he could have been done a while ago."

Teagle lay on his right side, drawn slightly into a fetal position. His hands were crabbed, the rictus also pulling his lips away from his teeth in a ghastly, uneven grin. The left eye was open, and, from where I stood, the right eye was, too, but they weren't working together anymore. You couldn't miss the wound, hair matted and scalp torn and the left ear nearly ripped off. What I expected would prove to be the murder weapon was lying a few feet from him, and Cross moved toward it.

She started to stoop, then caught herself. "Just what we needed."

Even from the doorway, you could see the hair and gore on the business end of the poker from Rush Teagle's wood stove.

I waited downstairs with Cross until the M.E. pronounced the body and the lab techs in surgical masks started their macabre rituals. Then we left her partner with them and moved up to Traci Wickmire's apartment. Cross had me sit on the floor in the hall outside as she interviewed Wickmire and I assumed Myra as well. While I waited, another detective from Homicide arrived and started canvassing the neighbors. Given the basement location of Teagle's apartment, I didn't have high hopes for that.

After half an hour, Cross came out with some keys in her hand. "Let's go downstairs."

"I doubt the air's much better yet."

She looked at me. "Darbra Proft's place."

I stood. "Hope you like eau de cat."

"Christ, Cuddy, you weren't kidding."

"I doubt anybody's changed the litter."

"So this is the way you found it?"

"This is the way Wickmire showed it to me, except for what I handled and what the cat might have moved around since."

Cross bent down to scratch Tigger behind the ears. "Ms. Wickmire seemed awfully touchy about her sexual preference."

"I got the same impression."

"You think it could have anything to do with this here?"

"I don't know. I didn't even know about her preference until an hour ago."

Tigger started purring and nudging his head hard into Cross's hand. She said, "Poor little guy."

253

"He may be eligible for adoption."

She looked up at me. "You figure this Darbra Proft is dead."

"The last link I can find with her being alive was Teagle."

Cross stood, went to the antique cherry table, and sat down. "Tell me."

I summarized my talk with Frank Utt at Jolly Cholly's.

She lowered her pen. "So, our 'foxy lady' makes a big deal about people knowing she's there, then doesn't bother to say good-bye."

"And whatever was in the motel sink, it doesn't look like it went on the convertible."

"We'll impound the car, run it through, and find out for sure." Cross fixed me with that good, intimidating stare. "So, what more do you have on this?"

"Nothing that makes any sense."

"Let's give it a try anyway."

We did.

She nodded, but more from resignation than agreement. "Generally, you get a killer finds a way that works, he sticks with it."

"The poker, you mean."

"Pok-*ers*."

"Granted, but why kill Teagle even if he did kill Darbra Proft?"

"I don't get it. Seems neither of your clients would've done it. Shit, the brother Proft'd pin a medal on him, maybe even split the insurance if Teagle'd just show the adjuster where the body was. And the widow—if Darbra was punching the husband?—old Pearl ought to have kissed Teagle, avenging her honor, so to speak."

"Cross, I think you have a warped view of human relations."

"It's the job, Cuddy. Makes you lose touch with the brighter side of life."

"Okay if I still look into Proft's disappearance and the Rivkind killing?"

Cross closed up her pad. "Give us a day first, let my people and me talk to these folks. Tomorrow's the Fourth. Take some time off, celebrate the founding of this great country of ours."

I wasn't going to argue with her.

21

"I THINK I'M MIMOSA COMATOSA."

"Have to learn to nurse them, counselor."

"But then all the bubbles go away."

"Life is compromise."

Her head resnuggled itself against the right side of my chest. "But not today, okay?"

"Okay."

We were lying on an old comforter Nancy had found in the back of her hall closet. The grass under us was short and sweet, the Parks Department having mowed it for the holiday.

More resnuggling. "It was a great idea, John, staying in the city like this."

The pleasure craft were politely jockeying for position in the Charles River in front of us, the MDC patrol boat herding them away from the dormant fireworks barge like a Belgian shepherd tending its flock. Three Hispanic kids were learning how to fly a kite with their father, the tail of the kite in red, white, and blue. A double date of college students roller-bladed by us, one couple expert and waving small American flags, the other awkward and holding hands to keep each other up. A fortyish guy in a beard, blue jeans, and no shirt strummed a guitar and sang old folk songs, mostly to himself until he noticed he'd attracted a gaggle of listeners and raised his voice a bit. He reminded me more of my squandered youth than Rush Teagle's curtailed one, but it was enough to make me turn back toward the boats.

I said, "You want anything more to eat?"

"Un-unh. Stuffed."

"Let me get up a minute, throw away the trash."

"Do you have to?"

"Unless you want bees."

"But this is so nice."

"And it will be again. Two minutes."

Nancy lifted her head, and I put my hands under it, lowering it gently to the comforter. "Thank you, John."

I gathered up the remains of two paper plates, a pear, an apple, two turkey and swiss croissants, and two bagels, one blueberry, the other sesame. Leaving the plastic cups and the jug of champagne and orange juice, I took the rest to the green trash can already overflowing like a sluggish volcano onto the ground around it. A little after noon, there were only ten or twelve thousand people on the Boston side of the river, maybe half as many across it on the narrower Cambridge bank. By seven P.M. the numbers would swell to over five hundred thousand to hear the Boston Pops annual concert and watch the accompanying fireworks display.

By the time I'd gotten back to Nancy, I'd seen both a pet rabbit and a tiny black pig—I looked at it three times, a pig—on leashes, walked slowly like show animals by their proud owners. A couple of dogs wrestled around the bushes by the lagoon, but otherwise the crowd was festive not restive, no trouble simmering anywhere I could tell.

Nancy said, "What kept you?"

I sat down just behind her head. She was wearing a pink

halter and white tennis shorts, the sun bringing out the freckles on her shoulders the way it already had the ones across her nose. She had amber sunglasses that reflected the light, so I couldn't tell if her eyes were open or closed, but I'd have bet on closed.

"It was a minute-thirty, tops."

"You lie, John Francis Cuddy."

I thought briefly about Abraham Rivkind, the man who never lied, but I hadn't been there to find his body, so he still seemed more a problem to me than a part of real life.

"You're beautiful, Nancy Meagher."

"What?" The sunglasses came off, the eyes wide open, looking back at me upside down.

"I said you're beautiful. I would have used your middle name, too, but it occurred to me I don't know it."

She said, "That's because I never use it," but I had the feeling she wanted to say something else.

I used the pads of my index, middle, and ring fingers to rub circles lightly in the scalp above her ears. "How come?"

"How come I never use it?"

"Yes. It isn't on your diplomas or bar admission, and I've never seen your driver's license."

"Because it's a funny name."

"Tell me."

"I'm embarrassed."

"Then I really want you to tell me."

"Why, so you'll make fun of me?"

"Yes."

"Run up and down the river, yelling it to people, who'll point at me and laugh?"

"Only the beginning."

Nancy brought her right hand up to mine, running her nails along the veins on the back. "I like the way you say that."

"Me, too."

"John, I . . . we've been close for a while now, but I've

never felt closer to anyone than I have this last week with you."

"Even though I was in New Jersey for part of it?"

"Especially because of that. You being gone for a while after we had that talk cinched it."

"Now I feel like a horse."

The nails bit in a little. "A stallion."

"You'll turn my head."

"Seriously, John."

"Okay. Serious."

"This past week, I felt as though we crossed some kind of line that had been there, ever since I met you. A line I thought we'd cross by making love the first time, but didn't."

"I know what you mean."

Nancy nodded with her eyelids. "But now, I'm not sure how to phrase it exactly, but . . . you never told me I was beautiful before."

"Now I don't know what you mean."

"In the past, you've given me plenty of reason to think you find me attractive, and I've been paid a lot of compliments over the years, but they've been . . . qualified?"

" 'Smart-looking,' 'striking' . . ."

"I even had one date in college tell me I was 'amazingly photogenic.' "

"Like he was interested in you as album art."

"Or the way the other guys would nod and elbow each other in the ribs when he took my picture out of his wallet at the bar."

"I don't think I'd do that."

"I know you wouldn't. It's just that . . . well, if you're just pretty, you lose that as you get older. You lose a lot of things, but never—"

"Somebody thinking you're beautiful."

"The right somebody, anyway."

I leaned over and kissed her upside down.

Nancy let my lips go with the half-smile. "You taste like mimosa."

"Is that a veiled request?"

"It's a holiday, and you're making me feel like I don't have a care in the world."

I refilled her cup from the jug. "Save some room for tonight."

"The party, you mean?"

"Buffet and bar both."

"That's not till seven, right?"

"Right."

"And it's just across the street."

I pointed toward the tall, balconied building, then realized she couldn't see me doing it. "Fifty feet from my doorstep."

Nancy sat up and twisted at the waist, taking the cup from me. "In that case, we'll have plenty of time to work off this meal before the next one."

"What did you have in mind, counselor?"

Over the rim she said, "Giddyap, horsey," and giggled into her drink.

Being able to walk to the party meant I didn't have to move the Prelude from behind the building, which was a real advantage. Some of my neighbors were gone, but apparently not for the night, as they left trash cans at the curb-cuts of their spaces. Maybe that would discourage the frustrated who couldn't find a legal spot to leave a car, maybe not.

Norm had one of the penthouse units in the skyscraper across Beacon Street. The doorman was prepared for us, his eyes lingering a little less on me and a little more on Nancy in a floppier pair of shorts and a sheer silk blouse that let even the casual observer guess the color of her bra. The guy working the elevator was less discreet, but I was feeling good and let it pass.

As Nancy and I rode up, she silently mocked the operator's goggle-eyed look to his back, and I laughed just suddenly enough for the guy to turn and ask if everything was all right. I told him it was.

The elevator opened onto a large anteroom, with mirrored closets for coats. At the end of the mirrors the living room began, a broad, windowed expanse facing north toward Cambridge. There were already forty or so people in the room, a half dozen more out on the sixty-foot balcony, admiring the sunset. One of them was Elie from the Nautilus club, setting up a tripod camera to take some slow exposures of the western sky.

From my right came, "John. Glad you could make it."

Norm looked like he'd just stepped off the cover of a calypso album. Sandals, white duck pants cut ragged at the shin, and a billowy, double-pocketed white shirt.

I said, "Where's the straw hat?"

"Wind took it. How's the shoulder?"

"Much better."

"And the knee?"

"Same. Thanks for the advice."

"Nothing you wouldn't have learned on your own."

"The hard way."

"The usual way."

I introduced him to Nancy.

Norm said to her, "Let me give you guys the Cook's tour."

With a wave of his big hand, he took in the buffet and liquor tables with catering staff in magenta vests. There was a den, a guest bedroom, and a magnificent master bedroom suite with access to another long but empty balcony looking south over Back Bay. Norm led us back to the bar.

"I've got more folks arriving. Just mill around. Lots of different people and two balconies, no waiting."

As Norm moved off, Nancy said, "Nice man."

"The ones who make it on their own generally are."

I ordered a screwdriver for me, but just a tonic water

261

with lime for Madam Mimosa, whose head wasn't used to drinking through the afternoon. I saw somebody else from the club, but Nancy tugged on my arm, and we went back through the master bedroom and out onto the empty balcony there. The rooftops in front of us were at least fifteen stories below, giving a perspective of the neighborhood I'd never really had. "I'm surprised there're so few roof-decks."

"I feel like Mary Poppins," said Nancy.

"Flying over Victorian chimneys."

"Umbrella above my head, other hand on my hat."

"So long as you don't break into song."

"Julie Andrews I'm not."

I looked at her, the half-smile looking back. "Remember today, when you said I'd laugh if you told me your middle name?"

"I remember a lot about today that I liked."

"Well, if you promise you won't laugh, I'll tell you what Hollywood figure you remind me of."

"Uh-oh. Do I want to know?"

"Your choice. But you have to promise not to laugh."

"Okay, I promise."

I said, "Loni Anderson."

"Loni . . . ?" A turn away, then an abrupt choking sound, the hand in front of the mouth, followed by a sidelong glance and a deep, strong laugh.

"Staunch of you, Nance."

"Oh, John . . . I'm sorry . . . but . . . Loni?"

"Your smiles."

"You're not kidding."

"I'm not."

"John Cuddy, the things you see in people."

At that moment, another couple came out and asked if they could join us. We kicked introductions around, they from a nice suburb named Sudbury and having spent an hour trying to park "the Volvo." She knew Norm because of the real estate business, he ran a bookstore in Framingham. We left them to the view. As we walked back through the master bedroom, I heard her say to him. "From the street, you'd expect there'd be more roof-decks."

We took Norm's suggestion and milled around, spending a lot of time with Elie and his date, a woman who worked with the severely retarded. We spent a little less time with a sculptor and his poet girlfriend, a police commander Nancy knew slightly and his wife, a school principal, and a gay couple who owned an art gallery on Newbury Street where probably nobody in the room except Norm could afford to shop. Noshing from the buffet, we spent considerably less time with a stockbroker and her husband, a retailing executive who kept eyeing two fashion models in their early twenties, and the models themselves, Nancy's hold on my hand and forearm becoming stronger the longer we were with them.

Norm asked everybody for their attention, and I realized that it was dark outside, the lights from the MIT buildings across the river twinkling through the glass.

He said, "Only a few minutes now. I'm going to put the concert on simulcast. When the fireworks start, the balcony should hold most of us, but please, no stamping of your feet, especially not in time to the music."

Nancy leaned up to my ear. "Why not?"

"The force of all those feet could weaken the thing structurally."

"Really?"

"It's why when you march soldiers across a bridge, you tell them to go route step, meaning not in rhythm with each other."

"Otherwise the bridge would fall down?"

"Been known to happen. Remember that hotel thing out in—"

"Oh, yeah."

We grabbed some drinks and moved onto the balcony. The Hatch Shell looked like a miniature scallop, all lit up.

The crowd was barely distinguishable, only the occasional flashlight or lantern showing you people in its beam. There were so many boats on the river around the fireworks barge, it looked like a flubbed special effect. Twenty- to forty-footers stern-lashed together. Little black commando dinghies riding the endless chop next to canoes and even a few kayaks. The music from the Hatch Shell was barely audible, the stereo inside the living room really letting you know where the orchestra was on its way to the *1812 Overture*.

When John Williams signaled his people to strike that first chord from the overture, there was a swelling roar from the crowd. More lights appeared on the barge, and the voice level on the balcony rose as well. People dah-dahed toward the crescendo, and when it came, the fireworks display began.

Norm's building was positioned so that the fireworks were shot toward us, their trajectory bringing the exploding flowers into our faces like a 3-D movie. The first time it happened, I gripped Nancy's hand so tightly she had to say, "John, that hurts a little."

"Sorry."

She had a touch of concern on her face. "Remind you of something?"

"Only for a second. I'm enjoying it now."

It was hard not to. The crowd went nuts over both the music and the display, the latter building itself to a thundering peak of teardrop colors in impossible combinations and blinding white flashes and explosions that pushed every other sensation of any kind to the side.

When it finally died, there was a grayish-blue cloud over the river and the smell of cordite in the air. We applauded and whistled and cheered with everyone else, Nancy hanging back on the balcony as the rest went in to freshen drinks and compare notes.

Nancy looked up at me, but without the half-smile this time. "John, can I ask you a question?"

ACT OF GOD

"Sure."

"It's something I never ask you about."

"That's okay."

She took my right hand in both of hers. "The fireworks. What did they remind you of?"

I shrugged and looked away, trying not to breathe too deeply the cordite smell. "The war."

"But what part?"

I looked back at her. "Specifically, you mean?"

"Yes."

Watching her, I said, "I had to go out to a fire-base with one of my men, pick up an artillery lieutenant for some things he did to a bar girl in Saigon. The MPs liked to send an officer to bring back an officer."

"Go on."

"We had to stay over, wait for a chopper the next day. The Vietcong decided to hit the base that night. The first few rounds of mortar fire came in before the flares, guys running around, grabbing weapons, and trying to put on their boots. The mortars were behind a hill, and somebody called in a fire mission—artillery from another base—to knock them out. As I'm hunkered down, the flares are breaking over our heads, everything spotlit, like the lights panning a crowd at a rock concert."

"Like tonight's crowd on the river," she said quietly.

"Like that. Only back then most of us weren't watching. I couldn't help it, though, Nance. The flares and the mortar rounds—I mean, guys were being killed and wounded all around me, and I was scared, but in its own way, it was . . . so beautiful."

Nancy searched my eyes for a moment. "That's the first time you've ever told me anything about your time over there. Really told me."

"Like you said, it was the first time I was asked."

She brought her hands up around my neck, mine going around her waist.

Nancy said, "Eugenia."

"What?"

"Eugenia. My mother was reading a Russian novel the week I was born and convinced my dad that 'Eugenia' was the most beautiful middle name an Irish lass could have."

I leaned into her, a hug rather than a kiss. "Your mom was right."

22

"Mr. Proft."

With the perpetual grin, he looked away from locking a nondescript two-door Ford Escort at the curb in front of the pharmacy. Looking back to the keys, Proft pocketed them under the white lab coat.

"Mr. Cuddy. You're certainly the early bird, aren't you?"

I'd been parked on the street for maybe twenty minutes. "I was hoping to catch you before things got too busy."

"Is this about that Rush Teagle person?"

"Partly. I thought as my client you might also be interested to hear what I found out in Jersey."

"Yes." Proft frowned. "Yes, I should have led with that, shouldn't I?"

I didn't say anything.

He swung his head around. "Our bench, then?"

"That would do fine."

The long legs carried him across the street like a spider moving to the corner of its web. Sprawling over the bench, he said, "Well, I guess you tell me, eh?"

I sat on the other end. "Just after I spoke to you last, I got a call from Traci Wickmire."

"So did I."

"You did."

"Yes. Well, I imagine it was after you saw her. And Darbra's somewhat ... reordered apartment? I understand it was quite a mess."

"You haven't been over there."

"No. But from what Traci told me, you went through it rather thoroughly."

"You have any idea what someone might have been looking for?"

"None," said Proft.

"It appeared that the somebody had a key to the place."

"Perhaps it was Darbra herself, raging."

"Over what?"

"Over whatever it is that's made her vanish on us."

I stopped. "What else did Wickmire tell you?"

Heels on the ground, Proft rotated the toe end of his Hush Puppies in the air, as though he were limbering up his ankles. "She seemed rather put out about the cat."

"More like his litter."

"Yes." The grin curled some. "She even asked if I were interested in coming over and cleaning it up."

"I take it you declined."

"Perhaps we *are* getting to know each other, Mr. Cuddy."

"How did you know about Teagle?"

"Various ways. One, my Escort was on the fritz, so I had to take it into the shop on Friday and was without transportation over the long weekend. I just picked up the car this morning, in fact."

"What was wrong with it?"

"The mechanic said he couldn't find a thing. Just a gremlin, I suppose."

The curled grin.

I said, "So you had no way to get around the last few days."

"Correct. Accordingly, I was pretty much housebound, and therefore heard about the Teagle incident via radio and television. I also received a call from a friend of yours."

"From Homicide?"

"Yes. A rather gruff woman, from her telephone manner. Do you suppose she doesn't enjoy her work?"

"What did you tell her?"

"Just what I've told you. I never met the man, though I wasn't—and remain *un*—surprised that Darbra had one or more in her life."

"I don't suppose anybody was with you when Teagle was killed?"

"Not knowing when he was killed, I really couldn't say, but I doubt it. I stayed in most of the time these last few days. You see, when you deal with people for a living, it's awfully nice to be without them for a period, not having to say anything, just . . . living."

I watched him.

"So, Mr. Cuddy, is this where I should ask about how you spent my money in New Jersey?"

"I found the place where she stayed. The motel owner there said—"

"What was the name of the place?"

"The name?"

"Of the motel, yes."

"Why?"

"If Darbra has passed from us, I really would like to know the name of the last place we know she was happy."

"Happy."

"Well, yes. Aren't people generally happy on their vacations?"

I took a breath. "Jolly Cholly's."

"No."

"Yes."

"How positively . . . banal. How perfect for her."

"The motel owner says she wasn't alone."

"She never has been for any considerable period."

"He said Rush Teagle was with her."

"Teagle?"

"Yes."

Proft stopped, tapping a long index finger at the corner of his mouth. "No . . . no, that doesn't seem right."

"What do you mean?"

"Well, to hear you and your friend Detective Cross, this Teagle wasn't a big-spender type."

"You'd be right there."

"Darbra wasn't—but I suppose we should give her the benefit of the doubt and still use the present tense, shouldn't we? Darbra *isn't* the type to bring a toy with her to the toy store."

I thought back to Teagle's comment about bringing sand to the beach when he lied to me about going with her. "She'd have gone alone?"

"Or brought someone to buy toys for her."

I thought about Abraham Rivkind and Roger Houle. "The motel owner also said that she was very friendly to everybody."

"Friendly? You mean in a flirting way?"

"No. At least he said no. More outgoing."

"Outgoing? Darbra would be outgoing only if it pointed the way to more toys for her."

"Meaning more money."

"Yes. She's always been quite taken with money and what it could buy. We never had much as children, you see."

"Until your mother died."

"Yes, but we were hardly children when that happened."

"I spoke to the officer who investigated her death."

"Oh, good for you. What was his name?"

"I forget."

Proft winched the grin up a little more. "Mr. Cuddy, you're not coming to distrust me, are you?"

"He thinks it may have been more than an accident."

"Then he and I disagree."

No change in the grin. "Mr. Proft, the motel owner—"

"I'm glad we haven't finished with New Jersey. It hardly sounded as though I'd gotten my money's worth so far."

I was getting good at taking deep breaths. "The motel owner said that he didn't exactly see Darbra check out."

"Leave the motel, you mean?"

"Yes."

"How does that make a difference?"

Proft seemed to be going dense on me. "It means she may not have actually gotten back here that Saturday."

"But you said her suitcase . . . ?"

"Yes. But if somebody, maybe Teagle, did something with her or to her, that somebody would have her keys and be able to make it look like she got back."

"When really she never did?"

"It's a possibility."

Proft came up to speed. "Which would explain why no one heard from her. . . ."

"Except Teagle, supposedly."

"And why she never changed the cat litter."

"You thought of that, did you?"

He looked at me. "Seems obvious."

"You also think it kind of strange that one man Darbra was seeing and another she might have been seeing are both dead the same way?"

"Teagle was killed with a poker, too?"

"Cross didn't mention that to you?"

"No. Perhaps you should have warned me, before she spoke to me."

"Warned you?"

The grin arched again. "As your client, don't I warrant some prophylactic advice?"

271

"You want some advice, I'll give it to you. You ought to think about the cat."

"Think about it?"

"In case it needs a new home."

"Isn't that what pounds are for?"

"You wouldn't want it, then."

"I enjoy my life the way it is, Mr. Cuddy. Clean, pure. I dislike . . . encumbrances, animal or human."

William Proft gave me his most engaging smile, but it was kind of hard to look at.

Over the receiver of the pay phone outside the pharmacy, I heard, "Homicide, Cross."

"It's Cuddy."

"What?"

"Okay to talk to people other than my clients?"

"Yeah."

I thought I heard her chewing. "Anything on the crime scene at Teagle's that you can tell me?"

"Time of death's kind of a wide bracket. Saturday morning to Sunday, at least four or five hours before you found him."

"Prints?"

"The place was lousy with them, especially on the musical stuff."

"How about the poker?"

"Nothing readable, except for some of Teagle's own."

"You doing eliminations on the guys in his band?"

"Yeah, we already had them in."

"See them yourself?"

"Yeah. Not what you'd call appetizing young men, except maybe the drummer, he let his hair grow past the scalpline."

"You wouldn't have a name and address on the one with the dreadlocks?"

"The Chinese kid?"

272

"I thought he might be Korean."

"Uh-unh. Chinese. Howard Ling. But the whole band's got at least partial alibis. Sixty anxious patrons, pounding their beers on tables, waiting for Teagle to show for the set."

"I'd still like an address on this Ling."

"Hold on."

I tried Pearl Rivkind's number, braced if her son Lawrence answered. But nobody did, and there was still no tape after ten rings. I hung up, thought about it, then decided to find their street.

It was in a subdivision built maybe a decade before, enough time for the shrubs around the houses and the trees between the lots to look as though they belonged there. The houses were mostly split-levels, the Rivkinds' chocolate-brown garrison the exception with brass lampposts staked at the ends of a driveway that led up a modest slope to a two-car garage. The grass had been cut, and a Mazda sports car sat on the macadam outside the closed garage doors, but there were also three separate bundles of translucent green plastic on the lawn near the front stoop. Each bundle was the size of a piece of split firewood.

I left the Prelude at the end of the driveway and walked up to the car. The hood of the Mazda was in the shade. I felt the metal. Cool.

Moving along the path to the stoop, I checked the little green bundles. Boston *Globe*s, for the last three days. I had a sinking feeling as I reached the stoop itself.

The bell produced a sequence of chimes inside, but nothing else. I knocked, waited, then knocked louder. Stepping down from the stoop into the shrubs, I shaded my hand at the glass in a front window. The repose of an empty house, something flickering from the rear of it like a fluorescent bulb about to go bad.

I was halfway around to the back when a cruiser with a rack of bubble-lights on its roof pulled up in front of my car, slanting in to block it and the driveway at the same time. Smooth.

The first cop out was a tall black male on the passenger's side of the car, facing me. The driver, a shorter white female, stepped onto the pavement but kept her door and her options open.

The male cop said, "Mind coming down to see us?"

"No."

I walked down the path and the driveway. The male cop stayed on my side of the car, the female standing in the angle of her open door, hands where I couldn't see them.

When I was about ten feet from the male cop, he said, "Mind telling us what you're doing?"

"I have some ID, inside left jacket."

"Let's see it."

"I also have a Chief's Special over my right hip."

The black cop looked at me almost sleepily. "Nice of you to mention it."

I went into my coat pocket for the holder, then stepped close enough to hand it to him. Reading, he said over his shoulder to the partner, "John Francis Cuddy, P.I. from Boston. Want to call it in?"

She said, "Right."

I said, "Can I have that back?"

A sleepy smile. "When it checks out."

A minute later the partner said, "He's licensed."

The male cop folded my identification and returned it to me. "What's your business here?"

"I'm working for the woman who lives in that house."

"And what would her name be?"

'Rivkind."

"First name?"

"Pearl."

"Husband and son's name?"

"Son's Lawrence, husband's Abraham, but he's dead. Mrs. Rivkind is about five feet tall, with—"

"You're working for her, how come you're visiting when she's not here?"

"I didn't know that."

Over his shoulder again, the male cop said, "What do you think?"

"I think he's legit."

"Same." Then to me, "Mrs. Rivkind and her son, they took a little time off, go away over the Fourth, put aside the memories for a while. The family's been real active in town here, supporting this and that. People are real sorry about what happened, looking out for them now."

"Glad to hear it. Which neighbor called me in?"

The sleepy smile. "This street, Cuddy, it has a thousand eyes. Just so we don't get any more calls though, how about we move our car and you move yours somewhere else?"

"Fair enough."

23

WHEN I PULLED TO THE CURB OUTSIDE ROGER HOULE'S HOUSE IN
Meade, there was no sign of him or his neighbor, Mrs. Thorson. However, this time the front lawn was mowed, the
clippings either raked off or captured in some kind of bag
so that his place looked the same as the other mini-manses
on the street. Turning off the engine, I could hear the sound
of a hammer. Bang-bang-bang, then a pause, then one-two-
three again. Getting out of the Prelude and walking around
the back of his house, I found myself almost marching in
time to the rhythm.

The hammering got louder as I cleared the corner on Mrs.
Thorson's side. This time I saw Houle from the front, and
he looked a little better than the first time I'd met him. The
face under the bald head still seemed haggard, but he'd
shaved that morning, and there was some color on his arms
below a breast-pocket T-shirt. He stood on a ladder leaned
against the potting shed, which was almost finished, the
glassless windows showing what would have been a bright,
airy place for a person interested in gardening to work.

Houle had a magnetized hammer in his left hand, holding a nail by its head as he positioned a section of green, tweedy shingle with his right on the sloping roof of the shed.

He was about to drive the nail when my movement caught his eye. "You're . . . ?"

"John Cuddy, Mr. Houle. I was by here last Thursday?"

He seemed to have to focus on that. "Oh, right. About Darbra."

Nodding, I glanced over at his wife's garden, less to check on the plants and more to check on the covered urn. The other vases and his redwood lounge chair were still in the same positions, which let me see more quickly that the urn wasn't.

Houle climbed down from the ladder, slipping the handle of his hammer into a loop on a leather carpenter's apron, then unstrapping the apron like a cowboy reversing his gun belt. "What can I do for you?"

"There've been a few developments I thought you should know about."

Houle looked at me carefully. "Something's wrong, isn't it?"

"Yes."

"More than just Darbra being off somewhere."

"I'm afraid so."

He shook his head. "It just doesn't stop." Walking, almost shambling over to the corner of the shed by the fertilizer bags and tools, Houle pulled the other lounge chair by its foot, the back wheels making tracks in the grass. "The arm of this thing's like a little desktop, in case you need to write something down."

He seemed to be functioning a lot better. I said, "Thanks."

Houle sat on his lounge sidesaddle, like he expected maybe to get up again soon. "I wasn't in real good shape last time I saw you."

I eased into the other one. "Pretty understandable."

"That first week . . . I didn't wash or look after myself. . . . Wouldn't have eaten anything if it wasn't for a neighbor."

"Mrs. Thorson?"

Houle narrowed his eyes. "How did you . . . ?"

"I met her coming in last time."

He shook his head again. "Sorry. I don't remember much about . . . that."

"You seem to be doing well now."

Houle grunted. "Sometime Friday, I got up, looked in the mirror, and got a little scared. Up till then, I was mostly . . . numb. But I looked at myself, and I saw one of those guys you try to avoid when you go into the city, mumbling to themselves on the street in torn clothes and dirty shoes. That was when I showered and shaved. Cut myself to pieces, hadn't tried to take a beard off since college. But it brought me around, a little."

He looked toward the garden. "Then I came out here, saw the ashes—the urn, I mean, and said fuck the law, said it out loud, and spread Caroline among the flowers, where she belongs." Houle moved his head the other way. "Then I saw the shed over there, halfway done, and figured I could work on it some, and that brought me around a little more. I'm building it better than it has to be, but . . ." Just a shrug.

"I'm sorry to have to do this, but I need some more information."

Houle came back to me. "Look, I'm sorry. You've got a job to do. I don't remember what all we talked about last time, so you might have to repeat some of it for me."

"Since I spoke to you, somebody went through Darbra's apartment."

"I know."

"You do?"

"Yeah. I got a call from a Boston detective. Police, I mean. A woman. It was only . . . Sunday, maybe, but I don't remember her name."

"Sergeant Bonnie Cross?"

278

"Right. Cross. She asked me where I was on Saturday and Sunday both, and I told here I was here. I'd been here all week. Then I asked her why she wanted to know, and she said some guy Darbra knew was dead." Houle looked at me harder. "You told me about some ... men she was seeing, right?"

"Right."

"Good, because that's what I told her—Cross, I mean. I didn't know the guy—God, it's terrible, I can't even remember what she said his name was."

"Teagle, Rush Teagle."

"Teagle, right. Teagle. She said he was dead, and did I know him, and I said no, I didn't. Then she asked me if I had a key to Darbra's place, and I said I did, and she wanted to know if I still had it, and I said I thought so, but with everything else, I didn't know where it was."

"Did Cross also ask you if you knew any reason why somebody would search Darbra's apartment?"

"Yeah. I told her no. I mean, it's not like I bought her jewelry or something, and Darbra never had more than a twenty-dollar bill in her purse. Even that wouldn't last the day, the way she bought herself little things."

"What kind of little things?"

"Oh, I don't know. Trinkets, knickknacks. They were all over the apartment."

I thought about the Hummels and other figurines.

Houle said, "I always figured she was just compensating."

"Compensating?"

"For being a little kid and poor. Like she never got presents from her mother except at Christmas and birthdays, and then probably not enough for her."

"Darbra ever mention anything about somebody buying them for her?"

"No. I bought her some of the Hummels, but ... wait a minute, you asked me about one of the guys at her store, right?"

279

"Right."

"Rivlin?"

"Rivkind."

"Right, right. That Cross asked me about him, too."

"What about him?"

"Did I know if Darbra knew him, then about him being killed. She—the policewoman—wanted to know where I was then."

"You told me Denver."

"I told Cross the same thing. She said could I prove it, and I told her I guessed I could, but the receipts for the plane and the hotel and restaurants—you know, the expense account stuff?—all that was at the office. So I called the secretary this morning to messenger Cross what she needed."

"Mr. Houle, you know anybody who'd have reason to hurt Darbra, or get somebody like Teagle to maybe do the job?"

"Hurt her? No. Darbra . . . Darbra can kind of rankle you, you know? Or fly off the handle, like she did with me in that restaurant."

"When you thought she was acting."

"Right. But she could do that, kind of put on an attitude for the occasion. She did it with me, often enough."

"I don't get you."

"With, uh . . ." Houle looked over to the garden. "With like . . . sex games in her apartment."

I thought about it. "But nobody who hated her."

"Unless it was reciprocal."

"Reciprocal?"

"Her brother, Wee Willie. She couldn't stand him. I think I told you that, or at least his name."

I'd also told Houle that I was working for William Proft, but I let it pass. "Darbra ever say anything about her brother threatening her?"

"No. No, nothing like that, ever. Just that she hated him and hated that she had to split the money from her mother

280

with him. That's about all she ever said to me about Wee Willie, except for his . . . preferences."

"What do you mean?"

"His . . ." Another look at the garden, shorter this time. "His sexual preferences."

"What were they?"

"That's just it. Darbra told me she didn't think he had any."

I was thinking the same thing when Houle said, "Look, I don't want to seem . . . touchy, but it's kind of hard for me to talk about these things . . . here."

"I'm sorry I have to ask about them."

He nodded.

Aware of the last few days with Nancy, I said, "One thing that might help."

Houle looked harder at me again. "What's that?"

"Time. It's been a while since I lost my wife, and over time, it gets easier."

He nodded, the eyes starting to fill.

I said, a little quickly, "You ride it out, somebody else can matter again."

Houle rubbed the back of his wrist across his nose. "Yeah, thanks."

Watching him dam it in, I really didn't want to stay or say much more, but I couldn't be sure Cross thought to tell him something he might not have realized on his own. "One last thing, Mr. Houle?"

"Yeah?"

"Both Abraham Rivkind and Rush Teagle were killed by fireplace pokers."

"Fireplace . . . ?"

"Pokers. And as I said, it might be that both Rivkind and Teagle had relationships, sexual relationships, with Darbra Proft."

He just stared at me. "So?"

"So you did, too."

Houle stared some more, then started. "What? You mean . . . ?"

"I don't know what I mean, but I don't think it's only coincidence. I think you ought to be careful, just in case."

He worked his hands together, like he was washing them rather than praying with them. "Jesus, you mean like . . . hire a bodyguard?"

"I don't know. I don't even know you well enough to give you advice. And I don't want to scare you unnecessarily. But it's something that comes to mind, and I wasn't sure you saw it."

Houle swallowed hard. "Another Ex-Lax."

"What?"

A few tears, the eyes bewildered. "Another laxative. God taking them so he can really shit on you."

I stood up, said again I was sorry for his loss, and left him, Roger Houle now looking not that much different than he had the first time I'd met him.

The address Cross had given me for Howard Ling was in Allston. It turned out to be a brick building just off Brighton Ave. with a hardware store on the street level and three floors of apartments above. I found a metered space a block down, then walked back, the entryway next to the hardware having an unlocked outer door and just the word LING and an oriental character handwritten under the middle buzzer.

Instead of pressing the button, I climbed the stairs. The second floor smelled strongly of garlic, the next like the vent from the kitchen of a Chinese restaurant. There was only one doorway on that third floor, so I knocked. I heard a kind of growling, more human than animal. I was about to knock harder when the door opened, a hissing voice saying something in a language that might have been Chinese.

Looking into the apartment, I saw the kid with the dreadlocks standing in front of me, the one Rush Teagle had called "Hack." He wore black jeans and no top and held one of those small, strawed boxes of Gatorade in his hand. Behind him, an Asian man in his forties was lying on the couch. The man wore just a strappy T-shirt and boxer shorts. One leg was half off the bed, the sock half off the foot, and one arm was up and around the neck, as though he were trying to put himself into a half nelson. The man was snoring irregularly and giving every indication of sleeping off a monumental drunk.

The kid didn't like me at his doorstep, but the way he looked behind him told me he didn't like the man being awakened even more.

Quietly, I said, "Why don't we step outside, Howie."

In the hissing voice, he said in English, "Don't call me that."

"Fine. Outside still looks better."

Another look over the shoulder. "All right, all right."

He did something to the door lock with his free hand, then came out, closing the door behind him so that it barely clicked shut. The corridor had a black rubber runner tacked down here and there with carpet staples, the runner buckling at the beginning and end of each flight of stairs. The walls were plaster and painted pumpkin-orange, but there were enough crumble spots that the white showed through, like mold on a damp vegetable.

Howard Ling said, "What do you want?"

"First things first. What should I call you?"

"Hack. That's my name."

"Not according to the police, Hack."

"They need the righteous one for their paperwork, that's like their problem, not mine. I didn't have anything to do with Rush getting killed, man."

"Kind of an abrupt segue, don't you think?"

Ling took a sip of his Gatorade. "I don't know what to think."

"You and Rush and the other two were supposed to do a gig on Saturday night, right?"

"We already told the cops everything."

"Indulge me, Hack."

"Why should I? You gonna beat me up?"

"Maybe we could just wake your dad, have him talk it over with you."

"He's not—" Ling caught his voice rising, lowered it. "He's my stepfather."

"Where's your mother?"

"Out buying him more booze so when he wakes up, he'll drink some more and go back to sleep."

I took a breath. "I'm sorry."

Ling seemed to soften a little. "You don't see it much in us. Drunks, I mean. Not a very 'Chinese' vice, you know?"

"About that night."

"What night?"

"When Teagle was killed. You guys had a gig, right?"

Ling got more tired than soft. "Right." He took another sip.

"And Rush didn't show."

"Right. But we didn't like know he was dead."

"When's the last time you saw him?"

"I don't know."

"You don't remember the last time you saw your friend?"

"No, man, I don't."

"How many friends you have get killed?"

Almost a smile, the kid's face angelic. "Like Rush, just two. First was this crackhead, he smoked a pipe with the wrong dude. The other took a little speed one night, thought the Mass Pike was the Daytona 500, and crossed the median doing about a hundred and five."

I just looked at him.

Ling said, "The rest of us, we're just like waiting our turn."

"You ever figure Teagle'd be next?"

"Never can tell."

"He ever talk with you about anything besides music?"

"Sure. Rush, he never stopped talking, said it was important for his lyrics."

"His lyrics."

"Yeah, like he had to keep hearing the words out loud, not just in his head, make sure they sounded good together."

"What did you talk about?"

"What difference does it make?"

"It might help find who killed him."

A longer drink. "So what?"

"You don't care who killed your friend?"

"Man, if it's not the drugs, it'll be the air or the water or microwaves or cellular phones. We're all gonna die from this planet, you know?"

"What if it was connected to the band?"

"It wasn't."

"How do you know?"

"Rush said . . ."

Ling bit on his lower lip, a pouting angel now.

I said, "What did Rush say?"

"Aw, man, he just said that the boss guy at his woman's store got killed that way, so I like don't see how him getting it is connected with us, all right?"

" 'His woman' meaning Darbra Proft."

"Yeah. She was old, but thought she wasn't, you know?"

"Tell me."

"Aw, she'd come to our gigs, like the one where you saw us?" Ling warmed to his subject. "Only she'd dress up like she thought she should, not real grunge, but kind of . . . pseudo grunge, you know?"

"Like she thought she was copying you, but didn't really know how?"

"Yeah. Yeah, like that." Ling seemed to remember who he was talking to and dropped the warmth. "Only she was just another groupie lay, and kind of old for it."

"Teagle brag about that?"

285

"Rush, he liked to brag about a lot of things, man. That was Rush, what you need in a lead."

"Confidence?"

"Flash and sizzle, dude. The stud on the come. The audience feels that, they're with you, rocking. They don't, you might as well be the Beatles."

Who didn't fare too badly for themselves. "What else did Rush brag about?"

"Fuck, all kinds of shit. The time he was on tour opening for this group just got a major record deal, the convertible he got with the money from that, the other money he—"

Dead stop. I said, "What money is that?"

More Gatorade. "I don't know, man."

"Hack, what money are we talking about now?"

"I don't know."

"Hack."

"Look, dude, I can't tell you what I don't know."

"How about telling me what you do know?"

"Aw, Rush, he was bragging about what he was gonna do with this money he was getting."

"For what?"

"I don't know."

"How much was it supposed to be?"

"I like just don't know, man."

"Well, what was he bragging he'd do with it?"

"Get a new guitar, upgrade some of our rack—the amps, that kind of thing."

"For the band, you mean."

"Yeah."

"So how much would all that cost?"

"Depends."

"On what?"

"Whether it's new or used, what quality. The usual."

"Give me a ballpark."

"Couple, three thousand, maybe."

286

"You guys have anything planned that would bring in that kind of money?"

"You shitting me or what? The most, like the absolute excellent *most* we ever took down was five hundred, split four ways."

"So how would Teagle come into a few thousand or more?"

"I don't know, and he didn't say."

"When was this?"

"When was what?"

"Teagle bragging about getting this new money."

"I don't know, man. He did it all the time, like I—"

"But when did he start?"

"Start bragging about it?"

"Yes."

"I don't know. maybe a month ago?"

"A month ago."

"Yeah."

I thought about it. Roughly the time Darbra broke off with Roger Houle and started in with Rush Teagle. A week or so before Abraham Rivkind died.

Ling went back to his straw, but it quickly made that tank-empty, sucking sound. "Hey, dude. Okay if I go back in now?"

"Aren't you afraid of waking your stepfather?"

"Yeah, but I gotta study."

"Study what?"

"Accounting, man."

"Accounting?"

Ling threw the empty box over his shoulder onto the black rubber runner. "Yeah. You don't think I want to live in this shithole forever, do you?"

24

I STOOD ACROSS THE STREET FROM VALUE FURNITURE, LOOKING UP
at the facade and the roof line with its finials and flagpole
that reminded Abraham Rivkind of a place I'd have thought
anybody would want to forget. Then I went in through the
main entrance and received the standard greeting from
Karen, wanting to know if she could help me in any way.
I asked her about Finian Quill.

"Gee, I'm sorry but I don't think Finian's here right now.
Can someone else help you?"

I said I'd see Mr. Bernstein instead and already knew
the way.

The grand ballroom staircase to the second floor was
empty as I climbed it. Only a smattering of customers
browsed among the dining room sets on the second floor
and the bedrooms on the third. As I moved through the
padded swinging doors on the fourth, Joel Bernstein was
just coming out of the men's room, hitching his suit pants
a little against the suspenders. He stopped hitching as soon
as he saw me.

"You're back?"

"Afraid so."

Bernstein ran a hand through the black clots on his head. "Look, I'm sorry I got kind of hot at you there."

"It happens. Forget it."

"No, really. I know you're not trying to rip off Pearl or anything, it's just that the pressure around here, me trying to do it all...." He made the harsh, blubbering sound.

I said, "Can you give me a couple of minutes?"

"Why not. Take my mind off all the other things I can't change."

I followed him toward the partners' office, the door just before it open. A Latino woman was sitting behind Darbra's desk, briskly sorting through papers.

I spoke to Bernstein's back. "Replacement?"

"What?"

"The woman in Darbra's office."

"Oh, her." He sagged into his desk chair, waving me toward one of the captain's chairs. "Temp. Beverly got her last Friday. Seems to be working out."

"Meaning you might take her on full-time?"

"Yeah, there's a need for it." Bernstein tilted his head, the neck so thick there was little or no difference in width between it and his jowls. "You had any luck finding Amelia Earhart?"

"You think Darbra flew away on her vacation?"

"Couldn't drive. At least, she said she couldn't, one time I asked her to use my car, pick something up for me. Way she said it at first, I thought it was like one of those coffee things, you know?"

"Sorry?"

"Like in the old days, you could ask a secretary to get your coffee? Now, it's like sexual harassment you even suggest they could do something for their salary besides type and file."

"But Darbra said she couldn't use your car because she didn't know how to drive."

"Never learned, she said. Mentioned it a couple times, often enough so you believed her. At least, I did." Bernstein tilted his head the other way. "So, you didn't answer my question."

"No, I haven't had much luck finding her."

"Goofy broad. Wait a minute, can't say 'broad' nowadays, either."

"Mr. Bernstein, when we went through Darbra's desk, I didn't see any keys."

"Wouldn't expect you to."

"She kept the key to her office in her handbag?"

"Yeah. Where else would it be?"

"I was wondering if she kept any spares here in the store."

"Spares. You mean like to her house?"

"Apartment."

"Whatever."

"Yes. A key to her building and front door, maybe."

Bernstein thought about it. "Beats me. Why?"

"Somebody searched her apartment, really tore it apart."

"Maybe a burglar. They read the ..."

"Read what, Mr. Bernstein?"

He pursed his lips. "I was going to say they read the death notices, you know? Break in when they think there's nobody home."

"Except we don't know Darbra's dead, do we?"

"No. We don't."

"And there hasn't been anything in the papers about her disappearance."

"Right."

"And whoever it was didn't break in. They used a key."

Bernstein looked at me, through me. "I told you, I don't know anything about her keys."

"You read about the guy killed in her building?"

"Enough people get killed in this city, you don't keep track of them."

"This is kind of a special guy. He's the one Darbra went to New Jersey with."

"New Jersey."

"On her vacation."

"She never said anything to me about it."

"Not even about the boyfriend?"

"Especially about him, whoever he is."

"Or was."

Bernstein just looked at me this time.

"A Detective Sergeant Cross didn't get in touch with you?"

He chewed on the inside of his cheek. "Yeah. She got in touch."

"So you knew about Rush Teagle being killed."

"I heard from this Cross that a guy Darbra knew got killed. That's it."

"Cross ask you about where you were?"

"Yeah, she did."

"What'd you tell her?"

Bernstein flushed, his voice with an edge on it. "Ask this Cross, you know her so well."

I didn't want to lose him just yet. "I stopped by Mrs. Rivkind's house a few hours ago."

He seemed to defuse. "She back yet?"

"No. Do you know where she went?"

He waited a moment. "Pearl and Larry, they went away for a couple days, clear the head about Abe."

"Any idea why she waited this long?"

"This long?"

"Given that her husband died over three weeks ago?"

"I don't like your attitude. Pearl's got the right to grieve the way she wants to. We all do."

I remembered how Bernstein had used anger the last time

to deflect me from asking him about Abraham Rivkind and Darbra Proft.

"One last question."

"Good."

"You think there was anything between your partner and Darbra."

He lurched forward in his chair. "Get out."

"This isn't just a missing-person case, Mr. Bernstein. It never has been. If you know something that could help the police with who killed Abraham Rivkind or Rush Teagle, you'd best tell somebody soon."

He started to rise, struggling with both his weight and his attitude. "Get the hell out of my store!"

My store.

"Mr. Cuddy?"

I turned in the corridor. Joel Bernstein had trailed me to his office door, then slammed it behind me. Beverly Swindell was wearing a rust-colored skirt and a maize blouse that day. She had a sheaf of green and white computer printouts in her hand and a worried look on her face, darkening it to a less milky shade of brown.

I said, "Don't worry. I'm leaving quietly."

Swindell cradled the printouts under an arm. "Why are you here at all?"

"Some things have happened."

She seemed to gird herself. "Now what?"

I looked back at Bernstein's door. "Your boss told me to get out of his store."

"Joel's still very upset. We all are." Swindell stopped. "Is there something you need from me?"

"It might help."

The bookkeeper shifted the printouts. "These can wait."

"Your office?"

She shook her head.

* * *

Grgo Radja said, "This table okay for you, Mrs. Swindell?"

"It's fine, thank you."

"And the gentleman?"

Radja had seated us while giving Swindell the impression he'd never met me before.

I played along. "Fine, thanks."

The restaurateur took her order for coffee and mine for iced tea. He bowed very slightly, the lapels on his double-breasted suit, blue this time, spiraling a little as he did.

Swindell said, "It feels comfortable being here, even though the place is empty this time of day."

"Mrs. Rivkind told me her husband used to eat here a lot."

"Yes." Swindell put her elbows on the table, letting her palms lay on top of them. "Abe used to take all of us out to dinner here, sometimes in a group, sometimes just individually, find out how we were doing, did we have any suggestions for running the store better that we might not want to put into writing or say in front of somebody else. Even when times were bad—businesswise, I mean—Abe would always say he remembered a time when things were a lot worse—not businesswise—and reach for the check."

The waiter in the black Eisenhower jacket came by with our drinks, serving them with a flourish and apparently knowing how Swindell took hers because he brought it with cream and maybe sugar already mixed into the cup. After we assured him we didn't need anything else, he went back into the kitchen.

I said, "Mrs. Swindell, did Mr. Rivkind ever talk to you about the time he was in the concentration camp?"

Her brows went up. "The camp?"

"Yes."

"Why?"

"Mr. Bernstein told me the front of the store looks like a picture of the entrance to Buchenwald."

Swindell hunched a little on the elbows, not drinking her coffee. "Joel also tell you that was why I got hired on originally?"

"Yes."

"Well, the Liberators, that was why Abe gave me the chance, but not why he kept me on."

"Why did he give Darbra the chance?"

Swindell's face darkened again, deeper now than her untouched coffee. "Her brother said something to Pearl, and Abe got it into his head that the girl was an orphan."

"Because of her mother being killed?"

Again the eyebrows went up. "Killed? I heard she fell from a building."

"There's some question about the 'fell' part."

"Oh." Swindell pushed her coffee away. "Oh, my."

"What's the matter?"

She looked up at me. "I just thought."

"What?"

"That there was something about that girl from the first time I saw her."

"Something?"

"Something . . . evil might be too strong a word for it. More like . . . a twist."

Bernstein had said the same, something off about her. "Go on."

"I sometimes . . . sometimes I thought Darbra was working with us as part of something else."

"How do you mean?"

"Well, like I told you before, she was always trying to do things a little different than what you wanted?"

"The paperwork example."

Swindell's head bobbed. "It was almost that she was . . . using the job, not trying to learn it, but more learn from it. Only not to do it better. Just to do it differently, like . . . vary it, keep her interested in it without trying to better herself at it."

"Any idea why?"

"I got the impression . . . Maybe I shouldn't say this."

"Maybe you should."

A hesitation. "I got the impression that Darbra was just using us, too. Like her in here that night, kind of using me as an audience for a little scene she was playing with that poor man she threw the wine at."

"Again, any idea why?"

"No. None."

Swindell seemed sad, and I regretted having to add to it. I said, "Have the police been in touch with you about Darbra's boyfriend?"

"The boy who was killed in her building?"

"Yes."

"They came by Sunday, just before we were closing, and talked to us."

"Us?"

"Joel, me. Finian, too, I think."

"I tried to see Quill today. Karen at the door said he wasn't around."

"I don't know where he is. Joel might."

"I think I'll have to skip that."

Swindell tried a smile, but it didn't work. "Everything's been kind of a mess since . . ."

She didn't have to finish it. "What did the police ask you?"

Swindell looked at me a little sharply. "It's okay for me to tell you that?"

"Unless you don't want to."

Another hesitation. "Don't see that it makes any difference. They—this policewoman—asked me did I know the boy, a musician?"

"Rock band."

"And I told her I didn't, and Darbra never mentioned him."

"Did Cross also tell you how he was killed?"

"No."

Something in Swindell's face made me ask it differently. "Did you read about it?"

She shook her head but said, "Yes. In the *Herald*, yesterday, but the paper didn't say anything about Darbra, just the address, which I recognized."

"Recognized."

"From Darbra's personnel file. For her W-4, health plan, that kind of thing, I had to send notices to her apartment."

"She ever mention keeping a spare key around the office?"

"No. She kept things pretty close that way."

"What way?"

"Personal things. Didn't really talk to me about them. Didn't really talk to anybody at the store about them, far as I know."

Darbra, the butterfly at the Jersey shore with Teagle, the caterpillar in her cocoon at work. "Her apartment was ransacked by somebody last Thursday into Friday."

"Ransacked?"

"Yes. Anything she could have had that somebody would want?"

Another head shake, this one slow. "Wouldn't know to tell you. Like I said, she wasn't the confiding type."

"Cross also ask you where you were when Teagle was killed?"

"Yes." A little defiance behind it.

"And I should ask her?"

"No, I'll be happy to tell you. I was at the store Saturday into Saturday night and all day Sunday, working with Lupé."

"Who's that?"

"The temp in Darbra's office."

"So you were breaking her in."

"That's right. She's a good girl, learning fast."

"And you were working Saturday night, too."

"Like I said."

"Was Joel Bernstein?"

Swindell stood. "You'll have to take that up with him."

As she walked out, I guessed I'd be paying for the drinks.

"Look this way at things. She not throw it in your face."

I said, "The way Darbra would have?"

Grgo Radja shrugged as he sat in a different chair than Beverly Swindell had used. He glanced at her full cup, clean spoon.

"There was something wrong with the coffee?"

"I don't think so."

The hooded eyes moved to my iced tea. "Yours?"

"We just didn't get around to them."

"You want try something else to drink?"

"This is fine."

"I don't want force you, but maybe you join Grgo in some slivovitz?"

"What is it?"

"Brandy from plum, Croatia drink."

I wondered if this meant he wanted to talk to me, especially given how tight he'd been about Abraham Rivkind and Darbra the first time I'd seen him. "Sure, thanks."

Radja bellowed out a foreign word, which brought the waiter running, then conversationally, "Slivovitz," and something else.

The waiter reappeared with a brown bottle, squat and oval, and two bell glasses half the size of a big brandy snifter. The waiter poured several ounces of the slivovitz into each glass. Then he left the bottle on the table and went back to the kitchen.

I said to Radja, "If you'd like to smoke, I don't mind."

He picked up his glass in both hands, rolling it between his palms like a potter with clay on a wheel. "The cigar is for me a sometime thing." He looked to his hands. "This warm up the brandy, more flavor, but maybe you try first, see you like it."

I took a sip. Fiery, with a flavor like the plum sauce for a Szechuan moo shu. "Excellent."

"Yes, so. Cannot find the slivovitz here now, because of the wars over there. Slivovitz I think is only thing we agree about, Serb and Croat. In my country, they . . . but you not here to learn more about Croatia, eh?"

"No, I'm not."

Radja nodded, more like a slight, sitting bow, and inhaled over his glass. The smudgy eyelids got dreamy, then he tossed half the drink at the back of his throat, making a thick sound of satisfaction. "Only a little is enough, you do things right way."

"That's true."

The eyelids blinked slowly. "So, this Darbra, you find her?"

"Not yet."

"You still ask about Mr. Rivkind?"

"If you feel like talking about him."

"No. Not to tell you things. Maybe tell you not to ask things still."

I took another nip of the slivovitz. "Why is that?"

"What can you find to help him now?"

"I'm trying to help his wife."

"Same thing. A man and his wife, no good to find things, push things out can't help nobody."

"What kind of things?"

"Any kind. Mr. Rivkind, he good man. He no kind of man for you to ask question about."

"It's my job."

"Maybe you need other job."

"I like this one."

In a lower voice, Radja said, "Maybe better you find other job still."

298

I tried warming my glass the way he had, my shoulders square to him. "Is that a suggestion or a threat?"

Radja shrugged, the beard riding his collar like a surfboard on a wave. "Croat like me, we don't make threats. We just see what is right, and we do that."

I said, "Grgo, there some reason you didn't want Mrs. Swindell to know we'd had a talk already?"

He considered it, like he'd prepared a speech about it. "Mr. Rivkind good to me, save my restaurant because he bring his people here. I don't want these people think Grgo talk to you. I don't want you talk to these people, these good people, give them pain in their heart."

"Somebody already did that, by killing Abraham Rivkind. Darbra Proft is involved in this somehow, and I hope to find out how and why."

The eyelids seemed to get blacker, the beard bristling now. "Pain in the heart is terrible thing. I know that, you know that. People, they maybe die from it."

Grgo Radja tossed the rest of his slivovitz at the back of his throat, rose, and gave me the same slight bow he'd used before. Then he picked up the bottle and moved with deliberation toward his kitchen.

25

I WALKED FROM THE RESTAURANT BACK TO MY OFFICE. CHECKING for messages, I had only one I cared about.

The chocolate-brown garrison looked much as it had earlier that day, with the twin lampposts at the foot of its driveway and the Mazda coupe near the garage. However, the car was on the other side of the driveway now, and there were no green plastic newspaper bags on the path or lawn.

Leaving the Prelude at the curb, I went up the drive and the path to the front door. The bell chimed inside, and I heard a young male voice call out something I couldn't catch. A few seconds later, the door swung open.

Larry Rivkind scowled at me. He had on jeans again but a different polo shirt, and his skin seemed a shade or two darker, as though he'd been working on a tan. "What are you doing here?"

"Back from your trip, Larry?"

"What business is it of yours?"

From a few rooms away, Pearl Rivkind's voice said, "Larry? Larry, who is it?"

The boy didn't answer, just posturing for me. "You tell my mom about our fight?"

"No."

Rivkind's face looked skeptical. "How come?"

"You were upset, had a right to be. I was just a convenient target."

He seemed to turn that over. "Mr. Forgiveness."

"Can I speak to your mother?"

"Why?"

"That's kind of between her and me."

"Larry?" Closer now.

Rivkind stood aside dramatically. "I can't stop her from being stupid if she wants to be."

"Larry, who—"

Pearl Rivkind stopped cold when she saw me. Without makeup, the lantern jaw really dominated her face, which still looked weary but somehow brighter than when I'd seen her in my office. There was some color in her cheeks, and the big brown eyes were clear and wide. She wore a lightweight pink sweat suit with white strings in the front tied like a ribbon on a present. There was a dish towel in one hand, the other looking a little wet and red.

"John, I called your secretary."

I said, "My answering service."

"Oh. Yeah, maybe. She didn't seem to have any information, said I'd have to talk with you."

Without looking at her son, I said, "That's why I'm here. Is there some place we can talk?"

Larry Rivkind said, "I'm going up to my room. Call me if you want me, huh?"

Pearl Rivkind nodded at her son without looking at him, either. As he left us for a stairway on the right, she said, "Kitchen all right, John?"

"Fine, Pearl."

301

We moved through a tasteful living room in which the furnishings seemed perfectly proportioned for the space and color-coordinated with each other. The kitchen had a bright, peened linoleum floor in yellow with matching appliances and daisy wallpaper. There was a breakfast nook with high-backed benches that were quaint but somehow too small for the wall and Palladian window they abutted. The window reminded me of the ones at Value Furniture.

"You want to sit in the nook, I'll make some coffee?"

"The nook's fine, but no coffee, thanks."

"Tea? Tonic?"

Rivkind still used the old New England expression for carbonated drinks like Coke or Pepsi. "Tonic would be good."

"We got Sprite or Diet Dr Pepper."

"Sprite, please."

"Ice?"

"Not if it's already cold."

She went over to a large double refrigerator, stopping on the way for a pair of tall, crystal glasses. Opening the door, she pulled out a two-liter bottle with both hands, then couldn't turn the top.

I said, "Can I get that for you?"

"No, thanks. Larry has to go back to his job soon, and I need to be able to do these kinds of things for myself." Rivkind tried the dish towel to help her grip. I heard the fizz noise that meant she'd been successful.

"There." She used both hands to tilt the bottle and fill the glasses. Rivkind seemed to perform each task carefully and slowly, as though it were ritually important to do it right.

"Where does Larry work?"

"Up in New Hampshire. Kid's camp. Imagine, he goes through Harvard, degree in philosophy, and he wants to be a camp counselor?"

"Maybe it gives him a chance to think out what he really wants to do with his life."

ACT OF GOD

Rivkind brought the glasses over and sat down across from me. "You know, this is almost the only thing we brought with us from the old house."

"This nook?"

"Yeah. Abe and me bought it for our first place together, because we were just kind of scraping by. Then, when the store was doing well back in the early eighties, we moved here. Good idea, and we gave our old furniture to Hadassah, let somebody else get some use from it. All but this little nook, where we'd have our coffee every . . ."

Rivkind looked away from me, out the window, biting her lip as she seemed to check the shrubs for flowers. No tears, though. "Your Sprite, it's all right?"

I hadn't tasted it yet. "It's fine, Pearl."

She nodded, still at the bushes.

"You and Larry went away for a while?"

"Yeah." She came back to me. "Yeah, I'm sorry, I guess I should have called you."

"No problem. I stopped out here once today, but it was on my way. The police swung by, let me know everything was okay."

"Everybody's been real good that way. Mr. Khoumanian, across the street, he mowed our lawn. Then his back went out, he couldn't get over to pick up the papers, but he said he called the cops on somebody this morning. I'm sorry if they scared you or anything."

"They didn't. How was the trip?"

"It was good, John. Real good. A chance to get away, have some fresh air. This is where I want to be, this house, I mean. At least for a while. But getting away like that, Larry taking care of all the arrangements . . . for the trip, I mean. It's funny, how your child comes to be an adult and take care of you when you need it. All Abe's stuff is done except for the lawyer and"—she looked at me differently—"I guess, for you."

I drank some of the Sprite.

303

"You found out anything, John?"

"Not really."

"Does that mean you think it's hopeless?"

There was emotion behind her voice, but it was hard to gauge which one it was. "I've talked to everyone I can think of, except your son."

Rivkind bit her lip again, then tasted her Sprite, more for something to do than something to drink. "Larry, he's like my lawyer, he doesn't think it's so good for you to be working for me."

"I'd still like to talk to him."

A nod. "I'll go upstairs, try to get him to."

She slid out from her bench and stood, but didn't move right away. "Back there in your office, you told me . . . you said being widowed, it . . . passes with time?"

"Some, anyway."

"How long does it take, John?"

I just shook my head.

"So you got my mother to do your dirty work."

Larry Rivkind lay on a platform bed, his head and shoulders against one of those corduroy back rests at the wall. There were a couple of football posters in his room, and a framed program showing a hockey player in full stride wearing a crimson uniform with HARVARD across his chest and the legend NCAA NATIONAL CHAMPIONS—1989 beneath the player. A fourteen-inch television with a cable box was on a low bureau, the station MTV or VH-1. The sound was off, the rock group mouthing their lyrics in pantomime.

I said, "How do you mean, 'my dirty work'?"

"You know what I mean. Sending her up here because you knew if she asked me to talk with you, I'd do it."

"I figured you might do it anyway."

"Why should I?"

"Because I spared her some heartache, not telling her about you swinging on me in your father's store."

"Yeah, well, heartache, that's something you're just trying to bring her more of."

"She has questions, and she wants answers to them."

"Even if it means ruining my dad's memory for her."

"Is that what the answers would do, Larry?"

He turned away from me, looking at the figures gyrating on the small screen.

Very slowly, he said, "Was my father having an affair with somebody? I don't know. If my mother found out he was, would it kill her? I don't think so. But it would sure as shit ruin a nice part of her, a part of what she believes in, what keeps her going through all this."

"Do you know anybody who had a reason to kill your father?"

Another scowl. "No. He was the best. The kindest, I mean. He hated violence, hardship. He once told me he had to lie all the time in the camp, lie to stay alive. He said he'd never lie again."

"Larry—"

"That's what you just don't seem to understand. If he told my mom he was faithful, he was. You never knew him. I did. Let me tell you a story, something my father told me once and said he never told even my mother or his partner, Joel. This middle-aged couple was in the store, almost twenty years ago. They saw Joel and asked him if he had a blue couch. Now Joel, he's more the buyer than the seller in the place, so he hunts up my dad and asked him, 'Abe, we got a blue couch for these people here?' And my father, he looks over at the couple, they're from our temple and he knows them, thinks they're kind of obnoxious. But he also had this young couple, nice Spanish people, he told me, who'd saved up for a down payment on a couch and they needed a blue one. Now, my father had two blue couches in stock, and he'd shown both to the Spanish couple, but he didn't know which one they were going to take, they were supposed to come in the next day and decide. So my father says to Joel, 'No, we don't have a blue couch,' because in fact they had *two* of them. You see what I'm saying?"

"Your father couldn't bring himself to lie to his partner for the Spanish couple."

"That's right. He wanted them to get the couch they wanted, but he couldn't bring himself to lie to Joel about the stupid stock. So instead he just kind of hid the truth."

I felt a penny drop somewhere inside my head.

Larry Rivkind looked at me. "You see, he couldn't even deceive his partner without telling the truth."

"So, was my son any help to you?"

"Maybe. Back in my office, you told me you asked your husband if he'd ever been unfaithful to you."

Pearl Rivkind looked up at me from the bench at the kitchen window. "That's right."

"Do you remember the exact words?"

"What, Abe's?"

"Yours and his."

"This . . . this is important?"

"Maybe."

Rivkind looked out the window. "We were . . . in the bedroom, and I said—what was it? Oh, yeah."

She told me, and I felt the other penny drop.

My client looked back up at me. "So tell me, you think my Abe lied to me?"

I watched her face, the lantern jaw, the big brown eyes holding a lot of hope in them.

"No, Pearl, I don't think he did."

26

—————————

"AH, JOHN CUDDY, ISN'T IT?"

"It is, Mr. Quill."

"What's this now? I thought we'd reached a first-name basis."

"Where's Karen?"

"The greeter? She's off on break somewhere. Perhaps the employee lounge. I can fetch her if she's there?"

"Don't trouble. Who will I find on the fourth floor?"

The skin around the ruined but somehow regal nose wrinkled a little. "Why the usual, I expect."

"Thanks."

"Can I escort you up there?"

I stepped around him. "Won't be necessary."

"Joel's not here. He'll be gone for a couple of hours."

"That's all right. You're the one I need to talk to."

Beverly Swindell looked up at me. Then she used a stapler to anchor some printouts on Rivkind and Bernstein's partners' desk. "Here or my office?"

"Wherever you'd be more comfortable."

Swindell heard something in my voice. "My office, then."

We moved down the corridor toward the doorway to the back staircase, turning in at her door, which she closed behind me as I took one of the conference chairs in the corner. She pulled back one of the others and sat down, folding her hands on the tabletop like a fifth-grader who took school very seriously.

I said, "I figured it out, but I don't know what to do with it."

Swindell kept an even gaze. "Figured what out?"

"What happened here that night. But it still doesn't make much sense with everything else."

"I don't understand you."

"Abraham Rivkind never lied."

"That's right."

"His wife asked him if he'd ever been unfaithful to her, and he said he hadn't."

The even gaze. "If Abe said that, then—"

"Not quite."

A couple of blinks.

I said, "He didn't quite say that, because Pearl didn't quite ask him that. What she asked him was, 'Abe, you having an affair on me?'"

The blinks stopped.

I took a breath. "And Abe said, 'No.'"

Swindell's fingers meshed a little tighter. "Then he was telling the truth."

"Yes, he was. Because he wasn't having 'an' affair, he was having two."

"I don't know what—"

"It's what Grgo was trying to keep from me, that you and your boss were having an affair, only I wasn't sharp enough to notice it the first time I talked with him in the restaurant. I thought he was just steering me away from Rivkind and Darbra Proft. Grgo tried to be a little more direct today, but it still didn't hit home until Larry Rivkind told me a story about two blue couches and a young couple who wanted to buy one."

Swindell looked at me, not so evenly now. "That was almost Abe's favorite story, Mr. Cuddy."

"His son told me that Rivkind never mentioned it to his wife or his partner."

There was a surge in her voice as she said, "He told it to me. How he managed to avoid telling a lie and still kept somebody from being hurt. He said he'd been able to do that in the camp—Buchenwald—a few times, and whenever he thought of it, it always made him . . . cry."

I said, "You can say something to me if you want to, or you can just listen."

Swindell shook her head.

I took another breath. "You were all working that Thursday night here, Finian Quill down on the first floor, Bernstein and Rivkind in their office, you in yours, running the daily numbers. As Quill was closing up the front entrance, Bernstein went to the men's room. My guess is Rivkind picked that time, when he knew his partner would be gone awhile, to call Darbra, maybe to set something up, maybe just to say hello. But Darbra was out that night, so he got her answering machine. The call showed up on the telephone company's local line records, which made the police aware of it, but Darbra told them the message was just dead space. That's not quite true, is it?"

Swindell gave me just the even gaze, hands still folded in front of her.

I said, "Abraham Rivkind was on the telephone leaving Darbra a message, a message you overheard when you came into his office with the printouts. You couldn't believe your ears, that he'd betray you like that. Without thinking clearly, you pulled the poker from its holder. Hanging up the phone, Rivkind heard that noise behind him and started to rise and turn. And then you hit him, in anger and with strength, and he fell to the floor."

Swindell could have been a statue.

"When I finally saw it, I thought you must have just panicked after that, run to the end of the corridor and pushed the panic bar itself on the staircase door, started yelling. But that wouldn't have given the 'burglar' enough time to get down the stairs before Finian Quill heard you screaming from the rear door on the first floor. So I'm guessing you walked from Rivkind's office to the end door, opened it to set off the alarm, then hurried back to Rivkind's office before screaming and running again to the door, screaming down the staircase where Quill heard you on his way back in from the alley and Bernstein found you on his way back from the men's room."

Swindell opened her mouth, but it wasn't as though she was addressing me. "At first, it was because I needed the job. Fifteen years ago, I didn't know much, but I wanted to learn, needed to learn, so I joked around with Abe, didn't try to encourage him along, but didn't discourage him, either. He wasn't . . . forceful. I'd had some bad experiences with that kind of man. I wasn't real good-looking, just good-looking enough to get bothered by men. But Abe was gentle, kind. He was just right, in a lot of ways. So we had . . . I don't know, it's awful hard to call it an 'affair,' but I guess that's what it was. We'd see each other here, and we'd have dinner at Grgo's or drinks at some other places. Once in a while, we'd slip off to some motel or other, and Abe would pay cash and wink at the clerk, and—I don't know, that makes it sound kind of dirty, but it wasn't. It was . . . he was sweet, the nicest man to me I ever had."

Hearing Swindell talk about it, I suppose I should have felt more. After all, crime of passion or not, she'd still brutally killed Abraham Rivkind. But I'd already made up my mind on what to do about that. For Pearl's sake.

Swindell jerked her head up suddenly, as though she

thought I wasn't paying attention. "Then Darbra came to work here. I noticed it right away, her . . . twitching herself past Abe, hanging on his words, his arm, just here or there, but no question. I kind of denied it, denied it to myself, and I never asked him about it straight out, but it was like telling my head that my hand wasn't in a fire. I suppose I shouldn't have been so surprised. I mean, if he cheated on his wife with me, why shouldn't he cheat on me with somebody else? But all I know is that night, when I came into his office and—"

"Found him dead on the floor, you did what anybody would have done."

Swindell blinked. "What?"

I said, "When you found Abraham Rivkind dead on the floor, the poker nearby, you did what anyone would have. You panicked and ran for help. Joel Bernstein and Finian Quill, picking up the poker as they did, unfortunately ruined any fingerprints the police could have found on it."

"What . . . what are you saying now?"

"I'm saying there's no physical evidence to prove who killed Abraham Rivkind, so it's hard for me to tell his wife it was anything but a burglar who killed her husband, who wasn't having 'an' affair on her."

I wondered if I'd changed gears on Beverly Swindell a little too abruptly, but she began to bob her head. "You're not going to tell the police about me, are you?"

"Tell them what? You haven't confessed anything. They should have been able to find out that a dead man had an affair with one of his employees, an affair that would break his widow's heart if she found out about it. With no physical evidence, it's a long stretch to the employee being the killer, what with other people like Joel Bernstein and Finian Quill around to back up the burglar story. At best, the finger starts pointing at anybody in the building that night, and with opportunity and probably their own motives, at least Bernstein and even Quill look like a lot of reasonable doubt to

311

me. Maybe the employee would get convicted, but I'd bet against it. And all this about 'Honest Abe' would have to come out for no good reason."

Swindell set her jaw. "My time in this life, I haven't met anybody who gives away something for nothing."

"And you still haven't."

"What do you want, then?"

"I want to know what happened to Darbra Proft and why her boyfriend, Rush Teagle, got himself killed."

A determined tone. "If you believe I lied to you and the police before, then you don't have any cause to believe me right now."

"I'll believe you."

Swindell paused, then swung her head slowly, keeping her eyes on me. "I don't have any idea what happened to that girl or her boyfriend or why. I swear to you I don't."

I let out a breath. "I was hoping otherwise."

She just kept swinging her head.

I stood, pushing back my chair, then snugging it under the table. "Good-bye, Mrs. Swindell."

As I got to the door, I heard behind me, "Should have been his wife."

I turned. Swindell was speaking to her clasped hands.

"What?"

She looked up, unfolding the hands in an almost supplicating way. "Abe shared things with me. Not just food or some laughs or a bed now and then, but things he cared about, like his time in the camp or that story about the Spanish couple and the couches. I should have been his wife, not his girlfriend."

I said, "Jesus Christ," and Beverly Swindell probably thought the surprise in my voice had something to do with her.

27

YOU HAVE THE INDIVIDUAL FACTS, BUT THEY NEVER COME TO-
gether because you run into them separately, from different
people who don't seem involved, or much involved, in your
problem. And then you remember something, or hear it next
to something else, and it's like one of Nancy's computer
searches, where she asks the machine to find a phrase within
a certain number of words from another, and it hits you.

But it hitting you and you proving it are two different
things. Especially if you're trying to protect someone like
Pearl Rivkind and her memories of her husband as you're
doing it. I stayed at my place solo that night, not answering
the phone, just thinking about what I needed to find out the
next morning.

"Hold me up and fan me quick."

"Mo—"

"I don't see you for what, months at a time? And now
it's three times in a week?"

He was leaning back in his desk chair, the dead cigar at

the corner of his mouth. I took the chair in front of the mound of paperwork on his desk.

"I need some help, Mo."

"Huh, tell me about it. You need help? I need help. First I don't have any story ideas, now I got too many."

"Too many?"

"Yeah, I got this story here about Chinese fortune cookies."

"Mo, my—"

"Did you know fortune cookies don't come from China?"

"No, Mo, I didn't."

"Well, they don't. At least, the Chinese don't have them over there now, so this guy down in Brooklyn—a Chinese-American himself—he's going to export them back to China. Can you imagine that?"

"Sounds like a pretty good—"

"I mean, we Americans, we don't know from these sayings, are they authentic, you know? Tell me, John, you open a fortune cookie in a Szechuan place here, can you tell whether Confucius or whoever actually said some of the things in there?"

"Probably not, Mo."

"Huh, probably is right. I remember this one company up here, they did reverse fortune cookies."

I had to ask. "Reverse fortune . . ."

"Cookies. Cookies, you know what I'm talking about here, right, John? I mean, these hard, sugary things you break apart and read the little slip inside there."

"I get the picture, Mo."

"So, okay, this company up here, they make cookies with terrible fortunes in them, like 'You will get syphilis and your brain will rot,' and so on."

"I wouldn't think there'd be much market for that sort of thing, Mo."

"Neither did anybody else. I don't think the company's still around."

"Mo—"

"But this guy in Brooklyn, now, how do you suppose he's going to know if his sayings are right for the real Chinese over across the Pacific, huh? I mean, how are they going to react, he sends them fortunes that aren't quite kosher?"

"Sounds like a genuine problem, Mo."

"Problem, huh. That guy's problem pales in comparison to the other story idea."

"What's that, Mo?"

Katzen removed the cigar from his mouth and regarded it disdainfully. "Condoms."

"Condoms?"

"Yeah. The city council's going to make all the bars and restaurants in Boston have coin-operated condom machines in the rest rooms."

"I must have missed that, Mo."

"Yeah, well, it's going to be kind of hard to miss them, I'm thinking. Most of these places, they got a men's room the size of a broom closet, you can barely turn around in there by yourself, and you're going to be doing your business with this machine staring you in the face? I remember when I was young—this was quite some time ago, John, believe it or not."

"I believe you, Mo."

"I remember we used to carry the little buggers around in our wallets, hoping we'd get lucky. Only in those days, lucky meant once, so you'd have just this one in there, and you'd be praying your mother wouldn't go into your bedroom to put some lunch money in the wallet and see the thing and have a heart attack and die, right there at your bureau, and all the family would know when she was found with the thing in her hand that you're the one who killed her, killed her stone cold. And the problem was, they always got ruined in there, anyway."

"Ruined, Mo?"

"Yeah, ruined. I mean, you keep that wallet in your back pocket, you're sitting on it all day, every day. You never

315

thought to, like, replace the thing. I mean, you know you haven't used it, there's no reason to go through the agony of buying a new one. And that's what it was, too. Agony, John. That movie got it right, there."

"Movie, Mo?"

"Movie. Film, whatever. *Summer of '42*, when the kid goes into the pharmacy and tries to buy a condom."

Pharmacy brought me back to William Proft and his sister. "Mo, I wonder if—"

"Now they got whole stores of them."

"Whole stores, Mo?"

"Yeah. Condom stores, with corny names. They got one over by you there in Back Bay, whole place is like a card store except instead of catchy verse they got legions of latex."

"That's pretty catchy itself, Mo."

He gestured with his cigar. "What is?"

" 'Legions of latex.' "

Katzen pointed the cigar at me. "I can't use that, John."

"Why not?"

"You can't make fun of this stuff anymore, not with AIDS and all. It's off-limits, unless you want to do a serious story on it, and I'm not sure I'm in the mood for a serious story today."

"Then the fortune-cookie one sounds like a good bet."

"Yeah."

"You can do it like spaghetti."

"Spaghetti?"

"Yes. The way Marco Polo brought spaghetti to Italy from China."

"Italy? I'm talking Chinese restaurants here, John, not Italian ones."

"Mo, what I mean is—"

"Who ever heard of a fortune cookie in an Italian restaurant?"

"Nobody, Mo. That's—"

"Wait a minute. You know, that's not such a bad idea. Why not have fortune cookies in all your ethnic restaurants. The Italian places, Irish pubs, the kosher joints in Brookline there. That's actually a great idea for a nice light story. Only now"—Mo suddenly looked gloomy—"now I have three story ideas I got to choose from."

"Mo?"

He didn't look up.

"Mo?"

"What?"

"I need to see some more articles from your morgue files."

"More?"

"Yes, and another favor."

"You come in here, bothering me three times in a week, and now another favor, too?"

"It might be worse than that, Mo?"

"Worse?"

"You may have to call in a chip or two for me."

"From where?"

"Your friend at Logan Airport."

"Let me get this straight."

"Okay."

"You're this private investigator named John Cuddy, right?"

"Right."

"And you're calling me about that crash outside Washington, D.C."

"That's right."

"What do you want from us?"

"Since your agency investigates these things, I thought you might be able to help me with some questions I have."

"Look, I've known Mo Katzen a hundred years, but you I don't know from a hole in the ground."

"I don't think what I'm asking is all that secret. I just need to know it fast without going through a lot of reports."

317

"Wouldn't matter anyway."

"I'm sorry?"

"I said, wouldn't matter anyway. The reports aren't admissible into evidence."

"Who said anything about a trial?"

"Why else would a private eye want information about a plane crash, you're not going to use it to sue somebody?"

"I'm just trying to track someone down."

"We don't release whether a given person was a passenger on a flight. Neither do the airlines."

"I already know the passenger was on the flight from the *Herald* articles Mo dug out for me. I just need to know what happened."

"What happened?"

"To the plane."

"The plane would still be in a hangar down by D.C., lying in pieces after they reconstructed it, as far as they could."

"No, that's not what I mean. I just need to confirm some things about how the crash itself occurred."

An exasperated sigh. "This is for Mo, right?"

"Right."

Some shuffling of papers. "Tell him he owes me."

"I'll tell him."

"Dinner at Dunfey's Parker House."

"He's already looking forward to it."

"All right, I got the report in front of me. What do you want to know?"

"I want to know if there was any possibility the plane was sabotaged in any way."

"What?"

"The news stories dealt with the incident and even quoted some of the passengers. What I need to know is whether what the papers said was the cause is the only possible cause of the crash."

"Look, I don't spend that much time reading the papers. Don't tell Mo that, all right? I don't want him having a

318

stroke on my account. But you want, I can tell you what the report says on causation."

"Please."

More shuffling. "You want all the surrounding stuff, or just the conclusion?"

"Start with the conclusion."

"Okay, I'm reading this, now. Let's see. . . . 'Therefore, it would appear that the sudden, unpredictable ascent of the flock of geese into the flight path of the aircraft was the cause of the engine failure, and that no pilot action could have avoided that failure or the incipient crash.' How's that?"

"No indication of any other cause, then."

"No."

Despite the magnitude of the tragedy, I found myself smiling a little.

The voice said, "We get these once in a while, pal. The lawyers like the one you probably work for, they'd like to have you believe that everything is somebody's fault, but once in a while, we get one of these."

"I understand."

"Know what we call them?"

"Them?"

"A crash like this one. Do you know what we call it?"

"No."

"Just an act of God."

I stopped smiling.

The voice said, "Hey, you still there?"

"I'm here."

"Tell Mo I'm free tomorrow night."

"Tomorrow . . . ?"

"Night. For that dinner at Dunfey's."

"Oh, right. I will. One last thing?"

An impatient "What?"

I asked the question.

"Of course we do."

319

"Where would it be?" I said.

"Be? Probably down in Washington. No reason to ship that kind of thing back up here. The families sure as hell wouldn't want to take them home and watch them."

I thanked her and hung up the phone in Mo Katzen's office.

"Hello?"

"Mrs. Thorson?"

"This is she. Who is this, please?"

"Mrs. Thorson, this is John Cuddy. I'm the investigator who spoke to you last Thursday."

"Oh, yes. You'll be pleased to know that Roger is doing much better."

I said, "I'm glad."

"Yes. He actually came over to dinner with my husband and me last night. He seemed, well, if not over what happened to Caroline, at least on his way back to life."

"I was wondering, I really don't want to disturb him by dredging up memories, but you mentioned that you took videotapes of him and his wife."

A pause. "Yes?"

"For the case I'm working on, it would be a real help if I could see one of those."

Another pause. "See one?"

"Yes. I know it's kind of an odd request, but—"

"Oh, no. It's not that. In fact, I'm glad you called me instead of Roger."

"You are?"

"Yes, I have a number of them you could look at, but he has only the one."

"Only the one?"

"Yes. It was a tape I took of them at a little going-away party we had just before one of their vacations. It wasn't much, really, just drinks and some silly gifts, all of us waving good-bye and them waving back. You know."

"I can picture it, I think."

A third pause. "They were such a lovely couple. Roger borrowed that tape from me, oh, a month or so before Caroline was killed, but naturally I haven't had the heart to ask for it back."

"Naturally," I said quietly.

28

It was a condo complex spread up a hill overlooking Route 1A in Swampscott, about twelve miles north of Boston. I'd had to do some driving around to locate the right unit in a brick building with white trim around the outside doors and windows. At the main entrance, I rang the bell under the name JORGENSEN.

Before I could say anything, a woman's voice came over the intercom. "You're a doll, Janey. Come on in, I just have to put my shoes on."

The building door made a buzzing noise, and I pushed through it.

There were two units on the first floor of the entryway. The door to the rear one was open, soft rock coming through it. I walked down the short hall and knocked on the jamb.

"Janey, you don't have to—who are you?"

The woman looking back at me was in her mid-thirties, with a youthful face and trim figure in slacks and a short-sleeved knit jersey. She had one foot in a slip-on sandal, the other foot next to its mate, the toenails painted shocking pink. The only thing spoiling the picture was the cast on her right arm, elbow to hand, the fingers showing dark, as though ink-stained.

Staying in the hall, I took out my ID holder. "Becca Jorgensen?"

She used her good hand to brush brown, ringletted hair out of her eye. "I said, who are you?"

"My name's John Cuddy. I'm a private investigator from Boston."

I held up the ID, and Jorgensen looked at it from across her living room, though she was too far away to read anything on it. Her voice gave me the impression she didn't trust me. "I don't have time for anything right now."

"I can come back another day, but I need to talk with you."

"About what?"

"About the flight to D.C. you were on, a week ago Friday."

The voice got frosty. "We're not commenting on that."

"This doesn't have anything to do with a lawsuit against the airline."

"Right," in a tone that meant she wasn't close to buying it.

"Ms. Jorgensen, I—"

The phone rang but she ignored the noise, just keeping me in sight. "You'll have to leave now."

I didn't say anything. There was a tape machine next to the ringing phone on the little table near her kitchen, and I had the impression she couldn't wait it out.

Glaring at me, Jorgensen used her left hand to pick up the receiver. "Hello? . . . Janey, where . . . Oh, no, Janey. . . . Well, when's the last time you started it? . . . The lights on? How . . . Okay, okay I know you didn't do it on purpose. . . . Right, right. . . . I guess I'll have to call—just a second." Jorgensen kept her eyes on me. "Listen, there's a guy here . . . No, not him. This guy claims he's a private investigator."

I walked toward her, holding my ID out in front of me. She flinched at first, then glared harder.

Three feet from her, I stopped, the hand with the holder at eye level to her. Into the phone, Jorgensen said, "Janey? His name's John Francis Cuddy." She recited the rest of the information on the thing. "What? . . . I don't know what you're supposed to do with it, just make sure you remember it for the police. . . . Right, right. I'll call you in five minutes."

Hanging up the phone, Jorgensen said, "She doesn't hear from me, my friend's calling the cops."

"Dead battery?"

"What?"

"Your friend Janey. Dead battery in her car?"

Guardedly, "Yes."

"And because of your arm, she was supposed to drive you somewhere, right?"

Still guarded. "Maybe."

"Tell you what. My car's just out front. I'll drive you, and we can talk on the way."

Shaking her head, having to use the good hand again on her hair. "I'm not going to talk with you, now I'm supposed to take a ride with you?"

I took out my wallet and started doling things out to her. "Driver's license, with photo. Permit to carry a concealed weapon, also with photo. My passport would take a while, but I can give you the names and telephone numbers of three or four Boston cops who'll vouch for me."

Jorgensen caught herself smiling. "And for your driving?"

"If I didn't have this doctor's appointment, there's no way on earth I'd be doing this."

I nodded. "Given the reason you need the appointment, I hope the airline's picking up the tab."

She turned in the passenger's seat to look at me. "What do you mean, 'the reason'?"

324

"I read some newspaper articles about the crash. One profiled how you broke and burned your arm."

Jorgensen looked back out the windshield, not saying anything.

We stopped for a red light. "It must have taken a lot, going back inside that plane after the little girl."

Nothing at first. Then, "She had braces."

"Braces?"

"Not on her teeth, on her legs. Like from polio, only I guess it couldn't have been polio she had, this day and age."

"Probably not." The traffic light changed. "Do you remember another passenger with a limp?"

"Just from preboarding."

"You mean helping some people onto the plane before you let everybody on it?"

"Yes. The little girl, somebody else helped her on, but I kept track of her." Jorgensen suddenly seemed to want to talk, her face still straight ahead. "We were a lifeguard flight, so I was thinking about sick people."

"Lifeguard?"

"Yes. When a plane is carrying donated organs—for transplanting into somebody else—the air traffic controllers add 'lifeguard' to the flight number. So we'd be like "Flight four-zero-five Lifeguard.' When you're carrying organs, speed is of the—what's the expression?"

"Speed is of the essence?"

"Right. Once we were airborne, the captain used that, talking to the passengers. To tell them how . . . lucky they were to be on the plane, because the tower would give us expedited consideration for routing and landing. Anyway, since we were a lifeguard flight, I was thinking about sick people, and when the little girl wasn't in my section, I switched off with one of the other attendants, so I could be near her. She was only seven or eight, had the cutest little face, dimples to drive the boys wild. When the . . . when we went down, we only had a few seconds warning from the cockpit, not even enough time for most of the passengers to panic or anything, unfasten their seat belts. The cabin ... the fuselage just split apart and burst into flames. It was ... unbelievable, really. One second, you're on this approach, everything just fine, smiling with relief that you have only the return hop back to Logan, and the next minute it's like ... some kind of nightmare in hell, everybody screaming, the walls opening up, the section behind you just ... just not there, not there anymore."

Jorgensen was speaking more to the windshield than me.

I made a left turn. She said, "The second right after this one."

We slowed down for it. "You said there was another passenger with a limp?"

Jorgensen's head came back to me. "What?"

"You said there was somebody else who needed help preboarding?"

"Oh. Oh, right." Eyes front. "A blond woman, with a limp. She was kind of crying, almost didn't make the preboarding, like she was ... preoccupied, thinking about something."

"Did you get a good look at her?"

"Pretty good. I would have tried to help her, too, when we ... when we hit, but she was in the section that ... was gone."

I reached into my suit pocket to get the photo I'd been carrying around for a week. "Was this the woman?"

Jorgensen looked at it. "I don't think so. The hair is wrong, and she's—this woman's too young. The passenger had sunglasses on, but she dressed and ... she was just older."

I took the photo back. "Did you speak to her?"

"A little."

"Do you remember what she said?"

"Just introduced herself, thanked me for helping her."

"Introduced herself?"

326

"Told me her name, said she really appreciated the help because she was going to D.C. to see the Wall."

"The Vietnam Memorial?"

"Yes."

"Do you remember her name?"

"She said it was 'Hool.' I made a mental note, thinking 'Heated Pool.' Word association, you know, 'H' for 'Heated' with 'Pool' is Mrs. Hool."

"Why did you do that?"

"In case she might need anything on the flight. You keep a little more track of the people who preboard."

"Why the 'Mrs.'?"

"Excuse me?"

"Why did you say 'Mrs.' Houle?"

"Oh. Her wedding rings. I didn't ask her about it, though. Thought it might have been her husband."

"Her husband?"

Jorgensen looked at me. "You know . . . on 'the Wall?' "

"I understand. Anything else?"

"What do you mean?"

"Did Mrs. Houle say anything else to you?"

"I don't think so. She seemed to be in pretty good shape, except for the limp."

"How do you mean?"

"Well, when I took her arm, it seemed pretty strong under her clothes. Toned, you know?"

"But she didn't say anything else?"

"Not then."

"Then?"

"Not as I found her window seat for her. Just later."

"Later?"

"After the aisle seat arrived. We were only about two-thirds full, so there was going to be an empty middle one between them, but this Mrs. Hool said she had to change her seat."

"Why?"

327

"She didn't say. A lot of people with disabilities like an aisle seat, but just as many go for the window, since you don't have to get up to let other people out all the time. This time, though, when the woman who had the aisle seat arrived—kind of late, just barely made the flight—we're about to shut the door when Mrs. Hool told me she had to change her seat."

"But she didn't say why."

"No. And the way she was, I didn't ask her."

"The way she was?"

"Kind of weepy and all, tissues in her hand, rubbing under her eyes."

"The way she'd been as you boarded her?"

"Yes, only . . . more so? I guess she was thinking about the Wall."

"Then what?"

"Well, I got Mrs. Hool out of that row and then aft maybe ten, twelve rows. That made the difference."

"The difference?"

"Yes. The way we . . . hit, she probably would have been okay, because I think the fat lady walked away without a scratch."

"The fat lady?"

"I'm sorry. I shouldn't say that. The aisle seat, she was pretty heavy."

"The woman who would have been next to Mrs. Houle."

"Right. Well, a seat away, like I said."

"Because of the middle one being open."

"Right."

I thought about it. "The seat that Mrs. Houle changed to, was that a window seat, too?"

"No. No, it was a middle seat. I was afraid the other people in her new row would give me a hard time, too. You know, you figure, the doors are sealed, you've got that middle seat free, but they saw her limp and the aisle

328

seat in the new row got up so Mrs. Hool could get in the middle."

"You know the name of the heavy woman?"

"No."

"Her seat number?"

"Well, it was the row just forward of ..." Jorgensen closed her eyes. "On that aircraft, it would have been '13,' and 'C' for the aisle." She opened her eyes. "That's what's so ironic."

"The number, you mean?"

"Yeah. Mrs. Hool stays in 13A, she's probably okay, because the fat—sorry, the heavyset one, like I said, I think she walked away. Or ran away, like everybody else did."

"Except for you."

Jorgensen swung her head toward the windshield. "All the good it did."

"Your going back into that plane gave the little girl a chance."

"Not enough of one."

"The only one she had."

Jorgensen said, "It's the tall building in this mall."

I pulled into the parking area for a strip of eight stores with a four-story professional building at the far end of it. "Any way I can find out the name of the woman in 13C?"

"Not airline policy to release that."

"Could you find it out for me?"

She got frosty again. "Why?"

"Why should you find it out, or why do I need it?"

"Both."

"I need it because I think that flight revolves around a murder."

"Oh, great." Jorgensen looked at me as we stopped in front of the professional building. "So why should I find it out for you?"

"Same reason you went back in after the little girl."

Jorgensen looked at me some more, then shook her head. "God, I have to find another line of work."

I waited, but she didn't get out of the car.

Finally, Jorgensen used her good hand cross-body to yank on the door handle. "There's a pay phone inside the lobby. I'll call somebody, but it'll probably get you just a name, not an address or anything."

"That'd be more than I have now."

"What I mean is, the woman might live in the Washington area. She could have been heading home instead of down there on business or something."

"That would make things harder, but I'd still like the name."

Jorgensen got out of the car, closing the door with the window still down. Then she leaned in. "Thanks."

"The information more than covers the ride."

"I didn't mean for the ride. I meant for what you said about my giving that little girl a chance."

Despite the bad arm, Becca Jorgensen trotted into the lobby.

The name could have been "Smith." Even "Taylor" or "O'Brien." Fortunately, it was 'Iturraldi." There were none in the Boston White Pages, and only two in the rest of the metropolitan area. The first was a dead end, no female in the family. As I dialed the second, first initial "K," I began to picture myself sitting in the Boston Public Library, going through the shelves of nationwide directories, trying all the ones around D.C.

Then a woman's voice answered. K. Iturraldi heard me out, then said, "Yes, that was me," and "Sure, I can see you."

Half an hour later, I parked in front of the address she'd given me over the phone. A small cape, it had a nice lawn and hedges trimmed in the shape of popover tarts.

I walked up the front path and rang the bell at the side

of the screened door, the inner wooden one standing open. A large figure filled the foyer, and I found myself smiling as she moved closer to me on the other side of the screen.

A wave preceded her, washing over me before she asked if I was the private investigator. A wave of perfume, Shalimar or Opium maybe. K. Iturraldi reeked of it.

29

As I drove out there, I thought about how to play it. Maybe it would work and maybe it wouldn't, but either way, I'd have tried.

I left the Prelude in front of the house and walked up the flagstoned path. At the door between the white Doric columns I pushed the button and heard the deep, bong-bong chiming inside. This time he answered the door.

"What . . . ?"

"I'm afraid I have to bother you again, Mr. Houle."

His hands were empty, his clothing just shorts and another T-shirt with a breast pocket. The chin forced the rest of his face into a smile. "Sure. Sure, come on in."

I let him precede me into a living room with a traditional sofa and love seat arranged around a marble fireplace. On the mantel sat the covered urn I'd last seen in the garden my first visit there.

Houle said, "Take the couch, it's more comfortable."

I did as he moved to the love seat, some newspapers scattered at the base of it. Houle stepped over them but instead of settling into the love seat, he perched on the front cushion of it. "Caroline was always after me about leaving papers on the floor like this."

I nodded. "I take it you really didn't get around to spreading the ashes."

Houle looked at me strangely, blinking rapidly. "What was that?"

I gestured toward the mantel. "The urn there. You told me yesterday that you'd spread the ashes in the garden your wife loved so well. Since the urn's still here, I'm guessing you were mistaken, that you just haven't found the time yet."

More blinking. "That's pretty . . . harsh, don't you think?"

"Harsh. Now that's a word that could cover a lot of ground, Rog."

The blinking stopped.

I said, "Abraham Rivkind's death was harsh. The plane crash was harsh. Rush Teagle's death was harsh. The only death I'm not sure of is the fourth one."

"I . . . I don't know what you're talking about."

"I think you do. It was a hell of a plan, Rog, and it should have worked. And it would have, except for those darned geese."

Houle's face seemed to cave in. "What . . . what the hell are you trying to do to me?"

"Nothing worse than you've already done to others. Let me outline things for you, in case some of the details have slipped your mind, all the pressure you've been under lately."

Houle didn't sit back. He didn't move in any way.

I said, "A while ago, you started losing interest in your wife. Divorce didn't make much sense: The real money in the marriage, like this house, came from her side, and trying to make it on your own in real estate with this economy didn't look too appealing. So, you stuck it out. Then, about a year ago, along comes Darbra Proft."

My mentioning her name seemed to hurt him.

"You fell for her, hook, line, and sinker. But she wanted a lot of nice things, and you didn't really have the discretionary income to provide them. However, the two of you saw a way, a way that must have made a lot of sense the more you thought and talked about it, even though it was a little different from how Darbra had earned her last grubstake."

"I don't know what you're saying."

"Pay attention, Rog, it'll come back to you. Six years ago, Darbra killed her mother, pushing the woman off a roof for fifty thousand in life insurance. About four months ago, Darbra was running low on money and would have done the same to her brother, even tried to get him to check whether the policies were still in effect, so there'd be no inquiry on record from her. But then she probably figured, and rightly, that two insured, accidental deaths in the same family circle within a decade was pushing it a little. On the other hand, there was your wife. Darbra was younger than Caroline, but looked old for her age, and she'd spent some time as a stage actress. Not a very good actress, but then, she didn't need to be. Just good enough to fool a friend from a distance and strangers up close. Darbra got a job at Value Furniture, to give her a little cover and enough money to tide her over. Then you borrowed a videotape of a party from your neighbor, Mrs. Thorson, so Darbra could bone up on your wife's limp, posture, mannerisms. You and Darbra had a violent breakup scene in Grgo's restaurant, kind of overdone by her, as you said, though I heard you were very convincing. About the same time, Darbra wheedled some vacation time from her new boss to take a trip to New Jersey, to give both her and you perfect alibis.

"The plan was for Darbra to dye her hair blond and come back up here from New Jersey by train. Her aunt Darlene said she loved to ride trains as a kid, and it fit in perfectly. The day of your wife's flight to Washington, Darbra takes the Amtrak from Newark to Boston. She comes out here, probably by cab to an address a few blocks away. Then she walks over to this house. Tell me, Rog, was Caroline already dead by then?"

No response, the eyes seeming to look not at me but inward.

"I'm guessing she wasn't, that you'd want Caroline alive as long as possible, in case Mrs. Thorson or another neighbor popped over to wish her well on the trip. I also believe you'd want Darbra in on the killing. That's the one death I can't describe for you, so let's hold it for now. At some point, Darbra goes up to your wife's closet, dresses in one of her outfits, and puts on her sunglasses. You call a cab for Darbra, and then pop next door yourself, so that Mrs. Thorson gets a look only from her door of a cab pulling away and through the passenger window her 'friend' Caroline's classic wave, something Darbra had practiced from the video. The plan from there was for you to go to Mrs. Thorson's for dinner, to bring your cellular phone and to act naturally, at some point noting with concern the fact that your wife hadn't gotten in touch with you after her plane landed. Then we'd have an investigation, which would show that Caroline Houle had gotten the assistance of a flight attendant in preboarding, introduced herself even, and definitely had been on the plane when it arrived in D.C. The authorities would search the Washington area for the woman, nobody but you and Darbra knowing that Darbra had changed in the ladies' room at the airport, gone to the train station, and taken the Amtrak back to New Jersey, to finish out her vacation and round out her alibi. How am I doing so far, Rog?"

He lifted his chin a little.

"I'll take that as confirmation for now. There were also some things you didn't know about, of course. A couple of people told me Darbra was somebody who couldn't leave well enough alone, who couldn't resist trying to do someone else's idea one better. She probably figured she had a little more experience in the area than you did, thanks to her mother's situation, but I'm thinking she probably also didn't quite trust love to be enough. So Darbra didn't just get a job with Value Furniture, she seduced one of the bosses into an affair with her, to make it look like she was in the process of acquiring another 'sugar daddy' and easing off with you long before the breakup scene at Grgo's. She also wanted a little extra alibi the day of the killing, somebody to convince the motel owner at the Jersey shore that she was 'in the shower' that Friday night when she would have been on the Amtrak coming back from her flight to Washington. Maybe also some help with the videotape and transportation while she was in Jersey itself. So, about a month ago, Darbra started up with Rush Teagle and brought him into the 'vacation' part of the plan. Given how Teagle behaved, I think he must have been promised a couple thousand dollars by Darbra for helping her, because he bragged about being in line for some new money to his band before the fact. That Friday night at the motel, though, he probably waited for Darbra till he fell asleep, maybe from all the beer the motel owner saw in the room. I'm guessing that the next morning, Teagle woke up, saw Darbra wasn't back, and turned on the TV while he tried to figure out what to do. The plane crash would have been on any news broadcast along the Northeast Corridor, and Teagle must have realized what happened. He threw his and Darbra's stuff from vacation into his convertible and hightailed it back to Boston.

"From your reaction the first time we met, Rog, you had no idea about these other men in her life. You didn't even know Abraham Rivkind had been killed, because it happened while you were out-of-state on business, and I'm betting Darbra didn't breathe a word of it to you, for fear of making you skittish about her being close to two deaths in a few weeks' time. Unfortunately, though, the Friday your wife died here Darbra also inconveniently 'forgot' to bring back to you Mrs. Thorson's videotape of the party. Do you think Darbra thought of that tape as insurance, too, Rog? Insurance on your honorable intentions toward her? Either way, there were other little quirks, like Darbra staining the motel sink with her hair dye and coincidentally getting a seat on the plane too close to a woman who bathed in perfume, forcing Darbra to move because of her allergy. But these other things, Rog, they were nothing compared to the biggest quirk of all, the ultimate irony."

I looked up at the urn. "The fact that the plane, the one your wife would have been on, goes and crashes, completely by accident, killing Darbra in her place."

Houle moved his head a few degrees at a time, like a bolt being turned by a ratcheting wrench. He stared up at the urn.

I said, "When I visited here last Thursday and told you Darbra had 'come back' to Boston after you knew she'd died, it really rocked you. I took it for sincere reaction to the death of the woman you loved, and it was. On account of Darbra, that is. But that made you realize that Darbra could have left the party videotape, and maybe other incriminating evidence as well, in her apartment. So you went there, used your keys, and ransacked the place. When you didn't find the tape, you tumbled to another unpleasant possibility. There might be somebody else in on the game, the somebody turning out to be Rush Teagle."

Houle spoke for the first time in a long time. "Bastard."

"I was the one who told him about Darbra's place being searched, and he seemed awfully interested. Unfortunately, I'm also the one who told you the name of the young guy Darbra was seeing. When an unidentified young guy calls to blackmail you using the videotape, you kind of put two and two together, maybe even noticing his name over a buzzer at the apartment house when you went there to toss Darbra's place. You go along with Teagle over the telephone, then return to the apartment house and unlock the front

337

door of the building with your key. You use some kind of ruse to get Teagle to open his apartment door in the basement. What'd you do, Rog, impersonate a cop?"

Houle looked at me.

"Anyway, you get into his place, maybe carrying a weapon of your own, but lo and behold, there's a fireplace poker there. You remember I told you that's how Rivkind was killed, while you were in Denver, so you figure using the same kind of weapon is the perfect way for the cops to think Rivkind and Teagle must have been killed by the same person, who couldn't be you. Tell me, did you find Mrs. Thorson's videotape in Teagle's apartment?"

Houle just kept looking at me, eyes piercing me, really seeing it now.

"I'm guessing you did, Rog. I'm guessing you figured at that point you were home free. A little covered in blood, maybe, and still distraught over losing Darbra, but at least well-off and in the clear on all the killings. Except for one thing."

Houle opened his mouth, then closed it again without speaking.

"Not curious, Rog? Come on now, we've gotten this far together, you don't want to know the one glitch you can't fix?"

His hands started flexing.

I said, "The other videotape."

"The other . . . ?"

"When I was here the first time, remember? You were going on about having to claim the body, how they conducted the identification, the video monitor in the room."

"No."

"They do keep a copy of that, Rog."

"No!"

"Before they release the body, they make a tape of it, to show the injuries. A tape that will also show the half of the face that wasn't burned, the features belonging to Darbra Proft, not Caroline Houle."

He squeezed his eyes shut.

Now for the play. It would work, or it wouldn't. "I haven't told the cops, yet, of course."

The eyes opened, blinking. "What . . . ?"

"I haven't told the cops yet, because I wanted to learn about the one thing I didn't know. Exactly how Caroline died."

I suddenly stood and started through the house toward the back. "This way to the garden, Rog?"

I walked as briskly as my braced knee would allow, so he'd come after me quickly. I heard his steps behind me right away.

I went out the back door, the flowers and shrubs in front of me, the new potting shed to my left. The plastic bags and garden tools were all arranged in the shed now, as though someone had just straightened it. I turned around to face Houle, putting the shed to my right.

He came through the door and out, hands still flexing, something off about his breathing.

I said, "There was only one real problem with your original plan, Rog. Since your theory was that Caroline disappeared in Washington while you were alibied by the Thorsons up here, it would look kind of funny if her body turned up around the house. Damned complicated to get rid of a body, too. Woods? Always hunters and hikers, poking around. Water? Boaters and fishermen. Look at that guy on the sailboat, the lobstermen bringing up the woman he'd weighted down and sent overboard. So, what to do, what to do?"

I looked over at the shed and snapped my fingers. Houle shifted his feet, moving closer to it.

"A little creative concrete, Rog? It'd mean you'd have to live here forever, just in case a new owner wanted to tear down the shed, tear up the concrete under it. But what better way to hide the Massachusetts body of the wife who disappeared in D.C.?"

Houle's breathing was getting more irregular, his head now shaking a couple of times like a fighter trying to clear it. I wasn't sure he was seeing his chance.

"What say you pick up one of those long-handled shovels, Rog, and we do some archaelogy?"

I'd tipped him, but the way he kept his eyes on me while reaching out and grabbing the handle told me he'd been thinking it before I said it. He brought the shovel into both of his hands, first like Little John with a quarterstaff, which would have been a lot more trouble. Then he switched to a baseball grip, a leftie, and swung at me forehand. I jumped back, the knee twinging as I torqued it. He swung backhand, striking me on the left bicep and knocking me downward as I drew the Smith & Wesson Chief's Special worn over my right hip.

From the ground, I could see Houle raising the shovel above his head, like a man with a maul to split firewood. When the shovel came forward, I fired three times into his chest and rolled left, the shovel hammering my right shoulder as Houle's face thumped into the lawn about where my head had been.

"So, what made you think it was this guy Houle?"

Bonnie Cross was sitting in one of the redwood lounge chairs, using the wide drink arm on it to hold her pad as she took notes. A detective from the Meade town force and a state trooper in plainclothes attached to the county district attorney sat on lawn chairs flanking the lounge, both men deferring to her. Roger Houle had already been pronounced by a pathologist from the Medical Examiner's officer, his body gurneyed out toward the driveway. A couple of EMTs from the ambulance had looked over my bruises and said they didn't think I needed X-rays, but they weren't doctors themselves, "So who knows?" At the shed, lab techs were still tutoring a crew of hardhats with picks and mallets on the finer points of excavating an area where a body might be found.

"Cuddy?"

"Sorry. Still a little in shock."

"Right," said the town detective, no sarcasm in his voice. Yet.

Cross didn't look at him. "So what made you think this Houle was the one?"

"I don't know. Little things bothered me. Darbra supposedly came back from New Jersey after a week away, but she didn't bother to change her cat's litter or let the person feeding it know she was back. Teagle claimed he'd gotten a note, but I found out in Jersey that while he'd been with her there, she wasn't seen leaving with him."

Cross said, "Making Teagle look good for killing her there."

"Or at least losing her there. But it seemed hard to believe that Proft's disappearance and Rivkind's death weren't connected, and that's what kept things clouded."

"Clouded," said the statie.

"Yes," I said.

Cross flipped through the pages in her pad. "So Houle and Proft decide to ice his wife and fake the wife's disappearance, but the plane crash screws that up. Teagle tries to blackmail Houle, and the kid gets killed for his trouble."

"Right."

"And you figure we're going to find Mrs. Houle under the shed?"

"Based on the way Houle was raving at me toward the end."

The townie took out a pack of Marlboros. "About that. You say he came at you with the shovel."

"Right."

"And you didn't have time to show your gun before you had to use it?"

"He'd knocked me down and was standing over me, about to split my head open."

The townie lit a cigarette. "Doesn't say much for your agility, you can't clear your holster before a guy with a shovel gets close enough to whack you."

"I've been having some troubles with my knee and shoulder." I pulled up my left pantleg so he could see the bottom of the brace. "My doctor can give you the medical backup, you need it for the reports."

The statie said, "You're a little hurt, it was kind of stupid coming out here alone, what you suspected and all."

"That's just it, though. I only suspected. There wasn't any solid evidence of Houle being the killer except for suspicion and what I hope you find under that shed."

"You mentioned shock before. Seems to me you aren't exactly broken up over shooting this guy."

"I'm not. He killed two people in cold blood, his wife and Teagle."

Cross said, "So you came out, figured to trap him in some kind of statement."

I turned back to her. "That's what I was hoping for. And he gave me some of it, like I've already told you. The rest I'm just filling in, but I think I'm right about most of it."

The townie drew on the Marlboro. "Of course, with our citizen dead here, we'll never really know for sure."

I said, "Even if he'd given himself up peacefully, a lawyer would have told him to take the Fifth when you questioned him and to stay off the stand come trial."

The statie said, "Meaning we'd never really know, period."

"That's right."

The townie coughed, stubbing out his smoke on the lawn. "Par for the course."

Cross folded her pad. "So what about Rivkind?"

I looked at her. "What about him?"

"From what you're saying, this Houle did a copycat on

Teagle to throw us off because Houle was two thousand miles away when Rivkind got killed."

"That's what Houle told me, anyway."

"He had his real estate company send us stuff that bears that out."

I nodded.

Cross didn't. "So, who killed Rivkind?"

"Can't tell by me."

Cross looked at the town detective and the state trooper. All three shook their heads.

From over by the shed, one of the lab techs said, "Hey, Sergeant?"

Cross twisted around in the lounge. "Yeah?"

"We got a white female, one of these plastic fertilizer bags over her head."

Cross and the other two left me for something they could believe in.

I went down the steps and opened the door. The wiry waiter in black came halfway across the empty dining room, then recognized me and hurried back toward the kitchen. Grgo Radja came out and we met at the center of the room.

"You here for dinner, still too early."

"Just for a talk."

"I talk all I want with you."

"I think I figured out who did the killings."

The smudgy eyelids closed halfway. "Yes, so?"

"Maybe we could sit for a while, go over it."

Radja watched me a moment, then indicated with his head to follow him to the table we'd used before. He didn't take out a cigar or call for drink.

After we were in the chairs, he folded his hands on the tablecloth. "So talk."

I told him about Roger Houle and Darbra Proft and what they did to Houle's wife.

JEREMIAH HEALY

"I tell you first time I see you, there is something wrong with that Darbra. But man she throw wine on, him, too?"

"Yes."

A sad ticktocking of the head.

I said, "But he couldn't have killed Abraham Rivkind."

The eyes came all the way open. "How so?"

"Houle was out-of-state. Now that he's dead, though, there won't be a trial in his case, so it doesn't look like there'll be any more investigation into Darbra or the Rivkind killing."

"Houle is dead, no more police or you about Mr. Rivkind?"

"Not about his killing or ... anything, I would guess."

Radja smiled, the hooded eyes almost closing. "You understand me last time, maybe?"

"Maybe. Finally."

"Better you did. You have time for plum brandy with Grgo?"

"A little slivovitz would be nice."

Radja smiled some more and yelled in Croatian toward the kitchen.